THE DOHLEN INHERITANCE

Land Hadeln

THE DOHLEN

INHERITANCE

Tessa Lorant Warburg

T_TP

THE THORN PRESS

First published by The Thorn Press in 2009

Copyright © Tessa Lorant Warburg 2009

The moral right of Tessa Lorant Warburg has been asserted

This book is a work of fiction. All of the characters and their life stories are the product of the author's fertile imagination. Some of the events happened to a real family who lived in the Villa Gehben, Altenbruch, Cuxhaven, Germany between 1908 and 1938. A few of the older inhabitants of Altenbruch may think they recognize several character traits of the main protagonists, but this book is *not* a bio-graph of the Gehben family, it is a work of fiction loosely based on that family.

ISBN: 978-0-906374-06-1

The Thorn Press
thethornpress.com
Lansdowne House
Castle Lane
Southampton SO14 2BU, UK

Printed and bound in the UK

DEDICATION

This book is dedicated to my daughter Madeleine Warburg without whose constant, enthusiastic and inspirational support it would not have been written.

BY THE SAME AUTHOR

Fiction: written as Emma Lorant
(Tessa Lorant Warburg with Madeleine Warburg)
Cradle of Secrets
Lullaby of Fear
Baby Roulette

Non Fiction, written as Tessa Lorant Warburg
A Voice at Twilight (Diary of a Dying Man), Oddfellows Social
Concern Book Award 1989

Non Fiction, written as Tessa Lorant
The Batsford Book of Hand and Machine Knitting
The Batsford Book of Knitted Laces
Yarns for Textile Crafts

THE HERITAGE OF KNITTING SERIES:
Tessa Lorant's Collection of Knitted Lace Edgings
Knitted Quilts & Flounces
Knitted Lace Collars
Knitted Shawls & Wraps
The Secrets of Successful Irish Crochet Lace
Knitted Lace Doilies

Earning and Saving with a Knitting Machine
Choosing and Buying a Knitting Machine
Yarns for the Knitter
The Good Yarn Guide

Jeremy Warburg and Tessa Lorant:
The Grockles' Guide

Richard Warburg and Tessa Lorant
Snack Yourself Slim

ACKNOWLEDGMENTS

I would like to thank Madeleine Warburg for her help in editing this book. Thanks are also due to Gillian Geering for her generous and unstinting help and support with some of the historical background, as well as her painstaking copyediting. I am grateful to the members of the Blue Room Writing Group 2007/8—Deanna Dewey, Janet Elliott, Mo Foster, Evelyn Harris, Mike Hayward, Jenni Jacombs, Glen Jayson, Donna McGie and Mike Plumbley—for their reading of, and commenting on, the complete MS. My thanks also to Katharina Bosch, Diana Shaman, Anna Starkey and Richard Warburg for their valuable contributions. I am particularly grateful to Irmgard Schwenk, a family friend and resident of Altenbruch, Germany, for her help in finding sources for several of the myths and legends of the area, particularly those put together by Eberhard Michael Iba in *Hake Betken Siene Duven,*. My thanks also to the publisher for the generous permission to translate a number of these myths and legends and insert them into the novel. These wonderful stories are not well known outside the local area and deserve far greater recognition. I have adapted some for English-speaking readers as well as clarifying their relationship to *The Dohlen Inheritance*. It is truly astonishing how many of these stories point, in essence, to the reasons several of the characters in the book act the way they do.

Last, but by no means least, my appreciation and thanks go to the Town of Cuxhaven and the village of Altenbruch for their generous invitation in 2008 to attend the 100th anniversary of the building of the Villa Gehben, the ancestral home of the Gehben family. The Villa, built by Ernst Julius Gehben, is a showcase of Art Nouveau architecture. It now serves as Cuxhaven's City Hall and has become a major tourist attraction. My sister Diana and I, granddaughters of Ernst Julius, were wonderfully feted and given many mementoes of the village and the family. I would particularly like to mention Ortsbürgermeister Jörg-Heinrich Ahlemeyer and his wife Ingrid, Erhard Holthusen, Hermann and Trude Meyer, Karl-Wilhelm and Inge Tiedemann and Hans-Jürgen and Lilli Umland. They and the village of Altenbruch created a memorable event of which I am sure my grandfather would have been very proud. It also gave me the final impetus to publish this fictional saga based on a family that has become part of the local lore.

Hake Betken Siene Duven is a comprehensive collection of myths and legends of the "Land an Elb- und Wesermündung", that is the North German fens bordering the estuaries of the Elbe and Weser rivers, put together by Eberhard Michael Iba and published by Männer vom Morgenstern in 1993, ISBN 3-927-857-41-6.

PROLOGUE

THE AMERICAN DREAM

The first part of the nineteenth century was a particularly turbulent time in German history, and saw the end of the Holy Roman Empire. By 1860 famine was widespread and people despaired of the future. That's when Emil Julius Dohlen, youngest son of the wheelwright of the coastal village of Schwanenbruch, decided to change his life.

He'd always been a good boy, done what he could to help his family. Starting out before dawn he once again hoisted his father's best cartwheel onto his back and trudged the thirty kilometres to the nearest market. He spent all day trying for a sale, but he had no luck. And that meant carrying the heavy wheel all those kilometres back, as well as bringing home the bad news.

That's when Emil knew he'd had enough. If he wanted a decent future he'd have to fashion it. He decided then and there that Germany was not the place to do it. So he put on the best of his home-spun clothes, proud of the mother who had so lovingly woven the material from tufts of fleece she'd garnered from thorn bushes growing on the marsh. He would follow her lead; use his imagination to create a better, richer career than following in his father's footsteps.

Emil set a jaunty sailor's cap on his head and left the two-room cottage snuggled within the shelter of the dyke. He had no money, and only one day's ration wrapped in his kerchief. His only other possessions were the smile on his face, an optimistic temperament and the determination to win.

The sixteen-year-old offered his services to all and sundry, but he got more kicks than jobs until he wormed his way into the good graces

1

of a captain sailing for America. To the Land of the Free, the country of enterprise, where there's work for all seekers and the streets are paved with gold. He got himself a passage in return for washing dishes, sluicing decks and sleeping where he could find the space.

The youth was allowed to eat his fill for the first time in his life. He reckoned that even if he had to spend his time journeying back and forth across the Atlantic he'd be better off than in his native land.

Emil was lucky; his boat docked in Manhattan, on South Street at Coenties Slip, a short walk from Wall Street. He stepped off the gangplank, sank to his knees, picked up the dirt and kissed it. He knew he'd arrived in God's own Country.

The youth got back to his feet, stood tall with his cap in his hand, smiled. He remembered the old German saying:

Mit dem Hute in der Hand
Kommt man durch das ganze Land.

Cap in hand
Helps you find the Promised Land.

And, sure enough, he soon landed a job sweeping the floor of the New York Stock and Exchange Board at a dime a day.

Emil wasn't just hard-working and agreeable; he also had a good business head on his shoulders. He'd been enterprising enough to shake the dust of the Old Country from his feet. Now he was determined to make a success of life in the New World.

When the brokers who worked on the floor of the Exchange got hungry they sent young Emil uptown to fetch their lunch. It soon occurred to the lad that he could prepare sandwiches before he came to work, save himself the long trip uptown and make some money on the side, selling his offerings to the brokers. He saved a few cents a day, going without food himself, until he had enough money to buy the ingredients to satisfy the brokers' quick-snack appetites.

At that time a large percentage of people living and working in Manhattan came from Germany. Emil knew exactly what they liked to eat. Thick, well-filled sandwiches made with sturdy slices of rye bread

2

stuffed with good German sausage, ham or beef. He added mustard and garnishes as well. The fledgling businessman sold his first day's concoctions within minutes. Encouraged, he bought more supplies to make the next day's fare.

Emil's business grew. Soon, too busy to sweep the Exchange floor, he saved his money and bought a stand to sell his wares on Wall Street. People flocked to buy. And then he had a better idea. He'd open an Eatery within a stone's throw not only of the Exchange, but also of the new buildings he'd heard were being planned for the whole financial sector. He found the shell of a warehouse abandoned after the 1835 fire, and renovated it.

The business prospered. Emil listened to the brokers as they discussed their shares, saved his money, invested wisely. He didn't restrict himself to equities but bought into real estate as well. His favourite investments were Lower East Side tenement houses, built right where the workers needed a place to live. Nor did he stop there. With no running water in the tall, overcrowded buildings Emil saw the potential for public baths, places where the East Side dwellers could soak city grime from their bodies, relax—and be happy to pay a small price to do so.

That's when the poor wheelwright's son from a tiny village nestling below the dyke became rich beyond his wildest dreams. The only things he lacked were a wife and family. Then, out of the blue, fate brought a young woman from Schwanenbruch to fill that gap.

The Villa

PART 1

FORCED LANDINGS

1913–1916

THE DYKEMAN

A long time ago, when Schwanenbruch was just a tiny hamlet and the dyke was still low and narrow, the sea cut a breach in it. And the water poured through, threatening the whole village. The villagers' houses, their barns, their farm animals, their livelihood. Even their lives were no longer safe.

The wind blew hard across the Elbe estuary, pushing heavy North Sea rollers against the dyke, splitting it, breaking through.

So the village sent their strongest men to repair it. They toiled day and night to patch up the dyke. But nothing worked. Nothing they did held against the fierce sea, or the breakers whipped high by the cruel wind.

That's when a stranger walked past the village workers. From Hamburg, the big town upstream along the river Elbe. Wearing an expensive coat, and with money in his pockets.

The village men grabbed him and trussed him up. They ignored his cries, refused to touch the money he held out to them, pleaded with them to take.

They didn't utter a single word. Not to each other, not to him.

But they made a bigger slit in the dyke, longer and wider than the sea had made. They lowered the stranger into his watery grave, let the wind carry his cries away. And they shovelled the wet dark silt over him until his nose and mouth were covered up. So that he couldn't cry out any more. Or so they thought.

The dyke held from that moment onwards. But the dykeman's cries can still be heard when der Blanke Hans—the foaming North Sea—rages across the flat marshes of Land Hadeln. And one day—one grim, unforgettable day—the dykeman will rise out of his grave. And he will get his revenge on the villagers of Schwanenbruch.

CHAPTER 1

Schwanenbruch, September 13th, 1913

Gabriele Dohlen, nicknamed Gabby because she talks so much, is alert and wakeful long after bedtime. She squints at the cot near her bed. No movement from her sister Doly, not even snuffles. No heavy breathing, either. Pretending to be asleep. The little sneak.

Gabby punches down the billowing Federbett and sits up, listening. And hears the sounds she knows are coming, the ones she's been waiting for.

Always the same. The rattles as her father's stick clatters against the metal railing beside the stoop, clangs the front door. Followed by softer noises, thumps and bangs. And then the swear words which rumble like thunder rolling across the North Sea mudflats. Growling and loud.

Gabby takes an enormous gulp of air and holds it tight. She's trained herself to count up to sixty without breathing. So that she can hear what her parents are saying.

Usually Vater is the one who tells Mutti what to do. But at night Mutti scolds Vater about drinking too much. When she thinks no one else can hear.

At first everything is comforting, familiar. Exactly like the noises Gabby listens out for every night. The slurp of her father's feet dragging up the stoop, the low grumble of the front door opening, the squeak of hinges as it swings wide, her mother's whispers.

But Mutti sounds different tonight.She's making odd mewling noises, like the new kittens.

Is it because she stubbed her toe on the big doll Gabby left lying in the hall? Pastor Bender gave it to Doly. It's much too big for her, so she put it in her cot, pretended it was her baby sister.

Gabby grabbed it when Doly wasn't looking, dropped it over the balusters. When Herta saw it she told Doly off for leaving her toys around. Then she sent Gabby to fetch the doll and put it away.

Gabby left the bedroom, but not to go downstairs. The hall was dark, and cold. The dykeman might come after her if she went down alone. She crept along the corridor, then came back, leaving the doll where it had fallen.

As she remembers her breath turns into pants and she feels sick. Does the dykeman know about the doll? Will he make Mutti fall over it and hurt herself? Should she run down, right now, and warn her?

She can't. Vater will shout at her if she leaves her room. Mutti is bound to see a big doll like that, it will be all right.

She hears her parents' boots scuffing the parquet of the entrance hall, then the wooden stairs. Herta will grumble about cleaning the black marks tomorrow.

Scrape, crash. 'Holy Moses, what the hell is this?' A thump, a flip-flop of something hard-soft on the floor.

The doll. Gabby gulps.

'Shsh, Emil. The servants will hear.'

It wouldn't matter if they did. Gabby's heard the servants talk amongst themselves. Ursula to Herta: "Had a good one on him last night." Herta to Ursula: "Can't hold it like he used to. Not like our blessed Pastor Bender. He's practically pickled now."

How can a man be pickled? Pastor Bender—even though he's her grandfather, Gabby always has to call him that—is her father's dearest friend. Because they were blood brothers before Vater left to go to America. Hundreds of years ago.

Gabby wrinkles her forehead to remember the year her father was born. She never can, she isn't good at numbers. Vater is old. He has crinkly white hair with bits of sandy stuff. His beard is made up of lots of colours, like the shells and crabs on the mudflats beyond the dyke. His eyebrows are all straggly and the same colour as the gingerbread men Rula bakes on St Nicolaus Day. He's the patron saint of children and fishermen. Vater calls him Santa Claus. And laughs and laughs. Everyone laughs with him. What's so funny?

'Can't a man get any peace around here?'

'Shuushh, Ehhmihl...'

Muffled words. Not just Mutti's usual worry about being overheard by Herta and Ursula. Fuzzy. Gabby shivers. If she keeps completely still, cups her hands behind her ears, holds her breath and doesn't move one tiny bit she might find out what it is.

'Holy Moses. Enough to make one break one's neck.'

'Listen Emil. I think...'

Doly begins to snuffle in her cot. Much too near Gabby's bed. Her name is Dorinda, but she can only say Dolinda, so she's Doly now.

Gabby clamps her mouth tight. She's nearly seven. Why does she have to share with Doly, who's five years younger? There are lots of other rooms in the big house. Herta says so.

''lo, Gabby.'

Busybody brat. Always spying on her. 'You're supposed to be asleep.'

'You not.'

Gabby feels the familiar knot in her throat. Doly has a knack of making her mad. 'Shut up.'

'Gabby bad.'

Gabby jumps out from under the fat duvet and grabs the cot bars. She stubs her large toe. It hurts. All Doly's fault. 'Shut up, you little toad...'

That mocking laugh. 'Gabby mad,' Doly lisps. 'Gabby velly mad.'

Hands suddenly moist with sweat, eyes smarting tears, Gabby shakes the cot. The stolid wood holds firm. She doesn't shout at Doly, in case it brings Mutti into the room. But she pushes a finger through the bars and pokes her.

Doly pokes back. 'Doly tell Mutti.'

'Isn't she sweet?' Herta always says, tucking Doly up, covering her with kisses, brushing back the bouncy ginger curls. 'The little innocent.'

Even Vater smiles at Doly, calls her his little Dresden doll, lifts her high, twirls her until she giggles and her curls fly round her head.

Never Gabby. Because her hair is straight. And already thin. The bald patch on the back of her head is getting too large to hide.

'Tell tale tit,' Gabby hisses. She moves to the door, puts her ear against it.

Another deep breath as Gabby counts again. '...twenty-one, twenty-two...'

Vater's loud singing: *'He, Du mit den Lockenkopp...'* The words sound different when Herta and Ursula sing them, even different from Mutti.

'Your father spoke only English for almost fifty years,' Mutti told her. 'That's why you can't always understand him.'

Vater prefers English, says it's better than German, easier to use when doing business. Maybe if she learns English Vater will talk to her.

The singing turns to cackles. *'He, Du mit den Lockenkopp—Hey, you with the curly mop.'* Is he singing about Doly's hair? Because there's lots of it and it's so pretty? Mutti's is set in rigid waves. Her hat sits on top, even indoors.

'Emil, please.'

A grunt, a shuffle.

'...fifty. Fifty-one...'

'Ooooh...'

Gabby listens harder. What's that sound? Not her father's feet dragging up the stairs, nor his body humping from tread to tread. It's her mother, crying. Why?

'Ahhhuuuhhh...'

Low. In pain. Louder.

'Emil...'

A faint hiss, a rattle. Is Vater hitting her?

'Help me, Emil!'

Weaker now, the words all gurgled.

'Aaauuhhh.'

More like a wail.

Gabby turns to Doly. Completely still. She stares at the bedroom door. Should she go to Mutti? Will Vater yell at her? Tears itch and prickle.

'Help!'

Her mother's voice much fainter than before, but unmistakable. Mutti needs her. Gabby searches for her slippers...

'Herta!'

No time for strict rules about bare feet. Gabby rushes to the door, pulls at the knob. Hot, damp fingers can't turn it.

A bump, several more, the deep snore which tells her Vater is out cold.

The doorknob turns. Gabby creeps out to the banisters, looks down on a grey huddle which must be her mother. She tiptoes to the stairs, listens. Snores from her father—but in the pauses Gabby can hear her mother's rapid, panting breaths.

What's wrong with Mutti? Goosebumps down her spine tell Gabby what she doesn't want to know. Something awful, terrible; has the dykeman come, will he drag Mutti to a watery grave?

Then all is quiet again. Maybe everything is all right. It's draughty in the hall, cold and dank. She longs for her warm bed.

'Help!'

Mutti needs her. She has to go. Gabby creeps her way down the high treads, hears her mother moan, sees her father lying several steps further down.

'Mutti,' she whispers. And again, louder.

No answer, no movement.

She leans towards her. An odd, metallic smell. 'Mutti! What's wrong with you?'

'Get Herta, Gabby.' Her words like caws. Like the rooks in the big oak.

What is that smell? Not Schnapps. She'd recognise her father's brandy.

She hurtles up the stairs, on up the second staircase to the servants' quarters, pummels on the first door. 'Herta! There's something wrong with my Mutti. Wake up, Herta!'

Nothing stirs. Gabby's screams echo round the stairwell.

Doors open, lights come on, heads appear, hair covered in knitted caps, long nightgowns making ghosts of well-known figures.

'What on earth is the matter, child?'

'Die Mutti,' Gabby sobs. 'Something's wrong with my Mutti. She's been hurt. She's bleeding.'

Her mother—her energetic, efficient, no-nonsense mother—is lying helpless on the stiars and Vater, strong powerful Vater, isn't doing anything about it.

CHAPTER 2

Schwanenbruch, September 13th, 1913

Broad bodies flatten Gabby against the wall. Voices ricochet like Onkel Wilfred's repeater shotgun exploding at flocks of thieving starlings in the cherry orchards. Black corpses plunging down.

Disjointed syllables change to words, assume meaning. 'Oh-my-God. Get the doctor, quick.'

Gabby crouches in the landing shadows. She watches Ursula lumber up, her arms grabbing Mutti's legs. Hat and hair askew, Mutti's head is upright against Herta's chest. The three women struggle past, undulating like a monstrous serpent, splattering liquid. Gabby's arms ache to embrace Mutti, to protect her. 'You're hurting her.'

'Get back to bed, child.'

'What's wrong with my Mutti?'

Herta—dear sweet patient Herta—heaves a broad hip against her. 'Bed.'

Barked syllables stab through Gabby's brain where they spread like fog, slowing thought and action.

Below her Vater's lion mane shakes anger. 'God dammit. Is someone going to see to *me*?' He humps to his knees, twines his arms round the banister. A lurch up the stairs.

Gabby sees Herta throw Mutti's shawl round Ursula's shoulders,

13

push her towards the stairs. 'He's got to come at once. No time to lose.'

Ursula's gown whirls past Vater.

'Damn you women. What's all the fuss?' Vater's hand grabs at Ursula. '*He, Du mit den Lockenkopp.*'

But Ursula's hair is straight. Plaited into one long coiled snake twisting down her back. Strong nut-brown hair which glows. Gabby thinks of her own wisps. Neither brown nor blonde. Flaxen, Mutti says. More like mouse. Gabby longs to have shining chestnut hair like Ursula's. Or even Herta's stiff grey which still grows full and strong.

Ursula brushes Vater's hands away, clomps to the front door. Gabby knows he'll send her packing to-morrow, the way he did Anna when she answered back. If he remembers.

'Emma! Where are you, woman?'

'She's up here, Herr Dohlen.' Herta is standing by Mutti's open door. 'Try to get up to the bedroom. She's started.'

'Holy Moses! Has her time come already?'

The new baby. That's what it is. 'Due any moment,' Herta told Rula yesterday. 'Have to watch out, she's always quick.'

Is that all? Gabby feels cross. Mutti's got her and Doly. And Moppel. The only boy, the one that counts. Is she having another baby because she wants another son?

'She's haemorrhaging, Herr Dohlen. It's bad.'

'Holy Moses! Where's that damn doctor.' A sob at the end of the roar. 'Don't I pay him enough to come when he's wanted?' Vater's grip on the banister rail hauls his body up two treads. He falls back with a crash. Herta's body, facing the bedroom, swivels round. She goes down to him.

Gabby slips into her mother's room. She edges past the dressing-table. Silver brushes, silver comb, silver mirror back. Emma Dohlen engraved on all of them. In hard-to-read curling letters.

Mutti's black hair is spread like a spatchcocked bird on the pillow. Her special sheets are soft and silky, pearly white. They show up oozing tentacles of colour, like a giant octopus clutching around her, growing fat.

'Gabby...' A low murmur. A trembling hand points at her neck.

'What's the matter, Mutti?'

14

'My big girl.' Her fingers sign to come nearer.

Gabby perches on the edge of the bed. Where it isn't smeared.

'Take it, Gabby. To remind you.' The small hand with the wide wedding ring points to the locket round her neck. 'Remember, Gabby. Always remember.'

Great-grandmother Emma's locket. The one Gabby will inherit one day. Not yet... Not yet!

Gabby stares at the locket, large and clumsy, solid gold in a heart shape. The lower half has September 27th, 1825 scrolled into the metal. In ornate twining letters, with small wedding bells set around the date. The top is embossed in diamonds. Two interlocking letters, E and H, are topped by the famous Lieblingsblüte, the legendary flower of truest love. Shown by a huge white pearl set below a small black one.

The locket is always there, always round Mutti's neck. It can be opened wide to show two tiny smiling faces. Great-grandfather Hinrich, his dark luxuriant hair and beard framing a healthy robust complexion, and Great-grandmother Emma, a Dutch coif covering her head and shadowing her features. They face each other, for ever smiling their adoration.

Mutti singsongs their love story time and again. The precious, bell-shaped white flower with the black centre is famous in the little town of Hagen. A truly rare flower, hard to find. Said to grow only on the spot where virtuous Hiltrud shed bitter tears when her brave husband Heino was killed defending her virtue. The legend says that lovers who find the flower together, and pluck it, will always remain united in their love.

Great-grandparents Emma and Hinrich found that special bloom, the lily-white flower with its dark interior, which grows nearby and in no other place in the whole world. And when they found it Great-grandmother Emma whispered the secret of what she lacked, of her unfortunate inheritance, to her ardent suitor. Quite sure that, in spite of finding the Lieblingsblüte, he would reject her because of it. Pale, delicate, brave, she waited for his verdict. Head bowed.

And Great-grandfather Hinrich sank to his knees, right there in the meadow. Emma was such a little thing that her bowed head was almost level with Hinrich's proud one when she was standing and

15

he was kneeling. He combed his fingers through his luxuriant locks, tossed them at her, picked the precious flower, laughed and held it up to her.

'Don't you worry yourself about that, my love,' he said as he embraced his sweetheart. 'I have enough for two.'

'The doctor's coming, Mutti. He'll make you better right away.' Gabby presses the limp hand, lets go in case she crushes it.

'Take it.'

Gabby doesn't want to, shudders back.

Mutti's head is raised off the pillow. Glassy eyes stare deep into Gabby's. Commanding, unmistakable.

She puts her hands around her mother's neck, unclasps the golden chain and holds the locket up.

Mutti's eyes, bluer now, begin to smile. Gabby dangles the locket towards the bedside table. 'No.' Her mother's body arches.

Gabby folds the locket tight inside her hand. 'Shall I get Herta, Mutti?' Is this how babies are born? They jump out?

The mound of body sags, the dark head sinks into the pillows. Slow pants for air, eyes showing white. A searching hand tries to find Gabby's arm, misses.

Gabby catches the hand between her palms, cradles it, wedging the locket hard, enduring, between the two of them.

'Be good to your brother and sister, Gabby.' Mutti's arm grows limp, her hand slips away. 'My poor children.'

A dread Gabby's never known before blots out awareness. She clutches the locket inside her palms until the clasp draws blood. She presses harder, welcoming pain.

'What the hell...' Vater's raw voice pulls her away. 'This is no place for you, child.' Strong fingers push down on her head, move to her shoulders, propel her out.

Gabby stumbles along the corridor. She hears Vater's breath rasp, hears him choke. The sound of loud weeping.

Love for her parents fragments into splinters of fear not even Vater can turn away. The bedroom door slams shut.

16

CHAPTER 3

Schwanenbruch, September 13th, 1913

Gabby creeps back into her bed and pulls the bedclothes over her head, trying to blot out what's happening around her. Her mother's image appears to her, the way she was earlier when Gabby came home from school.

Mutti was waiting by their gate as Gabby hurried back to be on time for the Mittagessen Rula was preparing. The midday meal is always served at noon. On the dot.

Rula promised Gabby she'd have her favourite dessert one more time this year, made with the last of the summer fruit. Rote Grütze mit Vanillesauce, gooey and thick, the red jelly is her special favourite. Served with vanilla custard. Making lovely yellow swirls in the dark red pudding.

Gabby took off her satchel, stepped nearer her mother, caught a glimpse of her smile. So sweet and gentle. Nearly as good as a bear hug from Herta.

'Frau Dohlen is a strange one,' Gabby heard Herta tell Rula. In the kitchen while Rula was kneading dough. 'Doesn't even hug her babies, let alone her children. I wonder how she ever came by them.'

And Rula laughing, crashing the sourdough on the floured table, pushing the heels of her strong palms into it. Making it smooth and shiny. Letting it rise.

Mutti used her fingertips to adjust the large taffeta ribbon Gabby was wearing. She's taken to plaiting a big coloured ribbon into Gabby's hair. An ornament which adds bulk to the flaxen wisps, disguises her high forehead, covers the bald patch.

'Too clever-looking for a girl. We want to show off those forget-me-not-blue eyes of yours. Such an unusual colour. Smile, Gabby.'

Gabby's more interested in how she can use her eyes than in how they look. 'I'm the best reader in my class, Mutti. Fräulein Winter said...'

'You don't have to be the best.'

That's not what Vater says. She's heard him roar that only the best is good enough.

'You just have to do your best,' Mutti murmured.

Gabby looked at her mother, waited for the big hat which always covers her mother's head and shades her face to move up and down. Approvingly. She watched for the strong black circle of shadow to sweep from Mutti's throat down to her bosom, and back again. It didn't move down. Instead, Mutti's head tilted a long way back so that Gabby could see her eyes. Shining. The way they do whenever she talks about coming back home to Germany.

'Where did we come from, Mutti?' Gabby asked. On cue. She likes to go through the same question and answer routine. Time and again.

'Why, from America, Gabby. We lived in the state of New Jersey. In Wyckoff, where you were born.

'Is that near New York, Mutti? Near the skyscrapers?'

That soft laugh. 'Very near. Your father had business to see to in Manhattan every day. On Wall Street. He took the ferry across the river Hudson. Haven't I told you that?'

'Why did you and Vater come back to Schwanenbruch?'

'Lots of reasons. Because I didn't really like it over there. All those parties. Invitations from people I didn't know. And they wear such formal clothes. Besides, it's so hot in the summer, so clammy.' She paused, her eyes silver fishes darting in clear water. 'Your father didn't mind coming home.' She pointed to their house, to the second floor, at the huge double windows surrounded by decorative wooden panelling. Large letters are chiselled into the woodwork:

OB OST OB WEST TO HUS OM BEST

'East or West, home is best. That's what I always say. And your father agrees with me.'

Those words are easy for Gabby to read. But they're not written the way they're spelt at school. Maybe Vater doesn't understand Plattdeutsch any more. 'He's always sailing back to New York, Mutti.'

'For business, Gabby.' Delicate fingers stroked her face, lifted her chin. 'You know he was born here in Schwanenbruch.'

'In the last but one house in the Westerstrasse. And Pastor Bender was born right next door.'

'Quite right. Your father and my father, your grandfather, were boys together. Just think, that was well over sixty years ago. When there wasn't even a street. Ours were the only two houses there. A long way out of the village.'

'The last ones before the dyke.' Gabby always worries a little when they come to this part. Does Vater know about the dykeman? That one day he'll take his revenge on the oldest village families, on the people who lived in the two little houses which stand close to the dyke? Where Rula is now. And Onkel Palter.

The large hat shook up and down in agreement. Like a mother raven flapping her wings. 'It's where I was born as well.'

'And you looked after your younger brothers and sisters, didn't you, Mutti.'

'When my step-mother died.' This time the shadow moved from side to side. 'Tante Hannah and Tante Martha were too young to be at school. But we were in the parsonage by then.' She looked down at Gabby, her features shadowed, her feelings hidden, and put her arm round Gabby's shoulders. A loosening blending touch, safe haven even if der Blanke Hans were to hiss and foam right over the dyke.

'Now, do you remember in which year of Our Lord we came home, Gabby?' Mutti's finger pointed up to the inscription painted in huge curly white lettering arched high under the eaves of their house, her voice urgent, as though the answer were more important than anything Gabby learned at school.

19

Gabby did a little dance in her dainty patent-leather shoes. 'Nineteen hundred and eight.' She knew Mutti would be proud she could say the big number.

'Very good, Gabby. You're getting better at large numbers. That's when you were only one year old, a little baby.' Her mother's laugh wind-chimed in the Indian summer sun. And the St Nicolaikirche bells, housed in the round bell-tower across the road from their villa, boomed once, then sounded back twelve dings.

'The date tells us that our lovely house was built the year your father brought us home. Now, can you read the words?' Sparkling eyes were raised to the eaves, her finger pointed up to the lettering again. As though she'd never done it before.

1908

DEUTSCHE ART TREU BEWAHRT

No need. She knows them by heart. 'German Ways Upheld with Praise.' She rolled the syllables slowly around her tongue, deciphering them. So Mutti would know how good she was at reading.

'I suppose you don't really need to. You've heard me repeat them often enough.' She put her hand out and brushed a willow leaf from Gabby's dress. 'The leaves are turning already.'

Gabby drew back, pushing the large ribbon straight again.

'The real question is, do you understand what they mean?' She gripped Gabby's shoulders and stared into her eyes.

Gabby twisted her head away.

'I'd like you to remember those words, Gabby. They're there to remind us how proud we are to keep our German traditions alive, to keep faith with them.' Her hands pressed hard on Gabby's shoulders. 'Honour, loyalty and duty are the most important ones.'

'That hurts, Mutti.'

'Together with honesty, diligence, sobriety, responsibility, discipline, courage.' Determined fingers dug off the virtues. Then stopped as Mutti leaned against the railings. 'Aahh.'

'Are you ill, Mutti?'

'A little tired, Gabby.'

She stared at her mother's swollen tummy. The new baby's in there, Herta said. She didn't say how it got out, and when that would be. And whenever Gabby asks such questions even Herta gets annoyed.

CHAPTER 4

Schwanenbruch, September 13th, 1913

Doly lies curled up in her cot, left thumb in her mouth, knees drawn tight to her chin. The slats look blacker, more menacing, than the dark all round her. She's longing for strong arms to swallow her up, for puckering lips to kiss her. There's no one. She kicks against the imprisoning bars, stops when she feels the pain.

Freckles of light filter through from the hall outside. She opens her eyes wide, tries to focus. A threatening wardrobe seems about to swallow her up, then to retreat. She clutches her bedding round her, determined chin above it, tightening her fists.

Doly pushes her thumb deep inside her mouth, bites it to stop from crying out. If she makes a noise, even shows she's awake, Gabby will scream at her, rock the cot from side to side, pushing her hard against the bars.

She'll wait for daylight, for Herta or Ursula to pull back the curtains, to gather her up in arms which always smell of soap, to heave her into the air and catch her, then to cover her face and hair with wet smacking kisses.

Doly sucks at her thumb. After Mutti she loves Herta best. And sometimes Vater. He sits her on his lap, and runs her ginger locks through his fingers. She loves the feel of his hand through her curls, shakes her head to feel the weight of it. Even if she can't see her hair she can toss it, feel it flow around her, know that it isn't thin—like

22

Gabby's.

More noises from outside, lights flashing on and off. She cowers away from the dark cot slats on the white bedding, hunches into herself, cramming fingers on top of the thumb in her mouth. She longs for warm sweet-smelling arms around her.

Doly leans back against a toy, feels sweat creep down her back as it makes a noise. She holds her breath: whisperings, Vater's gruff shout, then gentler tones which sound like Herta. She shudders herself upright, grabs the cot bars, clutches a corner of the duvet. Time to get up? Where's the light from behind the curtains? She swallows a sob, desperate for someone, anyone, to comfort her.

'You'th 'wake, Gabby.' The words slip out even though she knows Gabby will jump out of bed, snarling, and cuff her head.

But Gabby doesn't snarl, or even snap. She's crying, hard enough for Doly to hear through the banging doors and clumping footsteps.

Doly's heart beats even faster, she feels herself choke as she watches a slash of yellow light slither up to the ceiling. Her sister's got up, pushed their door half open. Streams of light turn the dark bars on Doly's cot into sharp long knives of shadow.

'Be good, Doly,' Gabby's cracked voice comes nearer, then breaks into sobs. 'Vater is very upset,' Doly makes out.

She pushes her head down, on to the mattress, burrows under her Federbett. Herta said it was dangerous, the plump comforter could suffocate her. She doesn't care.

'How long ago?' A loud male voice booms through the billowing feathers.

Doly pokes her head out to listen. 'About half an hour, Herr Doktor.' Ursula's voice, gulping and fearful.

'Where is she?'

'If you would follow me upstairs, Herr Doktor.'

Slow footsteps on the wooden treads, the growl of hobnailed boots. More words, her parents' bedroom door bursts open, then closes.

Doly tramples the comforter away from her. 'Gabby.'

'What?' Her sister's voice, subdued with crying.

'Wha's 'at?'

'What's what?'

'Tha' man.'

'The doctor. There's something wrong with Mutti,' Gabby rushes out in whispers. 'I don't know what's the matter with her.'

She shuffles over to the cot and lays her head against the bars. Doly stares at her. She's different, changed, doesn't bully or threaten. She's just a thin dismal shadow in her nightdress, her figure haloed by light from the door.

'I's 'fraid, Gabby,' Doly murmurs at her.

'We have to be very good, Doly.' The normally determined voice is raspy, as though Gabby has a cold. 'Our Mutti is very ill.'

The sound of their parents' bedroom door opening again.

'Emma. Don't leave us, Emma.' A long drawn-out wail. Is that... *Vater?*

Doly puts out her hands, finds Gabby's. They stretch both arms towards each other, clasp tight, the cot bars hard against their bodies.

Herta leans round their door. 'Get back into bed, Gabby. And you, Doly. Lie down. Your Mutti isn't feeling well, the doctor's here to put it right. Help her by being good girls, now. It will all be better in the morning.'

Such a long speech. Doly knows right away that something very, very bad is going on. Even Herta doesn't say much to them. "Children should be seen and not heard" is the longest speech Doly can remember.

'Go back to sleep now.'

The door clicks shut.

Last time he asked for 5 Pfennig. Rula says that's hardly anything. There are 10 Pfennig in a Groschen, so he wasn't even asking for a Groschen.

He can often coax a little out of Vater if he can get him on his own. That's hard because Gabby and Doly always poke their noses in. And Vater forgets about his only son and heir, and turns to Doly. Watches her twirl herself around, making her skirts stick out.

Vater's face changes, his eyes go soft, he even smiles. He likes Doly's stupid dancing. All right for girls. What's a boy supposed to do? Vater ignores him.

But Moppel knows a trick or two. His favourite is the money chair. Big and black, made of leather. In the study, right underneath the portrait. Vater sat in that chair and let the painter stare at him while he worked. For months and months. The whole house smelled of paint. Horrible.

The picture's eyes look so much like Vater they make Moppel jump. As though he's really sitting in that chair. Moppel waits for Vater to leave before he dares go in. Then he runs right up to the chair and clambers on.

Vater's coins jingle in his trouser pockets. A habit he's picked up in America, Mutti says. Loads spill out when he's sitting down. Into the folds of soft leather at the sides.

Just like the magic barrel in the fairy tale. You drop money in and when you take it out there's more to pick up. The chair's exactly the same. Even when Moppel's sure there's nothing more, twisting his fingers under the leather and into the stuffing will often get him another coin. Real treasure trove. Mostly Groschen, but Pfennig pieces are worth collecting, too.

One day he found a Goldmark: a real Mark coin. Made of silver, not gold, but still based on the value of the metal it's made of. Vater explained all that. Moppel knew he had to find a grown-up to give him change. Rula said she didn't have that sort of money. Told him to go to one of his uncles.

Onkel Wilfred offered him 5 Groschen. Small eyes nearly shut, teeth showing.

Moppel knows there are 10 Groschen to a Mark. 'Did you m-make a m-mistake, Onkel Wilfred? Isn't a Mark w-worth m-m-much more than that?' Nervous because Onkel Wilfred stood with his feet wide apart. Cigar glowing

The stern look changed to a grin. 'Think so, do you, my boy? Well, if you don't believe me, you can always ask your father what it's worth.'

That's when he looked for a secret place for his coins. Found one in his bedroom: the little hole behind the window sill. No one but Gabby would know to look for it there. And she isn't allowed in his room.

Moppel slides off his bed, moves over to his hiding place, digs his fingers into it, feels the hard coins. Strokes them. Enjoys them.

A new noise outside his bedroom. He jumps away from the window, back into his bed. Not footsteps along the corridor... Someone clip-clopping up the stairs, lighter boots than earlier on, firmer steps.

He knows whose they are. His hair prickles, sweat pours from his armpits, feels cold. He shuts his eyes and pulls the Federbett round himself, up to his chin. Still freezing.

'What's happening? Why are the lights on? What's going on here? Emma? Are you there, Emma?'

That shrill terrifying voice. Tante Hannah.

She came to live with them. Ages ago. On Easter Sunday. He had to give her one of his Easter eggs because she's Mutti's baby sister. She's supposed to look after the three of them, take them for walks. Teach them folk songs, read them fairy tales.

She doesn't do any of that.

What Tante Hannah does is to march them along the cobbled streets, then out on the dirt road to the dyke. She leaves them there, huddled against the fierce wind. They crowd together and try to find shelter behind a tamarisk bush or a rugosa rose.

'Stay there, you brats,' she shouts as she runs off. 'If you've moved even a centimetre before I get back, the dykeman will get you.'

The story of the dykeman is the one story Tante Hannah does tell them, time and again. It's seared into Moppel's mind.

He watches her open mouth. Showing black stumpy rotting teeth. He knows exactly what she means. She'll bury all three of them if they don't do what she says. Bury them just like the villagers buried the dykeman. Alive. So no one will ever find them again. Or hear their cries.

'A solid body is the best bulwark there is against the threatening sea,' twisted lips spill out at them, and she laughs. Hard and mean. 'Just you remember that.'

In spite of Tante Hannah's threats the children don't do exactly as they're told. She can't bury all three of them, they mumble at each other. Vater will stop her. They choose to forget that Vater is away a lot. Sailing to New York.

They wait a few minutes after Tante Hannah has gone. Then they climb to the top of the dyke and watch her as she runs towards the pebbled beach, her skirts held up above the little streams crossing the short-grassed moors. To meet a man. Is he the dykeman?

Scared, they scramble back down the steep bank, scrabble against it. And keep watch for the long black shadow which will cover them when Tante Hannah reappears above them.

'What are you gawking at?' she shouts as she comes closer. 'Didn't I say I'd be back right away?'

Moppel hates her. The fat ungainly body, the oily thick black hair, the dark pock-marked complexion, the blisters on her big lips. He could put up with all those, but not the snarl behind every syllable, the spite every time Mutti's back is turned.

'Moppel smashed another of your special cups,' Tante Hannah lied to Mutti. Last Sunday. She did it herself. The clumsy fat thing swept it off the dresser as she turned. Her swollen leaking lips sneered. 'I told you not to let him have a proper one.'

She changed the cup for a mug. Thick and heavy. 'I keep telling you, Emma. You have to be much stricter with the children. You spoil them rotten.'

Now Tante Hannah's penetrating voice pierces the silent house.

'Emma?' she calls out. 'Is everything all right?' She clatters up the stairs. Grit grinds into the wooden treads, makes a scrunching noise. 'Are you there, Emma?'

A door kicks open.

'What's going on, Ursula? Where's Herta?'

No one answers her.

Moppel creeps under his Federbett. All is silent again except for the echo of Tante Hannah's voice, the click-clack of her boots clattering on the landing.

31

CHAPTER 6

Schwanenbruch, September 14th, 1913

'You're wanted, Gabriele. Your father wants to see you in his study.'

Herta is calling her Gabriele. Something's dreadfully wrong. She looks beyond Herta, at the door.

'You're to get dressed before you go to him. Hurry up and wash.'

'Is Mutti...?'

Herta's skirts swish as she turns away and lowers the side of Doly's cot. 'Don't pester me with questions. And don't forget to brush your teeth.' Face hidden by Doly's curls, words hard to make out.

Why is Herta so cross? Gabby fingers the heart-shaped gold in her nightdress pocket. Did Mutti tell Herta about last night? Was it wrong to take the locket from around Mutti's neck? Did that make her worse?

If she's been really bad, if Mutti's being ill is all her fault, Vater could make it turn out right. Vater can do anything. Gabby closes her eyes to imagine the worst. He could give her a whipping with his belt. The way he always threatens to do with Moppel. Then Mutti would feel better right away.

She brushes tears from her eyes. If Vater punishes her, everything will be as it was. Before last night.

But will he? Vater always says whipping is for boys but he's never actually beaten Moppel. Or anybody else. He doesn't even kick Jemima's kittens out of the way, like Onkel Wilfred does. He thumps his stick and roars, and everyone does exactly as he says.

The lump in Gabby's throat feels fiery. 'What's wrong with Mutti, Herta?'

The grey head is turned away. 'You'll find out soon enough, my girl.' A growl as deep as that of the Riesenschnauzer Onkel Wilfred keeps to guard his barn. 'Hurry up. Put on your Sunday best.'

Gabby watches Herta force Doly into clothes she's grown out of. 'You have to show respect,' she keeps muttering. No kisses for Herta's little pet this morning.

'What are you gawping at, child?' Gabby jumps at the harsh tone. 'Didn't you hear me? I said get dressed.'

'The blue dress?'

'What else? Have you got more than one Sunday best?' Herta's body lumbers to the wardrobe, pulls out the stiff taffeta. 'Get going, child. Your father's waiting for you.'

'Is he very angry?'

Herta stares out of the window. 'Angry? I suppose he is. He's lost so much.'

Gabby feels terror constrict her throat, stiffen her arms. Then relaxes. He's lost the locket, that's what Herta means. But it was Mutti's... She slips the golden pendant from nightdress to apron pocket, wills her heart to stop pounding.

'Come along, Gabriele. Don't dilly-dally.' No longer cross. Just sad. Tears in her soft crinkly eyes. 'Poor little mites,' she whispers into Doly's curls. 'What's going to happen to you now?'

Grown-ups often call the three of them 'poor'. When they don't know Gabby's listening. Vater is very rich. A millionaire, Herta is forever boasting. What can they mean?

'Where is my Mutti, Herta?'

Herta's round body shakes, producing a sound Gabby's never heard before. It sends shudders through her.

'What's wrong, Herta? Are you ill?'

She slumps back in the rocker, Doly on her lap. Sways back and forth, drawing deep breaths. A massive handkerchief floats out of her pocket, covers her face, she blows a trumpet sound.

'Go and see your father, Gabby. Now. There's something he has to tell you.'

Gabby's legs are wooden as she walks away from Herta, from Doly. She steps out of the nursery alone, her dress tight and stiff, long sleeves and edgings of spiky starched white lace holding her in a vice. She pulls at it, feels the lace tear, stops. "Ask, and it shall be given unto you," she hears her grandfather's voice.

'Please, lieber Gott, make me good and make my Mutti better,' she prays. Over and over again. So that God is bound to hear. Because He can make anything happen.

There's no one on the huge landing, not even Moppel. Vater's study door is forbidding, closed. Gabby knocks with timid weak taps.

No answer brings relief. Gone out maybe. To see Pastor Bender, the way he does. Gabby pictures her grandfather. Black coat with tails, neck circled by a stiff white collar, hymn voice. The large nose Herta says is pickled shines red like Rote Grütze.

Her grandfather is the same age as her father. How can that be? It's a riddle no one will solve for her. And, though she knows it's wrong, she doesn't like Tobias Bender. Tight small eyes, a drippy nose, batwing ears. All topped by his bald head which glistens, adorned by a few white bristles like a worn-out brush.

Herta tells Ursula that it's Pastor Bender's fault Vater goes out every night. Old bender Bender she calls him when he isn't there. But she's all smiles and curtsies when he speaks to her.

Gabby taps louder. Rat-a-tat repeats shrilly round the vast stairwell. Knockings of nervousness make her flinch.

'Come.' The unmistakable roar.

The doorknob, set high, is difficult to turn. She uses both hands.

'Herein,' he shouts again. 'Holy Moses! What are you dawdling for?'

The double doors spring inwards. Gabby is lost in space facing the back of her father's enormous chair. Black leather wings hide his body.

'Du da. I said come in.'

Gabby walks in with shoulders back, head high. 'Here I am, Vater.' Her taffeta skirt rustles as she rounds the chair and fronts him.

'So it's you, my girl. Emilmann with you?'

Vater always calls her brother Emilmann. From a song he likes to sing. A little man called Emil. A little *man*. Girls don't count.

'Herta said you wanted to see me, Vater.'

The flashing eyes dull, eyelids half-closed. Thick brows bush together over a long thin nose.

Gabby concentrates on the rugged facescape. Her father's beard, still with bits of the red colour Mutti says his hair used to be, is all over his cheeks. But there's a bare strip under the chin. And two bald patches of skin between the beard, with a narrow hairy cleft under the lower lip.

'Yes, Gabriele.' He seems to be looking at her, yet not seeing her. 'There's something I have to tell you.'

'I didn't mean...' Gabby begins to falter.

Vater's head jerks up. 'Mean? Mean what? What's that you're drivelling about?'

He must know about the locket. She'll give it back to him, then he can look after it. Mutti's too ill. Has he noticed her apron pocket's lopsided with the weight? She never wanted to take it, doesn't want it now. She fishes it out.

His eyebrows sweep up in outrage. 'What's that you've got there?'

She holds it out. 'It's Mutti's locket, Vater. The one she always wears, the one with the tiny pictures.' Splutters of phlegm go down the wrong way. 'I...a-a...I'm s-sorry, V-Vater. I didn't mean to take it. She asked me to, she wanted me to have it. I'd rather you took it, honestly.'

'Locket?' His eyes blank out. 'Goddam. You mean those miniatures.' His eyelids close again. 'That's not what I wanted to see you about. It's your mother, Gabby.'

Terror filters through her. She has to stop him telling her. 'I didn't mean to make her worse,' she interrupts, not caring. 'She called me...'

He's really angry now. Shoulders all bunched up, long nose with white lines down the side. His teeth bared like Onkel Wilfred's Schnauzer when he kicks him. 'What are you babbling on about now, Diern?'

Calling her lass? He hardly ever uses the local dialect, only the servants do.

'I didn't mean any harm.' Her voice is too loud and clear. She puts her hand over her mouth.

'Harm? What's that got to do with it?'

Hands at her side she holds herself upright, as tall as she can. 'You'd better beat me, Vater. Then she'll be well again.'

The bearded jaw drops down, his lips cover his teeth. 'Beat you? Holy Moses, child. What the devil d'you take me for?'

'She's tired out because I went to see her,' Gabby wails. 'It was all my fault. I shouldn't have...'

Her father grabs the sides of his chair, motions to her to get his stick, holds it. 'No, Gabby. It was not your fault. Your mother became ill...'

'Ill? She's ill? She's going to get better, then.' Her feet do a sort of jig, she starts towards the door. She'll go and see Mutti right away.

'Stand still!' Vater bellows, half-rising from his chair. 'Stay exactly where you are. I didn't say you could leave.'

'I want to go and see my Mutti,' Gabby howls, already by the door. Strength spurts through her body. The big man in the chair might be her father, and all powerful, but she has to go to her mother. To return the locket. Otherwise...

Vater leans forward and begins to lever himself out of the chair. His right hand, stiff and slow, moves towards his waist.

Gabby's heart pounds. She's disobeyed him to his face. He's going to take off his belt, beat her.

The hand pushes past his waist and grasps the walking stick balanced against the chair.

'Not yet,' he says, his voice a low growl. 'You can't go and see your mother yet.' He clumps towards Gabby, left hand held out.

She puts the locket into it.

He takes it, opens it, stares at his wife's grandparents eternally smiling at each other.

"They were so in love," Gabby hears her mother's voice. As though she were in the room standing right beside her. "And they had a long, long life together."

She looks up at her father, sees a large single tear in each eye.

He blinks, holds the locket out to Gabby. 'She meant you to have it, Gabby,' he whispers. 'Put it on.'

She turns to the door, leans against it for support. He said "Not yet. You can't go and see your mother yet." A throb of hope. 'Is she asleep?' The drumming in her ears is louder.

36

'Asleep, yes. Your mother is asleep, my child.'

Gabby keeps very still. Her Sunday dress crisps round her, not moving. Light reflects from dainty black patent-leather shoes and twinkles into her eyes. Her lips quiver, tears spill. She turns her back on her father.

He fumbles the locket around her neck, fastens it with shaking hands.

Gabby's shoulders sag. One last chance. 'Are you going to beat me now?' Vater can do anything. He could make it all come right. If he beats her.

He takes her shoulders, twists her to face him. She isn't ready for what she sees. Stooped body, pain in his eyes. 'Is that really what you thought I was going to do?'

'You have to punish me, Vater. Because I went into her room last night. That's why Mutti's still sleeping.'

'Eternal sleep, my child.'

Eternal is what Pastor Bender says in church. It's no use. Gabby sees the time has come. She can't stop him, can't block her ears. 'Will you sleep with her, Vater?'

'She will rest in the Mausoleum, child.' The whisper of falling autumn leaves.

Vater's little house in the churchyard. 'It's cold in there. All that white marble. It's icy cold.'

'Your mother will not wake again, Gabby. She will not feel the cold.' Choked caws like the black ravens in the elms. 'Your little brother is sleeping, too, Gabby.'

'Emilmann? Emilmann is asleep?'

'Emilmann? Of course not young Emil.' Voice roaring again. 'Don't be so damn stupid.' He puts his left hand on her right shoulder. 'The new baby, of course. He was born dead.'

'Dead?'

'How many times do I have to tell you?'

'I want to see her,' Gabby says. No longer afraid. 'I want to see my mother.' She shrugs her father's hand off her shoulder, fingers the locket now dangling round her neck. Her voice doesn't falter, doesn't beg. She simply states her wishes. Just like Vater. 'I want to see my Mutti one more time.'

His face is rigid, his mouth set. 'I'll take you to her.' He takes her hand and, as he does, his strength flows to her.

Gabby is to remember all her life that power belongs to whoever demands it.

FLOTSAM AND JETSAM

No God-fearing marshland pastor ends his sermon without the words: 'Gott schütze das Land und segne den Strand—May the Lord safeguard our land and bless our beaches.' Not, perhaps, the most Christian of sentiments. Reinforcing, as it does, the ancient rights of salvage. Nevertheless the prayer is answered often enough. Which is how the St Nicolaikirche came by its magnificent predella, consisting of intricately carved sections which, together, make up the backing of the altar.

One dark stormy winter's night a Swedish vessel bound for Hamburg was wrecked off the Schwanenbruch coast. The boat smashed against the rocks, her crew lost their lives, her cargo littered the beach.

The ancient law was invoked. Flotsam and jetsam could properly be collected by the villagers. And the most precious pieces, no doubt destined for a Hamburg church, were rushed to the safety of the nave to embellish the altar of the St Nicolaikirche. Which they have done ever since.

CHAPTER 7

Schwanenbruch, September 15th, 1913

'Na, Emil.' Tobias Bender's grief twists at him, tells him what his son-in-law must be going through. He walks over to his old friend, arms extended.

There's no answer from the sorrowing widower. He's sitting in the rocking chair beside the four-poster. Emma's body is stretched out on her back, peaceful and pallid. Discreet binding around her face keeps her jaw up. The solid mass of black hair set in rigid waves is incongruous against the ashen face, the waxy hands are curved around her stillborn son. Her eyelids are open. Herta has dressed her in cornflower blue to match her irises.

Emil sways, silent and unresponsive, a letter clutched in his hand.

'Emil, old friend.' The pastor voice is a weeping willow murmur. Autumn fingers, serried and yellow, curl round the grieving widower's shoulder.

Emil shrugs off the hand, heaves himself up. The rocker teeters back. A wild lunge clatters his cane against the still-swinging wood. 'Damnblast.'

Tobias Bender pushes stubby hands behind the tails of his black frock coat. He walks up to his daughter's corpse. Was he to blame, encouraging her to visit Emil, giving her marriage to such an old man his blessing? Surely not. Her choice was already very restricted by the time she married.

'My precious girl gone so soon. She was always a good wife to you.'

'Holy Moses! Ever hear me complain?' Emil kicks the rocker across the room.

Tobias feels a keen loss. Emma was his eldest daughter, his favourite. Always so loving, so dutiful. Only a toddler when her own mother died, yet she willingly took on his household when he lost his second wife. That second widowing left him with nine motherless children to bring up, the youngest only two. But Emma coped. Only a teenager herself, but she managed very well. Who'll take on *her* little ones?

'Come creeping in to see what sort of send-off I'm planning for her?' Emil's tall body is bowed. It still towers over Tobias.

'Can't a father say a last goodbye...'

'Maybe your mind's on other things. You're usually after something. What now? Another fat donation for your precious church?' Dark eye sockets smoulder at Tobias. 'Another stained-glass window?'

Tobias turns his back on Emil, bends over his dead daughter and strokes the delicate ivory hands. The fingers are already turning colour. 'In the midst of life we are in death,' he whispers. He pulls his child's lids down, presses them shut.

Tears slide down his smooth beardless chin. 'The Lord's peace be with you, Emma, my girl.' He pulls a large handkerchief out of his pocket, blows into it. Stares at the body of his latest grandson. A full head of hair, eyebrows and eyelashes. He hasn't got the rotten gene, but he hasn't got life, either.

'We can't brood here all day, Emil. Let's go to the Schleuse for a Schnapps...'

'I'm staying with her.' Emil grabs Tobias's shoulders and pushes him towards the bedroom door.

Tobias sighs. Why mourn by turning on his old friend? Why hold him responsible for Emma's death? Makes no sense. He's always been a good father to Emma. Made sure her children went to Sunday school. Taught them himself.

Emil Dohlen huffs his shoulders at the bedroom door, slams it shut. As though the lifeless wood had killed his beloved Emma. The whole house reverberates.

41

One thing he's sure of. It's all her father's fault. The old soaker was the one who persuaded him to spend hours away from her, drinking far too much at the Schleuse Inn, gossiping with the landlord, playing cards. He should have spent that time with Emma. Would have done, if it hadn't been for Tobias. Is that how Emma's father, a pastor, should behave? Is that the example he should be setting his flock?

Damn bloody Schwanenbruch. If he could bring the wretched house, the whole village, crashing down, he would. Leave the stinking mean-spirited place and join his little Emma in heaven.

Tobias's gentle daughter came so unexpectedly into his life. Knocked, unannounced, at the door of the New Jersey ranch he was so proud of. Sent by her father.

Feather of a girl he thought when he saw her. Reckoned she'd blow away at the slightest sign of a breeze. Looked in her late teens, though he knew her to be in her middle twenties. Creamy, delicate skin. Baby doll features.

'I'm Emma Bender,' she said, head tilted back. Perky as a sparrow. 'My father would never forgive me if I didn't take the chance to call on his oldest friend.'

'How come you're here?' he asked her. 'Are you joining your brothers in Nebraska?'

'I've just come from there,' she told him, fluttering her eyelids. 'Not the right place for me. I'm on my way back to Germany.'

They hit it off right from the start, in spite of the huge difference in their ages. Who would have dreamt she'd be the first to go?

Emil brushes his hand down the damask cheeks, picks up the rigid fingers, kisses the tips. He sees how she twinkled up to him on dainty feet, peeping from under her wide-brimmed hat, a saucy smile showing even teeth. So vibrant, so full of life, cornflower blue irises widening, darting at him, peppering him with one question after another. Tiny waist, small enough for his hands to circle, delicate bone structure, bustling behind. The clincher was that quick decisive movement of her head. Cocked sideways with an impish grin. It captivated him.

He found the right wife at long last. Decided then and there to show her the exciting New World he chose to live in, to teach her all it stood for, to keep her there.

And Emma was so willing, so eager, to be the one to mother

children for him, to give him sons. Sure that a strong man like Emil Dohlen would override her gene, assert his own abundant hair, pass it on to his children.

One thing he couldn't cure her of. She insisted on wearing that damned locket day and night. Wouldn't change it for the beautiful pearl necklace he bought for her. Smiled, but shook her head. Said she couldn't put on both. Told him that old story about the wretched Lieblingsblüte. Time and again. That story of her grandparents' romantic troth passed down through the generations. Repeated endlessly to encourage those girls who, not only deprived of their own crowning glory, knew that each of their children stood a fifty-fifty chance of inheriting the gene. The fairytale romance proved they could find a husband in spite of sparse or absent hair.

Holy Moses; all that sentimental claptrap he had to listen to. Damned caricatures of her grandparents in that clumsy locket, grinning at each other for ever. But he liked the way it made Emma's eyes glitter. Still, darned if he was going to repeat what some other man had said. And got so wrong. The whole caboodle passed down to each one of his own children. And Gabby saddled with the damned locket now, fastened tight around her young neck.

He didn't pick a bloody flower, but he did go down on one knee when he proposed to *his* Emma. Didn't he prove himself just as much as old Hinrich had done? Made it clear time and again that her stupid gene didn't matter to him. Told her often enough that he felt the same as that old bore. Put it a little better.

He lets the dead hand drop down, drapes it carefully around his second son, the one he always hoped for, a boy who might have shown Gabby's astuteness, Doly's spunk.

When Emma first saw Gabby, born to them at the Wyckoff ranch, she brushed her fingers over the baby's absent eyebrows, the tell-tale sign of their daughter's inheritance. That's when his little wife turned fearful. And made the decision which would change all their lives.

She took it—well, they both did—that, thirty-six years younger than her husband, she'd be the one to be widowed. That's why she insisted both she and Gabby would be better off back in Germany, surrounded by her family.

And he let her persuade him. Let her override his time-tested instincts, his judgement. He had the wretched villa built, brought mother and daughter back to Schwanenbruch.

Emma was wrong. Devastatingly wrong. She's the one lying dead. Leaving him saddled with three young children to raise. How come he turned into such an old fool? How in hell is he going to cope?

Emil wipes his nose on his sleeve. Begins to reread the last letter she sent him. On what he agreed would be his final business trip to New York. He only ever went there on business. And to get out of Schwanenbruch's stultifying clutches.

Schwanenbruch, September 5th, 1912.

Written just over a year ago. Only married eight short years. And so many months of those spent apart.

My dearest Emil,
You've been gone a whole fourteen days. I expect you'd like to hear how things are here, though there isn't that much to write about.

Why the devil did he rush back to the States so often? What was he thinking of, depriving himself of her company for such long periods?

Well, we did have a little excitement this morning: Beile turned up with a whole battery of henchicks, if you can call that news.

An image of his little Doly comes into his mind. She doesn't report news, she makes it. That little girl has spunk, causes plenty of excitement even though she's barely thirty months. Only last week, tiny toddler though she is, she climbed on to one of Hinrich's German Shepherds. Damned if she didn't hitch a ride on him. Laughed fit to burst when she fell off. Picked herself out of the mud, looked up to see who was watching her.

And they all clapped, enchanted by her pretty looks, her adorable antics. He had to snatch her up when he saw the dog was about to maul her. That's the child's problem. Not much common sense.

Now Gabby's quite another kettle of fish. Knows what she wants. Thinks everything through and applies that scheming little brain of hers. Spotted her need to speak English from an early age, pesters him to teach her. Obvious she's always known she wouldn't be spending the rest of her life in Schwanenbruch. An operator; a born operator.

Trouble is, her looks are already spoiled by her inheritance. Not enough hair even now to hide the high forehead, the questing eyes, the sharp features of a blue stocking. If she were a boy there'd be no question but she'd find a way to real success. A chip off the old block...

He pats Emma's cheek, the way he used to. His money, combined with Gabby's determination, will see to it she doesn't end up an old maid.

So when the little darlings are finally in bed, there's this uncanny silence. That's when I miss you most.

He really missed Emma that last time in New York, wandering around downtown Manhattan on his own. Wall Street, Broad Street, Liberty Street—his old stamping grounds, the places where the humble wheelwright's son from Schwanenbruch had the same chances as any Ritter's son, any nobleman's scion.

He loves the place, loved it from the moment his foot touched American soil. He loathes living in backward-looking Germany. That's why he sailed away at least once a year. To glory in his past. To visit the neighbourhood where he had his first bright idea: introducing snacks on Wall Street.

That's how it all began. When he first arrived at least a quarter of the local population was of German descent. Nothing to eat in downtown Manhattan then. So he made up sandwiches filled to overflowing with good German sausage. Offered them for sale in front of the New York Stock Exchange. Not a crumb left that very first day.

He made more, saved his pennies, listened to the brokers talk. Invested on their tips. Made enough to start his first eatery. Couldn't put a bite wrong.

We finally had that rain we've been longing for. It came a couple of nights ago, and the next morning everything looked lovely and green. All the same, there's very little water to show for it in the cellar reservoir.

Good little housewife, in that old-fashioned way. He put in running water, but she still collected rain water—just in case. Practically the same attitude as the women living in Charlemagne's time. Schwanenbruch is in a time warp. The villagers refuse to install running water in their houses, or decent sewers in the village. Why live in the dark ages when there's no need?

There is one story which will amuse you. On our way back from visiting Papa I almost burst into flames. An ember from his cigar somehow got lodged in my jacket, and no one noticed it. Suddenly my back began to feel oddly warm, then really hot. I got the thing off just in time not to get burnt, but that was the end of my beautiful suit.

Strange. He yearned for Emma during his last trip to the States, thought about his little family all the time. And that old feeling—of freedom, of emancipation—which always surged through him in the past, always made him feel heady, almost drunk with the power of the city, this time it just wasn't there.

Yet the moment he's back in Schwanenbruch he's bored. That's the truth of it, the big problem he and his little wife never managed to sort out. Emma wouldn't, couldn't, come to terms with living in America. He finds the old country altogether too stifling, too inhibiting. If only she could have brought herself to face the world, told it to take her or leave her. His fault. He shouldn't have allowed her to think herself inferior, hide herself away.

Next time I popped over to the parsonage, Papa immediately asked whether I'd come for the money to buy myself a new suit. Of course he gave it to me then and there.

Emma wouldn't handle money herself. She depended on her father to deal with the finances when Emil was away.

A real disappointment that Tobias didn't pay for the damage he caused. He used the funds Emil left with him. Every single one of the wretched Schwanenbruchers, even his old school friend, always on the make.

It's what he really likes about the New World. None of that handout mentality. People expect to earn their keep, and damned well do it.

The children and I crossed over the canal to walk all the way to Meyer's, just for a cup of coffee with him and his wife. Before we left he proudly, and ceremoniously, presented us with four very large apples. Of course I played up to him, made him feel the big man, as you would put it. He looked extremely pleased with himself.

Always so sweet, even to a heel like Meyer.

'How come you're not already married?' Emil asked Emma, almost first thing on meeting her.

She blushed. Deep crimson which stayed, embarrassing them both. 'I do have three or four admirers,' she said, eyes down. 'But there's someone special I haven't managed to forget.'

'Already married, eh?'

Her face went blank. 'No. He was free to do as he liked.'

She'd been turned down? Emil bristled at the very thought.

Her eyes stared ahead. 'Said he loved me, asked me to marry him.' A deep sigh. 'He wasn't from Schwanenbruch, so he didn't know. I had to explain the facts of the family inheritance.'

Facts which Emil knew—about Tobias—before Emma was even born, and which he knew applied to her as well. Actually, he found her translucent milky skin attractive, the lack of body hair reminiscent of classical paintings, an outward sign of an inward delicacy. Her baldness didn't worry him. She was always beautiful as far as he was concerned. He just made sure the hairpieces he bought her were the very best money could buy. Made her look younger, prettier, than the other village women.

And she had so much else to give. Her quick intelligence, her eagerness to please. The way her bright eyes challenged him, promising so much more than the simpering flutters of women with long eyelashes and flowing hair.

'You mean he couldn't take it?'

Emma drew herself up to her full height—a good head below him. 'He didn't pass the test,' she said, head high. 'Lucky for me. What use would a man like Kurt Meyer be to me?'

Quite right: Meyer wasn't man enough to take her on. 'Bloody fool,' Emil blazed, secretly delighted to get his chance. Wasn't that his forte, picking out winners others missed?

And revenge is sweet. By an odd twist of fate, so Emma thought, Meyer had to lease the farm he now works from Emma's husband. Because Emil, quick to see his chance, instructed Tobias to buy it from the original owner when he booked his family's passage back to Germany. Offered more than the market price but got his money's worth. Because from that time on Meyer had to lease from Emil. Damned heel was the one who had to solicit Emma's favours, defer to her. Doggone blackguard couldn't do enough for 'Lady Dohlen'.

Apart from that things are pretty much as ever. The usual chores, and so many of them. I always feel I have to carry the whole world on my shoulders.

That was Emma's big flaw. Not the one she was so ridiculously secretive about, but the way she worried herself sick. About nothing. Why did she care what the neighbours thought, or whether she was doing enough for the people of the village?

And that sturdy little Emilmann of ours really misses you. He runs round, plaguing anyone who'll listen to him, starting every sentence with: 'When my father gets back from America...'

Emil's spirits droop further. Emil Junior isn't the son and heir he hoped for. Doesn't have his older sister's boldness, her self-control, her persistence. Doesn't even have his younger sister's reckless courage, her gift for charm, her determination. All young Emil has shown so far is a bent to ask for hand-outs, and to take what isn't his. A petty thief, dammit.

There's one scheme the boy has dreamed up, just to prise a couple of miserable coins out of his father. He grabs hold of Doly, pushes her ahead of him into the study, then begs a few Groschen for them both.

Bad enough to use Doly as a decoy, but then only to ask for Groschen! Emil always gives Moppel what he asks for, Doly a bit more. She's the one who sings for her supper.

The little tot hands her coins straight over to her brother, not understanding their meaning, wanting to please. And Moppel's quick to grab them before Gabby turns up. She makes him give at least one back to Doly. What sort of man will a boy like that turn out to be?

'Who's going to come after you?' Emil remembers his mother asking him. Her words are always with him, they were so few. Like the first time he came back to see her, twenty years after he left, proud of his success, bursting to tell her all about it.

His mother was on her knees, cleaning the steps outside the old stone cottage, the last but one before the dyke. She looked up, nodded recognition. If she felt any strong emotions, she kept them to herself.

'Coffee's on the stove, my boy,' she said, pointing at the door. Squeezed the suds out of her cloth, sloshed the dirty water away, then followed him inside. As though he lived in the village.

She poured them both a cup, sat down, listened to his news. And never said a word about it either way.

Tobias was the one who pestered him to marry every time he wrote. Eventually sent his daughter round.

'Who's going to inherit all that wealth you've built up?' he pressed him on his visits home. 'Your mother's old, your brothers dead. High time you produced an heir.'

Finally his mother died. The cottage stayed empty until he gave it to Rula. No close family left.

Longing to hear your news, so write soon. I hope you're keeping well—of course you are. I'm not a bit worried on that account. And anyway, I have my little Emilmann to take your place should the worst happen.

My deepest, truest love,

Your Emma

Emil folds the letter, puts it in his breast pocket. He showed her a good time in the States, all right. Took her to see the new skyscrapers lining Fifth Avenue, persuaded her to ride the Coney Island roller-coasters with him. Such fun together.

And now his Emma is dead, and the child who might have been the kind of son he wants, needs, is dead as well.

Emil stomps round the room, his fury rising. She had no right to die, no right to leave him to keep the pot boiling in this bloody funk hole. Why did he let her drag him back? A damned softee in his old age.

Who's going to take on his children now? That awful trollop Hannah will have to fill the gap for the time being. Should be able to manage; Emma's already trained the wretched girl. He'll look out for a replacement as soon as he can.

Emil walks up to the window and sees Fritz Palter raking the first leaves of autumn into small heaps. What's the old fool doing, raking leaves? Waste of time. There'll be more leaves tomorrow.

CHAPTER 8

Schwanenbruch, September, 1913

Hannah Bender's childhood training, after her half-sister Emma's departure for the States, ensured suppressed feelings. Those which remained were strangled by her father's prayers for a pious daughter. Toys were pronounced to be temptations of the devil, sweets the cravings of a tarnished spirit, joie de vivre a sure sign of decadence. Each day Pastor Bender encouraged Hannah to greater achievements in humility. Godliness next to cleanliness meant hours spent scrubbing the Church steps to virtue. The sting of carbolic soap was there to purify Hannah's soul as well as the church entrance. Polishing pews to a shine which might mirror vanity was forbidden. That privilege was reserved for those whose reflection no longer pleased.

The zealous father succeeded beyond all expectations, instilling a lust for forbidden pleasures the devil might envy. Leaving Hannah poorer in spirit than a church rat.

It is two weeks since Emma's death and still Emil Dohlen hasn't reacted to Hannah's charms. Instead of turning to her for comfort he's locked himself in his study and only comes out for meals.

Hannah isn't the girl to give up easily. Rejection spurs stronger action. She'll honour her half-sister's memory, show her own deep loss by wearing black for a whole year. Making do with the old serge her sister-in-law Gerda lent her simply isn't good enough.

Black is Hannah's best colour. It brings out the glossy jet of her hair, her most alluring feature. But old Dohlen hasn't even glanced at her. She needs the right material for a special mourning dress. Hamburg's the place where they have what Hannah's looking for. There are other attractions, besides.

One problem is that Emma can no longer slip Hannah the little extra for the train fare. Or anything else. The other is more intractable. She can't be seen to go on that trip at the moment. She has to consider people's attitude to Emma's brood. "Poor motherless little ones" is a phrase she's come to loathe the sound of. But can't ignore. Bound to be taken as unseemly if she were seen to be abandoning the damned brats just to go shopping. She'll try for the right material locally. Take Gabby with her and consider having a dress made for her as well.

'You can't go round not wearing black for your mother, Gabby. You're coming with me to get a mourning outfit made.'

'I've got my black armband on. Herta said...'

'Forget Herta. I'm in charge.'

Gabby cringes away. How can she be? She's only sixteen; Mutti said she would be like an older sister...

'Get moving, child. I haven't got all day.'

'You mean go to Frau Meininger's, Tante Hannah?' The worthy Frau runs the small dingy drapery in the village. Last time Tante Hannah tried to buy something there Herr Meininger told her she wasn't allowed in the shop. Herta dragged Gabby away before she could hear why.

'You have a better idea?'

'Mutti said...'

'Your mother's d... not here any more. You'll do as *I* say.'

'Yes, Tante Hannah.' Gabby follows her aunt, wonders how she's going to get out of having a dress made of scratchy material. When she and Mutti visited the shop, Mutti said everything was quite unsuitable. They had to go all the way to Cuxhaven to find material for a new dress.

'Guten Tag, Fräulein Bender.' Frau Meininger is standing in the door of her shop, smiling at Tante Hannah, ushering her in. Addressing her formally, the way she did Mutti. Why, all of a sudden?

Tante Hannah struts in, demands to see several bales, strokes a heavy silk moiré nestling among prosaic wools and cottons. Frau Meininger is eyeing her as she fingers the lush undulating fabric.

'The pattern is excellent. It disperses light in a way which will give a well-cut dress movement and style…'

'I can see that. Now, have you got something suitable for Gabriele? This is too old.'

'Of course, Fräulein Bender. Perhaps a light wool.' She drags a bale from the back of the shop, puts it with the moiré.

A thin dismal material Gabby finds depressing. Not only Herta; Rula said a black armband would show enough respect.

'How are things up at the big house?' Frau Meininger's eyes shift from the moiré to Tante Hannah's face. Slide away. 'It must be so hard for you. Losing your sister, coping with the grieving little ones.'

She doesn't look at Gabby, doesn't even greet her, acts as though she's not there.

Like the rest of the village, the worthy Frau refused to even speak to Tante Hannah after Pastor Bender threw her out of his house. Until Mutti took her to live with them in the villa. Then they were polite when Mutti was around. Why is Frau Meininger so friendly now?

'It's very sad, of course,' Tante Hannah simpers, her hands fondling the material. 'Herr Dohlen is so overcome with grief we hardly see him.'

True; Vater is hardly ever around. He eats alone, sits reading in his study, doesn't even joke with Herta and Ursula. Gabby's heard Herta say he's a reformed character as far as the Schleuse Inn is concerned. Only drinks a glass or two of beer, then spends hours walking the dyke and striding the moors. Gabby tries hard to get his attention, but he brushes her off, says he's too busy. She so wants him to teach her English.

'Poor little orphans.' Frau Meininger smoothes a small amount of moiré along her counter top as she smiles at Tante Hannah. 'What's to become of them?'

'Their father's still alive.' Tante Hannah's impressive eyelashes flutter. 'He may be nearly seventy, but he's as strong as an ox. Anyway, my nephew and nieces have plenty of relatives around.'

Frau Meininger unwraps the bolt of cloth, spraying dust. 'They'll need a mother. And you're their half-aunt.'

What does she mean by that? Surely Vater would never marry Tante Hannah! Gabby feels her face pinch, her eyes fill with tears.

Frau Meininger nods as she strokes the fabric along the grain. 'This is something I bought because I wanted to make myself a dress...'

Tante Hannah turns away. 'For *you*? I see.' Her hand is on the doorknob.

Frau Meininger walks round the counter, the material swinging loose between her arms. 'You'll want to see it in daylight. I won't get round to a dress for me, of course. The rest will go back to Hamburg.' She eyes Tante Hannah. 'About five metres? Just to be on the safe side.'

'I knew I could rely on you, Frau Meininger. Charge it to Herr Dohlen's account.' Tante Hannah's hand sweeps the air in a gesture of limitless funds. 'He wants his family to show their grief in a decent way.'

'Naturally.' The draper's wife bows low, cuts a nick and tears the material along the grain. 'Would you like my Lotti to make it up? She's the only one in the village who can handle such heavy silk. I'll call her down to take your measurements, shall I?'

Neither of them remembers Gabby's there.

CHAPTER 9

Schwanenbruch, September 1913

Hannah wants to see some changes in the villa, hasn't yet dared to bring the subject up. But there's one she's particularly impatient for. Why wait for the old man to woo her before she moves from the turret room above the servants' quarters to a first-floor bedroom? She isn't a servant, she's the children's aunt, Emil Dohlen's sister-in-law. Confronting the old tyrant with such a suggestion needs tactful handling but has to be done.

Hannah walks into the hallway from the garden, squints up the enormous stairwell and checks the first floor doors. All closed. She lifts the voluminous moiré skirt and rustles up the stairs, arriving breathless. Everything in the villa is on the large side, the stair-treads distinctly steep. No wonder Emma came to grief on them.

Hannah breathes hard. The double doors to the study burst open and Emil Dohlen lumbers out. A fissure the size of a chasm appears between his eyes as soon as he catches sight of Hannah.

'What the devil are you doing here?'

Hannah sweeps her skirts back. 'The stairs, Herr...'

'The back stairs will get you to your room, woman. I've told you I want complete peace and quiet in this part of the house.' Spittle hisses down his beard. 'I don't want jabbering females harassing me. Clear enough?'

'I didn't mean to disturb you, Herr Dohlen. I was just about to ask you to discuss a matter of great importance. You see...'

'My first rule is to keep out of my way. Even your tiny mind must be able to grasp it. I'm working.' The rumbling bellow echoes around the hall. 'If you can't follow simple instructions I'll make arrangements to replace you.' Emil Dohlen's face-hair bristles scorn. A drop trembles at the end of his nose as he takes in the new dress. 'No need to tart yourself up like a fat crow. A mourning band around your arm will do.'

The old dodderer must be getting senile. 'What I thought...'

'Thought?' The word explodes round the stairwell. 'Holy Moses, girl. That's not what I employ you for. I pay you to run my household and supervise my children's welfare. No more, no less.'

And you're a damned scrooge, Hannah thinks. But daren't meet his eyes in case he reads what's there. 'Of course, Herr Dohlen.' She begins a smile, sees him glower, backs away. The man's dangerous. Can't cope with his new situation. 'I just wondered whether it might be a good idea for me to sleep on this floor.' She does her best to imitate Emma's gentle voice.

Bloody enormous place but only three bedrooms on the first floor. Because the blue salon stretches along the whole width of the house. The rest is taken up with the master bedroom with a door leading into a huge bathroom next to the girls' room, then Emil's study and, right at the end, Moppel's relatively small bedroom.

'What's that supposed to mean? Precisely how d'you think you're going to arrange that?' Emil's eyes darken to the charcoal of smoked eel. 'Share the girls' room? I hardly think that's suitable.' His eyes glow fury. 'The hours you keep; the company.'

The walking stick approaches the hem of the new dress. 'I haven't been out since Emma...'

'What you do is your affair, nothing to me. Get one thing clear. I'm not having you sleeping in the girls' room.'

She has to bring it up now or forget it. 'What I was thinking of, Herr Dohlen, was to move into Emilmann's room. Then...'

'Young Emil? You want to share a bedroom with young Emil?' The walking stick the old man carries everywhere points wildly at Hannah as she retreats. 'Out of the question.' His mouth gapes open. 'You must be mad.' The calm of conviction.

Flamed cheeks droop as Hannah gulps for air. 'No, no. Of course not share with the boy.' Her voice the habitual whinge she hates herself for. 'I thought perhaps the children might all sleep in the big bedroom together, and I'd take over Emilma... young Emil's room. Then I can keep an ear out for them at night.' A tentative smile. Showing a couple of black stumps between healthy teeth. 'They do need looking after. Doly is still so young and very highly strung. She often has nightmares.' Claw-nailed hands spread in sympathy for the motherless babe. 'Herta was only...'

'You want to get out of sleeping in the servants' quarters.' Emil's pupils narrow to pinpoints of assessment. Reading her mind like the pastor reads the lesson. 'Well, never mind all that.' The stick brandishes skywards. Hannah's present bedroom, an enormous octagonal room built into a small tower, is reached by a spiral staircase leading up beyond the servants' rooms. 'The turret room will suit me very well. Tucked out of your way, for a start. I'll take it over.'

'You'd like me to sleep in the master bedroom?'

'You?' Saliva spurts down Emil's beard, his jaw low enough to show the wide papillae of his tongue. '*You* sleep in Emma's bed?' His face the purple of thunder clouds, his hands knuckled into fists. 'I'll sleep in my bedroom, work in the turret. Take young Emil's room, if you must. Lump the kids together. Just keep out of my damned way.'

Hannah bows at Emil, escapes. She's achieved the first part of her strategy. A promising start. She'll win the old bastard round eventually. She knows that now.

THE MOTHERLESS CHILDREN

A farmer lost his beloved wife and was left with motherless children to care for. He did his best for them but found he couldn't replace a mother's care, a mother's touch. So he asked his dead wife's unmarried sister to keep house for him, to look after them, expecting that the children's aunt would make a loving mother for them.

His sister-in-law was not at all like his wife. She shouted harsh words at the children and didn't give them enough to eat. She didn't even see to it that their clothes were clean.

One night the children were in their bedroom, crying before they fell asleep. That's when they saw the diaphanous form of their mother slide into the room and ran up to her. She comforted them, spoke gently to them, dried their tears until they went to sleep. The next morning each child found a clean vest on its chair.

The children grew older and learned to defend themselves against their wicked aunt. The mother's visits became fewer. Eventually they stopped because she realised her children no longer needed her.

CHAPTER 10

Schwanenbruch, November 1913

'My Mutti comes every night and puts my clothes out for me,' Doly tells Minni. 'She thinks I can't see her. But I can.'

'No, no, my little one. Your Mutti's gone away for ever,' Minni gasps at Doly. 'She's up in Heaven.' The new nursery maid is cycling across the moors towards her father's cottage. He's the lighthouse-keeper, the man who makes sure the boats which ply the River Elbe don't run aground.

Tante Hannah hired Minni a month ago. 'Are they treating our girl right?' Doly overheard Minni's father ask his wife the first time she visited. 'They say that young hussy Hannah has a sharp tongue in her head.'

'Hush now, Ulrich,' Minni's mother warned. Frown-smiling at Doly.

'Wha's a hussy?'

'Someone who shouts a lot,' Minni told Doly. Too quickly.

Doly and Minni have become best friends, united against big bad Tante Hannah. Doly is small for her age. She manages to squeeze into the basket in front of Minni's handlebars.

At first Doly was frightened at being shaken up and down. Scared she'd fall out, hit her head on the hard cobblestones. Or fall among the cowpats once Minni left the road and pedalled over the pastures leading to her home.

Only the first time. Now Doly understands how skilled Minni is and enjoys what feels like flying over the long stretches of flat marsh crossing the causeway.

'We have a very special lighthouse here in Schwanenbruch,' Minni tells Doly. 'It's called der Ochsenturm—the Oxtower. It was built hundreds of years ago.'

The structure, completely round and very tall, is higher than the Villa Dohlen. It reaches beyond the clouds and pierces the sky, a cream funnel with a black top among red evening clouds. Doly knows that means the lighthouse-keeper is even more important than Vater.

'Why are the clouds so pink?' she asks Minni as she's lifted out of the bicycle basket and carried into the little cottage beside the lighthouse. It's all in one with the barn, where the animals live and keep everything warm.

'Because the angels are baking bread.' Minni's velvet lips brush across Doly's nose, her soft arm covers her shoulders.

Is Minni an angel from Heaven? Large china-blue eyes and rosy cheeks are circled by silver-blonde curls all round her head. Like a halo. 'Are they baking it for my Mutti?'

'Of course they are. Your Mutti's gone to Heaven to be with the angels. And to smile down on her children from there.' Minni's hand strokes across Doly's ginger curls, her fingers lift her chin.

'Where's Heaven, Minni?'

'See those big clouds? See the way the light peeps out from behind them like the points of a gold-red star? Heaven's above the clouds, Doly. You can't see it, but it's there. You know it because the angels send the light down to earth.'

'So why can't I see my Mutti?'

'Because she's an angel herself now, a heavenly being. And they're invisible.'

Minni tells just the sort of stories Doly loves. 'Are they keeping her company, Minni? Singing the songs she likes?'

Minni dots her finger on Doly's nose. 'Of course they are, my pretty one. Your Mutti is enjoying herself in Heaven. The angels are dressing her in lovely clothes. Just look at those fleecy white clouds. They're using them to spin beautiful yarn to weave your Mutti's new dress. All white and silver. Can you see that silver lining in the clouds?

60

Now Doly understands. Mutti is too busy in Heaven to look after her children. That's why Tante Hannah is in charge and tells the servants what to do. She makes them wear a uniform and call her Gnädige Frau.

Why? That's what they called Mutti, but Tante Hannah isn't married to Vater.

CHAPTER 11

Schwanenbruch, Spring 1914

'Excuse me, Fräulein Bender. I just came in to finish setting the table.'

'Lay it for two.' Hannah is standing in the dining room, one of several reception rooms on the ground floor. It overlooks the garden at the back giving it a quiet sheltered air. The perfect place to set her special plan in motion.

'I beg your pardon, Fräulein Bender. What did you say?' Herta puts her tray down, looks at the huge table, waits.

At the head of the table, under the oriel window at the far end, gleam solid silver candlesticks and cutlery, ornate china belonging to the Schwanengeschirr, the swan pattern from Meissen, and some magnificent examples of Corning glassware Emil brought over from New York. Where Emma was concerned the old miser's purse was always wide open: a damask napkin is folded in a filigreed silver napkin ring, the letters E and D entwined in voluptuous enjoyment. The second ring, without its napkin, is placed beside it. The same initials, but on a smaller scale, are engraved on it.

From the day of Emma's death there's been only one place setting in the dining room. Emil insists that a fresh red rosebud be threaded through Emma's napkin ring every day. Fritz Palter couldn't believe that the rose was expected even after the first frosts. He sent a chrysanthemum instead.

The grieving widower roared his outrage. Ever since that day Herta reminds the old gardener to cover some of the rose bushes against cold weather. A new greenhouse was built and planted with special hot-house roses ready for the winter months. Regardless of cost.

'Lay two place settings.' Hannah's sharp elbow digs into Herta's arm. 'I know you're slow, Herta. Are you becoming deaf as well? Could make it difficult for you to keep your position here. This house needs competent personnel.' Hannah sweeps round from the bay into the main part of the dining room, Hausfrau eyes scanning the polished mahogany table, the twenty chairs set round it. 'Why aren't you wearing the uniform I ordered for you?'

Herta's nostrils widen, but her voice falters. 'I just thought...'

'You can safely leave the thinking to me. Just do exactly as you're told.' Hannah devours the room with her eyes, feasts them on the ornate ceiling. She has to admire Emma's taste. Each reception room was decorated to enhance the splendid Jugendstil style the architect worked in.

'As you wish, Fräulein Bender. Where would you like me to lay the second place?' Herta empties the tray holding the table setting.

Where would be least offensive? The other end of the table would signify the wife's position. Altogether too presumptuous. Placing another setting by Emil's would be worse.

Hannah focuses on the centre of one long side, by the bay window, light coming from behind. That's the right place, with more daylight coming from the imposing oriel higher up. The room's luminance will help soften her features, give her a gentle air. The sun will be setting during this evening's meal, but she has to plan for the future.

'Over there, Herta. Right in the middle.'

While Herta fetches the silver, glass and crockery for a second place setting, Hannah imagines herself in some of the villa's other rooms. The red living room, where Emma entertained her lady friends. Served them Kaffee und Kuchen in the afternoons. Rula baked the cakes, though Emma herself always made the coffee. Not exactly a small room, but the most intimate of the reception rooms. So far Emil Dohlen hasn't allowed anyone to touch it.

The second sitting room is a rather sombre combination of brown and beige, and very elegant. That's where Emil and Emma entertained together, where they invited friends and family.

The finest of the reception rooms is on the first floor. Named the blue salon because it is decorated and furnished in a melody of cerulean blue and gold, this room is only used for festive entertaining. Emil always insisted that it be turned into a ballroom once a year, on Emma's birthday, with the little alcove off the centre used to house the band. The delicate Louis Quinze chairs are lined up at the sides and the parquet floor cleared for the guests to dance on.

Hannah can see herself there next year. On August 1st, 1914, her husband Emil will lead her to start the dancing. She'll be dressed in a gorgeous gown of emerald green encrusted with pearls.

Herta clatters back and Hannah inspects her current surroundings. Not a bad colour-scheme. Emma had the dining room painted in cool shades of turquoise, highlighting the theme of loaves and fishes in the ceiling plaster-work outlined in gold. Voluptuous clusters of grapes form a rose for the magnificent art nouveau chandelier, interspersed with more modest fare of bread and wine served in sinuous horn beakers. Streamers, carefully outlined in gold, point to different species of fish at each of the four corners: sole, plaice, turbot and halibut. A full and fitting harvest from the North Sea.

How can she make sure there are no intimations of the wretched brats tonight? Emil has never tolerated their presence at his meals. He and Emma didn't dine in the middle of the day, German fashion. They adopted the American habit of a light lunch and entertained in the early evening. Or they ate in solitary state.

But tonight is crucial. There must be no noises off, no hints of Emma's children, when Hannah makes her first appearance in the dining room. Emil always asks Herta whether the children are being read to. Ursula can put the brats to bed tonight, as usual. Hannah will assure him she's already read to them.

As though it makes any difference what those children learn. Rich, aren't they? No need for them to bother about an education. They'll be able to do anything they like once they're of age. They'll have inherited their father's fortune by then.

Unless, of course, Emil marries again. And chooses a healthy young woman.

'He who pays the piper calls the tune,' Pastor Bender is fond of preaching. For once Hannah agrees enthusiastically with her sententious father's sentiments.

'Is this where you mean, Fräulein Bender?' Herta begins to lay the place opposite the bay window.

'You know perfectly well where I want it laid. On the other side, right in the centre.'

Hannah checks the grandfather clock in the hall. She's got ten minutes. The two younger children are already being put to bed. Gabby will be coming in from the garden any minute now. The child knows she has to be in her room by six.

Hannah goes into Moppel's former bedroom, powders her nose, dabs at her hair, puts perfume behind her ears. And adjusts a fine lace collar around her neck. She smiles at her reflection. She'll be in the dining room to greet Emil with his glass of Schnapps and his cigar. And then she'll go through to the kitchen and tell Rula to get ready to serve the meal. The way Emma always did.

Hannah is about to go down when she hears the door to Emil's study open with a crash. She stands frozen as she realises he's early. She hears him stomping towards the stairs, clodhopping down, opening the door leading to the kitchen quarters. He likes to chat with Rula occasionally, find out how things are in the house he was born in. Then he'll clobber his way into the dining room, help himself to Schnapps. All hell will break loose as soon as he takes in the second place setting and demands to know why it's there.

Herta will mince at him soon enough that it was "Fräulein Bender, Herr Dohlen" who gave her the order to set another place. If that's the way it plays out, Hannah is well aware the old tyrant will throw her out on her ear, without another thought. She has to get rid of that second setting before he sees it. Or find a way of accounting for it. She walks out on to the main landing, heart hammering inside her. What has she done?

''Abend, Tante Hannah,' Gabby greets her dutifully on her way in from the garden.

'Good evening, Gabby.' she calls, sensing a solution. 'There you are. I've been looking for you all over the place.'

'Yes, Tante Hannah?'

65

'Come into the bathroom for a moment.'

Gabby swings up the stairs, her clothes stained with mud, lanky hair untidy. Though Herta does her best to keep the children neat, she doesn't have Emma's touch. Gabby's hair is already very sparse, and now there isn't even a ribbon to give it body. Herta isn't skilled in such niceties, nor is she allowed the time to look after the children properly.

Hannah looks at the unkempt child with some dismay. Then suddenly smiles at her. 'I've laid a place for you in the dining room, Gabby. So that you can see something of your father.'

'Vater's invited me to have dinner with him?' The promise of an answered prayer lights fireworks in Gabby's eyes.

'The place is laid.' Hannah stares at the child's hair, her face. 'You are disgustingly filthy. You can't go down to him looking like that. I'll help you get yourself cleaned up, then you can go and join him. Hurry up, take those filthy clothes off and start washing yourself.'

Hannah, searching for a clean outfit in the children's bedroom, hears running water, the humming of a tune. '*He, Du mit den Lockenkopp*', Gabby's young voice sings out. She reappears within moments, face scrubbed clean, hair brushed back.

Hannah feels a pang as she looks at the seven-year-old. She has good features: a triangular face, a questing, turned-up nose, high cheek-bones and one of the smoothest complexions Hannah has ever seen. But the effect is spoiled by the straggly, thin, mouse-coloured hair which the child has slicked back. The style accentuates her high forehead, gives her a strangely owlish look. Then Hannah realises it's the lack of eyebrows and eyelashes which has this curious effect.

'I expect he wants to talk to me about Byron,' Gabby prattles, walking towards the table by the big window in the children's bedroom. A book of poems is lying there. She picks it up reverently, holds it in her hand. 'He said I could borrow his copy of *Childe Harold's Pilgrimage*, to see whether I could understand any of it.' She strokes the suede cover, checks that the ribbon mark is in the right place. 'I think he might want me to read to him during his meal.' Intense eyes move avidly across the pages she's just opened. 'Perhaps he's decided to teach me English.' A softness creeps over her face, emphasising its sweetness, its simplicity.

'Never mind all that,' Hannah mutters, her ear attuned to the sounds below. She can hear Emil Dohlen's stick tracking across the hall, visualises him opening the dining-room door. He likes to sit smoking a cigar while waiting for his meal to be served.

'Herta!' she hears the roar. 'What the devil is this?'

'Get going, Gabby,' Hannah urges the child. 'Can't you hear your father's shouting because you aren't there?'

'I've got to put a black ribbon on,' Gabby insists, side-stepping her aunt and rummaging in the bedside table drawer. She draws out a long wide satin ribbon and holds it against her head. The material, as black as her mother's heavy coiffure, shows the striking resemblance between mother and daughter. 'Vater would want me to wear it.' She tries to put it on.

Hannah, hearing further explosions from below, grabs the ribbon and manhandles a fistful of Gabby's hair. Some of it is left in her hands.

'You're hurting me.' Gabby has seen it too, is using all her will-power not to cry. It will never grow back.

'Stand still.' Hannah forces herself into gentleness, plaits the ribbon into the hair, ties the ends into a bow, strokes the child's hairstyle into place. 'Now, down you go.'

Gabby, clutching her book, skips down the stairs and straight into the dining room.

'Holy Moses, child.' Hannah can hear all the way up the stairs. 'What now, dammit? What are you doing here?'

Hannah tiptoes down the stairs and stands outside the door. Will the child involve her? Has the whole scheme backfired?

'I've l-learned the first v-verse, Vater,' Gabby gabbles, excited enough to trip over her words. 'I've learned it all by heart. Shall I r-recite it to you?'

'First verse? What first verse, dammit?'

'Of Byron. You gave me your book to look at. You said he was the greatest poet that ever lived.' The tone of awe makes her voice crisply clear.

The ticking of the grandfather clock emphasises Emil's silence. Hannah doesn't have to be in the room to know that somehow Gabby has softened her father's wrath, turned his voice gruff.

'And you've learnt it by heart?'

'The first verse, Vater.' The child's pride in her achievement is unmistakable. *'Cheeldey Harold toe tay darrk tover camay,'* rings out in singsong tones.

'Stop. Stop right there.'

Hannah cringes outside the door. The wretched child has obviously muffed the lines, ruined the whole thing.

Gabby stops, clears her throat. 'Wasn't that right?'

'You're murdering the words, child. It's in English, for God's sake. You don't say "ch", you say "tsch". And the last "e" is silent.'

'Tscheeld Harold...'

'"i" in English is pronounced like "ei" in German. Listen, Gabby.' The tone is encouraging now. 'Listen carefully and say it after me: *Tscheild Harold tu the daak tauer käm.'*

Hannah hears him pronounce the words which have no meaning for her, and which Gabby can't know either. She was only one when she left the States.

'Tscheild Harold to sa daak tauer käm,' Gabby mimics her father.

'No, no, child.'

The change is astonishing. Emil's voice has lost its roar.

'Not "sa": *the* is a sound we don't use in German. You say it by putting the tip of your tongue behind your front teeth, like this. *The.* Try it.'

'Tss.'

'No, Gabby. No "s". Lisp...*The.'*

'The,' she says. *'The.* Is that right?'

'Not bad.'

'Childe Harold to the dark tower came,' Gabby echoes her father.

American intonations, heard long ago in infancy, have obviously come back to her. Hannah grins to herself as she realises she's pulled it off.

'Am I speaking real English now?'

'Making an excellent start,' Hannah hears Emil Dohlen say.

Hannah's shoulders relax, her breathing returns to normal. She hears the door to the kitchen quarters open. Herta with the main course.

Hannah lifts up her skirts and sweeps up to her room. She'll get the old man yet.

THE PRINCE AND THE SMALLHOLDER

A smallholder living to the east of Schwanenbruch felt badly done by.
He considered it very unjust to pay tithes on land liable to flooding.
So he petitioned his prince, living on the far side of Land Hadeln. But
to no avail.

Undaunted, the smallholder refused to be defeated. He visited the
prince's castle, managed to obtain an audience, and carefully explained
how little the land was worth.

The fine lord turned him down again. But he felt sorry for the man
who'd had a long, wasted journey, and invited him to a feast to be held
that evening.

The prince's subject accepted with joy. He ate and drank the fine
food, sat on the resplendent chairs, took in all the expensive furnishings.
But he was by no means overawed, and acted like a man who knew his
worth.

'Not impressed by my splendid castle and fertile lands?' the prince
asked, surprised.

'I can see they're very fine indeed, your Grace. But I have just as
good at home.'

The great lord took that for a joke, and laughed. 'So you'll invite me
to sample your riches, will you?'

'You're more than welcome, your Highness.'

One fine day, out on a hunting trip near Schwanenbruch, the prince
called on the smallholder. The man greeted him cordially enough, but
didn't invite him into his house. Instead, he suggested he visit one of his
barns later that evening.

The prince accepted, and returned to find his subject had centred
a huge table in the barn, groaning with home-made produce. The table
was crammed with ham and sausages in every shape and form, eggs
from chickens, ducks and geese, rich farm butter, the heaviest cream
the prince had ever seen, the crustiest bread he'd ever tasted. And,

instead of chairs, the smallholder provided sacks brimming with the finest corn to sit on.

The prince stared, astonished. He agreed that the smallholder's meal was ample, and indeed very wholesome. But comparable to his own sophisticated fare? Well, hardly.

His host smiled. He pointed to the fertile green pastures around him, explained the intrinsic worth of chairs filled with the finest grain, and the richness of the meal's ingredients.

The prince laughed. He admired the fellow's pride in his own achievements and agreed that the smallholder had been right, that he'd given as good as he'd received. And he sat down and enjoyed the bucolic feast.

Now that the Schwanenbruch villager knew the prince understood his little joke he repeated his request. He pointed to the land east of the barn which was, as usual, flooded by summer rains. And consequently useless for growing grain.

The great lord smiled, nodded. 'You're a cunning old fox. But you've convinced me. I'll let you off paying tithe for the land east of this barn.'

Which is why the east side of Schwanenbruch has always been tithe-free from that time onwards.

CHAPTER 12

Schwanenbruch, October 1914

'Holy Moses.' Emil Dohlen turns to Wilfred Bender sitting on his right and drinking beer. 'Where's Theo got to?'

'He's...'

'Doesn't he know there's a war on? *And* it's our last game before Hinrich is off to join his regiment.' Emil puffs at his cigar, smoke aimed at Wilfred. 'I thought you told me we were starting at six.' He fishes a large gold fob-watch out of his pocket; his tap on the table opens the lid. He peers at the face held at arm's length. 'It's quarter past.' He harrumphs at the watch-face. 'I made a special point of getting here on time. You Benders are a hopeless bunch. Always some lame excuse.'

'Not the best-chosen adjective to describe Theo, Emil.' Hinrich Bender, the eldest of Tobias's second brood and Emma's favourite half-brother, finally persuaded Emil to give up his solitary life and join in the card-playing sessions at Wilfred's house. He hasn't been able to persuade the old man to spend more time with his children. All three try hard to please him. He's in his late sixties, getting on for seventy; doesn't he realise he's not immortal? 'I was at the farm this morning. His stump is giving trouble.'

'That a fact?' Emil snaps the lid shut, puts the watch back in his pocket. 'He usually manages with a Schnapps or two. Knows he can rely on me to bring enough to help him out.'

The four men meet to play cards in Wilfred Bender's front room. Wife Gerda and daughter Ulrike are exiled to the kitchen on card-playing nights, only allowed into the Stube to serve the men snacks at regular intervals.

'Not just pain, Emil. He's got an attack of rheumatism in that leg.'

'Rheumatism?' Emil snorts round the low-ceilinged room. 'Holy Moses! How the devil d'you get rheumatism in an amputated limb?'

'Phantom pain. Apparently quite common.' Wilfred drains his beer, fills up the three tankards standing on the table.

'Wilfred here downs as much as Theo even without a wooden leg to put it in.'

Hinrich can see his brother-in-law is bored. And out for some sport at Wilfred's expense. The old man dislikes Tobias Bender's eldest son. Emil is only here because that's where the card game is.

'Sometimes I wonder whether he pours it into a secret barrel to get me to cough up more.'

Hinrich stands, walks to the window overlooking the dull waters of the Braake, the canal the villagers dug to protect them from flooding. 'I think Wilfred can fund his own beer, Emil. His business is doing pretty well.'

'Anything you say, Hinrich.' Emil turns a sharp nose, sits back in the upright chair lodged at the head of the table, stares at the men sitting round it. He grins; impish eyes focus across the yard at Wilfred's outbuildings. 'Your barn looks full to bursting, Wilfred. Not been a good trading year I take it. You've usually sold most of your grain by this time.'

Round unfringed eyes, ears set at right-angles to his toupee-covered head, a smile to split his face; Wilfred cultivates a clown disguise to hide astuteness. He knows he can't fool Emil, but he still broadens the grin into the village idiot look. 'I can't complain, Emil. The later I sell, the greater the profit. But I hardly have to tell you that.'

'So you won't be needing that loan you were muttering on about.'

Wilfred's eyes almost disappear behind angry eyelids. 'That's to build a second barn. Expand the business. My land's not fit for cultivation.'

Emil scowls. 'Any competent farmer could grow a grain crop on it.'

'It's always waterlogged, Emil. Summer and winter.' The whine is

72

habitual. It fades as Emil's nostrils fire disdain.

'What you mean is that if you can store twice as much grain as now, you can make a fortune out of your neighbours.'

'Anything wrong with that?'

'Good business, Wilfred. Which I applaud. Just one problem; I'm told you don't stick to your bargains.' Emil taps his watch, shifts it to catch the sun's rays, watches as Wilfred twists to avoid the dazzle. 'I heard you put the price up *after* you'd made a contract with Gerhard Mahler.'

Wilfred's thick neck reddens and widens. 'And you believe that liar?'

Emil nods, eyes sleepily affable. 'My tenant Meyer told me. He's got good reason to know.' He clicks his watch shut. 'I won't have you reneging on your deals, Wilfred. Not because I'm interested in your morals; they're entirely your affair. But you're my brother-in-law, so it reflects on me.'

Hinrich places himself between his half-brother and Emil. 'So how did it go yesterday, Emil? Who got the contract to make the new curtains for the blue salon?'

The last ball held there, six weeks before Emma's death, now over a year ago, saw the curtains burnt when someone placed the splendid candelabrum, all fifteen candles lit, too near the material.

Emil cackles. 'Worked out quite well. I commissioned Samuel Nussbaum.'

Hinrich can't help admiring the old trouble-maker. He's deliberately made a choice he must know the village will interpret as eccentric if not unpatriotic. Nussbaum has recently arrived from Danzig. Not just a Jew: an Ostjude, a Jew coming from the wildernesses east of Berlin.

'You gave it to Nussbaum?' Wilfred explodes. 'That damned runt of a pork-hater?'

'His choice of food is hardly my concern.' The cane thumps the floor as Emil walks over to the window.

'Wouldn't have thought he could have reached high enough to take the measurements.'

Emil has twelve centimetres over Wilfred who, at one metre seventy-five, is a mere two and a half centimetres taller than Nussbaum. 'He uses a step-ladder, like everybody else. I've yet to meet the man who can reach the top of any of my windows without one, let alone that huge oriel in the blue salon.' His hand brushes the top of Wilfred's curtain rail. He wags a blackened finger.

Hinrich laughs. The Villa Dohlen windows are famous in Schwanenbruch, the tales of their size wildly exaggerated. Village lore has it that the villa is so enormous because the dimensions were increased by a factor of three. Because imperial measure was read as metric, and metres were substituted for feet.

A completely unrealistic story. If it were true, the three and a half metre ceilings, already high by village standards, would have reached nearly twelve metres. Clearly absurd.

The truth, Hinrich suspects, is more banal. The German builders didn't read feet as metres, they read yards as metres and so increased all measurements by roughly ten percent. This had an effect, but hardly a drastic one. It explained, for example, why the treads on the stairs were uncomfortably high.

There was a more serious consequence. Emil was determined to have several stained-glass windows in his house, depicting the surrounding countryside as well as the famous swans which give the village its name. Naturally Emil wanted the best. So he took the villa measurements to Tiffany's on Fifth Avenue. Their recently-patented favrile glass was famed all over Europe and in great demand. The iridescent surface was achieved by spraying it with metallic salts while hot, a method not used on the Continent.

The Tiffany workshops translated the German measurements into imperial ones, and based the window proportions on them. Then Louis Comfort Tiffany sent the window sizes back in American units. The German builders presumably read yards as metres, so making the spaces for the windows too large.

Emil, still in New York while the villa was being built, had no idea that Tobias, entrusted with overseeing the work, had asked Wilfred to take over. And Wilfred, having consulted the architect, arranged for coloured-glass borders to fill the empty spaces. An excellent compromise. The windows were still splendid, though the borders could not equal the glowing colours of the Tiffany glass.

'Sacrilege!' Emil roared the first time he saw the results. 'Holy Moses; how in hell did this come about?'

Hinrich understands very well why Emil wasn't going to trust just anyone with his new curtains.

Emil takes a sip of beer, replaces the tankard on the table, begins to shuffle the cards. 'If Theo isn't here soon, we'll have to play pinochle.'

'So how did you choose?' Hinrich doesn't have to pretend, he's really interested in how Emil went about it. 'What made you go for Nussbaum?'

'Not that difficult. I had them all do their measuring and their sums. Checked those out for myself, of course. Had it all figured from the start.' Emil takes a childish pleasure in his feats of mental arithmetic.

He assesses the room, focusing on Wilfred's traditional windows. Small, conforming to the style of the house, making it easy to keep warm with a Kachelofen in the corner.

'I told them to send me written estimates. Anton Weber's was the lowest tender, so low I couldn't see how he could make a profit.' Emil's laugh sounds the trumpet secondary. 'Fact is, I don't think he estimated the cost at all. I reckon he had his assistant work the figures out before he came. Based them on average sizes is my guess. So he got them wrong. Bloody idiot.'

'So why didn't you give it to him?' Wilfred grumbles. 'Would have saved you a pretty penny.'

'That's how you'd have handled it, is it?' Emil takes another swig, wipes beads from his moustache and winks at Hinrich. 'Not the way I like to work.'

Wilfred's podgy fingers swell, redden, curl into fists.

'Peter Fissbad's estimate was completely over the top. Reckons I'm made of money, I suppose. A couple of seconds' thought would have shown him that if I am, there has to be a reason for it. I can tell a good deal from a bad one.' Emil moves his beer to the right, shuffles again. 'Then Samuel Nussbaum showed me his figures and breakdown: first class materials, bought at trade prices in Hamburg, first rate making-up at his premises in Cuxhaven. Showed me his profit margin, all above board. Must say I took to it.'

Wilfred's hands clamp round his beer mug. 'So that's the one you plumped for. All right for those who can afford it.'

'Thought we could have a bit of fun first.' Emil's soft tone concentrates his listeners. 'Even made sure young Emil was there to see how business should be done.'

'The boy? You got a six-year-old child involved?' Wilfred sounds peeved, irritated that Emil not only has money, he also has a son.

'Hardly involved. Told him to sit and watch how to go about it. Why not? He'll be taking over in a few years' time. The sooner he learns, the better chance he'll have to do well.'

'The kid already fancies himself a financial genius...'

'That's your opinion, Wilfred. When you have a son you need to train him from an early age.'

'So what was the great scheme, then?' Wilfred mutters into his beer mug.

Emil looks round, eyes challenging. 'I asked all three tradesmen whether they'd like to play cards for the job. Whoever won, I'd take that person's estimate. Usual rules of whist, plus we rotated partners at the end of each game.' He pauses. 'One other rule: said I'd call the end of the session. They all agreed.'

'You gave them so much choice,' Hinrich murmurs.

'I'm a fair man. I wouldn't have held it against them if they'd said no. I'd simply have taken the estimate I liked best.'

Wilfred's fingers clench and unclench round his tall tankard. 'And Nussbaum won?'

'Naturally *I* won.' Powerful frown lines distort Emil's face. 'What makes you think he plays the better game?'

Hinrich hides his smile with his tankard. Emil's competitiveness is irrepressible. And he is an outstanding player.

'Well...' Wilfred mumbles.

'That's precisely what they thought,' Emil bellows, banging the table with his fist. 'Thought of me as an old man. Never occurred to them I might win.'

'So they just wasted their time, amusing you.' Wilfred shuts his tankard lid.

'Nothing to do with entertainment. It was a business meeting.' Emil glowers round, but his eyes sparkle. 'I dealt the first hand, nothing special. The game was brisk. Nussbaum and I won easily.'

'So you reckoned he'd be just as good a partner for the curtains...'

'Holy Moses, Wilfred. Am I telling the story, or are you?'

Wilfred returns to his drink, shrugging his shoulders.

'We played three games, swapped partners each time. As it happens, I won with each of them.' Emil glares round the room, daring anyone to interrupt. 'Not that I didn't notice Weber and Fissbad playing badly to make sure I'd win. Damn fools, what do they take me for?'

'So Nussbaum was the only one who played properly?' Hinrich prods.

'Right, played to the best of his ability. And then I thought I'd really test them; Nussbaum and Weber were winning, so I made a deliberate bloomer. The trick was ours, Fissbad's and mine, but I pretended I didn't realise. Quick as a flash Nussbaum pointed it out to me.

'"Herr Dohlen," he said, his voice quite loud for such a little chap, "I think you've made a mistake. You're far too good a player to throw away a trump. Perhaps you'd like to reconsider?"' Emil's deep-set eyes and fiery beard sweep from Hinrich to Wilfred and back again. 'I put the cards down right away. "The game is over, gentlemen," I told them. "Herr Nussbaum has the job".'

The door opens and Theo Bender hobbles through, his wooden leg not fitted to his stump. 'Sorry I'm late.' He manages his crutches around the chairs and table, waving aside Hinrich's efforts to help him. He pulls out a chair, places his crutches against its side, and hops on his good leg to sit. 'Didn't mean to keep you waiting. Couple of things I had to do.'

He catches the admiration reflected in Emil Dohlen's eyes and smiles faintly as he pours the Schnapps Hinrich has readied for him down his throat. Then holds his glass out for more.

'Come on, Wilfred. Let's have another bottle.' Emil roars, leaning back and opening a cupboard just behind him.

Wilfred jumps up, takes out a new bottle of Schnapps.

Emil turns, snatching the bottle from him. 'We're here for a game of whist, man. You finally ready to start?'

'Of course, Emil. I was only getting...'

'Theo is ready, so is Hinrich. What are you dithering around for?'

Wilfred returns to his seat to shuffle the second pack, cards spilling over the table as he begins to deal. In his hurry a card turns face up.

'Redeal.' Emil Dohlen thunders. 'My God, Wilfred, I know you're a rotten player. But can't you even *deal* them straight?'

THE CHURCH WITH THREE SPIRES

The twin spires of the St Nicolaikirche—named after the patron saint of children, sailors, travellers and thieves—dominates the flat landscape of the Schwanenbruch marshes.

A long time ago two ladies of noble birth, accompanied by their young and devout lady-in-waiting, were sailing along the Elbe Estuary. Suddenly one of the terrible storms this region suffers from overtook their fine vessel. The ladies could tell that their boat was about to go under. Dismay turned to prayer. They and their lady-in-waiting stood on deck, hands steepled, arms interlinked, and prayed to be delivered from the elements. They refused to let go of each other even when the boat was sinking. And continued to pray while tossed into the raging sea and buffeted by high waves.

One particularly high roller carried them ashore. It deposited them on the rocky Schwanenbruch coastline. The two ladies were exhausted, cold, and bruised by the hard stones. But their young lady-in-waiting persuaded them to go on raising their voices to God in prayer. So sweetly did they sing their hymns, so loudly did they give praise to the Lord, that the villagers heard them above the wind.

All three were rescued, given dry clothes and good food, made comfortable. They rested in Schwanenbruch until they regained their strength. And in thanksgiving to the merciful God who saved them, and as a reminder of His great glory, the ladies used their enormous wealth to turn the St Nicolaikirche into the finest house of God in Land Hadeln. They took down the original spire and had twin towers built, one in thanksgiving for Fräulein Anna, the other for Fräulein Beate. Then added a shorter, squatter bell tower. Its golden-tongued bells peal the call to prayer, imitating their loyal lady-in-waiting on that stormy night.

That is why Schwanenbruch can be picked out from far away, the twin towers clear against the vast sky. They stand out, triumphant over the mudflats, bringing cheer to sailors and fishermen in trouble along the North Sea shoreline. But it is the bell-tower, with its golden-tongued bell, which peals out in fog to lead sailors safely home, and it is the glorious sound which announces the joys and disasters of the village.

CHAPTER 13

Schwanenbruch, April 1915

Emil Dohlen's practical jokes are legendary in the village. Gabby is particularly fond of the trick he played on an American business associate, the one she heard him tell Pastor Bender about. They both laughed so much they didn't notice her behind the door, listening.

Harvey Smith wrote to Vater, saying he was planning to visit Schwanenbruch. Vater put the letter in his pocket and strolled over the square to the Deutsches Haus. For a friendly chat with Franz Utter, the innkeeper. To warn him about a man with initials HS.

'Kind of an eccentric,' Emil mentioned casually. 'Name of Harvey Smith. Always travels under an alias. Tries to sneak out without paying his bills.'

'He's short of money?'

'He's a millionaire.' Emil slapped his leg. 'He just likes to see what he can get away with. Normally leaves by his window. Or down the fire escape.'

Franz Utter took Emil's visit as a special kindness. Forewarned is forearmed.

Emil answered Harvey's letter, welcoming him to his native village. Just one suggestion: maybe he should use an alias while in Germany. Some name which sounds a little less American. In these times of political unrest.

'One other fact I guess I should mention,' he wrote to his friend.

'The village can't afford the fire-tower bells we use in New York. You already know that our St Nicolaikirche is very special, and how it came to have three towers. I didn't bring it to your attention before, but you sure need to know. Our bells are special too. They perform a double duty: as church bells and as fire bells. If you hear them ring outside of a Sunday morning, don't stand on ceremony. Run for your life. Or jump out the nearest window.' A PS. 'At your age, you might think to take a ground-floor room.'

Franz Utter didn't worry when Hermann Smit asked for a room on the ground floor. HS, he told himself, forefinger tapping the side of his nose. Nor was he surprised to see his guest's luggage labelled Harvey Smith. Son Kurt will catch him fast enough if HS tries any tricks.

The village bell ringers practise on Thursday evenings. A high carillon rang out. Clear, but not the rhythmic call to worship familiar to all church-goers. A splendid new peal for Easter Sunday.

Harvey Smith knew precisely what to do. He opened his window, threw out his luggage, followed it. Right into the arms of stalwart Kurt Utter.

The Utters knew they'd be paid right away if they confronted Hermann Smit with Emil Dohlen. Maybe get a couple of Marks extra into the bargain.

It was a surprise to both parties to find Emil speechless with laughter. Even when he explained the joke to them they weren't entirely sure they understood it. But Pastor Bender was doubled up with laughter when he was told about it. And Gabby thought it wonderful, because she worships her father, every aspect of him.

'Come *on*, Moppel. Even a simpleton like you can pour water out of a jug.'

Doly's senses are on the alert. That bossy tone in Gabby's voice means she's planning to play another trick on her. Doly pulls bedding around herself, squeezes into the corner furthest away from the other two. Then fights the Federbett off, stands and grabs the rail. She won't let Gabby bully her.

Moppel strains his arms towards his sister, podgy hands puffed pink against the duck-egg blue of the china.

'Hold it up *straight*, stupid.'

'You do it, Gabby.' Nervous eyes flicker the corners of the room, the door, avoid the cot and Doly. Contracted muscles spasm his arms, lurching splashes of water on highly polished parquet.

Gabby moves out of range, arms folded across her chest, shaking her head. 'The boy is supposed to be the one to act.' Her imitation schoolmarm voice terrifies Moppel into obeying her. 'It's what boys do.'

Moppel brings his elbows back, hugs the jug to his chest, head bent down, tears and snot welling.

Gabby's eyes hawk at her brother, index finger stabbed at Doly's cot. 'You're such a *dolt*, Moppel.' The steaming hiss of a kettle about to boil.

Moppel's face is rigid. 'I don't want to...'

Doly bawls in self defence as Gabby pushes her unwilling partner forward. He stumbles, and the lip of the jug teeters through the bars, spilling water on Doly's mattress.

Piercing screams bring Herta and Minni rushing into the room. They're almost unrecognisable. Tante Hannah has forced them into uniforms. The two blundering women are encased in tight black dresses and adorned with starched white aprons and white caps. Doly, making tweeting sounds, calls them her penguins. Safe now they have arrived her cries turn into chirps, her arms flap up and down like wings.

'What on earth's the matter this time, Doly?' Herta pushes her elbows up and down to ease the starch.

Doly opens her mouth, juts out her chin and bobs her head back and forth, her lips formed into an opened beak.

'Is there something wrong with your neck, child?'

Minni laughs. 'She's being a baby penguin. But I think she's wet herself.' She leans over the cot bars and lifts Doly out.

Bird noises turn back to screams as Doly's fury overcomes her powers of speech.

Herta grabs her from Minni, puts her hand under her bottom, turns to Moppel and Gabby. 'Well? Just what have you two been up to?'

Moppel's eyes sink like currants in a bun. He tries to hide the jug behind his back.

'We haven't done anything, Herta,' Gabby says, shifting over to the window, nose wrinkling. 'I think Doly has wet her bed again.'

'Didn't,' Doly screams.

'That's what you think, is it? Wet the mattress without wetting her nightdress, I suppose?' She pats Doly's rear. 'Quite dry.' She settles Doly on her hip and pulls at Moppel's left ear. 'What are you doing with that jug, Moppel?'

'Thirsty,' he says, putting it to his lips and guzzling, water coursing down his cheeks. Loud slurping noises turn to belches he can't control.

'Poured some on Doly's mattress, did you, boy?' She twists the ear in her fingers.

'You're hurting, Herta.' He holds the jug out, imploringly, towards Gabby.

She turns her back, putting her hand over her mouth to hide her grin. 'I'll open the curtains, shall I, Herta?' She pulls at the cord of the heavy velvet covering the windows and lets the daylight in.

'That's a really naughty thing to do, Moppel,' Herta scolds. 'I'm going to have to tell your father.'

'No, Herta. Please Herta, it was just a joke...'

Gabby begins to giggle, then convulses into uncontrollable laughter.

'And what's so funny, Diern?' Herta stands watching Gabby, eyes cold.

'If you tell Vater, he'll just be proud of Moppel, think it was very funny. It really worked, Herta—just like one of Vater's practical jokes.'

CHAPTER 14

Schwanenbruch, April 1915

'What's all this racket I can hear?' The sounds of a female voice speaking High German. The clipped incisive syllables Tante Hannah favours over the local Plattdeutsch.

Doly stiffens, puts both arms around Herta's neck, burrows her head under her chin. She sees Gabby rush over to her day clothes, stacked ready on a chair, and begin to dress. Loud heels click closer.

'Well, children. That really sounds like quite a to-do. What on earth is going on?'

'Tante Martha.' Doly wriggles out of Herta's arms and runs towards her aunt. She remembers now. Tante Martha is sleeping in Tante Hannah's room because Tante Hannah has gone to Hamburg. *That's* why Gabby dared to try that trick with Moppel.

Strange how similar Tante Hannah and Tante Martha sound, yet how different they are. Tante Hannah is very round, with black hair, brown eyes, swarthy skin. Tante Martha has a peachy-cream complexion and high cheekbones. The slight build and twinkling searching eyes remind Doly of Mutti. And she has the same cap of dull lifeless hair which sits on her head like a hat. Except that Tante Martha's is light brown, not black.

Doly holds up her arms and squeezes her eyes tight shut. She can pretend Mutti's still there, about to pick her up.

Tante Martha lifts Doly high, shifts her on to her left hip. 'We don't want all this noise today.' She clasps her tight, nuzzles nose on nose.

Doly curves an arm around her neck and nuzzles back. Tante Martha takes it away and frees a wad of lifeless hair caught under it. She always shies away from real hugs. Just like Mutti.

But Mutti's in Heaven, and Tante Martha hardly ever comes to visit. And, though she likes her aunt, Doly likes Minni better. Tante Martha doesn't sit back on Vater's chaise longue and snore, and pretend the pestering Doly is a fly to be swatted away. And she doesn't encourage her to hide in cupboards and pretend not to find her. Tante Martha plays serious grown-up games.

'We could have a session of dominoes,' she tells the children. 'Then Gabby can show you two younger ones how to add up the pips; that will help you with your arithmetic.' The cap of hair nods. 'And while Minni's getting you dressed, I will read you some poems. It's never too soon to start on the classics.' She opens a small slim volume she draws out of her dress pocket and peers at it.

'Schiller is a fine poet,' she says, her eyes much bigger behind the glasses which she now puts on. 'I will read you some of his work.'

'My father only reads Byron and Shakespeare,' Gabby shrills, determined to be heard. 'He says Byron is the finest poet in the whole world.'

'Byron wrote in English, Gabby. He is a very fine poet, but he did not write in our language. We have our great poets, too, you know. Goethe and Schiller. And our very own Hermann Allmers, from Hagen, is an outstanding poet. I think you know his story about saving the dyke.'

Doly shudders the dykeman out of consciousness. Somehow, he and her father are muddled up in her mind. She hates Vater's spiralling echo of emphatic shouts demanding attention, clamps her palms over her ears at the first bellow. It's impossible to please him. The explosive laughter when she acts her party pieces are almost as scary as the strange long silences and gruff grunts he delivers most of the time.

'Vater says Byron is the best.'

Gabby's insistence on her father's choice of poet encourages Martha's pedagogic streak. 'Byron was a good poet, but not such an admirable man.'

Gabby shrugs, clearly unable to believe Tante Martha might know better than Vater. 'And Vater taught me how to pronounce English so that I can read it well. I've just learned a new poem.' She climbs on to a stool, faces everyone in the room and begins to recite:

My hair is grey, but not with years.
Nor grew it white
In a single night
As men's have grown from sudden fears.

'That's very good, Gabby. Very good indeed.' Tante Martha's head bobs at her, voice low, eyes round. 'Your pronunciation is excellent. I suppose you remember from when you were a baby.'

'Can you speak English, Tante Martha?' Forget-me-not blue pierces the room in self-satisfied victory.

'Not as well as your father, of course. But English is my special subject.'

Gabby hunches her shoulders, then rallies. 'Of course Goethe had great praise for Byron,' she announces. Pulpit voice. 'Vater says he was the most influential poet of his time in Europe.'

Doly bites her lower lip. Gabby's good at English because Vater teaches her. Why doesn't he teach his younger daughter? Why does he only notice her when she twirls her skirts for him? Doly wants to learn English, too.

Tante Martha relaxes, nods agreement, eyes back to the book.

Doly can sense another bout of poetry reading coming on. The whole thing is becoming a huge bore. She runs over to Minni doing up the last of Gabby's buttons.

'Boots,' she says, pointing to her feet. 'Doly wear boots.'

'Your Onkel Hinrich is coming over this morning. He's promised to take you out.' Tante Martha's radiance takes in all three children, her eyes soft and dreamy.

Tall, dark, handsome Onkel Hinrich is very special. He'll lift Doly up, throw her high into the air and catch her as she falls. Even Tante Martha turns gay and carefree when her brother is there.

Tante Irmgard and Onkel Hinrich have no children of their own. Instead Tante Irmgard rescues injured animals and Onkel Hinrich breeds German Hunt Terriers and German Shepherd Dogs. Doly adores visiting them—Onkel Hinrich lets her romp with his dogs for hours. He even puts her astride his larger ones and lets her ride them to his little house. Then he carries her indoors.

Doly loves their cosy living room with its low ceilings, the worn comfortable chair warmed by a rescued kitten, another holding a bird with a broken wing or a rabbit with a paw shattered in a trap. Occasionally Tante Irmgard comes across a trampled hedgehog. She guards all her charges until their wounds are healed. Then she sets them free.

Onkel Hinrich encourages Doly to help look after the animals. Which makes her feel warm, and loved, and needed. All she has to do is to be herself. She longs for a father like Onkel Hinrich. He loves her for what she is, she doesn't have to put on a star performance.

Doly turns to see Moppel crying in a corner. He's still afraid Herta will tell Vater about the trick he's failed to play on her. Why don't the grown-ups know it was all Gabby's idea? That she made Moppel do it?

She sidles up to Herta. 'Want go with Moppel,' she says, taking hold of her brother's hand. 'Go find Onkel Hinrich.'

'Don't you ever try that nonsense with your little sister again.' Herta shakes her fist at the cringing boy, points to the door. 'She's never done you any harm, the little angel.'

Gabby's head jerks back as she jumps off the stool, runs after them.

'And you too, Gabby. You should have been looking after your little sister,' Herta huffs at her.

Tante Martha catches Doly up in her left arm, grabs Moppel's hand, skips across the room, turns at the door. 'Don't worry, Herta. I'll make sure Doly is looked after properly.'

Doly grins over Tante Martha's shoulder with triumphant eyes. It feels good to win.

THE MUDFLAT GHOST

The island of Neuwerk, at first simply known as Oe, meaning the island, used to be the key to the rich fishing and shipping spoils offered by the Elbe. It was a great prize, coveted even by Hamburg, the big merchant city along the river. Fierce battles were fought to gain possession of it.

The island is still a favourite with local fishermen. They willingly walk many kilometres across the mudflats, fishing tackle slung over their shoulders, searching for the best fishing grounds.

The mudflat ghost is the Lorelei of the North Sea, luring innocents to their death. The best known story told is that of two fishermen, one young, one old, who are out for a day's plaice fishing. Suddenly they spot the figure of a woman standing a long way out on the Watt. She's beckoning to them, clearly inviting them to join her, pointing to a huge plaice she's holding upright next to her—a plaice as long as she is tall. She goes on waving as they watch, encouraging them to team up with her.

The older man mistrusts the whole apparition. 'It doesn't feel right to me,' he says. 'She's a long way away, and flood tide could catch us out.'

'Scaredy cat,' the young man mutters, then laughs. 'I'm off to get myself a decent catch for once. You'll be sorry later!'

The young man rushes off over the flats, keen to get his hands on as good a plaice as the the one he's just seen. But the older man is wary. He shouts after the young one not to trust the sighting, not to give in to the temptation. He turns round and goes home.

The young man is never seen again.

CHAPTER 15

Neuwerk, April 1916

'So that's the final deal, is it?' Emil Dohlen's voice is harsh with excitement. He's bored, stuck in Schwanenbruch with nothing special to do. Today's bet, to see whether he can beat his old friend Tobias in a race walking over the Watt to Neuwerk, will help ease the tedium.

'Exactly. I win, and you subscribe another Tiffany window for the St Nicolaikirche.' Tobias, as competitive as Emil, sounds confident. As though a new stained-glass window were already on Tiffany's order books. He's asked for a central one, larger than the other two flanking the triptych altarpiece.

'*If* you win.' Emil's large feet are bare. He pushes his big toe at one of the tiny crabs which scurry, like sideways lightning, away from him. 'If *I* win, you get Martha to postpone her teacher training and oversee the children.'

'Can't think why you're so set on Martha. Any number of young village women would jump at the job.'

Emil lengthens stride, not pace. 'Obvious. I want a relative to look after them.'

'Hannah's their half-aunt as well. And two years older. Martha's only seventeen.'

'I'm looking for someone who's really fond of them. And trustworthy. Just for a year. To give me a chance to make more permanent arrangements.'

89

As soon as Martha is installed Emil plans to take the next boat for New York. The dangers of crossing the war-torn Atlantic will, he is confident, make him feel alive again for the first time since Emma's death. He sees himself on deck, binoculars in place, searching for U-boats. Why would he care about dying? He's reached his allotted three-score years and ten.

He slaps Tobias on the back. 'Then I can get rid of Hannah. Can't stand that damn slut in my house a moment longer.' An experienced hiker, he's already in his stride, increases his pace. At least fifteen centimetres taller than Tobias, he's also fitter. But Tobias's wiry frame means he has less weight to carry.

'All *right*, Emil. I know how you feel about Hannah. But Martha's got to train for a career. No chance of the poor girl finding a husband. The cream of our young men are going to be killed in this lousy War. It's going to be a real blood bath before we're through.'

'Some will come back. She'll make a splendid wife.'

'The odds are set against her. You know she's got the gene.'

Emil makes an explosive sound which dies in the wind. 'So did Emma. Still married her, didn't I?'

Tobias trudges on, head thrust forward like a cannon ball. His dominant gene has been passed down to eight of his seventeen children: four from his first marriage, four from his second. 'All I'm saying is there's no need to make such a fuss about Hannah.'

'Make a *fuss*? I've been a bloody model of restraint.' Emil's feet leave deep indentations in the soft mud. 'I know Hannah's your daughter, Tobias, but she's still a rotten apple. You know it as well as I do. She's got to go.' He turns round, waits for his friend to catch up. '*You* threw her out. Left it to my sweet little Emma to rescue her.'

'For God's sake, Emil. I'm the *Pastor*. I could hardly stand by and watch while she carried on with a married man.' Tobias plays the turkey-cock, cheeks pink balloons. 'Anyhow, Emma offered to take her in off her own bat. Fond of Hannah, you know that. More like a daughter than a sister.'

Emil steeples his hands in mock prayer. 'Poor motherless child, raised her from the age of four,' he intones. 'Holy Moses, man. Affects my reputation as well, you know, sheltering an unmarried woman who's let herself be compromised.'

90

Persistence is one of Tobias's better qualities. 'Wasn't all one way. Emma said she needed help with the children.'

'Fat lot of help that gross floozy ever gives.'

'So what's the girl been up to now?' He trots to keep up with his impetuous friend. Takes a deep breath. 'She's not seeing that cad Meyer any more, I know that for a fact.'

'It's a question of the children.'

'You mean she doesn't treat them right?'

'What? How the hell would I know? Children are for women to look after. I'm talking about morals here. Damned whore's out late every night, caterwauling away on the street, right in front of the villa. Disgusting.' Emil's roar is amplified by the wind.

'What's that?' Tobias runs alongside Emil. 'Enjoying a kiss isn't a crime, you know,' he yells at him. 'Not even in our sanctimonious village.' Three strides to every two of Emil's, he keeps up. 'As long as the men aren't married, of course.'

'She's a slut, Tobias. And riddled with the fruits of it. Damn it, you've seen the pustules. You know as well as I do.'

'I would have thought having the pox is punishment enough.'

'I'm doing my bit paying for her treatment.'

'Can't you wait until she's cured?'

'I'll tell you exactly why she has to go. Why there's no time to lose.' He stops dramatically, then starts up again as Tobias charges past him. 'You'll hardly credit it, even with Hannah, but it's God's truth. Yesterday I was sitting in the tub, quietly enjoying my bath, when I heard someone in the bedroom...'

'That all? For goodness sake, Emil. Could have been Herta putting your clean laundry away.'

'...who walked right through into the bathroom...'

'So she forgot. You know none of us lowly villagers has the luxury of a bathroom. Yours is the only one in a private house.'

'Forgot? Holy Moses. She's supposed to oversee the children's bath time every day. Leaves it to Herta, needless to say.'

Tobias loses pace. Hangs back. 'I don't need the petty details, Emil. Just doing her job. Seeing to the linen or something. You're positively puritanical.'

Emil swivels round and shouts: 'Pranced up to me while I was lying in the suds in my birthday suit. Started taking her jacket off, dammit.'

Tobias catches up again. 'Come on, Emil. You always assume the worst.'

'I'm telling you straight. Stood there, eyeing my nakedness. At first I just looked back at her. Thought I'd stare her out. Anyway, I'd no idea what the hell she was up to. Thought she'd come to whine about some damned domestic row. Trying to catch me in a place where I couldn't get away. Something like that. She's always drivelling on about the servants.

'Nothing of the kind. Chucked her jacket behind her, leered at me. Sort of a twisted smile, showing those black teeth. Started unbuttoning her blouse...'

Tobias's face is puce. 'You're going too far, Emil. I don't believe a word of it. You're such a damned braggart.'

Emil shakes his head, hair wind-whipped round his eyes. 'I'm telling you the unvarnished truth. Undid all those damned buttons, one by one, while giving me the eye. Took the ruddy thing right off. A bloody striptease, Tobias. In my own house.'

Tobias hangs his head, jerks it up. 'You let her carry on, I gather.'

'I was in the bath, man. How the hell was I supposed to react? Anyway, there she was, her fat arms bare, starting to undo her skirt.'

Tobias's breath is rasping, his chest heaving.

Emil puts an arm around his shoulders. 'You all right?'

He twists away. 'Just sat back and watched her, let her get in deep?' His shouts are squeaky, high. 'Bastard.'

'Like hell I did.' Emil shouts back. 'What d'you take me for? Think I aim to get involved with that tramp, catch her foul disease? No, sir. I grabbed the sides of the tub. Hauled myself out. Splashed as much water over her as I could.'

'So she took off.'

'No such bloody luck. She stood and laughed. Pulled the skirt away from her, patted her arse. Smirked. Thought I was *encouraging* her by God.'

Tobias's eyes and mouth cod gape at Emil.

'That was too much for me. I grabbed the jug from the stand, dipped it in the bath water, hurled it at her.' He races ahead, forcing Tobias into a run to keep up with him. 'Most of it splashed on the floor. But she got the drift. Took to her heels.'

Tobias holds his right side. Breathes in short puffs. 'Easy, man. I can't keep up with you.'

'Better not take the bet then.' Emil pokes a mud-plastered foot into one of the small rills trickling through the mudflats. Swishes it clean. 'Spoilsport. No kind of fun to be had around here.'

'All right, all right. I'll take the bet. Hedgehog and hare, you bloody boaster.'

'You can see she has to go.'

'I can see you're determined on it. Hinrich could always...'

'Hinrich? Have you forgotten there's a war on? Hinrich's off on active duty next week. The Eastern Front. You want to saddle Irmgard with that whore? Hinrich will never stand for that.'

'Irmgard will be lonely, she might even welcome Hannah. Anyway, you got a better idea?'

'Pack her off to Nebraska. They're short of women over there. Can't afford the luxury of virgins.' Emil cackles. 'She's always on about how she wants to go to the States. This is her big chance.' He dips his other foot in water, cleans it. 'Never know your luck. Her boat could be torpedoed.' Emil guesses Tobias hasn't prayed for Hannah's death, but he has almost certainly put it to the Lord that if he needed her elsewhere, her father would carry the burden of her loss with dignity.

'That won't wash. The girl won't hear of going out West. Not after Emma's experience.'

'Dammit, Tobias. I'll foot the ruddy bill, whatever it is, to ship her off somewhere. Anywhere. Cheap at any price.'

Tobias walks on. 'We'll see. Bet still on, or are you chickening out?'

'You know better than that.'

Tobias picks up a tiny crab, watches its legs wriggle. 'Best keep within sight of other people. Don't want to spook the Wattengeist.'

Emil knows very well that the Watt can, like the desert, conjure up a mirage, a chimera of glimmering lights which the mind changes into familiar forms. Leading the over-confident astray. 'Holy Moses, man. We might as well be dead already if we're not willing to take a chance or two.' Emil's long legs spider over the mudflats.

'I'm not about to test our North Sea Lorelei.' Tobias shouts as he runs after his friend.

'So turn your deaf ear.' Emil yells back as he waits for his friend to catch up.

'What?' Tobias is panting, his face red.

'We're not bloody tourists, after all. *You* stay on the path of righteousness. If I walk fast enough to leave you far behind, that's my business.' He picks up a larger crab than Tobias's. 'You can always choose to be second.'

'Three hours brisk walking over the Watt will sort you out, old man.' Tobias bends down, puts the crab back in the rill. 'Start off fast if you want, you'll soon run out of steam. Reckon I'll catch you up in plenty of time.'

'My God, Tobias. Making me out too old to cope with Wattlaufen. All I have to do is put one foot in front of the other on springy mud. What could be simpler?' He stares at his feet. Walking the mudflats is a challenge he can still enjoy. He *wants* to make it dangerous.

Tobias shrugs away responsibility. 'Don't be so stubborn. You know the risks. I'm telling you now: I'm keeping to the marked-out path. And I've brought my watch so we're sure to make it back to Duhnen before flood tide.'

Emil grins as he remembers the last time the two friends did the trip. Not leaving plenty of time for the return journey could give the rushing flood tide a chance to overtake the unwary walker. Deep channels fill with water before the rest of the tide flows in, so cutting off both shores, and making it impossible to turn back or carry on. Emil dawdled on the way back, insisted on tracking seabirds through his binoculars. 'Keep your hair on; both of them.'

A tired joke, and one Tobias doesn't bother to respond to.

Emil and Tobias started out from Duhnen first thing that morning, right at the start of ebb tide. Plenty of time to walk to the island and back.

A thick sea mist covered the flats so that even the Neuwerker Turm wasn't visible. The sun's now shining through, thinning the mists, dispersing them. A glorious dawn pushes golden shadows ahead of them. A group of tourists, led by an experienced guide, can be seen following them.

'Seeing the sun rise over the Watt is something I never get tired of.'

Emil waves at his friend, strides away.

Slowly, imperceptibly, the distance between Emil and Tobias lengthens. Soon Emil is way ahead, his friend's rolled-up white trousers still visible, then merging into the specks of other walkers behind him. The sun is stronger. Brilliant reflections from the wet mudflats prevent Emil from seeing clearly.

He whistles to himself, unperturbed. The long, wide tongue of sand stretching out to the north west looks innocent enough, especially from a distance. But there are hidden hazards. The flats aren't flat at all, but a landscape of deep ravines and narrow-channelled tideways. The path to the island is clearly marked and the other walkers will soon catch up with Tobias. He can carry on without worrying about his old friend. He'll get to Otto's Gartenlokal, his favourite island inn, make the landlord write down the time of his arrival, order a drink and wait for Tobias to turn up.

The pegged-out way detours to the right for a safe return trip. Emil knows he has nothing to fear on the way out, the channels aren't a threat at ebb tide. If he takes the direct route, he'll gain even more time on Tobias.

He swings out, curls his toes round the hard ripples the retreating sea has left behind, enjoys the sensation. He looks ahead to see the uninhabited island of Scharhörn a few kilometres further to the northwest of Neuwerk. A menace to shipping because of the stony outcrops but a paradise for sea birds. He wishes he'd brought his field glasses with him. In spite of their weight, he would have enjoyed using them. And he could have checked on Tobias.

He arrives at Otto's pleased with himself. The door's still shut, and there's no other walker in sight. He can see the clock on the tower, hear it strike the half-hour—8.30. He's done the trip in two and a half hours. He sets off again, determined on a short walk towards Scharhörn. To get a closer glimpse of the birds which nest there.

Thirty minutes later he's back at base. Expecting to see Tobias sitting in front of the inn, or staggering towards it. He'll have a hard time persuading his friend that he really did win the bet.

There's no sign of the old parson. Emil mutters to himself, sits down on the wooden bench outside the pub, watches the other walkers dribble towards the island. Slow but sure, one after the other.

His old friend isn't among them. The pub door opens, people amble into the bar. Emil goes in with them.

Otto is away in Hamburg. Emil has to deal with a young barman he doesn't know. 'Did someone called Tobias Bender call in and leave a message earlier on?'

'We've only just opened.'

'We were due to meet here. He was on his way over from Duhnen.'

'Good three hours' walk, sir. He'll be along.'

'Dammit, I know that. I started out with him...'

'Can't really get lost on the Watt, sir. Not if you stay with the group.'

Emil starts to worry. He approaches the walkers he saw arrive first. They're enjoying a drink after their exertions.

'Did you happen to pass a friend of mine, walking by himself?' he asks them. 'About my age, much shorter, no hair at all. Rather a ruddy complexion.'

'We didn't catch up with anyone,' one of the young men maintains. 'We were the first.'

'No, no. I got here before any of you.'

He sees them grin at each other.

'My friend and I started out on our own before your party set off.'

The young man shakes his head. 'We didn't notice any solitary walkers. I thought it was supposed to be most unwise...'

'No problem if you keep to the marked-out path,' Emil interrupts.

'I suppose he could have missed the pegs. Foolish for an old man to walk alone. He might not be able to see well enough to stick to the path.'

Emil, restraining an urge to yell, leaves a message with the barman. Then laughs to himself as he realises what must have happened. Tobias is waiting somewhere else. Relieved, Emil scours the small island for his friend. He's nowhere to be found.

Really concerned now, he walks over to the drivers arriving with their horse-drawn carts loaded with tourists.

All insist they saw no sign of Tobias, no sign of anyone walking alone. It's as though his old friend had been a mirage, a Wattengeist. As though he never existed.

There isn't much else Emil can do. He has a new thought. A happier one. Perhaps Tobias has played a trick on him. Doubled back to Duhnen, is waiting there, laughing at him. The old rascal, who'd have thought he had it in him?

Emil can't convince himself. He leaves word at each island inn that he's offering a reward to anyone who can bring him news of his friend.

It's late now. Too late for Emil to walk back safely. Not much of a choice. Either he stays until the next tide goes out, or he tries to hitch a ride on one of the horse-drawn carts going back to Duhnen.

He chooses the ride. It isn't easy to persuade a driver to take him along because it means crowding the other passengers. A few Marks settle the issue. Emil strains his eyes for signs of Tobias, urging his companions to do the same.

Nothing, no one, to be seen. No sign of the man, no sign of anything he was wearing.

No sign of Tobias in Duhnen, either. Emil watches the tide come in, the water rushing towards the shore. Looks out for a body. Nothing.

When the sun has set he knows there's only one hope left. Tobias could have gone back to Schwanenbruch, may be waiting for him there.

Emil starts out on the trek back to his village with a heavy heart. Will he ever see his old friend again?

CHAPTER 16

Schwanenbruch, June 1916

Doly is in the garden first thing every day. Praying. First there's God, then there's Onkel Palter.

She waits by his special shed until he arrives. He's out and about from first light. Long before Doly is allowed to get up. Digging the garden, splitting wood, loading the wheelbarrow. His private space, he calls it. The garden of Eden for Doly. Which Tante Hannah never bothers with. So there's not a snake in sight.

'There you are already, my little one. Up so early?'

Doly holds out her arms, puts her hands around his neck as he lifts her, plants a firm kiss on both cheeks.

'Now to work.'

She watches Onkel Palter dig. Never tires of it. Watches the soft rich loam turn easily. Runs her fingers through it, enjoys the feel of moist soil, the earthy smell. 'Look at the worms. So many little worms, Onkel Palter.'

'Earthworms are a gardener's best friends, Doly. They aerate the soil, fertilise it.'

Doly picks out one of the worms, strokes it.

'Look in my pocket,' he says. Takes the worm, buries it. 'They don't like being out in the sun. And cock robin will make a meal of him.'

Doly reaches into the old man's jacket pocket. She loves the special smell. Of sweat, of fertilising dung. What will he have for her today?

A luscious raspberry? A ripe gooseberry? Perhaps an apricot from the greenhouse?

'Cherry earrings.'

'Put them on, my little princess. See how pretty you look.'

She hooks a pair of cherries over each ear, twirls to show them off.

'Come Doly. We're all finished here. I'll put you in the barrow and take you to Tante Palter. Let her find you a piece of cake and a glass of foamy milk straight from the cow.'

Of all the games she and Onkel Palter play, this is her favourite. He sits her in the wheelbarrow, pushes her to his home, lifts her out. Sits her on the best chair in the Stube—their front room. Next to Kaspar, the German Hunt Terrier puppy Onkel Hinrich has just given him.

This is a place where Doly knows how it feels to be someone's treasure. To be the only beloved nestling in the nest. Even better than Onkel Hinrich's house. She wishes she could stay for ever.

Nothing lasts. The morning break is over, Onkel Palter has to get back to work. And he takes Doly with him.

'I'll keep the cherries on until Minni comes.'

'Well, well. Wenn man den Teufel an die Wand malt...talk of the devil...'

Minni is walking down the garden path to greet them. Doly knows exactly what the devil looks like, and he bears no resemblance at all to Minni. She's the nearest thing to an angel in this world.

'Look at my cherry earrings.'

'Just like a beautiful princess, my pretty one. But better take them off. I passed your Tante Hannah on the street. If she sees you wearing them, she'll say you're pestering Onkel Palter.'

Doly feels the earth slipping away under her feet. What's wrong with cherry earrings? 'But, Minni...'

Onkel Palter pats Minni's arm. 'Things are going from bad to worse. I never get a chance to talk to Emil any more. Seems he's forgotten his old schoolfellow.'

Hinrich Bender, Emma's favourite half-brother, can hear screaming as he steps outside his cottage a few metres from the Villa Dohlen. A fox caught in a trap? A rabbit?

A child. Has Hannah gone too far, started beating the Dohlen children? His heart pounds as he sprints towards the sound.

'The Wassermann is going to get me. The Wassermann is going to get me.' Doly's high-pitched voice. Hysterical.

The Wassermann is the water sprite, the evil being which pulls children under water and holds them there until they've drowned, the one all Schwanenbruch children are always warned about. Hinrich rockets forward. The stream dividing the garden from his land is a death trap for small children. He sees Moppel hanging with one hand clinging to a willow branch, the other holding on to Doly. About to lose his balance.

Hinrich grabs Doly's arm and hauls her out. 'All right now, little one. I've got you safe.'

She's spluttering, choking, clinging to his neck. 'I could see him grinning at me, Onkel Hinrich. Waiting to get me with his transparent claws.'

Where's that gaggle of women who're supposed to be in charge of the children? Hinrich gathers the soaking Doly into his arms and holds her tight. 'The Wassermann can't hurt you now I'm here.' That's the problem. He isn't around that much, and all too soon he won't be around at all. Nor, apparently, is anybody else. Where on earth are they all?

Moppel unwraps himself from the willow branches. 'I fought him off for Doly. Didn't I, Onkel Hinrich?'

He pats Moppel's head. The boy has more courage than he's given him credit for. 'You're a brave lad, Moppel. Your father will be proud of you.' He jogs into the house with Doly. 'Herta! Ursula!'

Ursula comes running to meet them in the hall. 'It's Herta's day off, Herr Bender. She's gone to see her sister in Cuxhaven.'

' So what about Minni?'

'She and Gabby have gone to the market.' She notices the water pouring from the child. 'Oh, my God. Has the little one drowned?'

'Just wet through, Ursula. She fell into the stream. We need plenty of towels and a change of clothes.'

'I'll run a hot bath, Herr Bender.'

Doly is shivering with cold as Hinrich carries her up to the bathroom. 'Where's Hannah, Ursula?'

'Fräulein Bender has gone to see Lotte Meininger, Herr Bender.'

100

The dressmaker again? Hannah seems to spend most of her time having Emma's clothes altered to fit her. 'When?'

'First thing this morning. She said she needed to get some winter underwear made for the children.'

Ursula peels Doly's soaking clothes from her, tests the bath water, lowers the trembling child into the tub.

Doly clasps Ursula's arms. 'The Wassermann was going to get Kaspar,' she gasps. 'He only let go because I fell in.' She grabs Ursula by the neck. 'His nails were pulling at my legs.'

Hinrich is standing by the door, watching. 'Why were you out there on your own, Doly?'

'I was with Kaspar. He fell into the stream and got all wet. We have to dry him too.'

'Terriers shake water off themselves, Doly. He's got his fur to keep him warm. And he can swim.'

Ursula splashes warm water over the child. Her face is wet. Not from the bath water. 'I didn't even know she was in the garden, Herr Bender. Fräulein Bender said she was taking her along.' She swallows. 'Doly's been forbidden to be with Onkel Palter. Since yesterday.'

'Not allowed to be with Fritz Palter?' Hannah may be his sister but Hinrich can't stand the way she tortures—not too harsh a word—her charges. How come Emma couldn't see what was staring her in the face? 'Why?'

'Fräulein Bender says it stops him doing his job. But the little one was always safe with him.'

'I have to talk to you, Emil.'

'You're worried about all those debts your father left. I've told you, Hinrich, I'll take care of all that.'

Emil, eyes bleak and shoulders bowed, greets his favourite brother-in-law with outstretched hand. Ursula asked Hinrich to wait in the hall while she went to fetch Emil from his eyrie. Tobias Bender's disappearance, presumed death, has sapped his spirit, turned him into a total recluse. He spends all his time closeted in the turret room, catching up on the classical education he missed out on as a boy. He's taken to reading the classics: Tacitus, Cicero, Plato, sometimes Caesar for light relief. He doesn't even play cards any more.

Hinrich smiles wanly. 'It is good of you, Emil. None of us had the slightest idea he'd borrowed so much. To be honest, it never occurred to me that all those traders would lend him money.'

'I was his son-in-law.' Emil's voice is low and lacking energy. 'They knew well enough they'd get their money eventually. Forget about it, Hinrich. Your father always liked the good things in life. I'm glad he had the chance to enjoy some of them.'

'I'm afraid you miss him.' Hinrich is shocked to see the effect his father's disappearance has had on Emil. Away with his regiment, he hasn't seen his brother-in-law for about two months. The man looks really old, he'd say ten years older than when he last saw him. There's no time to lose in bringing up the subject he's been trying to broach for some time now. 'Actually, I came about something else. I thought that...'

'Your wife, I suppose,' Emil interrupts. 'Now that your father's no longer here you want me to look after her if anything happens to you.'

Hinrich's eyes soften. So used to being milked, the old man can't imagine he needs help himself. 'That's very kind of you, Emil. I knew I could count on you for that.'

'I'll see she's taken care of.'

There's a pause. The two men have gone through to the red living room, are sitting in Emma's favourite corner nook. Emil keeps it all arranged precisely as she liked it.

Both men focus on the Louis Quinze desk set in the window, the sewing basket still in its stand by the low easy chair she always sat in. Emma's presence is still strong.

Ursula brings in two mugs of beer. Hinrich picks one up, holds it aloft to toast his host and sips at the frothy liquid. 'How are the children, Emil? I came across Doly and Moppel this morning, but I've hardly caught a glimpse of Gabby.'

Emil looks at Hinrich sharply. 'They're fine. Why shouldn't they be?'

'Look, Emil. I don't want you to think I'm trying to get out of my responsibilities, but war is war. And this one is going to be longer than any of us thought. We have to take account of the fact that I might not survive.'

'I just said...'

'I know, it's very good of you to think of Irmgard. I was thinking about your children.'

'You think I might not last the War.'

'That's it precisely,' Hinrich agrees politely. Strange how even a man as strong as Emil resists the nearing of his own mortality. 'You always said you weren't happy leaving things to Wilfred. Poor old Theo can hardly cope with his own family. No chance of his taking on any more responsibilities, assuming he's still around. All my other brothers are in Nebraska.'

Emil levers out of his chair and prowls round the room, examining some of the prints of fishing vessels Emma collected, straightening them. He stares at Hinrich, the white ring round his blue irises now opaque, heightening the impression of irritability. 'I *have* given it all quite a bit of thought, you know. I haven't just buried my head in the sand.'

Hinrich nods, his tired face smoothing out a little. 'You've picked someone, then.'

'Friend of mine in New Jersey. Completely trustworthy.'

'New Jersey?' Hinrich's forehead creases into triple folds. 'The Atlantic's a battlefield. What good is someone in America?'

'The War will end eventually, Hinrich. In any case, what d'you want me to do? I've arranged for Hudwalker to handle my financial interests in the States. Apart from stocks, that's mostly Manhattan property. Brings in a good rental income. Crazy to sell. Walter Hudwalker is an honest man and that's a rarity. He'll look after everything the best he can.'

'How old is he?'

Emil laughs. 'You think he's my age. Well, I'm still up to working that one out. He's in his late forties.'

'And will he take charge of the children's education, their welfare? I was thinking particularly about that.'

'Holy Moses, Hinrich. This is turning into an inquisition.' He glowers. Sees the expression on his brother-in-law's face. 'Shouldn't be a problem. He's the Principal of a large school. His two daughters teach as well.' He stops by the window to relight his cigar, takes several puffs, shaky steps back to his seat. 'If I were a young man, I'd be in the Army too, you know. Not like Wilfred, skulking about in Schwanenbruch.'

'Wilfred isn't young, Emil. He's forty. Middle-aged. And being a grain merchant is an important job. The Army has to eat.'

The smokescreen between him and Hinrich gets denser. 'No one can protect their children from fate.'

'Yours are particularly vulnerable. They have no mother.'

'There's Martha.'

Hinrich's embarrassment shows in his heightened colour. He shuffles Emma's chair a few centimetres nearer to the place he remembers it used to be, keeping his face turned from Emil. 'Martha's a good girl but she's very young.' He blushes even more but carries on. 'She may not marry. You know very well she's unlikely to.'

'I married Emma. That little family problem didn't bother me.'

He turns round to face Emil, waves the smoke away. 'I think you should consider appointing a legal guardian, Emil.' He tries to lighten his words with another smile. 'A mature couple, a woman who would be glad to take on the children, a man who can handle at least the German side of the finances.'

'I have. You and Irmgard. You have no children of your own, you both like mine, I trust you implicitly.'

Hinrich sighs. 'It's supposed to be a military secret. I'm being sent to the front. And Irmgard isn't strong, Emil.' Hinrich looks grave as he smoothes his uniform. 'She's a sweet woman but she depends on me to make all our decisions. She won't be able to look after the children if something happens to me.'

'I'm not appointing Wilfred.'

'So go outside the family. What about the Alpersons?'

'If we're both for the chop, Hinrich, the children will have to go to the States. I don't want them confined to Germany. I told you: Hudwalker will take them on. He gave me his solemn word.'

'You really think he's up to it?'

'Good as anyone else,' Emil says, getting up and walking over to the window. 'No predicting the future. Who'd have thought Emma would die before me?'

'But she has. And you have to face that, Emil. You've got to find someone to replace Hannah. Now.'

Flickers of fury gather in Emil's rheumy eyes, surging adrenaline straightens his spine. 'I've looked into hiring a governess. And I'm seeing Martha next week, Hinrich. What d'you take me for? I've got it all in hand.'

CHAPTER 17

Schwanenbruch, July 4th, 1916

Emil Dohlen moves slowly towards the dining room. His normally expressive eyes are veiled, sunk in a trough of apathy. The familiar room, its turquoise colouring emphasising the green of the Schwanenbruch summer, reflects light from the highly-polished surfaces. Herta works hard to keep the whole villa as Emma liked it.

All the same Emma's light touch is missing. The room feels empty, sterile. The once dynamic house has become a living shrine.

Emil walks up to the long mahogany table, sees his sombre face mirrored in it, frowns and opens a heavy leather-bound volume he's brought with him. Julius Caesar's Gallic Wars. He opens it at the silver book-mark and begins to read.

A single place is set for him at the head of the table. There are no candlesticks, no rose, no Schwanengeschirr, no Corning glassware. Instead, a plain white soup plate stands ready. A smaller equally plain plate, covered by two thick slices of rye bread, sits beside it. There is no Schnapps, no beer. A drinking glass is next to an earthenware jug filled with water.

Emil Dohlen stiffens himself into his chair, levers his stick to the horizontal. Uses it to press the electric bell. It jangles loud enough for him to hear it all the way from the servants' quarters but it takes several minutes for Herta to appear.

'Komm schon, Herr Dohlen,' he hears her calling to him out in the corridor leading from the kitchen. Her breath comes in little pants and wheezes. Always so willing, telling him she's on her way. But getting old.

Herta heaves the door open with her hip. Puffs into the room carrying a large tureen of soup. She sets it down in front of her employer, her breath loud as she lifts the lid and begins to ladle the steaming mass into the soup plate.

'Mahlzeit.' She puts real feeling into the well-worn expression to enjoy the meal. 'Rula hopes you'll like the lobster bisque. She saved some butter specially. Did the best she could without cream.'

Emil grunts, puts his spoon into the soup, lifts it to his lips. He doesn't care what he eats. His once healthy appetite has gone since he lost his friend. No one to banter with, no one to walk with in the whole boring village.

'Is it all right?'

'Geht schon,' he says, crinkling his eyes, trying not to sound too indifferent. 'It'll do.' The bisque is tasty, but the silken feel of cream is missing. 'We all have to make sacrifices. The soldiers at the front have had nearly two years of it. Tell Rula I admire the way she manages without the right ingredients.'

'I will, Herr Dohlen.' Herta shifts her weight from one foot to the other. Emil frowns at her. All he wants is to be left alone. 'Rula thought, we all thought, you might appreciate a special treat for July 4th.'

He tries to concentrate. What is she talking about?

Herta brushes down her apron. 'Independence Day, Herr Dohlen. The mistress always ordered a special meal.'

He fights back tears, nods. His servants are Germans but still want to please their American employer. For Emma's memory. 'Fetch Hannah.' Voice gruff.

Herta's hand shakes. The empty ladle misses the tureen. Drops of soup splash on the polished table. She uses her apron to clean them up. 'You want to see Fräulein Bender now?'

'Is now not convenient?' Emil's voice is louder than he intended, his scowl darker. Why is he taking his frustrations out on old Herta? Does her level best, way beyond need.

'Of course, Herr Dohlen. I'm on my way.'

He's finally come to a decision. Hinrich has a point. Time he dismissed Hannah. Tobias has been missing for three months, presumed dead. Emil has thought about it from every angle but, dead or alive, Pastor Bender lost the bet. There's no question of funds for Martha's teacher training from her father's estate; Emil has paid off the creditors. And her brothers are in no position to pay for it. Ethically speaking, Emil reckons he's well within his rights to ask Martha to replace Hannah for a time.

School is about to break up for the summer holidays. If Martha takes over from now until the autumn of next year, she'll only miss one year of training. She's just seventeen, still very young. She can make up one year without real hardship.

That's all he'll ask of her. A single year. And in return he'll pay all her fees, and make her a generous allowance on top of that. He's already put her in his latest will, in case he dies before the year is out. Her cooperation will give him time to find a permanent substitute.

He has to act. Hannah is getting on his nerves more than ever. Lately she's started getting in his way again. Flaunting herself at him, apparently unable to grasp that he finds her totally repulsive. It's beyond him. Surely, with all the troops billeted around, there are enough young men to keep even such a rapacious female satisfied?

Hannah can hardly believe that the moment has finally come. She runs to her room, loosens her hair and brushes it shiny. She changes into her freshly-laundered Sunday blouse, plaits her hair into one long thick coil and brings it forward to point towards her bosom. Then she sprays herself with some of the perfume she's stolen from Emma's bedroom.

She walks rapidly down the main staircase, enjoying the loud echo of her boots on the bare wood. She goes into the red salon to fetch two wine glasses. Delicate ones.

Emil is sitting at the far end of the dining table. As usual. He's pouring himself some water, drinks it soberly. Ridiculous. She'll see to it that they have a decent bottle of wine with their meal every day.

'You asked to see me?' She's bitten her lips to make them red, and honeys the words to sound submissive. But she can't stop the curve of her mouth going wide, the glitter in her eyes. It works on all the other men, so why not Emil? 'I've brought two of the Corning glasses. I do hope you don't mind.'

Emil presses his stick against the bell. He stares at Hannah, his face impassive. No move, no word.

'Are you ready for the main course, Herr Dohlen?' Herta stands just inside the door, staring from Hannah to Emil.

'All right, Herta. You can serve it now.'

'Kutterscholle, Herr Dohlen. Rula's Dieter brought in his haul of plaice this morning. This one's the best of the catch.'

'Put it down, woman.'

'And bring some wine, Herta.' Hannah's voice is loud and incisive.

Emil swings his head up sharply. 'What the hell d'you mean by that? If I want wine, I'll order it.' He turns to Herta. 'You can go.'

'Sorry. I thought you wanted to drink to Independence Day.' Hannah bats her eyelashes, smiles as seductively as she knows how. 'And the fish wants to swim, Emil.'

'*Emil?* What the devil d'you mean by calling me Emil?'

Hannah looks at her brother-in-law. Has she misjudged the situation? What else could he have called her in for if not to ask her to join him for a drink?

Emil inserts his knife against the backbone of the plaice and parts it from the bone. Carefully, skilfully, he loosens the flesh. He places his knife on the side of his plate, American fashion, changes the fork to his right hand and picks a piece of the fish up with it. The mustard sauce Rula always makes to his directions is in a sauce-boat by the side. He pours some over the fish, dips the piece into it, and eats.

'Potatoes.'

Hannah moves nearer and pushes the heaped bowl of boiled potatoes towards him. Emil helps himself to several, pouring more sauce over them.

'Rula's a good cook. This plaice is excellent.'

Hannah stands, waiting. Emil Dohlen continues to eat. He doesn't look at her, doesn't ask her to sit down. He finishes the dark-skinned side of the fish, then turns it white side up.

Suddenly his sharp eyes are on her. 'I've decided Martha is to take over your duties here.'

A slow deep flush spreads over Hannah's cheeks into her hair.

'Martha? Martha is starting her teacher training course at the end of August. She wouldn't be able to stay for more than six weeks. At most.'

'Martha can only enrol if I pay the fees. Your father left nothing but debts. If I don't choose to pay, she can't take the course.'

'But, Herr Dohlen, you know she's really keen. You know she desperately wants to become a teacher.' Rush to her sister's defence. Show him how cruel he's being to holy Martha. 'And she's two years younger than me.'

Emil attacks the potatoes with his fork, pushing the prongs into a large one and breaking the flesh up. 'Exactly. She's still very young. She has plenty of time. I need her for a year while I look round for someone suitable to take on overseeing the children's care.'

'And what about me? I'm not suitable?'

'Right. You're not suitable.' He takes another bite of fish, helps himself to further potato, dips it into the sauce with relish. 'You're nothing but a tramp. An ugly bloated tramp I refuse to have in my house a moment longer. I want you to pack your things and go; immediately.' Hedged eyebrows huff into a ferocious bridge.

Hannah feels her body stiffen, her feet leaden. As though her boots have sunk into the floor and won't release her.

'Now.' The stick bangs on the table for emphasis.

'And where am I to go to?' The bitter taste of blood as her lips leak.

Emil takes his knife, cuts a large potato into pieces, replaces the knife on the side of his plate. He spears a piece of potato with his fork, puts it into his mouth. Masticates.

'What exactly do you expect me to do at such short notice?' Her voice is sharp. No point in placating at this stage.

His Adam's apple moves with the swallowed food. 'I'll pay your passage to the States. You've always said that's where you want to go.'

Hannah stiffens. He's hoping to kill her off, the way he put paid to her father. 'There's a war on. In case you haven't noticed.'

'Boats still cross the Atlantic. You'll find one. I'll pay for your stay in Hamburg until you do.' He peels back the white fish skin. 'On the Reeperbahn, perhaps. I'm sure you know it well.'

He's associating her with the red-light district. Blatantly. Stirring the fury waiting inside her, spurring it through young veins, reaching her brain. Hannah's hands twist the folds of one of Emma's old dresses, bunch them in front of her.

Bad move. Emil glances up, jerks his eyes away, He scrapes some fish meat from the bone, puts down the knife and forks some of it quickly into his mouth. 'It's your big chance, girl. Try your luck out West. Join your brothers in Nebraska.'

'*Nebraska?*' She spits the word out and shifts over to the window, shadowing Emma's dress. Her body blocks out light, casting deep shade over Emil's plate.

He stirs the food around. 'Good place to find yourself a husband. They're none too fussy.'

'Fuck Nebraska.' She heaves closer to Emil, body heat steaming from her. He doesn't react. 'A tramp, am I? That's what you think of me?'

He goes on eating. 'Precisely. And I won't have my children exposed to that.' He doesn't even flinch, uses his knife to separate more fish from the bone.

Hannah sees her reflection twitching in the polished table, angry eyes flashing back at her. She might as well go for it. She's been longing to get at the bloody tyrant. 'How the hell would you know, you impotent old man,' she explodes. Enjoys the feeling. 'Think you're so bloody marvellous. Just because you're rich.' Her elbows spread wide as she leans back, pushes out her bosom. 'Some things money can't do for you, can it?' She stares at the crotch of Emil's trousers, leers. 'Can't get it up for you, for a start.' Her nostrils flare. 'Can't do your fucking Bumsen for you, either.'

Emil's lips purse round his fork.

'My father always said you were a bloody Puritan. But then he hadn't a clue. Thought you were being loyal to Emma's memory. Truth is you're past it. Past sex, past friends, past life. Dead on your doddery feet, old man.'

He shows no sign of anger, or even annoyance. 'The language of the gutter,' he says, calmly pouring more water, drinking it.

Hannah takes her explosion as internal purification. Draws back her lips, not caring about exposing rotting teeth. 'Don't think I didn't see you in the bath. Small flaccid worm which stayed that way. That's all you've bloody fucking well got left.'

'I'm sure you'll find plenty of pioneers in Nebraska who have the equipment you require.' Emil helps himself to more potatoes. 'They're so short of women out West they'll even settle for you.'

'You're short of the right woman here.' Hannah walks up to Emil, hands on hips. 'If you think Martha's going to take you on, you can think again.'

His knife is poised to scrape more fish. He holds it steady as he looks at her, sober, detached. She stops, not coming nearer.

'I'm looking for the right person to care for my children,' Emil says, continuing with his meal. 'Not a replacement wife.'

'No knowing how many of those you'd get through,' Hannah growls. Spittle creeps down both sides of her mouth, it caverns wide. 'Look what you did to Emma.'

He stops pushing more food on to his fork. 'What the hell are you drivelling about now?'

'*You* were the one who brought on her early labour. You started it.' Hannah grasps the chair nearest her, bangs it against the table and back with such force it jolts Emil's plate.

'What's that?' Emil's eyes sink into deep hollows. His fork is packed, halfway to his mouth. 'Holy Moses. What garbage are you gibbering on about now?'

'Because of you she haemorrhaged, wasn't it? Poor little fool. She tried to help you up those high treads...'

'That's enough.'

'...used her body, big with child, to help you...'

'Halt's Maul.' he bellows. 'You bloody well shut your fucking mouth.'

'Killed her, that's what.'

'Button up those filthy lips, woman.' He gulps the fork load and swallows.

There is a moment when his face, his mouth wide open, looks almost like the fish he's been eating. Plucked from the sea, gasping for air.

'You're not going to shut me up this time.' Hannah shouts, her arms attacking the chair again, rocking Emil's plate hard enough to slide into his lap. 'All the cocksuckers around here know, they're just too mealy-mouthed to let it out.'

Hannah, taking in a deep breath for more insults, squints at Emil for a response, waiting for the outburst.

Not a single word, nothing. What she sees silences her, too. Emil heaves for breath, then gags, starts choking.

Hannah, heart startled into rapid beats, grabs the chair to steady herself. Emil isn't choking with rage, he's trying to cough up something lodged in his gullet.

Her arms tighten round the chair, a delicate strut snaps. 'And what about my poor old father?' she taunts, round dripping head thrusting at Emil. 'Did for him, too, didn't you?'

Emil rasps, trembling fingers groping for his stick. Hannah draws back, replaces the chair carefully in its proper place, clenches her lips tight, retreats to the other side of the room.

Uncertain fingers flail, can't grasp the stick. Emil's face whitens, then deepens into red, purple, a dark shade of blue.

He's asphyxiating. Must be a fishbone caught in his throat, swallowed because he was busy slanging her. He needs help, and Herta won't come unless he calls her. He's roared at her often enough about that.

All Hannah has to do is walk away and let nature take its course. A dead man can't fire her. She'll be on the spot, in charge. Hasn't he just said he hasn't talked to Martha yet? That means Hannah will have complete power over the brats, the house. And the money needed to run it. Not hard to get that out of Wilfred, left in charge while Hinrich is at the front. She knows a thing or two about her half-brother he wouldn't like his darling bore of a wife Gerda to know.

The dark irises glow. Hannah stands upright, walks backwards, slowly, until she touches the wall. Her heart beats faster, the lump in her throat is tight, then threatens to block off her breath. She leans back, eyes shut, as she waits for her breath to return. Then, opening her eyes, she watches Emil Dohlen struggle.

He claws desperately at the table, the sides of his chair. She doesn't move, doesn't flinch.

He tries again to grab his stick to press the bell. Can't do it. He tries holding his breath, expelling air. No good. The colour of his face grows darker, turns black.

Hannah levers herself up away from the wall and walks slowly, deliberately right up to Emil. Stands only a metre away. Watches him.

His eyes, popping their sockets, focus on her. Daring her, challenging her.

She grins. 'So you want me to go, do you, Emil, my darling?' Her tone is gentle now, almost caressing, her mouth opened full width. 'Then of course I'll do exactly as you ask. I'll go at once.'

And Hannah saunters to the door, opens it, looks out to see if anyone is there, sees the empty hall, crosses it and walks through the archway leading to the kitchen. She waits a few moments, until she's sure the old bastard is finished.

'Herta,' she calls. 'Where have you got to, woman? Herr Dohlen wants you to clear the main course. He's ready for his dessert.'

CHAPTER 18

Schwanenbruch, July 6th, 1916

'Stand still for just a moment, Doly.'

Doly skips away from Herta towards the window. 'Don't like ribbons.'

'Just for today, Doly. We have to put a black one in your hair,' Herta coaxes. Deftly she brushes a handful of springy ginger curls to one side and twists black taffeta around it. 'To show respect,' she says. 'It's only proper.'

Doly can't stand all the fuss. She hates dressing up for the grownups. But she is fond of Herta. She can tell something unusual is going on, that Herta needs her to behave. Has Vater asked to see her?

She hops from one foot to the other until Herta manages to secure the ribbon in her hair. It keeps sliding off. Herta uses hair grips to hold it in place.

'Good girl.'

'Can I go now?'

'Hold my hand, Doly. We'll go together.'

Doly allows herself to be led to the door of the bedroom she shares with her brother and sister. They went off earlier, before Herta came to pretty her up.

Ursula helped them dress. In their Sunday best, though today is Thursday. But Doly doesn't care whether they dress up or not as long as she has her freedom.

Herta opens the bedroom door and pulls Doly through.

She can hardly believe what she sees. The landing is crowded with people, all jammed up together, all dressed in black, all silent. Filing in a long line up the stairs, along the landing and round into her father's bedroom. Then out again and down the stairs. Indian file. Grown-ups playing games?

'Come *along*, Doly. It's important that you should see him, too.' Herta grabs Doly's shoulders and tries to push her towards the master bedroom.

Doly digs in her heels. 'Don't want to go in there.'

'Never mind want. In you go.'

She can't escape, too many bodies pressing in on her from all sides. She walks through the double bedroom doors and stops, holds her breath. There's a gleaming brown box, gold handles at its sides, sitting on a sort of platform in front of the bed.

Something stirs in her mind, some deep-down memory she'd much rather forget. Curiosity gets the upper hand. What are they all looking at?

More and more people are trooping into the house. Doly grabs hold of the doorknob, clings to it, refuses to go further in. The mutter of low voices rumbles like flood tide in her ears, the wet eyes of the women make her afraid, the glum looks of the men send shivers of cold sweat down her spine. What's it all about?

She cranes backwards. To watch the ascending march of waving clouds of broad black hats. She hears the rhythm of crunching boots under heavy swishing skirts, sees bareheaded men carrying hats, wearing their Sunday best.

She turns to look into the bedroom. The space between two women walking past gives her a momentary glimpse of Gabby. Standing right by the box. She'll know what's happening; she always knows everything.

Herta is trying to prise her fingers loose. Doly lets go of the doorknob, rushes up to her sister.

'What you doing, Gabby?'

'Shhh, Doly.'

Gabby also has a black ribbon in her hair. Two, actually. One plaited into the wisps to hide the bald spot, another to make a large bow.

Moppel is standing next to her, wearing his dark sailor suit with the big white collar. It makes his face look even rounder. His sandy hair, neatly brushed for once, is falling down to his shoulders. And he has a black armband on his sleeve.

'When's the funeral?' Doly hears Frau Meininger ask Herta in a loud whisper.

'The reception of the coffin will be in the St Nicolaikirche at noon today. Pastor Alperson will lead a memorial service there at nine o'clock tomorrow morning. The funeral service will take place in the Mausoleum Chapel after that; it's too small for anyone but family to attend.' Herta's words are eagerly listened to by a cluster of women just coming into the room.

'A terrible tragedy...'

'The poor little orphans...'

Suddenly Doly finds herself back in time. She hears, as though it were today, her father's thundering voice: 'My beloved wife is dead,' it announces. She thinks she sees the double doors of the study opening wide, sees Emil Dohlen stand, his rigid frame upright, steely grey eyes sparking fire. 'She was a good woman, and we will honour her by silence.'

As Doly stares into the past four men come in. Dressed in black from top to toe, their high stove-pipe hats making them extra tall. They stride into her parents' bedroom. Memory stirs again, stirs deep.

'She was a wonderful wife,' Doly hears her father's distinctive voice, as though he were standing next to her. 'And a devoted mother to her children. She will be the first to lie in the Dohlen Mausoleum.'

No further sound of human voice reaches Doly. All she can hear is the scrape of boots across wood, all she can smell is the acid of stale sweat, all she can see is the surge of a moving mass of villagers trooping up the stairs, shuffling their turn towards the bedroom.

Suddenly she wants to be with her brother and sister, to stand beside them by the big box. The moving bodies melt away as Doly pushes herself between Gabby and Moppel. Touching them. She wants to feel them, be sure they are there with her. That she isn't alone, that someone of her flesh and blood is beside her.

A coffin. The big box is a coffin. Doly is right beside it, her eyes just high enough to look in. Her father's body is lying inside, surrounded by a soft silky lining. He's dressed in the black and white of his tuxedo.

He's prostrate before her. The rough, loud, domineering voice is silent, the large tall frame lies horizontal, still. His eyes are closed, not flashing anger. And his hands are folded, inert, across his chest, not thumping his stick while he shouts an order.

She stares, fascinated by the change. He doesn't move, he doesn't speak, he doesn't demand obedience.

Doly grabs Gabby's hand. Her sister's face, pinched tight, is chalky white. The enormous black bow on her head almost covering her forehead hides part of her face as she bends her head and bows her body. The gold locket she always wears on a chain around her neck moves forward. Opens wide.

It gapes at the unmoving, unseeing face. Gabby takes her hand away from Doly, snaps the locket shut and drops it inside the neckline of her dress. Then she places a book beside her father—a small, white-leather volume tooled in gold lettering. Doly knows what it says, because Gabby has told her time and again. BYRON.

Gabby lifts one of her father's hands, sets the book on the hand below and replaces the other one. It slips back, limp, and the book slips with it. A murmur rises up from the people around. Onkel Hinrich steps forward. He retrieves the book and firms the hand into its decorous position. It remains where it was.

The understanding that her father is no longer even able to control the movements of his own hand, that he is helpless, overwhelms Doly. Her lips began to part, a titter tripping through small milk teeth. It turns into a cackle, and then a full uproarious belly laugh she can't control, can't stop. It rocks her whole body, convulses her, doubles her over, engulfs her. It's all so very ridiculous. That harsh all-powerful man has finally been defeated. That aloof unresponsive father she could never get close to, whose every word was law, who controlled each waking moment of her life, can no longer dictate what she is to do. Doly finds that, in some peculiar way, absurdly funny.

The laughter becomes higher, louder. Turns into shrieks as tears blind her eyes. Emil Dohlen is no longer there. He's dead.

With each peal of laughter Doly feels herself break loose from the past, float without hindrance or guidance. She can no longer bear all these bodies pressing round her. She wants to be free.

Doly, surrounded, can see people staring down at her. Scandalised. Herta's big hand gropes over her mouth to shut off the unseemly sounds.

With one wild whoop she uses her sharp teeth. Sinks them into Herta's hand.

Herta lets go and Doly charges head first through villagers stepping quickly out of her way. She careers out of the bedroom, down the stairs, past black-clad bodies cringing to the sides, and so into the garden.

She rushes past the serried flower beds, beyond the rigid rows of vegetables, through the carefully spaced orchard trees. Leaves all that behind and hurries to the wide acres of meadow leading to the Braake.

She pulls off the mourning ribbon, tosses it into the stream. And welcomes the wind blowing through her hair, the fresh breeze cooling her face.

And Doly begins to twirl, to jump, to dance. A wild war dance of freedom, of release. The father who didn't cherish her, the tyrant who frightened her, who made her feel inadequate, is dead. Long live liberty.

Doly has no inkling of her inheritance, of the oppressor deep within herself. No idea at all that freedom is a two-edged sword.

Schwanenbruch, July 7ᵗʰ, 1916

The wheelwright's son who made his fortune in America is buried on July 7th, 1916. As the cortège leaves the St Nicolaikirche on its way to the Dohlen Mausoleum, his eldest child, his daughter Gabriele, nick-named Gabby because she talks so much, lifts her bowed head.

And sees the Villa Dohlen across the road. She stares at the house her father built, raises her eyes to the eaves, sees the inscription there.

DEUTSCHE ART TREU BEWAHRT

German ways upheld with praise. Her mother's words come flooding back to her:

"Heroism, loyalty and duty are the most important ones. Together with honesty, diligence, sobriety, responsibility, discipline." And with the echoes, a glimpse of what her mother was trying to tell her. She feels her mother Emma's pride and joy in their heritage.

Now that both her parents are dead, who will uphold, treasure, the traditions so dear to them now? The small mouth sets tight, and Gabby steps away from her brother Moppel, moping, shuffling, scuffing aimlessly along the dusty road. She overtakes her sister dragged unwillingly along, grasped by Herta's hand. Doly is looking down at a straggle of feathers in her free hand, clutching the body of the small dead bird the cat brought in, kissing it.

Gabby marches forward, the locket her mother entrusted to her proudly displayed and swinging on her chest. She catches up with her uncles, ramrods her spine and marches in step with the men towards the Mausoleum.

She knows who will uphold the family traditions. Not her brother Emil, nor her sister Dorinda. She will be the one. She is the proud standard bearer of the Dohlen Inheritance.

PART 2

GHOST RIDERS

1916–1919

THE GHOST RIDER

When storm clouds gather over the coastal marshes der Schimmelreiter—the ghost rider—can sometimes be seen riding his white horse along the top of the dyke, silhouetted against a dark sky. Or he may gallop along the shoreline and into the waves, disappearing into the mists which so often shroud the returning tide. He lived over a hundred years ago and was the dyke baron elected to oversee the Schwanenbruch stretch of dyke. It meant he was responsible for making sure that his neighbours carried out their dyke duty.

No marsh dweller could expect to retain his land unless he kept his section of the dyke in working order. The dyke laws were fierce and uncompromising. Any man found to shirk his duty risked terrible reprisals. His right hand might be cut off, or he might be burnt alive. And he would know that his family stood to lose everything: their land, their house, their belongings, their animals. These would be handed over to the new landowner, someone who'd swear to carry out his duties without fail.

De nich will dieken, mutt wieken

Dyke unattended, ownership ended.

A strict tenet of the dyke association was never to build your section of dyke higher than your neighbour's. Which left the dykes at the lowest common denominator, and very vulnerable.

The shrewd new dyke baron worked out that, instead of piling earth as steeply as possible, the dyke would be stronger if the slope facing the sea were a gentle one. That way, he reasoned, the dyke would be less likely to be breached by a raging sea.

His neighbours didn't agree. The baron's ideas went against all tradition. How could he know better than generations of their forebears?

Finally the baron ordered his fellow landowners to build the new-style dyke outside the old, disintegrating one. At first they argued with him. Still, he was their dyke baron and in the end they had to obey him.

But there was one tradition they intended to stick to, come what may. No dyke would hold unless a living being, a stranger to the community, were buried in the earth during its construction.

As luck would have it the dyke builders noticed a thin, bedraggled, unknown gelding dragging himself over the moor as they were patting the last spades of earth on to the new dyke. The horse was skeletal, hardly alive, a white nag. Not hard to catch. The weary men grasped him by his straggly mane, dug out a pit large enough to hold his body, and forced him inside. Only his head was showing when the baron arrived.

'What are you doing with that animal?'

The burliest of his neighbours stood forward from the rest. 'We need to wall up something living to make the dyke sea-worthy,' he told him. Massive shoulders straight, a look of defiance in his eyes.

The dyke baron stared the man out, then walked right up to the terrified horse. With his own hands he freed him from the wet earth covering him, with his own coat he washed him down. And then he mounted him, dressed only in his shirt—a white-clad figure on a pallid horse, a Schimmelreiter.

Awed, the dyke builders gave way to horse and rider.

'If you can't build a dyke without burying an innocent animal alive, you'll never manage to hold out against the elements,' the baron warned his neighbours. 'So, finish the dyke or pay the penalty.' And he rode off, a shimmering form distinct against the dark horizon.

The dyke was finished, a good dyke which held the sea at bay. Until the night of the biggest storm for decades. Not an ordinary storm, but a wild screaming tempest which hurled gigantic waves against the dyke and tried to tear it down.

The landowners were out in force to tend their animals, ready to flee if the sea should win. True, the biggest rollers poured over the new dyke. But they didn't breach it. The dyke baron rode his horse inside its length, proud to see his theory proved right. Not a single break anywhere.

But his fellow landowners watched the enormous waves roll over the dyke and on towards the old one behind it. They realised that some of the huge breakers would be strong enough to breach the old dyke made weak by mouse holes and neglect.

The dykers panicked. They started spading earth from the new dyke to repair the old. The dyke baron returned on his white charger, urged them to keep faith, not to abandon the new dyke which would hold back the worst of the storm and minimise the damage.

The men ignored him and continued to spade earth from the new dyke to fortify the old one.

The white horse and his rider galloped from one group to another, begged them to stop, to reinforce the new dyke again. Too late. The sea saw its chance, found the weakness in the new dyke, rushed in and swept away men, animals and buildings, until only the old church tower—the stalwart Ochsenturm, serving as lighthouse now—remained standing.

Now, whenever a big storm threatens, the image of the Schimmelreiter returns. 'Hold fast,' he shouts his warning as he rides. A lone shimmering figure in the vast dark plain.

CHAPTER 1

Schwanenbruch, September 1916

'Why aren't you two up and dressed?' The bedroom light blazes on as Tante Hannah crashes across the room. 'It's six o'clock.'

Gabby sits up in bed and rubs her eyes. Heavy curtains keep out the fragile morning light. No neatly folded clean underwear laid out. The linen she wore yesterday, creased and muddled up, lies in a heap with her frock. Exactly as she left it. 'Where's Herta, Tante Hannah? She hasn't brought our things.'

'Herta?' The black plait snakes round. 'What's that to do with you, Gör?'

Calling her stupid brat? Gabby tries to swallow, gulps. Her throat's on fire. She's been waiting for Herta to bring the honey mixture, afraid to call out now that Tante Hannah sleeps beyond the bathroom, in Emil Dohlen's bedroom. Her aunt will pour cod-liver oil down her throat if she suspects Gabby's ill. And send her out into the garden to kill the germs.

'My clothes...' Gabby forces air over her vocal cords to hide the huskiness.

'No need to yell.' Tante Hannah's heels crunch the floor like a squashed cockroach shell. 'What clothes?' The menace of high syllables.

'My vest and knick...underwear.' The croaking she can't control.

'Underwear? What d'you think this is?' Clothes are swept off the chair.

'I wore those yesterday, Tante Hannah.' Lips stiff with the pretence of being well.

A hooting foghorn snort. 'Oh? So you wore them yesterday, did you, your Royal Highness? For one whole day?'

Gabby shivers. Her throat's been raw for days. Herta soothed it with the balm of honey and cider vinegar. No lemons because of the War. She smuggled in a little Schnapps to take the pain away. Gabby needs more. Urgently. 'Herta always...'

'Speak up, girl. I can't understand that mumble.'

'Herta...'

'That's enough about Herta. I *told* Emma that woman spoils you brats. She won't be doing that in future.' Hyena laugh.

Gabby finds it hard to breathe. Looks sidelong at Doly. Her sister's feet stick out of the cot which is, by now, far too short for her. She pulls herself upright. The knuckles grasping the rail are white.

Tante Hannah is wearing one of their mother's dresses. Patches of another material line the sides and underarms to accommodate her bulk. Her eyes attack the bedding round Doly's feet. 'What are you hiding under your Federbett?' The cot bars are set too close for her fat arm. She reaches over the rail.

Gabby can't speak, has to act. She grabs the water pitcher from the bedside table, aims. A trickle of water catches Doly's head. Is that enough?

'What the devil?' Tante Hannah barges her body against the cot. It judders.

'Sorry, Tante Hannah.' Gabby's normally clear bell-like tone is reduced to a whisper. 'I just wanted to put the pitcher on the tray.'

'That's Ursula's job.' She tears it out of Gabby's hand. 'Things are going to change around here. You three aren't special, you know. Just ordinary village kids. You'll do exactly as I say.'

The rabbit Doly rescued from Onkel Hinrich's garden yesterday is squirming under the duvet. The trap Onkel Wilfred set broke its leg. Doly kicks her bedding into a thicker heap. Bares small pointed teeth. Sharp as rose thorns.

'Yes, Tante Hannah,' Gabby chants.

Doly makes a face at the broad back. Sticks out her tongue.

Tante Hannah strides away, whooshes the curtains wide.

Gabby ruckles her nose at Doly, puts both thumbs in her nostrils, waves her fingers up and down. Stops as she sees their aunt turn. 'Herta says we have to change our underwear every day, Tante Hannah. And blouses and aprons.' Demure obedient little girl who does as she's bid.

'Herta said that, did she?' The snarl pulls the right side of Tante Hannah's mouth higher than the left. Showing black stubs glistening with saliva.

Gabby, trying to conform to household rules, blunders on. 'It was Mutti, really...'

'Even a stupid brat like you must know your mother's dead.'

Gabby's mouth stays open. Silent. Doly's eyes fill with tears.

'And so's that old tyrant. Which leaves me in charge.' The long braid snakes over her shoulder as she turns. 'I'm what you're left with.' She opens the window wide. 'It stinks in here.'

The first of the autumn storms blows in.

'Where's Herta...'

'You won't see her again. Insolent old hag.'

'She's my friend.' Doly's voice.

Great gulps of cold blustering air fill the room. Gabby pulls on her summer vest, longs for her winter one. Has Herta died, like Mutti? 'Is Herta ill?' A fit of coughing she can't control.

'Ill? Of course not. You can forget about that old woman. Always mollycoddling you brats. Her job was to do as she was told. Which was to pack her bags and leave. Last night.'

A cold hard claw grabs Gabby by the throat. Minni left the day after Emil Dohlen's funeral. Her father wouldn't hear of her staying in a household run by Hannah Bender. Who's going to be left?

'And yours is to obey me.'

'You're not my parents.' Doly's chin is tight, eyes sharp as needles, voice carrying venom.

'Too true. Who'd want to be?' She cuffs Gabby's head, flicks at the skimpy hair. 'Stupid, ugly brats.'

Yesterday she came at Moppel with the wooden spoon. Again. Because he was in the kitchen with Rula. Whack; the hard thud of wood against Moppel's backside, the howl of anguish. Whenever

Gabby or Doly anger their aunt she turns on Moppel. Who cringes against the wall as soon as she appears.

'Damn it, boy, take your beating like a man. Or I'll take your father's stick to you. Then you'll have something to howl about.'

Rula stepped forward, arms akimbo, and put Moppel behind her. She's bigger than Tante Hannah and not afraid of her. Does that mean Rula will be sent away as well?

Tante Hannah grabs the duvet off Moppel's bed, yanks him to the floor. He buries his head in his arms. She strides over to Doly's cot. She grasps the ends and shakes the heavy wood. 'You're not a baby any more. High time you had a bed. Herta's will do.'

Gabby pulls on her knickers, her dress, her apron, her socks. Puts on her shoes. Sees Doly put her foot over the moving duvet, a hand down to lift the bedding. Letting in air.

'And no trying to get back under the bedclothes, you lazy brat. You're old enough to dress yourself, my girl. Get going.'

Ursula walks in, neatly folded linen in her hands. 'Shall I see to the children, Fräulein Bender?'

'Where the hell have you been, leaving me to your chores?'

'You asked me to see to the laundry, Fr...'

Tante Hannah's hands crossed against her bosom. 'Gnädige Frau,' she snaps. 'You'll call me madam. I am the mistress of this house.'

Ursula's eyes flicker at Gabby. 'Shall I dress Doly, Gnädige Frau?'

'She'll dress herself. Start airing the beds. What else are you here for?' Tante Hannah's skirts swirl as she leaves the room, catch in the door as she bangs it shut. Four pairs of eyes watch as she opens it again, four pairs of lungs hold their breath. Until she's gone.

Ursula picks up Doly's duvet. To air it.

'No, Ursula. The bunny needs it.' The rabbit is lying still. Ears flopped. A stain of blood on the sheet below it.

Ursula bends to stroke the inert body. 'Poor little thing's past caring.'

'She's killed my bunny.' Doly screams. 'I hate Tante Hannah. I'm going to kill *her*.'

Ursula folds Doly in her arms, sinks into the rocker with her. 'It was too badly hurt, Doly. It didn't have a chance.'

'It loved me. It was my pet,' Doly sobs. 'All soft and cuddly.'

'You come on over to our house,' Ursula coos into the ginger curls. 'Play with our dog. And the two cats. Talk to Pretty Polly in her cage. Come after your midday meal.'

'Tante Hannah is a snake-devil and I hate her. Next time there's a thunderstorm God's going to turn her to stone.' Doly clambers off Ursula's lap and begins to pull on her clothes. Vest back to front.

'This way, Doly. See where Herta has put a mark? Remember to keep your clothes clean, children.' Ursula looks round, whispers. 'Your aunt has given strict orders. You're only to change them once a week.'

DEAD MAN'S DEAL

The hard-working father of a large and close-knit family loves to provide well for them. He's found an area of fertile soil in a remote place. He farms it well, so making sure his wife and children have a sound roof over their heads, warm clothes, enough to eat. He's hale and hearty, strong and fit.

Until the day he's laid low with a raging fever. He lies down on his bed to help him recover but he only gets worse. And finally he realises death is not far away.

The sick man worries day and night. His beloved wife and family will starve without him. His deepest regret is that he didn't have the wit to sell his most prized possessions, his two oxen. For which he'd already struck a good bargain but had neglected to clinch the sale.

The loving husband and father dies in spite of his devoted wife's attentions. His grieving widow stays at home crying with her children.

By chance the men who were keen to buy his oxen come back to the area and seek out his farm, determined to conclude the deal. They have no inkling of what's happened and so are not surprised to see the farmer leaning against his fence, smoking his pipe.

They walk up to him, finalise negotiations to both sides' satisfaction, arrange the place where the oxen will be delivered and leave.

Minutes later the two buyers remember that no date and time was set for them to pick up the oxen. They turn back and, since the farmer is no longer standing by the fence, they knock on his door and ask to speak to him.

'My husband? I'm afraid you're too late. The dear man died yesterday of a raging fever.'

Until that moment the two men had no idea that they've bought livestock from a dead man.

CHAPTER 2

Schwanenbruch, September 1916

'Someone's ringing the front-door bell, Tante Hannah.' Gabby's voice. Hopeful, inquisitive, confident.

She sees her aunt frown. Not expecting anyone, then. Servants and tradespeople always come to the back. Relatives and friends use the side door. Gabby has a momentary vision of tall Walter Hudwalker, she's seen his likeness in her parents' wedding-group picture, come to claim the three of them and take them to America with him. Then tells herself not to be so stupid. He may be their legal guardian, but he can't sail to Cuxhaven. German U-boats are sinking any foreign vessels entering the area, including American ones. Even if he was as brave as Vater, he couldn't get through.

She sees Tante Hannah undo her apron, slick back her hair, take a deep breath and open the front door. Slides after her.

A well-dressed young woman with a suitcase smiles a greeting. 'Good morning. I'm Hermione Sinker.' Gabby watches her aunt—no answering smile, just a scowl-blink of irritable eyes. 'From Berlin. Herr Dohlen is expecting me.'

An old story flits through Gabby's mind, rolls cold shudders down her spine. Is Vater looking out for them? Still making his presence felt?

'You have an appointment with Herr Dohlen?'

The young woman, smile fixed, nods. 'Indeed. Perhaps you would be kind enough to take me to him?'

Tante Hannah's eyes narrow. She'll take that as being treated like a servant, asking her to carry messages. Who could this lady be? A secretary for Vater? Perhaps a housekeeper? Gabby's brain works overtime, imagining release from her aunt.

'Sad news, I'm afraid, Frau Sinker. Herr Dohlen died two months ago.'

Determined grey eyes and sharp features whiten. '*Fräulein* Sinker. Herr Dohlen engaged me as his children's governess. To start after the summer holidays. I'm to teach them English.' She scrabbles papers out of her handbag. 'My terms of employment.'

Locked away in the Mausoleum with Mutti, and Vater still has a trump card up his sleeve. Gabby grins: the queen of spades—a woman from as far away as Berlin, bearing a contract signed by her powerful father—wins the last trick.

Tante Hannah shoves Gabby ahead of her, fills the door frame with elbows wide. She certainly won't want someone around who'll teach the three of them the language of a country sympathetic to the enemy. The elbows move up and down, like a fat old duck protecting her territory. Then she nods, slight crinkle of the eyes. 'I'm Hannah Bender, the children's aunt. Poor little orphans. I'm putting everything else aside, devoting myself to looking after them.' Tight lips widen a little. 'You'll understand that I expect to make my own arrangements.'

Fräulein Sinker's head is cocked to one side as she hears her out. 'How very devoted. The children are indeed fortunate. But you will forgive me, aren't you a little young to be in full charge?' Her eyes scan the young woman with assessing shrewdness. 'Surely you're not of age?'

Tante Hannah, much shorter than Fräulein Sinker, rises on the balls of her feet. 'I oversee the children's daily welfare. My brother is their German guardian.'

Not quite yet. Gabby heard Onkel Theo say that that still had to be ratified by a Cuxhaven court, but what else can they do?

'Herr Wilfred Bender. In the Osterstrasse.'

The suitcase lodges on the top step. 'Then I'd better discuss the matter with Herr Bender. Herr Dohlen arranged for me to stay a full year. He was most insistent. He even asked me to promise him that

I would honour the contract "whatever happens".' An outstretched right hand demands the papers back. 'At his age I quite understood his concern.'

Tante Hannah shifts her weight on to Gabby's slight shoulders, making her shorter. 'My brother doesn't live far from here. Gabriele's the eldest. She'll take you to him.'

'Perhaps I could leave my suitcase?'

Tante Hannah's skirts swish against it as she pushes Gabby forward. She grabs the handrail to stop from falling. 'Get your coat on, Gabby. I want you to take Fräulein Sinker to your Onkel Wilfred.'

CHAPTER 3

Schwanenbruch, October 1916

'Who that girl, Miss?' Doly is trying to speak English. She supplements her speech with gestures, points at a small assured figure on a sleek white gelding trotting round the parade ring.

'What girl?' The children started out by calling the new governess Fräulein. 'You are to call me Miss Sinker. Or you can say Miss for short. Your father made it quite clear. We're only to communicate in English.'

'Girl on horse, Miss.' When her brother and sister are at school Doly has Miss Sinker to herself. Today they are at the Schützenfest, the annual autumn fair held in the big field behind the Villa Dohlen. Doly loves horses. Particularly sleek big ones like the white gelding across the field. Ridden by a girl about her own age. Quite a bit bigger than Doly; maybe a year older. Smartly dressed in light grey jodhpurs.

Miss Sinker never speaks German to her charges. Which means Doly can't always understand her. Or can make out she can't.

'I've no idea, Doly. I don't know many people round here. We'll ask your Tante Hannah.'

Doly twists out of Miss Sinker's hand grip. 'No. Her not like anyone.'

'That isn't true, Doly.'

Doly shrugs. 'You no speak Platt. I hear her tell Tante Gerda. She say you go soon.' Her eyes are avid for the show ring. She can already feel the horse's withers between her legs, the reins sliding through her fingers, between her palms. She breathes in the acrid smell of horse-sweat, longs for the soft muzzle against her face.

Miss Sinker's in-drawn breath sounds like a wave breaking against the hard pebbles of the Schwanenbruch shore. She switches to German, aware her charge would pretend not to understand if she didn't. 'Of course I need to stay with you. Your father was very particular that you should be fluent in English, Doly. He knew you'd go to America once the War is over.'

Doly's intent, watching the girl riding the Schimmel. She can't be much older than Doly or she'd be at school. In any case, she's good. Bobbing as the horse trots, digging sharp heels into its flanks. Fearless and in charge. The sort of friend she's looking for.

'I'm going over.' Doly reverts to German in her turn. 'That woman waving at her must be her governess. You can talk to her.'

Miss Sinker grabs Doly's hand. 'Just what did your aunt say, Doly?'

Doly tries but can't pull away. 'Come *on*. She'll leave before we get there.'

Miss Sinker holds on, hurting Doly's wrist. 'Well? What did she say?' The racket of hailstones crackling on roofs.

'She was telling Rula.'

'Telling her *what*?' Thin hands on Doly's shoulders grip hard.

'Let me go.'

'When you've told me.'

'Cutting down on servants.'

'*Servants?*'

Doly can feel the shock waves, can't squirm out of the grip. Anger provokes the truth. 'Your salary's too high. She can get two housemaids for that.'

'I'm a governess, not a servant. Anyway, your father's estate pays. And where else is she going to find someone who speaks English really well? I lived in New York for seven years, you know. Until my father died and we came back to Germany.'

'She's taking the horse to the side, Miss.' Doly feels the momentary slackening, ducks away and hares across the field.

Miss Sinker follows as fast as dignity will allow. She walks up to a young woman smiling at the gelding's rider. 'Is that your little charge?

135

She's brilliant with that horse.' Miss Sinker's tones peal the highest of High German. Too high. Because she attended the Bismarck-Lyzeum, the best school in Berlin. And then went on to Berlin's Royal Friedrich Wilhelm University. The young woman's mouth drops open. She wrinkles her nose, turns away.

Miss Sinker tries a smile. 'She can't be very old, or she'd be at school.'

The young woman's nostrils flare as she takes in Doly's crumpled clothes. 'Just turned six. Lieselotte's tall for her age.'

'Our little Doly here loves horses, too. We wondered whether she'd be allowed to stroke him?'

'Better not. Lieselotte's used to horses. Her parents train them. She learned to ride before she could even walk.' The young woman sidles away.

The small girl on the huge animal pulls at the bridle and steadies the horse alongside them. Effortlessly. Doly puts out her hand to stroke him.

The young rider wriggles the tip of her whip under Doly's fingers, pries them away. 'He'll bite you.' Firm authoritative voice.

Doly, just able to reach the horse's neck, moves her hand down to his flank. 'Animals never harm people who love them.' The horse's head moves up and down but he stays. 'Yours, is he?'

The girl leans back. 'I ride him for my parents. They have ten horses.'

Doly moves her hand rhythmically along the flank. The horse's muscles roll. 'Only ten?'

Lieselotte leans down, her eyes search Doly's wide open upturned ones. 'For now. My father's thinking of buying another one.'

'I can't let you do that.' Lieselotte's governess puts her hands under Doly's armpits, lifts her away. 'Down right this minute, Lieselotte. Your father said you could walk Flitsi round the field once. No trotting.'

Doly pulls at the jodhpurs, points at the massive bulk of the Villa Dohlen. 'I live in that house over there. What about you? Where d'you come from?'

Lieselotte swings her leg behind her over the saddle, steps into her governess's outstretched hand. 'Lüdingworth. My father goes to all the Schützenfeste. He's a brilliant shot. A hunter.'

'And he's waving at us, Lieselotte. Time to go.' She turns to Miss Sinker. 'So you work at the Villa Dohlen, do you?'

'I'm the children's governess.'

'We know all about the Dohlens. Rich Americans, aren't they?'

'Herr Dohlen came from Schwanenbruch originally.'

The young woman frowns at Miss Sinker. 'I thought he was dead? Must be months now.'

'I'm afraid so.'

The Plattdeutsch has become broader. 'Not very patriotic, working for Americans.' She tries to help Lieselotte lead the horse. 'They support the enemy.'

'I can do it, Fräulein,' Lieselotte has a low voice for such a young child. 'You'll only upset Flitsi if you hold his reins like that.'

Her governess allows her to take the reins. 'Let's get a move on.' She twists her head back. 'I know, I know. Times are hard, and beggars can't be choosers. I hope you and your little girl enjoy the rest of the day.'

'I'm *not* her little girl,' Doly shouts. 'I'm Dorinda Dohlen. The villa is my father's house.'

CHAPTER 4

Schwanenbruch, October 1916

'What d'you mean, you want more money? It's what I always give you.'

Hannah is at Wilfred's place collecting the housekeeping for the following week. 'It's getting colder, Wilfred. I have to pay to heat that great barn of a place.'

The Cuxhaven court didn't take long to appoint Wilfred Bender acting guardian for the Dohlen orphans until "such time as Walter Hudwalker can take up his obligations". Theo is dying, Hinrich at the front. Leaving Wilfred in charge of German funds and Hannah in charge of the house. The court also declared the contract with Miss Sinker a cast-iron one. The governess is to stay.

Half-brother and sister exchanged glances during the hearing. The governess will stay for the time being. But not for long. They understand one another.

'So shut down some of those barn-like rooms. Don't need them, do you?' Wilfred takes a large key out of his pocket, opens the table drawer. 'Unless you're going to tell me Gabby entertains?'

Hannah watches the sly grin expanding her half-brother's face like the accordion he likes to play. It elongates the thin lips, fires his complexion, flickers through piggy eyes and on to his head. Unlike his father, he's chosen to wear false hair. Scheisskopf. The swinish bastard is salting loot away. Fact. Paul Brisling's a…well, a good friend of hers.

138

A corn merchant from Lüdingworth with a frigid wife.

'I do occasionally have guests myself, Wilfred. Paul Brisling and his wife came to coffee only last week.'

Wilfred clears his throat. Loudly. He raps the table with his fist.

Hannah is well aware of her position. Unmarried, under age. 'We use Emma's living room. There are standards to be kept up.' Wilfred's head is just like the pigs' heads hanging in the butcher's window. Only his ears are smaller.

'By getting rid of almost all the servants I suppose?'

He bloody well grunts like a pig as well. But Hannah can afford to smile. 'You told me to cut back, Wilfred. I think you mentioned that the finances wouldn't run to the kind of expenditure Herr Dohlen went in for.' The smile is spoiled by the black teeth. 'You told me yourself there was no need to keep quite so many people working in a house without a master. That they're better employed in the War effort instead of running after American brats.'

Wilfred's eyes narrow away. 'Gerda says they look unkempt.'

'Best if Gerda spent her energies on your own little darling. Ulrike looks a mess in those hand-me-downs from Theo's girls.'

Wilfred's fist curls tight. 'None of your concern.'

'Herr Brisling was telling me. A good grain merchant buys low and sells high. If he has the funds to buy at the right time. And storage space.' Hannah walks up to the window overlooking Wilfred's courtyard. He takes his wagon to pick up inland stock. Uses the barge to go further afield, up-river. 'How's the new barn working out?'

Paul Brisling mentions Wilfred. Often. He understands very well that the new barn Emil Dohlen funded is a huge asset. But barns start out empty. Could Hannah tell him where Wilfred borrows money to buy his grain? She murmurs endearments. How would a woman know such things?

Wilfred unlocks the table drawer, opens it a sliver, puts in a hand. 'How much more?'

'Half as much again.' Hannah winks. 'What really costs is that idiot of a governess. Been to Cuxhaven to consult that lawyer yet?'

Wilfred grunts. 'Country bumpkin isn't up to it. Has to be a Hamburg man before we can sort out that little lot. I'll see to it next week.'

'Never mind the damned lawyers, Wilfred. Pay her off. Give her half what she'd earn if she stayed. She'll jump at the chance.'

'You're out of your mind, girl. She'll get lynched even trying for another job.'

Hannah's mouth widens into triumph. 'Naturally she can't teach English in the present political climate. But she's from Berlin and speaks High German. The Brislingers will go for that. So their kids learn to speak something better than Platt.'

'Bloody snobs.' He counts out more money, Mark by Mark. 'You reckon?'

Dark hair glistens as she scoops it up. 'Then I won't have to pester you about rising costs.' She throws her shawl around her shoulders, makes for the door, waves a cool hand. They're not a kissing family. 'I think we're beginning to understand one another very well, don't you, brother?'

CHAPTER 5

Schwanenbruch, November 1916

Rula stands beside the kitchen table, the wood scrubbed to a pale beige. The moment he hears the tell-tale clatter of high boots Moppel skips behind the huge dresser, out of sight. Tante Hannah has issued a strict decree: no children in the kitchen. He can watch what's going on through the slits in the wood.

'Dinner for twelve, Gnädige Frau? It'll have to be fish. I'll see if Dieter can let me have a halibut. A big one.'

The War is taking its toll. Critical food shortages have spread even to country areas. Cold weather and gales are making them more acute. The local midday meal is the same every day. A mash of swede and potato, with herring only for those who know how and where to get it—and can afford it. Even Rula's skill can't hide the lack of lard, let alone butter and cream, to make a palatable dish. Sunday is the only day she's able to lay on a decent Mittagessen.

'I'm arranging a celebration for our new officers. They're ready to lead our soldiers into battle.' Hannah tones down the shrill in her voice. 'How much butter have we got?'

'Only a little.'

'Enough to make that wonderful mustard sauce of yours?'

Sturdy arms hold an enormous saucepan while it fills with water from a tap in Emil Dohlen's kitchen. Running water is a great boon. No other house in the village has it. 'We'll have to see.'

'Don't waste it on those brats.'

Rula's anger is never hidden. She bends down, opens the door to the wood burning in the range. 'They're growing children.' Dragon gusts blast through the room.

Tante Hannah retreats towards the door. 'They won't get the chance to grow up if our gallant lieutenants don't defend the Vaterland, Rula. We must all do what we can to support them.'

Rula scrubs the potatoes. Throws them into the saucepan standing on the stove. Peels swedes.

'Your son's one of them, isn't he?'

'My son is a sergeant, Gnädige Frau.' Rula puts a knob of pork dripping into another saucepan, allows it to heat up, chops several onions with her sharp knife, adds them to the sizzling fat.

The blend of odours makes Moppel salivate, slightly move the cupboard door.

'Who's that back there?' Shrill, menacing tone.

'Must be the cat, Gnädige Frau.' Rula moves over, rummages in the drawers above Moppel, stays.

'You'll have more ingredients to work with in the future. When all three children go to school in Cuxhaven.'

The drawer is violently shut, opened, shut.

'The school cart won't bring them back till after two. They can have their meal then. They won't need anything more that day.'

Rula doesn't utter a sound. She and Ursula are the only servants left in the huge villa. They grumble about finding it hard to keep up with the work. But they stay for the three of them, Rula's told Moppel. And Tante Hannah does pay them above the average. She can afford to now there are two servants where there were four and a governess.

The cook returns to her vegetables, stirs the onions with her wooden spoon. Slowly, thoughtfully. 'I'll talk to Dieter when I get home.' She adds carrots, cabbage and a large knuckle of pork. Lifts the enormous black kettle to add more water. Puts on the lid.

'You're a good cook, Rula. I'd hate to lose you.' Hannah grabs a chunk of carrot, bites into it, then spits it out. Her teeth can't cope. 'Tomorrow's party is for the junior officers from the military training camps. For the seven newly-fledged lieutenants and their commanding officer.'

'Yes, Gnädige Frau.'

Moppel has seen some of them. The camp provides a fresh contingent of young men every few months. Hannah admires the handsome captain, Hauptmann Kreps. Not a bad choice for a husband Moppel's heard her tell Onkel Wilfred. Tall and flaxen, with the bluest eyes she's ever seen. Rein Deutsch—pure German blood. A Viking.

CHAPTER 6

Schwanenbruch, Late Autumn 1916

'Quick. They're coming this way. Run.' Gabby herds her younger brother and sister ahead of her. Away from the house, into the garden at the back.

Tante Hannah's military visitors are early. Gleaming boots and uniforms, loud shouts, raucous laughter. Goose-stepping into the garden at the back.

Their aunt's orders are crystal clear. 'You brats are so scruffy. Keep out of sight. If I catch you near my guests, I'll use your father's stick on the lot of you.'

Clothes dirty and torn, what hair they have unkempt, the Dohlen orphans cower against hoar-frosted rose bushes, scamper to hide behind tree trunks. Gabby knows that anyone seeing them in this state will think they have a disease, something catching, won't want anything to do with them.

Three young men in dress uniforms crackle frost-bitten leaves under their boots, breath vaporised in the cold air. They stride across the spiky grass as though they own it.

'Hide.' Gabby whispers. 'Quick. Under the leaves by the bridge.' Onkel Palter built a pretty crossing across the brook. So Mutti's pale dresses wouldn't catch the mud as she walked from the villa garden to Onkel Hinrich's little patch.

The hump-back bridge catches autumn leaves, builds them into a

144

soft igloo of russet and gold. Dry and dense. Moppel dives in head first, crawls through to the dark. Doly follows in his tracks and Gabby scrabbles after them. They move close together, push leaves around to cover themselves, hold their breath.

'What the hell's that moving under there?' Staccato sounds of High German in a loud male voice.

'I'll be damned.' The softer swallowed syllables of a native of Berlin. 'A fox, maybe. Or a dog.'

The sharp end of a sabre cuts into the earth at Gabby's side. She puts her hands over her mouth to stop herself crying out.

'Something's hiding in there. Let's have some sport.'

Another sabre. This time it needles into Moppel's boot. He screams.

'What's going on?' Gabby sees a surprised face as a young man uses his hands to part the leaves. She pushes herself out and stands proud as he uncovers Moppel, then Doly.

She can see his eyes dilate as he takes in the leaves interwoven with her scanty hair—and gags. 'Village kids. What in God's name are you doing here?' He hauls them out.

'Village idiots more like. Filthy. And just look at their hair.' The second officer pushes his sword out to keep a safe distance. 'Sticking up like straw.'

Gabby brushes leaves from Doly and herself, remembers to try to adjust her hair. She finger-combs the sparse ends back, tries to adjust the ribbon slipping across the smooth pink bald patch as covering leaves slide off. She sees the young man gape and backs behind Moppel.

'Come to scrump what's left of the fruit, have you?' Good-natured, a second young man sporting a lieutenant's insignia helps Moppel stand. 'There can't be much left in the orchard now. A couple of shrivelled apples, at best. Maybe a pear or two. Hungry, is that it?'

Gabby shakes her head, pushes Doly to the front, pats her curls. She's the most presentable. Her hair, though coarse, is still that unusual ginger colour and very plentiful. For the time being.

The men stare at the children's mud-smeared faces, leaf-matted hair. Gabby sees pity mingled with disgust.

'No harm done, I suppose,' the first one rumbles, turning away.

'Reckon not. Shoo back to the village, the lot of you.'

Gabby steps in front of her brother and sister, stands tall. 'This is my father's garden. You're the ones who have no right to be here.'

The men in their bright, shining new uniforms burst into loud cackles. 'You'll get into trouble trespassing. These are the grounds of the Villa Dohlen, my girl. The most important house outside Cuxhaven,' the first one roars. 'Scat, or I'll haul you in to Fräulein Hannah.'

The dining-room table is set for twelve. The Corning glassware, the Schwanengeschirr china, the silver, the damask tablecloth and napkins. All gleaming in lights from the chandelier.

'Dammit, Hannah, what a God-forsaken hole this is. Nothing but blasted moorland and heath. How in the world d'you stick it?' A captain in dress uniform, followed by a lieutenant, marches into the room.

Hannah settles Emma's finest lace collar around her neck. It doesn't meet at the front. She's fastened it with Emma's largest brooch. 'It may be bleak, and a bit windy, but it's what makes us the people we are. Good sturdy North German stock. Bearing fine sons to defend the Vaterland.'

'Prost. I'll drink to that.' The handsome captain takes in the festive table, grabs the tankard of beer Hannah hands him, drains it.

'We can even beat the devil at his own game.' Hannah, head nodding with beer drunk on an empty stomach, holds up her glass, takes another good draught. 'Prost.'

'Bottoms up, devil beater.'

'All I can say is, don't mess with us. We're Vikings and not to be trifled with.'

Hauptmann Kreps stares at Hannah. 'I've heard you people have to cope with the harshest conditions anywhere in Germany. That you have a special saying for every three children born:

Dem Ersten den Tod,
Dem Zweiten die Not,
Dem Dritten das Brot.

The first will soon die,
The second always cry,
The third will eat rye.

He declaims the verse, unsheathing his sword and raising it high.

Leutnant Mauer raises his glass. 'What a death-blow to poetry.' He laughs uproariously at his own joke.

The Hauptmann quells him with a look. 'So we're the ones who're privileged to eat pumpernickel, are we? "Bon pour Nicol", Napoleon said.' The Hauptmann's fist crashes down on the table. 'Only good for his bloody horse, by God. Damn all Frenchmen, now and forever.'

Hannah's eyes sparkle. 'I've got something much better than bread for you. A whole halibut, cooked with plenty of butter and cream. A real banquet.'

She does what she can to please the Hauptmann. She feels the memory of his flashing smile. Smooth skin, cool fingers, a good swell in his trousers. Even better when he takes them off. She sees his eyes, hungry, take in her body. He focuses on her bosom, lingers there, moves to her rear. Her hips wriggle at the very thought of him. There's wet between her legs.

'And something good for the fish to swim in?'

Hannah has already made considerable inroads into Emil Dohlen's cellar. There are a couple of dozen bottles of wine left, and Wilfred has supplied the beer. At a price. 'There's enough wine for the fish to drown in.'

Three young lieutenants jostle into the room, their boots scraping the floor, sabres rattling at their sides.

'Quite extraordinary,' Leutnant Maximilian Glestner shouts. 'We've just had the most bizarre experience. In the garden.'

Hannah, seated in Emil Dohlen's place at the head of the table, frowns, then shakes her shoulders, widens her mouth even more. 'Make yourselves at home, do. Come and sit by me, Herr Hauptmann.'

The captain nods but settles on a chair one away from Hannah. Glestner is keener to slide in next to her.

'We were strolling through the grounds, round the back. More like a park than a garden, really. Old Dohlen must have had a packet.'

'He did,' Hannah confirms. 'He made his fortune in America.'

Glestner pushes his chair back and stands. 'What? That old man was an American?'

'Spoils of war.' Hauptmann Kreps lays a restraining hand on Glestner's arm. 'Means we can take it all over with a good conscience.'

The newly-fledged lieutenant sees the point, grins. 'Enemy territory.'

Hannah unfolds a pristine napkin, puts it on her lap. 'You soldiers are so wonderful, protecting us all. I feel quite safe with you around.' She arches her neck. Elegant as a swan's, Paul Brisling has mentioned several times. She fingers tendrils of hair around her ears, touches Emma's diamond ring. She's managed to squeeze it on to her little finger by using soap. Too bad if it won't come off.

'What was the great offensive, then?' Hauptmann Kreps narrows his eyes at Glestner.

'Not exactly an offensive, Herr Hauptmann. Reconnaissance, really.'

'So what was so weird and wonderful, Glestner?' Mauer claims Hannah's other side.

'What? Oh, yes. We were just coming up to that toy bridge over the brook when I saw something move. Leaves rustling, that sort of thing.'

'Military training,' Kreps says. Face straight.

Glestner guffaws. 'I guess. Feltwebel Hass, meanest sergeant in the Prussian Army, makes sure we never miss a trick.'

'A snake, was it?' Hannah's voice is husky. Like all the other locals, she's terrified of snakes.

'That crossed my mind. We've been warned about them often enough.'

Hauptmann Kreps stands, claps his hands, raises his glass. 'To the brave new officers of the Prussian Army.' Everyone stands to drink the toast. 'Well, get on with the story, Glestner.'

Glestner looks round. 'I saw these leaves, a sort of heaving under the bridge. Thought we'd amuse ourselves with the local wildlife.'

'You mean a fox...'

'Wasn't a fox. Or a snake. Or any other animal. Three kids. Filthy as hell. And the most peculiar hair on two of them, sticking up in spikes, leaves streaked in. A pretty little one, all ginger curls and violet eyes, but even her hair stuck out like Struwwelpeter's.'

'He's dreaming of his nursery days.'

'No, I swear. And the older boy and girl. My God, you should have seen them. Something really wrong with those two.' He points to his head. 'Degenerates.'

'Not right in, or on, the head,' another of the young men shouts. 'Most extraordinary hair. You could see it right off. Crying, the boy was. Bloody disgrace. The dolt was much too old for such girlish nonsense.'

'As for the older girl,' the third man broke in, laughing. 'I put my sabre out, just to fend them off, you know. Can't tell what disease one might pick up if one got too close. Damned if the little filly didn't push herself in front of the other two. Stood there, yelling at me it was her father's place and I was to get out of it.' He laughs again, eyes shut with the fun of it. 'Said if I touched her she'd strike me blind.' He frowns at Hannah. 'That some kind of local curse?'

'Village people are very superstitious.'

'Backward, I suppose. Anyway, we had a fair bit of sport after that. Pretending we were going to run them through.' The first man looks a trifle uneasily at Hannah. 'Not relatives of yours by any chance?'

Hannah giggles defensively, hands twisting round her glass. 'Nothing to do with me. You know I'm an unmarried lady.' She smirks at him. 'I'm waiting for the right man to come along.'

He leans away from her. 'Stupid of me. Of course.'

'So your idea of sport is to chase after three kids who aren't right in the head. That it?' Hauptmann Kreps puts his hand out and pours more wine into his glass.

'Couldn't resist it, Herr Hauptmann. They were asking for it. The older girl stood guard, and the other two scrambled back under the bloody bridge. Getting filthier than ever.'

'So you big heroes went after them.'

Seeing the wine bottle set down, Leutnant Glestner leans across, grabs a glass and fills it. He drains it in one gulp. 'That girl was still yelling blue murder. You'd think she really bloody owned the place.' He pours another glass, drains that. 'Howled at me that if I cut her in two, both parts of her would stay alive and blind me.'

Glestner grabs a bottle, pours again. 'That's when she dived under the bridge herself. It's much too low for us to follow her. Next thing we knew, these damned dogs set on us. No idea where they came from.'

'Dogs?' Hannah asks. 'What kind of dogs?' Thank God, attention was being drawn from the kids.

'German Shepherds, I reckon. Bloody great brutes.'

Who'd set Hinrich's dogs on Army officers? Hannah knew it had to be that old fool, Fritz Palter. Doddering around the garden, pretending to work. Time she got rid of him. He's Irmgard's father, but Hinrich's at the front. So that's no problem.

'Some old man with a stick was right behind the brutes, egging them on. That's when we decided to call it a day and come in here.'

Three more young men, their uniforms encrusted with medals, boots gleaming, swagger in.

Hannah waves gaily. 'Sit down do. Just leave three places at the bottom. For my nephew and nieces.' Rula has made it plain. She only stays if the children eat in the dining room when a meal is served there. No other cook to touch her before Hamburg.

More bottles are opened, the wine flows. Hannah rings the bell for the first course. 'Tell the children it's time to eat,' she instructs Rula. 'Why haven't you brought the soup?'

'They'll be here directly, Gnädige Frau. They've gone to wash their hands.' Rula's slow body moves away.

'They're to be sharp about it. They'll only have themselves to blame if there's nothing left.'

The door opens and Gabby walks into the room. Her hair is swept back, tied with an enormous ribbon which somewhat disguises its thinning. She's wearing a clean pinafore over her Sunday dress, her mother's locket swinging. She puts her hand over it, stills it, looks towards her aunt, curtsies. 'Mahlzeit, Tante Hannah.' No tremor in her voice.

The young men rise in unison, click their heels.

Glestner raises his glass. 'Mahlzeit, pretty little German girl.' Eyes on her tiny waist.

No sign of recognition. Hannah sighs her relief. 'About time, Gabby. Sit down, for goodness sake. Where are the other two?'

'Just coming, Tante Hannah.' The demure decorum of a little lady. A chair is pulled out for her. She smiles and sits down.

'Don't be so hard on her, Hannah. Such stunning blue eyes.' Leutnant Glestner takes in the child's figure, nodding at her fair hair. What he can see of it.

A cleaned-up Doly trips through the door, followed by Moppel in a crisp sailor suit. Glestner stares at the ginger curls, mouth falling open.

Doly tosses her head, glances at Gabby, grins.

'Where are your manners, children?' Tante Hannah's voice sounds almost maternal, but Moppel's lower lip begins to quiver.

'M-mahlzeit-t, T-tant-te Hannah.'

Rula barges the door wide with her hip, bearing a tureen of soup. She begins ladling it out. A few boiling drops splash on to Hannah's lap. She winces but doesn't say a word.

'So sorry, Gnädige Frau. Clumsy of me.'

The men glance from one child to another, eat their soup in silence. 'You have an exceptional cook,' Hauptmann Kreps says slowly, savouring the rich soup, the aromatic bread, drinking the wine. 'Good German stock, I'll give you that.'

The table is cleared, large plates are brought for the main course, mounds of potatoes arrive in steaming bowls. Then Rula comes in bearing a magnificent halibut on an imposing platter.

Doly stands up, nods a conspiratorial look at Gabby. She grins back, holding the locket out as though it were a weapon to protect them.

Doly climbs on to her chair, her face intense as she looks at the magnificent dish. Her voice is piping clear. 'Not that old fish again, Tante Hannah. Isn't that the one which already stank to high heaven yesterday?'

CHAPTER 7

Schwanenbruch, Autumn 1917

The wooden school cart taking some of the Schwanenbruch children to the Cuxhaven schools every morning leaves promptly at half past six every morning. It waits outside the Villa Dohlen, opposite the church.

The Cuxhaven schools only take the brightest children. The rest stay on at the village school. Gabriele Dohlen has been longing to go for some time now. So Tante Hannah's latest edict is welcome.

It's not quite as easy for Emil Junior. Boys and girls go to separate schools, so he'll be on his own. He's not looking forward to the bullying he's bound to be in for. But he has one secret weapon. His collection of coins, the ones he removed to Fritz Palter's garden shed. A long time ago, when Tante Hannah took over his room. He has two Groschen in his pockets now. Ready to bribe oppressors.

Doly sits on the hard cart bench, wedged between her brother and sister. Two boys opposite are kicking her legs. It hurts. She clamps her lips tight.

'You stop kicking my sister.' Gabby's shrill voice carries above the rumble of the wooden wheels, the clip-clop of hooves.

The driver turns, whip raised, crackling it above his head. 'If I hear a boy's been getting at a girl, I'll flog him to within a fingerbreadth of his life.'

The boys stop kicking. The three Dohlens don't have to talk to each other to realise that walking alone in the village will be dangerous from now on. They'll be more isolated than ever.

Doly knows that none of the other children in her class will be able to read all that well. No one goes to school till the age of seven. Except for her. Tante Hannah went to Cuxhaven to talk to the Headmistress. Explained the special circumstances, that Miss Sinker has already taught Doly to read though she's only six.

'It's so difficult, you see, Frau Schulleiterin. No mother at home to look after the little ones.'

'You are their aunt?'

'Their mother was my half-sister. Much older than me. I do my best, of course. It's such a great responsibility.' The woman's mouth is pursed. 'And such a privilege.'

The Headmistress looks at the bare ring-finger Hannah tries to keep out of sight. 'You aren't married?'

'My brother lives in the village.'

The Headmistress frowns. 'And what about the governess? There is one, surely?'

Hannah smiles. 'Of course there was. Such a shame Miss Sinker felt she had to leave. To take a position in a German household.'

The woman frowns at Hannah.

'You can't blame her for not wanting to teach children whose father was American, who are Americans themselves. Not when Germany is actually at war with the United States.' Hannah blinks her eyes. 'Your school, Frau Schulleiterin, will give these children a wonderful opportunity.'

'I don't know about taking Americans...'

'That's what I mean. Your superior will be impressed.' She pauses dramatically, smiles. 'Because you will teach them to become proper Germans, Frau Schulleiterin.'

There are forty children in the Erste Klasse, aged between seven and eight. Doly is six and a half. Nearly. She'll be seven in April. But she's not telling anybody that.

The moment she enters the classroom she sees the girl who rode the white horse at the Schützenfest. She looks at her hopefully, tries to meet her eyes.

Lieselotte is writing in her exercise book. The teacher directs Doly to a seat two desks away from her. Lieselotte doesn't look up.

'Dohlen, what are you gawking at? Take out your book and begin to read on page four.'

Doly is small for her age. She only just manages to touch the floor with her feet while she's sitting. She stands up to read. Does well.

'Teacher's pet,' the girl next to her hisses. The one behind her pulls at her hair.

'I'll get you in break time,' Doly spits out of the side of her mouth. Keeping an eye on the teacher.

'Oh, yeah? You and who else?'

'I can beat you at wrestling any day.' Onkel Hinrich taught Doly how. She's had a lot of practice with him. And his dogs. They never hurt Doly.

'No talking, Dohlen.'

Time crawls. Doly memorises her classmates' surnames as the teacher addresses them. Lieselotte's name is Waldeck. She reads fluently.

There's a twenty-minute break mid morning. The class files out into the playground. Whatever the weather, the children play outside.

'So which one of us are you going to fight first?' Inge Feldmann is bigger than Doly. But she's slow.

'I'll start with you.'

The real motive for the dare is to attract Lieselotte's attention. It doesn't work. She's playing hopscotch with two other girls. Apparently engrossed.

Doly's determined punches and clever holds give her the edge. She wins against several girls, then challenges the three playing with Lieselotte. And wins against them as well.

'You're the only one in the class I haven't fought,' she exaggerates, breathing hard. 'Think you can beat me?'

Lieselotte stands up. A head taller than Doly. Eight months older. 'Think I'm afraid of a dwarf like you?'

They roll over and over on the hard playground. Scratches along their arms and legs draw blood. All Doly's wiles cannot stop Lieselotte's parries. All Lieselotte's blows are ducked. The school bell sounds. The two girls stop, dust themselves down. Stare at each other, extend their hands.

Doly scoops blood from her forearm on to her index finger, mixes it with drops glistening on Lieselotte's wrist. 'We're blood sisters now,' she says. 'We'll stand against the world together for the rest of our lives.'

Lieselotte's steady eyes are fixed on her. For at least a minute. Then she nods her head in agreement.

Werner Schiffer is proud of his achievement. He got a 2 in German. His mother was thrilled and can't wait to tell his father. Who's keen eyes make him one of the best ship's pilots around Cuxhaven. He isn't often home. He left to join the German Navy at the beginning of the War. Now he's in the conning tower of a U-boat.

Werner works hard at school. He has no trouble getting 1s for arithmetic and geography, but his German is weak. He often gets a 4. Werner wants to be a Lotse like his father. He needs high marks all round.

Gabriele Dohlen is good at German. She's willing to read Goethe with Werner, as well as a book about a family called Buddenbrooks. By a German author. Thomas Mann.

'What d'you want to sit next to *her* for?' Helga Ketter squeezes in on his other side, between him and his brother Kurt on the right side of the cart.

Helga can't stand Gabby. Was often mean to her when they were at the village school together. And nags on about Gabby being an American. Werner knows they are the enemy, but surely Gabby is really German? She's lived in the village since she was a baby. Helga says Gabby has horse hair and, anyway, so little of it because she's not from proper German stock. That doesn't make sense. The Dohlens are descended from the Saxons, just like the rest of the Schwanenbruchers. The Benders are descended from the Frisians. So both sets of forebears are from old Teutonic tribes.

Werner doesn't much care about hair. Gabby is almost like a boy. She doesn't go on about babies and clothes. She talks about the War, knows lots about the Battle of Jutland. And how the *Lusitania* was sunk by German U-boats and the effect this has had on the progress of the War. Whether it eventually brought in the Americans. How that will affect what happens after it's over. Whichever side wins.

Gabby reads loads of books. Even English ones from her father's library. She reads aloud with Werner every day, on their way to and from school. She helps him understand the books he studies in class which are the same ones she reads in school. Because they're the same age.

'D'you like my new ribbon?' Helga is pulling at Werner's arm.

'It's very pretty.'

Gabby never says, but Werner knows she wants him to look out for her brother, all on his own in the boys' school. He's not very good at fighting. He hunches in a corner of the playground by himself. Sometimes a knot of boys crowds round him. They punch his head, call him turnip-top.

He doesn't fight back. His hair does look like the withered leaves on a turnip. Bristly straw-coloured stuff which stands in awkward spikes. That's not Emil Junior's fault. The bully boys back off when Werner glares at them. He's a good fighter. Three elder brothers have made sure of that. The other boys keep their distance, including the bigger ones.

School Cart on a Feastday

CHAPTER 8

Cuxhaven, Winter 1917

Inspection for head lice takes place every month. Gabby sits huddled into herself, touching the locket hidden under her clothing, while the new inspector walks from child to child. The old one knew about her hair, knew that it might be coarse and scanty, but it isn't lousy. Gabby tries hard to think of that as a plus. Deep down she'd welcome any kind or condition of hair. Tangled, frizzy, short, long, whatever colour. She isn't a bit fussy. Truth to tell she'd even welcome nits, because they would prove she was—well, like everybody else. As it is, even the lice don't think she has proper hair.

The girls have been told to undo their plaits and remove all ribbons. The inspector stands behind the children sitting at their desks. He combs through their hair with a metal comb dipped in carbolic after each use. That stings.

'What's wrong with this one?' The metal comb digs into Gabby's scalp. 'Her hair's very thin. Why there's a bald patch right in the middle.' Gabby had to take off the ribbon she uses to hide the round of pink hairless skin. 'She got ringworm, by any chance? That's highly contagious. She'll have to be sent home.' He takes a step backwards.

Gabby tries to stop her eyes watering. She fingers the shape of the locket inside her vest. Wearing jewellery to school is strictly forbidden. She doesn't care. She never, ever, takes it off. Not even for a bath.

Fräulein Lener rushes up to the new health inspector, whispers. 'In the family, Herr Gesundsheitsführer.' Gabby, like everybody else, can hear the sibilant syllables. 'Hereditary, not catching. The Herr Doktor has assured us of that.'

'What are you whispering for, woman?' He jerks the comb away. Awkwardly.

Gabby can feel some of her hair coming out with it. That won't grow back. 'You're hurting me.' she cries out. To stop further depredation. It isn't true. Pulling her hair out doesn't hurt, because the roots aren't properly embedded. That's the whole trouble.

'Hereditary,' the teacher mumbles again to the impatient health inspector. 'Only the children of afflicted adults inherit it. A dominant gene.'

'Donnerwetter. Some people shouldn't be allowed to breed.' He passes on to Helga Ketter, on Gabby's right. 'This one's got the thickest hair I've ever seen.' He pulls the girl's head back by the mass of loose hair hanging down her back. 'Haven't you been told to plait it really tight? Anything loose allows the head lice to get in and breed. You're completely lousy, Gör. Stand over there.'

The girl stands, humiliated in front of the whole class. 'Not even the nits can stand your hair,' she taunts Gabby as she leaves to sit in the part of the classroom reserved for the unclean. Until they can be dealt with. Eventually each louse-infested head will be soaked in a mixture of cod-liver oil and paraffin, then covered in a cloth which will be left on for two hours. They'll wash their hair when they get home. Stinking all the way back in the cart.

Any girl found to be infested with head lice for a third time will have her hair cut short. Helga has been found lousy twice and is now in grave danger. Gabby knows she holds her responsible.

Gabby realises she's in trouble as soon as the school cart stops outside the Villa Dohlen and they all jump off. The girls form a circle round her, chant about her lack of hair. Helga is the first to tug at her ribbon. Gabby is terrified they'll pull out more hair on the pretence of stealing the ribbon. She has to distract them.

There's a bench where the cart stops. Gabby ducks her head, covers it with her arms, charges through and jumps on to the seat.

'You wouldn't be allowed to live here if you weren't rich.' Helga is in

158

hot pursuit. 'You soon won't be because America's joined the War.'

Gabby can't fight nearly a dozen girls. She'll have to hold them off with words. Even if she has to embroider the truth a little.

'We're not really Americans.'

'What are you, then? French, by any chance?'

Gabby is blessed with a loud penetrating voice. 'We're just as German as you are. My father emigrated ages ago because his family couldn't afford to feed him any more. Besides, there was no work for him in Germany, no future. But when he married my mother they decided to come back to Schwanenbruch.'

'Back to a poor village when they lived in New York City?' Helga's scornful laugh eggs on the others. 'Maybe the Americans wouldn't let your mother stay. Turned her back because…'

'She missed Schwanenbruch.' Gabby shouts. To drown what Helga is saying. 'You can tell from the wording carved into the house. See?' She points to the woodwork above the second-floor window facing the front.

OB OST OB WEST TO HUS OM BEST

'East or West, home is best. They even had it written in Plattdeutsch because they were so homesick.'

A murmur of approval as the girls step back a little. Gabby should stop now she's ahead. But she can't resist the chance to tell a good story.

'What's really exciting is that we're descended from the White Pirate.'

Helga Ketter pounces at once. Her special gift is to spot injudicious words. 'What White Pirate? I've never heard of him.'

All Gabby can do now is turn into Scheherazade. 'Because you aren't descended from him. My mother's family is.'

'You mean the Benders who're always on a bender? That shiftless lot of vagabonds?' Helga turns to the other girls. 'Tobias Bender had seventeen children, and only four of them still live in Schwanenbruch. The rest are scattered all over the world. What kind of family is that?'

'Emigrating isn't shiftless.' Gabby's pedantic streak wins out. 'The Benders came from Friesland. It's a Dutch province now.'

'So who cares about Frieslanders? Just another lot of foreigners.'

'You should. They're descended from the Frisians, a Germanic tribe who lived in this area before the Saxons came down from Holstein and pushed them west. They settled in the Netherlands. The Frieslanders were the dyke builders, the ones who made it possible to farm land reclaimed from the North Sea.' She turns to Helga. 'The stuff that's made your father one of the richest landowners around.'

'You just said you were descended from a pirate.'

Gabby's mind is working at lightning speed. 'He *was* a Frieslander. They're a seafaring people.'

'A common criminal, you mean.'

'It was forced on him.'

'Oh yeah?'

The crowd is turning hostile again. 'I'll tell you why. The first people to farm the marshes were peasant farmers from inland. They hadn't a clue how to protect their land from the sea, let alone how to win more from it.

'But they'd heard about the expert dyke builders from Friesland. So they invited them to live with them and, in return, make their acreage safe. And when they'd finished they tried to send the newcomers packing. They refused to let them own any land themselves.'

'So what? Why should the marshmen have given the Frieslanders land? It wasn't theirs.'

'Because they wouldn't have had nearly as much without them.'

The girls are standing round Gabby in a semi-circle. Which grows larger as even the boys join in.

'The Frieslanders weren't going to put up with that sort of rubbish. They took their speedy little boats and built a secret harbour in the swamps. Then they raided the settlements. Now they were pirates who terrorised the local villages. Led by der Weisse Pirat.'

'Why a white pirate? Sounds like a blackguard to me.'

'Because his hairless scalp reflected light from the sea at night. Striking terror into the hearts of his enemies. The farmers were lousy sailors. As soon as they saw the white head they knew they were in big trouble. They didn't know what to do about it, though. Running away would be cowardly. Staying around put them in the gravest danger.'

'Why were they so afraid of him?' Helga's voice trembles. 'Was he

160

terribly fierce and brutal? Did he pillage and rape?'

'He was brilliant at strategy, stronger and taller than the other men. And there wasn't any need for rape. All the girls were longing for him to carry them off.'

There's no sound from her audience. She's got them hooked.

'And as he had no wife, he chose a local girl. He went into one of the biggest farmhouses, saw the women spinning by the fire and picked the one he thought the most beautiful. Then he carried her off with him and made her his bride. That's how he founded Schwanenbruch.'

Gabby looks round. Most heads are nodding with understanding.

'You all have Frieslander blood in you by now. That's nothing to be ashamed of. They're independent folk, hard-working and sturdy. Which they need to be able to cope with the constant floods which are a fact of life when you live below sea level.'

'So you're saying that's what started this baldness in your family?' Helga's voice is soft with malice. 'Some good-for-nothing vagabond with no hair sneaks in, abducts a healthy German woman, then fathers bald children on her.'

'He wasn't a good-for-nothing. If it hadn't been for the Frieslanders, none of this land would be arable. None of us would be here.'

'You wouldn't be.' Helga pats the ample hair under the towel. 'Not much of a loss.'

'What you're forgetting is that the White Pirate fell in love with the girl and decided to settle down. And no one dared to attack the village because he lived in it. So it's not just our family he helped. The whole of Schwanenbruch is here because of him.'

THE OXTOWER

After the early marsh settlers built dykes and won land from the sea by the sweat of their brows, they lived for a while without their own church. But keeping Sunday holy according to God's word meant giving praise in their very own church.

Two new settlements, both too poor to afford a church, but rich enough to build one if they pooled their resources, asked the Bishop for guidance on where to build their shared House of God.

The Bishop was a wise man. He told the villagers that the Almighty was the One to decide the place where they should build their place of worship. All they had to do was yoke two oxen together, one from each settlement, and then drive them off. Wherever the oxen settled down to rest, that would be the place to build their church.

Both settlements agreed the Bishop's inspiration came from God. But, being men, they wanted to make sure God helped their own village rather than that of the neighbouring one. So the two strongest oxen, one from each settlement, were tethered together. The villagers from both sides were quite sure that their beast would pull the yoked pair towards his own settlement. And the stronger ox would, naturally, win.

The animals were duly tethered together. People from both sides cheered and yelled. They rattled spades against cartwheels to make more noise. They charged at the beasts when they seemed to lose interest and to flag. Until the time came when both oxen sank down exhausted. At the site for the new church.

No man in his right mind would have chosen that spot, because it was slap in the middle of the wettest marsh as well as much too near the sea for comfort. But God had laid down the rules and mere men had to stick by them.

They began to build their church. They started with the belfry and built the highest tower they could manage. Then they called it the Ochsenturm—the Oxtower—in memory of the way it came about. An enormous, solid tower which stands to this day.

CHAPTER 9

Schwanenbruch, February 1918

'Just follow me.' Doly's whisper promises conspiracy. Of a most important kind. Lieselotte has ridden Flitsi to Schwanenbruch. To deliver a haunch of venison to Rula, and to visit Doly. Lieselotte's father knows nothing about that.

Herr Waldeck's opinion of the Dohlens isn't high. Emil Dohlen's trips to the United States were viewed as disloyal. Coupled with rumours of other irregularities Karl Waldeck will not tolerate.

'Surely the children can't be held responsible?' his wife asks. Carefully. Her husband's temper is notorious.

'Not yet.' A growling paterfamilias guarding his daughter. 'Give them time. The leopard doesn't change his spots.'

'We'll take him to Onkel Hinrich's meadow.' Doly takes Flitsi's bridle and leads horse and rider to the side of the villa. Along the path which leads to Hinrich Bender's smallholding beyond the garden. Out of Tante Hannah's sight.

It's hard to get used to, but the meadow isn't Onkel Hinrich's now. He was killed fighting on the Eastern Front. In Russia. The telegram said he died a hero's death.

Doly's tears have run out. Her eyes are brittle as though she has a fever. She doesn't walk beside the gelding. She runs. 'We can jump Flitsi over the fences my uncle built.'

'Jump him?'

'Why not? You scared?'

'Why should I be? I'm a good rider.' Lieselotte dismounts. The two girls walk on either side of Flitsi through to the primitive jumps Onkel Hinrich built to train his dogs. He couldn't afford a horse. On his last leave he promised Doly that he would get money from Onkel Wilfred. So she could have a pony of her own.

'There's plenty of pasture for him,' Onkel Hinrich. 'My meadow's big enough to keep a pony all year round. The money to buy him is yours now, after all. Don't see how Wilfred can argue with that.'

Onkel Wilfred never argues. He smiles, then acts. Doly listens to Rula and Ursula talking. 'Wilfred Bender takes Hinrich's hay crop when he feels like it. Doesn't pay Irmgard a penny. Then he stores it in his barns until winter. Then he sells it.'

'What about Irmgard? Can't she say she wants her money?' Rula asks, banging her oven door and threatening the rising of the bread.

'Can't say boo to a flea, that one.'

Doly's last memory of Onkel Hinrich is precious. A piggy-back ride around the garden. Jogging round the meadow. 'Leave it to me, Doly. I'll make sure you have your pony.'

Tante Irmgard said she couldn't afford to feed two large dogs, so Doly offered to look after Ruffer and Rupus. Rula made sure Doly had all the scraps from the villa kitchen to feed them.

Onkel Wilfred said Doly couldn't have a horse because they were all needed for the Army. It's true that Lieselotte's father had all his horses requisitioned. Except for Flitsi. He has a special dispensation so he can work the Waldecks' land.

Herr Waldeck also uses Flitsi as a hunter. Rides him a long way inland to find wild boar and deer. Meat the government doesn't know about. Lieselotte has ridden over today because Dieter was due back from a fishing trip last night. The Waldecks hope for a large cod. Fair exchange for the venison.

The girls ride Flitsi in turn. Walk, trot, gallop. Jump. They sail him over the dry branches Onkel Hinrich intertwined on his last leave. For his beloved dogs which are no longer there.

Tante Irmgard let Onkel Wilfred have them as guard dogs for his barns. Such a tragedy that the poor dumb animals tried to find their way back home and never made it. Who'd have thought it? Onkel Wilfred only lives a few hundred metres down the Braake. How could such intelligent dogs lose their way like that?

'Boring,' Doly shouts, clearing the tangle of brushwood with half a metre to spare. 'Let's go for a real ride. Let's sit on him together and ride on the Watt.' An excited gulp as she tries for real adventure. 'Flitsi's quite ghostly-looking from a distance. Let's pretend to be the Schimmelreiter. We can go by Rula's house and see if we can fool her into thinking she's seen the ghost-rider himself.'

It's ebb tide on the Schwanenbruch shore. A pale February sun illuminates the day, the mudflats will be empty. The two girls clamber into the same saddle. Hair flying in the wind, shouting with joy as they clatter over the village cobbles on their way to the dyke. Right to the top. Looking out to the estuary spread before them on the other side.

A thick mist hangs over the water. Suspended, like a veil. Good cover against prying eyes. Doly feels the freedom of the wide horizons. 'Let's take our clothes off. And Flitsi's saddle. Ride bare and bareback.'

Lieselotte dismounts. Pulls off her shoes, her socks, her apron. Shivers with cold and stares at Doly. Who's taking off her dress, her vest; only her knickers left. She steps out of those, lets them drop on the beach, laughs.

Lieselotte takes off the rest of her clothes and unsaddles Flitsi. Gives Doly a leg-up and is pulled up after her. They ride across the mudflats, Lieselotte's arms wound tight round Doly's waist. Doly's hands grip Flitsi's mane and they fly out to sea. Wind singing in their ears, firm Watt under Flitsi's hoofs. The freedom to do exactly as they please. Their screams mingle with that of seagulls, their laughter roars with incoming breakers.

'Turn back.'

Doly is deaf. She urges Flitsi on.

'Turn back now, Doly,' Lieselotte shouts in her ear. 'The tide's coming in.'

Flitsi's turned round, heads for the shore. They think it's the shore, but they can't be sure. The mist has turned to fog, the sun has gone, daylight is fading.

Foghorns hoot. They keep the sound behind them. Don't say a word to each other. Urge Flitsi forward.

He snorts, slackens speed, obeys. Only the noise of the waves following behind, the muffled sound of Flitsi's hoofs on solid seabed. No seagulls shriek. No fishermen casting their nets. They are alone on an empty expanse of mudflats.

Doly, in front, can see a dim outline. 'There's the shore.'

Visible because the Schwanenbruch beach is not like the one at Duhnen, not made of smooth sand. It's covered with large, light-coloured, shifting shingle which makes a formidable barrier before it gives way to stubbled sedge and twitch grasses.

The horse is tired, pushed too hard. He stumbles. The girls' legs freeze against his sides. They don't spur him on. He limps.

'He's hurt himself, Liesi.' Doly slides off, strokes Flitsi's flank. Lieselotte slips off as well. The two girls walk the horse over the treacherous pebbles, a long way to the short-grassed foreshore.

The fog is denser now. They run up and down the grass but can't find Flitsi's saddle. Or their clothes.

'What are we going to *do*?' Lieselotte howls. 'My father'll never let me into his house again if he finds out Flitsi's lame.'

'We can use Tante Irmgard's shed to bed him down tomorrow...'

'Tomorrow? He needs to be kept warm all night if he's to recover.'

Doly puts her arm around her friend's neck. 'So let's keep him moving. We'll find somewhere warm to settle him.'

'In the village, you mean? Walk through the village with no clothes on? I'd rather die.' Tears and sobs as full horror dawns.

'We'll go by Rula's house.'

Lieselotte runs ahead, pulling Flitsi behind her. 'You know which way to go? We could be kilometres away from there.'

Doly catches up, grabs her friend's arm. 'Don't panic, Liesi. We can't just charge, we have to think our way out of this. Use our brains.'

'If you're so clever...'

'I've got it.' Doly is jubilant. 'We're all right. Look over there. Why didn't I think of that before?'

'Look where? I can't see a bloody thing in this damned fog.'

'The Oxtower, you goose. The lighthouse. See that glow? I know exactly how to get there blindfold.'

'*Lighthouse*? How's a lighthouse going to help us?'

166

Doly is running now, pulling the horse and urging Lieselotte after her. 'The lighthouse-keeper's cottage, dimwit. Minni will lend us clothes.'

'You mean a family *lives* there?'

'In the cottage right by it. After you, Minni's my best friend. I used to visit all the time. Half the cottage is a barn. Really warm. We can stable Flitsi there until the morning.'

Doly leads confidently on, finds the barn door at the far end, creaks it open. And sees candlelight outlining a pair of trousers. And other disembodied clothes.

She backs behind Flitsi. His heavy breathing fills the barn.

'Who's that?' Minni's voice. Fearful and thin. The candle is snuffed out.

'It's me, Minni. Doly. And my friend Lieselotte and her horse. We need your help.'

'*Doly?* Has your Tante Hannah...?'

An arm stretches out, touches her. Powerful and hairy. It draws back.

'Hold on a minute, Doly.' Minni's voice.

'Can't, Minni. We're frozen because we took our clothes off. And Flitsi's saddle. So we could play ghost rider.'

The laugh which greets this information sounds masculine, and relieved.

'Shh, Liebling. My father'll hear you.'

Now Doly recognises the laugh. Minni's boyfriend, Gunther. Strong, handsome, smiling Gunther who looks for her after dark. When she creeps out of her parents' house and meets him on the other side of the dyke. He must be here with her.

The rustle of straw as Doly can see the dim outline of a large form moving. Splitting in two as a soft white form moves ahead of a larger taller one.

'Best not to tell my father anything,' Minni whispers. 'He always makes such a fuss.'

The larger body, what light there is reflecting from white skin, moves to the side, turns a broad back. Gunther relights the candle, takes hold of Flitsi's reins and leads him to the back of the barn.

Minni is naked too. And giggly. 'Here, you two can use my apron and my petticoat.' She hands pieces of discarded clothing to the girls. 'I'll slip up to my room and find you both some bits and pieces. Then we'll go in.'

'Never thought girls would be so adventurous,' Gunther says, voice muted. 'Tell you what. I'll cycle to the villa. Explain you're staying the night because you're nervous about riding through the fog.'

'What about my father?' Lieselotte moans, draping Minni's petticoat around her neck. 'He'll flay me alive if I don't come home tonight.'

'Don't worry.' A lion purr. 'I'll cycle on to Lüdingworth and explain. Your mother'll be so happy to hear you're safe, she'll think of a way to talk the old man round.'

'You can't, Gunther. The whole neighbourhood'll find out you were with me. And split on us to Vater.'

Doly's soft giggle sets the others off. 'They won't. We'll say we met Gunther on the way. And he's such a gentleman, he offered to lead two lost and frightened little girls to the lighthouse cottage. Where the keeper and his wife insisted they stay the night.' She grins. 'Herr Waldeck will probably offer you a large Schnapps.'

Minni gives her a hug. 'I always said you were a clever one.'

'We can get our clothes back at first light tomorrow. It'll be easy to spot the saddle as soon as the fog clears. Flitsi will be fine by then, Liesi. Look, there's hardly a sign of a limp.'

CHAPTER 10

Schwanenbruch, October 1918

'Don't be ridiculous, Gör. Of course you can swallow. You're lucky to have something *to* swallow. Many people have to get by on no more than two pounds of potatoes a week.'

Gabby's throat has been burning. For three days now. She feels hot, then cold. Today she can't even manage the porridge Rula cooked. Made from a precious store of gleaned oats.

'What's wrong, Gabby? Why aren't you eating your breakfast?' Rula is by the door, her broad brow creased into three horizontal lines. 'Aren't you well?'

Gabby's eyes moisten as she points to her throat. 'Can't swallow.' She puts down her spoon, pushes away her plate. Leans her head on her arms.

'I'll fetch the doctor, Gnädige Frau.' Rula puts a hand on Gabby's forehead. 'That girl's not well. She hasn't been eating properly for days.'

'Say aah.'

Gabby opens her mouth, tries. No sound. The metal spatula presses her tongue down. She chokes.

'All right, child. Let's take your temperature.' The thermometer tube is icy under her armpit. 'Sit quite still.' The doctor rummages in his bag. 'Now then, Hannah. Why wasn't I called before?'

169

'The child didn't say a word before this morning.'

The stethoscope, a metal necklace round his neck, is raised. 'I'll check her breathing. It's pretty clear she has acute tonsillitis. There's only one solution. We'll have to take her tonsils out.'

Gabby shivers. Is he talking about an operation? Theo's daughter Anna had her appendix out. There's neither ether nor chloroform around for civilian use. Four men held her down. Her screams were heard from the Osterstrasse to the church. Six hundred metres.

'Who's in charge here?'

'Why me, Herr Doktor. My brother...'

'Rubbish, woman. Your brother Wilfred's the German guardian, isn't her? He's to come right away.'

'I'll send...'

'You'll fetch him yourself.' The doctor's head jerks towards the door.

Hannah stands square, hands on waist, mouth wide.

'And make sure you bring him back with you at once. Clear?'

'But...'

'What are you waiting for?'

Skirts swish as Hannah's boots ravage the floor. Fury crashes the house door shut.

'How long has this been going on, child?'

'A...few...days...' Gabby clutches her burning throat, lunges at the jug to pour herself some water.

The doctor puts both hands on her shoulders, pushes her back into her chair. 'Bring her a glass of Schnapps, will you, Rula? The child can hardly speak.' He examines the thermometer. 'Hmmm. Has this happened before?'

'Every...now...and...then.'

Gabby sips the liquid. Slowly, thankfully. Herta always laughed when she told Gabby she had her first taste of Schnapps when teething. She likes the tang, the euphoria which follows. Herta used to smuggle pain-killing amounts to her when her throat was particularly bad. Rula's more cautious.

'Drink up, my girl. It will do you good.' He pours more Schnapps, looks over thick glasses at Rula. 'Has she complained about her throat before today?'

'Not that I've heard, Herr Doktor. But then I don't suppose she'd dare.'

The house door opening, banging shut. The clatter of two pairs of boots. Onkel Wilfred, cigar blazing, followed by Tante Hannah. Gabby gasps, chokes on the smoke.

'Put that thing out, man.'

Scrunched-up slabs of cheek cover smouldering eyes. He hands the cigar to Rula, waves her out.

'The child has a high fever. No question about it. Her tonsils will have to come out.' The doctor scans the thermometer again. 'The question is: do you have the authority to allow me to operate?'

'I'm in loco parentis, Herr Doktor.' Widening nostrils snarl his voice. 'But what is all this? Just because some whiny brat maintains she's got a sore throat? Trying to get out of school, I'll be bound.'

'I think you can safely leave the diagnosis to me, Herr Bender. My professional assessment is that the child has a bad case of tonsillitis. This is not the first time, she's had recurrent episodes. If we just leave it, we run the risk of her contracting rheumatic fever.'

The room whirls around Gabby. She feels faint. This doctor called when Mutti died. He came to the house when Vater choked. Will he make her die, too?

'Serious, is it?' Onkel Wilfred grabs Gabby's glass and drains the rest of the brandy.

'That sort of infection can trigger heart problems in later life.' Emphatic shaking down of the mercury. 'Herr Dohlen trusted me. If you refuse permission, I will telegraph Herr Hudwalker. Wyckoff, New Jersey, I believe.' The thermometer stabs like an accusing finger.

Onkel Wilfred thrusts ox shoulders at the doctor. 'How much? The money's running out, you know.'

The doctor's mouth tightens into a thin red line, dividing a long nose from jutting chin which points a seething Adam's apple. 'My fees won't be beyond your means, Herr Bender. Full barns in winter mean good business. I'm prepared to wait until you collect your money.'

Work boots smear mud into the red salon carpet. 'Bloody fuss. When?'

'Now.' He turns to Rula hovering with a kettle she's brought from the kitchen. 'I'll need you to fetch Ursula. And another bottle of

Schnapps.' Gabby sees him extracting metal instruments from his bag. He's going to cut her, let her bleed to death.

She's woozy, but knows she's in danger. She stands, tries to run, stumbles because her legs won't function. Onkel Wilfred and Tante Hannah grab her arms as Rula and Ursula rush in.

'Drink this, Gabby.' Another glass of Schnapps. Big. Like the one Vater used to drink.

They hold her mouth open, pour the alcohol down her throat. The doctor cuts her tonsils out. But Gabby doesn't scream. Because she can't.

Schwanenbruch, November 1918

'How much money have you got, Moppel?' Gabby's voice is still husky. The cold, the lack of nutritious food, make it hard for her body to recover from the operation. But she can make herself understood.

'Money?' Moppel puts his hands into his trouser pockets. Balls them into fists. 'Haven't got any. Where would I get money?'

'I know you've got a stash somewhere.'

'Haven't.' The fists move his pockets tighter together as his shoulders hunch into a carapace.

'Don't lie. I can always tell Tante Hannah.'

'What's there to tell?'

Gabby pulls a piece of pumpernickel out of her apron pocket. 'My share of this week's bread. I kept it all for you.'

Eyes swivel on hungry stalks. 'It's only worth about 20 Pfennig. Tops.'

'You'll get your money back, Moppel. With interest. I have to send a telegram to Herr Hudwalker.'

'What for?'

'We've got to get away from here. He has all of Vater's American money. He can buy the tickets for our passage.'

'He's in charge of Vater's money?' Moppel straightens, takes his hands out of his pockets. 'Like Onkel Wilfred?'

'Not like Onkel Wilfred. Vater chose him. He put his name down in his will. He couldn't come and fetch us because of the War, but that's over at last. I wrote to him once.'

'Yeah? How did you know where to write?'

Gabby sighs. 'I told Tante Martha I wanted to thank him for the volume of Longfellow he sent me. She gave me the address.' She holds up a piece of paper. 'I'm going to ask him to send us tickets for America right away. Otherwise they'll kill me. And you and Doly will be on your own.'

'I haven't got much.

'Can you get some more?'

Moppel fidgets, shuffles his feet. 'Will he let us have some of the money?'

'You mean Mr Hudwalker?'

'Yes.'

'I expect so. It's ours.'

'Onkel Wilfred gives me money sometimes; when I help him with his business.'

'So you can get some more?'

'You promise Mr Hudwalker will pay me back?'

'Cross my heart and hope to die.'

'It'll take me a while to get it together.'

CHAPTER 11

Cuxhaven, January 1919

The clerk at the Cuxhaven Postamt stares at Gabby. At her thin hair. Does he recognise her because of it, or is he simply ill-mannered because she's a child?

'What are you doing here on your own, Diern?'

'My aunt sent me to ask you to telegraph an important message. She isn't very well.'

'That so. Let's see it.' He takes the exercise-book page Gabby is holding and reads the message:

HILFE—HELPEN. SENDE TICKETEN TU AMERIKA FUR
GABRIELE, EMIL AND DORINDA DOHLEN. NOT GOLD.
HOCHACHTUNGSVOLL, GABRIELE DOHLEN. MR WALTER
HUDWALKER, 1244 MAIN STR, WYCKOFF, NEW JERSEY,
U.S.A.

Fräulein Sinker stayed long enough for the Dohlen children to understand, and to be reasonably fluent, in English. But not long enough to teach them how to write it.

The clerk polishes his glasses, puts them on again. 'This is complete rubbish. You playing some sort of prank, Gör?'

Gabby gulps back tears. 'No, no, Herr Postbeamte. It's written in English.'

'English? What are you talking about?'

'It's to be sent to America.'

The clerk's glasses have slipped to the tip of his nose. 'So it is.' He scans the page again. 'You've got relatives there, have you?'

Gabby swallows. It is unwise to admit to American family ties, even though the War is over. Four million American troops entered the War when Germany was weak from fighting the French and the English. Without them Germany would have won, or so Onkel Wilfred maintains. Now they are imposing a harsh peace. 'A family friend,' Gabby whispers.

Suspicious eyes blink. 'Thirty-two words. 3 Marks 50 to include the sending fee. You got that?'

Gabby digs into her apron. Moppel gave her a handful of coins she hasn't counted yet. She has 30 Pfennig of her own. She puts all the coins on the counter. Her eyes are too blurred to add them up. 'I thought it was seventeen words. Is this enough?'

The post office official licks the carbon of his pencil, checks again. 'No. You have to include the address, and each digit counts as a separate word. No punctuation marks allowed. Spell out abbreviations, so write Strasse for STR. What's MR supposed to be?'

'It's the same as Herr.' Gabby's fingers are hot and sticky. She spent hours constructing the message. She can only guess at many of the English words.

'How much have you got?'

Gabby has been counting the coins on the wooden top. '2 Marks 60,' she croaks, her throat tight as well as sore.

'Enough for twenty-three words.' He gazes at her, sees the tears brimming. Makes a calculation on a pad. 'I can't help you much because it's in English. Put Amerika instead of U.S.A. and save two words. Can you think how to leave out seven more?'

The tears are falling now. Gabby crosses out 'HILFE', 'AND', the first 'DOHLEN' She debates whether to cross out the 'MR' changed to 'HERR' and the 'HOCHACHTUNGSVOLL'. Leaving out some sort of greeting would be so rude...

'Is it a town or a village? D'you need the number as well as the street?' the man behind the counter asks.

Gabby smiles her relief. There are street names and numbers in

Schwanenbruch. No one ever uses them. She's seen letters from Mr Hudwalker addressed to Onkel Wilfred: Herr Wilfred Bender, Schwanenbruch, Hannover, Deutschland finds him. The postman knows where everyone lives. She writes the message out again in perfect capitals.

HELPEN SENDE TICKETEN TU AMERIKA FUR GABRIELE EMIL AND DORINDA NOT GOLD HOCHACHTUNGSVOLL GABRIELE DOHLEN WALTER HUDWALKER MAIN STRASSE WYCKOFF NEW JERSEY AMERIKA

The clerk reads the new message, counts the words again. 'Correct. Wait here.' He disappears into the back.

Gabby can hear the clicking of hammer against plate, spelling out the letters in Morse code. Silence at last.

'Tell your aunt the message will arrive before it's sent.'

Is he playing a trick on her? Has he sent someone to the school while she's waiting, guessing she's playing truant? She tries to calm the wild beating of her heart. Why would he be suspicious? She's twelve. Many children have already left school at her age.

'They haven't taught you much at school, have they? There's a time difference between Germany and the East Coast of America. Six hours. Herr Hudwalker will be woken up by the telegram boy between three and four in the morning.'

CHAPTER 12

Schwanenbruch, February 1919

'What the hell's got into you, Hannah? Not like you to hold back when I'm putting money into your hand.'

Wilfred Bender counts the weekly ration of Marks into Hannah's palm. Fixed after he and Hannah paid off Miss Sinker.

'What am I supposed to do with this?' Hannah looks at the notes and coins, closes her fingers over them, turns her hand over and deposits the money on the wooden table on which Emil Dohlen played a weekly game of cards. Can he see what's happening? Does he know it's the place where the thirty pieces of silver are doled out?

'Not much left in the account. That villa eats money.'

Because it reflects the liberal 'borrowing' Wilfred has gone in for. 'D'you know what a loaf of bread costs today?' Hannah shrieks at her brother. '70 Pfennig. 70, Wilfred. And I can remember the time when I thought paying more than 30 was daylight robbery.' She glares at him. 'I can't manage on the usual amount. You'll...'

'What d'you think the rest of us live on?'

She's pretty sure she knows what Wilfred lives on. But decides not to say.

He takes her silence to mean he has outmanoeuvred her. 'I let you have a bloody fortune. You're spoilt, Hannah. And you've lost your touch. You can't even handle the children.'

Hannah feels wretched. The War may be over, but things have got much worse. The young men training at the nearby garrison have gone. Germany is virtually in the grip of civil war. There's talk of famine in Berlin, even in Hamburg. Schwanenbruch will survive because the North Sea gives as well as takes, but still...

'What d'you expect? They're the most self-willed brats I've ever come across. And I can hardly take a stick to the girls.'

Wilfred isn't in the mood for excuses. 'I've sent a letter to Hudwalker. We can't keep the children here. There isn't enough food for any of us, let alone three Americans. And you're right about the Mark. It's losing value every day.'

'Hudwalker? You mean that American?'

'The children's legal guardian. They're his responsibility. I only took the kids on out of the goodness of my heart because they couldn't sail safely. Now the Americans have won, it's up to him to take over.'

'Very true.' This is beginning to sound promising. A few dollars would translate into a lot of Marks. Hudwalker might not even realise that. 'So you told him to send you extra funds?'

'How else d'you expect me to foot the expenses for their trip?'

'Trip? You mean you're sending them off to America?' She feels a sudden chill in spite of the heat of the room. Where will that leave her? She should have known Wilfred was up to something. That benign expression is always a warning sign.

'The children ought to be with their guardian. That's what their father would have wanted.'

'And what am I supposed to do?' Hannah's blotchy complexion is greyer now. And she has lost weight. Like everybody else.

Wilfred shrugs as his smile grows broader. 'About time you got yourself a husband. Rather thought men were your speciality. What the hell's stopping you?'

'It may have escaped your attention, Wilfred. Half the young men didn't return from the War. I'm not exactly overwhelmed with offers.'

'Should have collared the young lieutenant while the going was good. Thought you'd have had the sense.'

'That jumped-up cowherd?' She's not about to tell her brother that Maximilian Glestner, son of a well-to-do dairy farmer, practically ran away at the suggestion of marriage.

178

'You set your cap too high, my girl. The Hauptmann always knew he could do better. Anyway, the Prussian Army's hardly the career it was.' Steely eyes assess his half-sister. 'Martha's the one who's done best out of all this. Teachers are bound to be in demand.'

'What the hell has Martha to do with it?' Hannah is still resentful that Wilfred actually forked out money, even if it was old Dohlen's, for her younger sister's teacher training while *she* was expected to play the skivvy looking after the brats.

'Knew what she was doing when she turned down looking after the kids. Never did understand why you were so keen. We all knew they'd go once the War was over. Which leaves you high and dry.'

Hannah's scowl would slay a lesser man. 'Got some sort of wily scheme in mind, have you?'

Sly eyes disappear in a grimace. 'I could try to wangle you a passage on the same boat as the children. Since you're their aunt. Steerage maybe. If Hudwalker's willing to let you travel with them, you'd be allowed up to First Class during the day. To look after them.'

'What a caring brother you are, Wilfred. And then what?'

'Well, then you're in America. New York streets are paved with gold they say.'

'But I'm supposed to carry on, to the sun-baked dirt of Nebraska, no doubt? That what you have in mind?'

'I can't force you to go, Hannah. But I'm closing down that great white elephant as soon as possible. Let the rats have it.' Wilfred goes over to his table, picks up the notes and coins, pockets them. 'If you don't want to take the money, don't. I'll assume you've resigned your position.'

'Resigned?' Hannah gapes at her brother, mouth cavered in surprise.

'Pack your things and go right away, if that's what you want. Gerda and Ulrike can move into the big house, look after the kids until they leave. I don't care either way.' Wilfred opens his cupboard, takes out a bottle of Schnapps. And two glasses. He pours a measure of spirits into each. 'Let's drink to the end of an era.'

'Drink to the defeat of Germany, you mean?'

A fist comes crashing down. 'Bloody hell, woman. Drinking's all I've got left. I'm too old to forge a new Germany. I have to leave that to the likes of you, God help us all.'

'You think things are ever going to be the same again?'

'Not a chance in hell. The Allies are making us starve until we're nothing but skeletons. Some dues are more personal than I expected. Hudwalker couldn't possibly have got my letter yet. He must have worked it out for himself. Or been told what to do.'

'Worked what out?'

'That the children have to live in America now. The orders arrived by special courier this morning. Sent by the American War Office would you believe.' Wilfred tosses back a glass, refills it. 'A letter demanding that the Dohlen children, being American citizens, be repatriated as soon as possible.'

'The American *War* Office?' She reaches for her glass and downs it in one. 'They wrote to you out of the blue?'

He nods. 'They're making sure of their pound of flesh. The *Imperator* was skulking in Hamburg until the War ended, now she's anchored off Schwanenbruch.'

'How can the children go on that? It's a HAPAG boat. A German line.'

'Exactly. She's sailing to England as part of the reparations due from Germany to the Allies.'

'War reparations? Conditions of surrender, you mean? I thought they hadn't signed anything yet.'

'Foregone conclusion. Meanwhile they're going to fit one of our best boats out as a Cunard liner, renaming her *Berengaria*. She sails for Southampton on April 30th, and the children are to sail with her. Then the authorities will make sure they're transferred to a boat sailing from there to the States.'

'So there's nothing we can do.' Hannah's voice has lost its power.

'Not a damned sausage.'

'So what d'you want from me?'

'I'll spell it out for you, my girl. You're going to spend next week kitting them out in the best gear you can muster. Go to Cuxhaven. We can't have them looking as though they'd come from the poor house.'

She swallows, pours herself another drink, pulls out a chair and sits down. 'You're saying their passage is already booked?'

'I told you. We're to put them on the tender from the Schwanenbruch pier. The rest isn't our responsibility. Hudwalker will meet them in New York, take them to live with him and his family. In New Jersey.'

Hannah sets her elbows on the table, leans her head against her hands. 'You've done all this without *any* reference to me?'

'Me? I'm just as surprised as you are. I've just got through telling you the War Office sent their ultimatum. Stirred up by Hudwalker, no doubt.' He downs another glass of Schnapps in one. 'All I did was pay you to oversee the children and the running of the villa. A job.' He takes the rejected money out of his pocket, presses it into her hand. Pulls a thick wad of notes out of the table drawer. 'This should be ample for a decent set of clothes for the children.'

'And what about *me*, Wilfred? What am *I* supposed to do?' She riffles the money as though it were a pack of cards. 'I see you can dish out handsomely when it's in your interest.'

'What d'you want from me, Diern? I've offered you the chance to go over with the kids, and all you do is snarl.' He grabs another wad of notes. Thinner. 'If you won't go to America, have this.' He clears his throat. 'On one condition. You get out of Schwanenbruch.'

'Think you can dump me like a piece of shit?'

Wilfred counts the notes out on the table. A reasonably impressive amount. 'In your shoes, I wouldn't make a fuss. Who knows what those Americans'll do if they hear about Prussian Army officers all over Emil Dohlen's house.'

He's got a good point. Conquering heroes demand retribution. Sweat oozes in drips down Hannah's neck. She takes the mound of notes, tidies it, looks at her brother. 'Not enough, Wilfred. I could mention a couple of things to the Americans myself.'

Wilfred's small eyes are almost shut. She knows he can't afford a hostile sister. One who's been part of his little schemes. 'I know it's hard on you, Hannah. Why won't you hear me out?'

'You can make me a better offer, is that it?'

He puts his hand over hers. She draws away.

'Thought you always wanted to go to America?'

Hannah's pasty face shows up the unattractive pimples. The hair which was so glossy only a few months ago is drab and untended. 'Haven't I made it clear? You can forget about bloody Nebraska, damn you. It wasn't good enough for Emma, and it won't be good enough for me.'

Wilfred nods. No eyelashes on his lids. Which gives him the look of a lizard waiting to strike. 'Who's talking about Nebraska? I mean New York. There's a small place called Brooklyn. It's becoming quite fashionable. People like to settle their families out of town and commute to Manhattan. Anton Weber's joining his brother there. In two months.'

Hannah's eyes brighten. 'You mean they need an assistant? I could work in a drapery?'

He pours more Schnapps. 'That's the best you think I can do for my little sister, is it?' Wilfred widens his eyes. Small, round, intense. 'Anton Weber's visa includes his wife, Hannah.'

'Hannah Weber's dead, Wilfred. She died of the 'flu last week.'

He nods, making no attempt to hide his pleasure. 'Exactly. Fool enough to visit her mother in Hamburg. What did she expect? People are dying like flies. Damned Spanish plague. Just like that dirty lot to spread disease.'

Hannah frowns. 'I can't see how that...'

Wilfred grins. 'Says Hannah Weber on the visa. I'm sure he'll want to marry again. I'll offer him the money for the tickets. Bloody good dowry.'

'But he's *your* age, Wilfred.' Tears are starting in Hannah's eyes. 'More than twice as old as me.'

'Didn't stop you trying for old Dohlen.' He put his hand over hers again. 'So you'll end up a young widow. There aren't even any children to get in your way. What more d'you want?' His eyes move slowly over her face, her body. 'All you have to do is get married before he sails. Make yourself look like the visa photograph.' He leans back in his chair to look at her. 'Get rid of some of that hair. Then dye it grey or wear a wig.' He cackles. 'That should do the trick.'

'My hair?' She can't stop herself putting a hand to the masses coiled on her head.

'What the fuck are you worrying about? *You* won't have a problem growing more.' The eyes are baleful now.

He's going to a lot of trouble to be shot of her. Must think she has something big on him. No proof, worse luck. 'But Weber, Wilfred. A boring little draper from Cuxhaven.'

Wilfred snorts, gathers phlegm, spits into a handkerchief. 'You've been through a whole battalion of fancy officers, woman. Not a bloody hint of a proposal.' He looks her up and down. Dispassionately. 'You said it yourself. Half our young men are dead, killed in that bloody War. Take your chance while you can, my girl. Go to America and work hard. When Weber dies you'll be a desirable widow. Show some bloody sense for once.'

Marry Weber. Live in Brooklyn, New York. She nods at her brother. 'All right. Set it up.' Things could have turned out worse.

184

PART 3

YANKEE DOODLERS

1919–1922

THE HOODWINKED DEVIL

A young lad sold himself to the devil. He made a contract with him, signed in blood, that he would give his soul to him in three years' time provided the devil fulfilled his three wishes.

The first wish the boy asked for was that he should have as much roast meat and other delicacies as he could eat. The devil easily fulfilled this wish, and the stripling happily ate his way through a mountain of food during the year. He grew fat and lazy.

When the year was over the devil asked the lad what his second wish might be.

He replied that he wished to have enough money to afford his every whim, however expensive.

'No problem,' the devil assured him. 'That's a simple enough wish to fulfil.' And rubbed his hands against his tail, in preparation for the final wish and the handing over of the foolish lad's soul.

The youth enjoyed his wealth during the year. Bought expensive clothes, a gold watch, even a house with the richest furnishings he could find. The devil watched, smiled. He would soon have his reward.

As was to be expected the time came for the naming of the third wish. The devil arrived promptly, grinning, sure of his reward.

'So what's it to be this time?' he asked, his hoofs making marks on his victim's beautifully manicured lawn.

Now the young chap knew very well that his future depended on what kind of wish he asked for at this stage. If he wanted to escape the devil he'd have to think of something to outwit him. In other words he would have to set him a task he couldn't actually carry out. But what could that possibly be?

He plied the devil with food and drink, ushered him into his best room, played for time. Then suddenly he had a brain wave.

'My last wish is very simple,' he said, patting the devil on the shoulder. 'I want to show you something. I want you to get hold of that something and make a knot in it. D'you think you can manage that?'

'Why ever not?' The devil tapped impatiently on the lost soul's splendid mantelpiece. 'Let's get it over with, then. What is it you're going to show me?'

With that the endangered one turned his back on the devil and let out such a loud and foul stink that the devil had to hold his nose before he could breathe.

'Right, now, get hold of that and make a knot in it!' the clever lout cried out, triumphant.

The devil gagged. 'Do it yourself, you stinker,' he shouted. He took to his heels and ran out of the splendid house, defeated by a mere mortal. But he made sure that the house fell down.

Even so, for once the devil was deprived of his booty.

CHAPTER 1

New York Harbour, Summer 1919

Gabby's on deck at dawn. It's not that she thinks the Captain lies, but suppose he miscalculated the time of arrival? She could miss the Statue of Liberty her father adored, its 1903 plaque commemorating The New Colossus. She knows it by heart—because her father was at the ceremony, declaimed it proudly whenever he could find occasion.

> Not like the brazen giant of Greek fame,
> With conquering limbs astride from land to land;
> Here at our sea-washed, sunset gates shall stand
> A mighty woman with a torch, whose flame
> Is the imprisoned lightning, and her name
> Mother of Exiles. From her beacon-hand
> Glows world-wide welcome; her mild eyes command
> The air-bridged harbor that twin cities frame.
> "Keep, ancient lands, your storied pomp!" cries she
> With silent lips. "Give me your tired, your poor,
> Your huddled masses yearning to breathe free,
> The wretched refuse of your teeming shore.
> Send these, the homeless, tempest-tost to me,
> I lift my lamp beside the golden door."

Mother of Exiles, Emma Lazarus, 1883

Gabby can hardly wait for the Manhattan skyline. She couldn't bear to miss that. Her father's loud voice comes back to her, repeating the story of his arrival:

"I disembarked with just the clothes on my back. And enthusiasm. Willing to work, keen to turn my hand to anything legal. Carting loads from the docks, sweeping floors, the streets. That's how it all began.

> *Mit dem Hute in der Hand*
> *Kommt man durch das ganze Land.*

> *Cap in hand*
> *Helps you find the Promised Land.*

"Manhattan was very different then. No skyscrapers, no elevators. No Ellis Island. I just walked ashore. Not even the Statue of Liberty." Gabby hears the loud ticking of the grandfather clock as he thinks back. *"I remember the dedication of the great monument as though it were yesterday. Bedloe's Island, October 1886. A great day.*

"Some of my money built the skyline hundreds of thousands now long to see. I'm really proud of that. I knew this country was exactly what I was looking for the moment I set foot on land. I picked up the dirt and kissed it."

Gabby has the deck to herself and finds a good vantage point, waits. She watches as a huddle of tall grey buildings rise slowly out of the morning mist. The sun behind her rises. It gilds the great statue, fires the flame. Gabby watches the enlarging buildings. It's as if all the marshland churches were gathered together, looming out of the sea. With one big difference. There are no church spires. These tall grey buildings are temples to Mammon, not houses of God.

She watches the dawn rays light up a myriad windows. Eyes winking at her, greeting her. She's an American citizen who asked to come home. Will she fit in, be a worthy daughter to her father? Is he proud of her for seeing to it that the three of them are returning to the city he helped build?

Moppel and Doly are early birds as well. They stand by her, watch as the sailors lower the gangplank. They stare at approaching American

189

heads, hear the tramp of American boots clattering up to greet their loved ones. Or to meet First Class immigrants, some of whom will be selected for further questioning on Ellis Island. Where all steerage passengers go, and many are turned back.

'You must be Gabriella. Welcome to the United States: Glory, glory hallelujah.'

A deep baritone is rumbling above Gabby's head, emerging from a towering, thin body. All she can see clearly is a neat column of waistcoat buttons. Done up, crossed by a watch chain.

It's hotter than she's ever known it. Humid as well. She's wearing her new Sunday best, as decreed by Onkel Wilfred. It's choking her. Because she's buttoned up as well. It's only right and proper.

Gabby leans back against the deck rail to get a wider angle. A face with a thin, pointed, close-shaved chin. Lips pressed together, topped by a moustache. A hovering Derby hat.

'Yes. I am Gabriele.' She rounds her shoulders to blend into the crowd. Will he think her too ugly for America? Send her back because of her scanty hair?

'I remember the day you were born as though it were yesterday. Your mother was a lovely lady. God calls his angels to Him.'

Gabby feels blood rushing to her cheeks, so tiresomely obvious through her delicate skin. Her mother was lovely. She's an ugly child whose hair gets thinner every day. She blushes her shame. Then remembers she's the eldest. It's her duty to greet her guardian properly.

'You are Mr Hootvalker?' She tries to remember the way her father said it. The phonemes come out like Onkel Wilfred's.

'We say Hudwalker, Gabriella.' His right hand appears from somewhere, grabs hers, shakes it. 'I've waited many years for this reunion. Last time I saw you you were in your mother's arms. Such a wonderful little lady.'

The second odious comparison. Will he accept her only because she's Emma's daughter?

'You're the spitting image of her. Your father must have been so proud of you.'

Gabby blinks tears away. Then finds herself distracted by her guardian's clothes. It's Saturday, but he's wearing a white shirt. Topped with a wing collar and a bow tie. There's a time difference, she remembers. Maybe it's Sunday in New York?

'My name is Gabrieyley.' Gabby enunciates pedantically, the way Tante Martha does. 'Vater always called me Gabby. It is easy to say in both English and German.' She's less nervous when she thinks about Vater. Mr Hudwalker is the guardian he picked out for them. Specially.

Grave brown eyes show no hint of amusement. 'I beg your pardon. Gabrieyley,' he repeats. An accurate imitation. 'We must be sure to get that right.' He clears his throat. 'We don't favour nicknames in our community. Christians should use their God-blessed baptismal names.'

Mr Hudwalker is the head teacher at Wyckoff Grade School. "Americans use a different system from ours," Tante Martha explained. In the precise way Mr Hudwalker speaks. "American children start school a year earlier than we do. Eight grades from six to fourteen. Some go on to High School after that."

Mr Hudwalker moves past Gabby, holds out his hand to Moppel. 'Ick freit mick düchtig, dick zu trebben—Very happy to meet you, Emil Julius Junior.'

His German sounds jerky, unsure. Plattdeutsch vocabulary, High German intonation. The children look at each other, their eyes expressive. He'll understand what they say to each other.

'An honour to meet the son and heir.'

Moppel's sailor collar is damp with sweat. He flourishes his cap off his head. Draws himself up, extends his hand and shakes Mr Hudwalker's as though he were a grown man. 'Wery happy to meeten you, sir. My father spoken off you wery good.'

Gabby's head jerks at her brother. His English isn't as good as hers or Doly's but he's obviously boned up on it. There's a surprise.

Moppel uses his cap to fan himself. Smiles.

Mr Hudwalker pumps Moppel's hand up and down. 'A real pleasure, Emil Junior. Glad to have you with us.'

Doly edges past to join the bustle of disembarking passengers.

Mr Hudwalker is not as lethargic as he looks. He twists away from Moppel, runs after her. 'Hold on there now, Dorinda.' Moderatesounding tones carry further than Gabby would have guessed.

Doly both hears and reacts, and clearly remembers Miss Sinker's lessons. 'How do you do, Herr Hudwalker. I am Doly.' Several top teeth are only half-grown. Giving her speech a whistling quality. When she's nervous.

'Delighted to make your acquaintance.' Brief pause. 'Well now, young lady. More people here than you're used to. Best if you stay with us, so you don't get lost.'

Doly stops. 'Is that your horse?' Her index finger points at a grey hitched up to a four-wheeled carriage below them on the wharf. 'He is beautiful.'

The sombre face deepens into sterner folds. 'He's pulling a hackney carriage. They're allowed alongside for the convenience of First Class passengers so their luggage can be loaded right on. We can hire one to take us and your cases back home to Wyckoff.'

'Vere are zee automobiles?' Moppel's face is intense.

'Why, that's right. I bet you've never even seen a car. They're not allowed here. You'll see them crowding the streets. Messy, noisy things. We can...'

'I like horses.' Doly flits down to the animal. Strokes his neck until the cabby takes her hand away.

'Don't get him excited none.'

'We'll hire him, Dorinda.' Mr Hudwalker, out of breath, nods at the driver. 'To cross the Hudson River to New Jersey. That will furnish you with another fine sight of the Manhattan skyline.'

Doly's eyes grow large. 'You mean the horse is going to swim?' She giggles. 'I understand. He will trot across the river bed. Like going to Neuwerk at ebb tide.'

The high starched collar makes it hard for Mr Hudwalker to show surprise. Except for his eyes, which bulge. 'The horse, child? My goodness, no. We have a ferry to take the whole carriage over.'

'We are going on a ferry with the horse?'

'Exactly right. The *John G McCullough*, named for the man who reorganised the Erie Railroad. People like to live over in New Jersey and commute to Manhattan to work.'

'We take the school cart.' Gabby is keen to show her understanding. 'From Schwanenbruch to Cuxhaven and back every day. An hour there and an hour back. On a good day.'

'That so, Gabriella—Gabrieyley. We need to find your baggage.' He leads them along the wharf, on to a large shed. 'See those big letters hanging up?' He's grabbed hold of Doly's hand. 'I guess you already know the letters of the alphabet?'

'Of course I do. I am eight.'

'You'll find your luggage stacked under the letter your last name starts with.'

Doly is roughly half Mr Hudwalker's height. She has no trouble pulling him. To where a large D is dangling from the wharf shed beams. 'D is my special letter. DD for Doly Dohlen.'

CHAPTER 2

Wyckoff, New Jersey, Summer 1919

A large woman, in a black dress topped by a bonnet in spite of summer heat, is waiting outside a massive brick building. She approaches the hackney carriage as it pulls up, spreads her arms wide.

'Welcome to New Jersey.' She embraces Doly's shoulders, helps her down. 'I'm Elsa Hudwalker my dears. Call me Mother...'

'You are not my mother.' Doly clutches a small bedraggled toy dog to her chest.

'I know that, dear. Mother *Hudwalker* is what I have in mind. We'd like you to call us Father and Mother Hudwalker.' She pats Moppel's head. 'We're not aiming to take your parents' place, but we're here for you.' She walks up to Gabby. 'I was matron of honour at your parents' wedding.' Tears fill her eyes. 'I held you in my arms when you were a few months old. Your lovely mother was so proud of you.'

'This is your house?' Doly looks towards the flight of steps leading to an imposing arched entrance. The place is enormous. Larger than the Villa Dohlen. As wide as two ordinary houses on either side of the front door. A clock tower on top.

'Why yes. We live right here. Dorinda, isn't it?'

'My name is Doly.'

'We don't use nicknames...' Walter Hudwalker begins.

Doly plants her feet apart. 'This is the name I gave myself because I could not pronounce Dorinda. I said Dolinda. Now everyone calls

194

me Doly.'

Elsa Hudwalker shakes her head at her husband. 'She's very young, Walter. And Dorinda isn't exactly a name we would have chosen, is it now?'

'What's that?'

'Dorinda, Walter. Not even a German name that I'm aware of. Spanish I think. I guess Doly will be just fine.' Mother Hudwalker turns to the child, beckons her towards an unpretentious building at the side of the brick-built one. 'Come right on in.'

'You mean that log cabin? That is where you live?'

'Log cabin?' Walter Hudwalker laughs. Loudly. Eyes turned to marbles. 'This is what we call a clapboard house. I guess it might look small to you, compared to the house your father built. I heard tell that turned out too large for his liking. We like to be modest in our use of God's gifts. Wood is a great building material.'

'You mean it's a village house, like Onkel Hinrich's?' Doly remembers the snug Stube, loving faces, pets all around.

'A cottage? I guess not. We have all the modern utilities. Most everyone has running water and electricity. And central heating.' A superior smile.

'Our villa has running water.' Gabby sounds nonchalant.

'Is that a fact?'

'And my father had electricity cables brought from Cuxhaven. To make ours the most modern house in Land Hadeln. To please my mother.'

The first pang of homesickness overwhelms Gabby as she thinks back to Schwanenbruch, to their lovely villa. She sees it towering over the flat marshes, just like one of the churches looming out of the mist ghosting the moors. The light there is nothing like as garish as the bright merciless sun now beating overhead.

Father Hudwalker climbs his stoop, opens his front door. Steps aside. 'This is your home now. Come right on in.'

The entrance leads straight into the living room. Though at most half the size of the Villa Dohlen's red drawing room, it's stuffed with furniture. A pianola is in central place on the wall opposite the door, topped by a glass-fronted cupboard holding china. Dark-stained pine soaks up what light is allowed to seep through heavy drapes on either side of small windows. A table in the centre is set for eight. The earthenware plates are crowded together.

'And these here are our girls: Gertrude and Hildegarde.'

Two stolid females, hardly distinguishable from their mother, nod at the new arrivals.

Doly stares around the living room. 'This room is very dark.'

'Best to keep the sun out so it doesn't get too hot.' Mother Hudwalker opens a door at the far end of the room. 'You up there, Bertrand? Come on down.'

'Bertrand is Father's nephew.' Hildegarde fingers Doly's sleeve. 'His family came over from Hamburg a few years ago. He likes to help out.'

'So very obliging.' Gertrude puts a fingertip on Doly's toy dog. 'Needs a wash, I guess.' Doly darts away. 'He helped move my things to Hildegarde's room. So you two girls can take over my room.' She stares after Doly. 'It has its own bathroom. That'll give you the opportunity to wash that toy.'

'Bertrand is a real wonderful boy. He repainted the church in the spring vacation.'

A freckled friendly face grins round the staircase door, a hand lifts in a salute.

'We have brought a present from Onkel Wilfred.' Doly points at a sealed wooden crate the hackney driver set on the floor.

'That's real friendly of your uncle,' Mother Hudwalker purrs. 'We'd best open it down here. Don't you agree, Walter?'

His hands fold together as though in prayer and he bows his head. 'The Lord giveth and the Lord taketh away. We're happy to welcome you to our humble home. No need for presents.' But his eyes are benign.

Bertrand opens the door to the right, walks through, fumbles in a drawer. He returns with a hammer and screwdriver, levers nails out.

'Thank you, Nephew. Yes, indeedy. The good Lord always provides. What have we here? Something quite heavy and made of glass. Preserves?'

'There are more bottles.' Doly smiles, confident of the Hudwalkers' pleasure. 'We haven't got much food or many clothes in Germany. Onkel Wilfred found these bottles in Vater's cellar and had them packed for you.'

'Let's see now.' Father Hudwalker fumbles through the straw and lifts up a coloured bottle. Brushes the straw away, reveals the label. *Fine Champagne 1811—T. Hine and Co.*

The upward lines of brotherly love turn down as the warmth of the room seems to turn to frost. 'Schnapps.'

The neck of the bottle is held between the thumb and index finger of Hudwalker's right hand. The full length of a thin disapproving arm holds it away from him.

Doly slips across the room and huddles between her sister and brother.

Bertrand's face is split in a wide grin. 'Schnapps? That's some kinda liquor, ain't it?'

'Isn't it, Bertrand.'

'Sorry, Aunt Elsa. Isn't it?' He giggles. 'I guess that's real friendly of your uncle.'

'Take a hold on yourself, Bertrand.' Father Hudwalker's cold voice. 'This is no joking matter. I'd like to hear you explain to these young people.'

Bertrand swallows, wipes his eyes with an enormous spotted handkerchief, clears his throat. Grim Hudwalker faces wait for the revelation.

'Your uncle couldn't know this here's a dry household.'

Three stunned white faces stare at him from across the room.

'Means we don't touch drink. Uncle Walter here is active in St Luke's, OK? That's the church right by the side of the house. He's the lay preacher. That's like a pastor. Preaches most every day. After school.'

'You mean you do not drink anything?' Doly's voice is a whisper.

'That's about the size of it. Most Christians round here took the pledge years ago.'

'You do not become thirsty?' Doly is near to tears. 'I am burning in this heat.'

'Why, goodness me, what am I thinking of? The poor child has no idea. She means she wants some water.' Mother Hudwalker reaches for three tumblers from her dresser, puts them on the table. 'Gertrude, if you wouldn't mind. Go fill the pitcher.'

Water gushes in the kitchen. Noisily, in fits and starts.

'What Bertrand was trying to tell you is that we belong to the Temperance Movement. We've made a solemn promise never to indulge in alcohol of any kind.'

Gertrude returns, the pitcher in her hand. 'I guess they need to know a little more, Father. Tell them about the 18th Amendment. Passed on January 16th of this year, even though Wilson was set against it. Prohibition becomes Law on January 16th, 1920. Not long now.'

'Exactly right. Spirits are the worst kind of alcohol.' Father Hudwalker holds the bottle as though it might explode. 'What you children don't understand is that spirits are made from grain. That isn't right. So many people starving, yet good grain is distilled into alcohol. We need to divert that waste and concentrate on growing wholesome food.'

Walter Hudwalker strides into the kitchen. Followed by wife and daughters. The thud of hammer on screwdriver, a plop as the cork is forced in. The gurgle as the liquid pours, very slowly, down the drain.

Bertrand winks, goes over to one of the trunks, opens the lid, scrabbles about in it. Brings out Gabby's two large leather-bound volumes of Shakespeare plays. He beckons to the Dohlen children. They approach.

He removes three bottles of Schnapps from the straw, hands them over, gestures at the clothes. Gabby buries them in the trunk.

'Old fool'll pour it all down the drain,' he whispers in Plattdeutsch. Manhandles the Shakespeare, shoves it among the straw. Rummages through the trunk again. Brings out the bust of Byron Gabby made Ursula pack.

'That is my...' Her voice fades away as Mother Hudwalker returns.

'Why, that's a real great present. How thoughtful of your uncle to send us that.' She takes the bronze, sets it aside. 'Father Hudwalker will be so pleased.'

He walks in and dumps the emptied Schnapps bottle in the crate. Spots the bronze. 'Just the one bottle? Among other presents?'

'One more, Uncle Walter.' Bertrand eases another bottle out.

Father Hudwalker returns to righteous execution in the kitchen.

Doly slurps her water, smacks her lips. 'That tasted really good.' She holds her glass out for more, spills some as Mother Hudwalker bustles up and pours. 'Sorry. I am just so thirsty.'

'Why, you poor child. I'll get a cloth.' She rushes out.

'Attagirl.' Bertrand slaps Doly's shoulder, fishes out the last bottle, spirits it away in the trunk.

'I'll get Junior here to help me take the luggage up to the bedrooms, Aunt Elsa.' Voice very loud.

'Hold on there, Bertrand...'

Gabby and Moppel grab one end, he hoists the other up the stairs. 'C'mon,' he urges. 'Junior's room. Back of the closet's a good place.'

Doly stays slurping water as Walter Hudwalker returns from his crusade. 'What about wine, Father Hudwalker?'

'That's alcohol as well, Doly.'

'But it is made from grapes.' She can't subdue a tiny twitch in the corner of her mouth.

'That's different, Doly...' Elsa Hudwalker begins.

'All right, Mother.' He draws himself up to his full, and considerable, height. 'Let me explain. All alcohol is the work of the devil. I hope you children understand that I carry out God's law. I know you're too young to have indulged. And pray the good Lord you never will. This time Congress is on our side. The United States aims to set an example to the whole world.'

Doly's new incisors gleam. 'Vater said it was God's own country.'

CHAPTER 3

Wyckoff, New Jersey, 1920

'Hey, Fritz. What you doin' over here? Don't you know we beat you hollow?'

Moppel, officially answering to Emil Junior now, is surrounded by boys a year younger than he is. Father Hudwalker enrolled each of the Dohlen children one grade below their age group. To allow them to learn English and to catch up on their American lessons.

Emil grasps he's in a place where his crew-cut sheaf of coarse hair and eyebrow-less face are assumed to be part of his German heritage, not his family one. He can handle that. He likes it here. A place you can do business. His allowance is in dollars. Strong currency.

'My family isn't German, guys. My father was an American. So I am too.'

'No kidding. Your Pop's American?'

'He worked on Wall Street.'

'Wall Street? You mean he's rich?'

'He's dead. But he was a millionaire. The Principal was his best friend, so he's our guardian. That's why I'm living in his house.'

A circular shuffle round, soft body boy-handled until Moppel thought he'd be one big bruise. But he kept mum; the Cuxhaven school taught him more than German. 'That so? How come you're from Germany? They're the enemy.'

'My father had business there. He died during the War, and we couldn't get away. U-boats and all that garbage.'

The circling slows. A poke in the ribs. He bites back tears.

'Got any dough?'

'Some. Father Hudwalker's in charge. Won't let me have none too much.'

The shoving is transferred among themselves. 'But he can git some, right?'

'Sure thing.'

'If you needed it real bad, he'd fork up?'

What are they getting at? 'He'd have to. Doesn't belong to him, it's mine. He's looking after it, is all.'

An older boy—dark, swarthy—saunters over. Grade eight. One above Gabby and the highest class. 'That a fact? So you c'n finger it any time?'

The underlying threat makes Moppel sweat. But there's admiration in the boy's eyes. 'Father Hudwalker takes care of all our expenses.'

'OK.' The boy's shoulders are massive. 'Live in his house, that what you sayin'?'

'Yeah.'

'No kinda action. You wanna join our gang? We hang out after school.'

'You bet.'

'Mind you straighten up'n fly.'

'Sure thing.' He has no idea what's expected, but he'll muddle through somehow. A boy who survived Tante Hannah can cope with a couple of kids.

Anyway, this is the place where Vater made his money. The streets may not be paved with gold; Wyckoff's are more like old mud tracks without even the cobbles they have in Schwanenbruch, but that's no big deal. The point is that even boys do business; real business. No hanging round to come of age, no listening to elders. This is the country where you're judged by what you are, not by what your parents do. The land of real opportunity, of freedom from the past. Moppel is positive he's going to follow in Emil Senior's footsteps. Do better, even. Right here.

Doly sits on her bed, bounces until the springs squeak. 'I hate it here,

Gabby.'

'I know. It's boring, boring, boring. I reckon Tante Hannah was better than those everlasting sermons from the Ugly Sisters. Honestly revolting, so to speak.'

'She was slicker than snot on a glass doorknob, but most of the time we didn't even see her. Ma Huddy's always after me to cover myself. In this heat.' Doly grins at her sister. 'I miss Lieselotte—can't find anyone worth playing with. Let's go home.'

'Some chance. They won't let us.'

'Why ask? Let's be stowaways. On a liner to Cuxhaven. Or Hamburg. Anywhere. Vater used to Shanks's pony home from Bremerhaven. We can, too. You game?'

'They'll catch us.'

'C'mon. We'd be on our way by then. They won't turn the boat round just for us.'

Gabby stares out of the window. 'They'll send us back. The Uglies will crow.'

'So what. Let's give it a try.'

'Count me out of hare-brained schemes. Much better if you wheedle old Huddy to let us go for the summer vacation. He likes you.'

Doly stands to increase the springy effect. 'He does not. He practises Christian charity on me. He only *likes* Moppel.'

Gabby sighs. 'Because he's a boy. And he thinks he's going to be just like Vater.'

'Moppel? Even Huddy can't be such a dope.' She grabs the book Gabby is reading. 'He'll listen if you ask him, Gabby. He thinks you're clever.'

'I've tried. He won't hear of our going back.'

The squeaking stops. 'Why not?'

'He blathers on about how he gave Vater his solemn promise to take care of us. And Moppel likes it here. Anyway, who'd keep an eye on us in Schwanenbruch? Even if we could cope with Tante Hannah now, she's married.'

Doly jumps higher with excitement. 'Out of our hair?' Giggles. 'Well, you know what I'm saying.' The jumping stops. 'Doesn't mean she won't come back.

'Oh yeah? She married a Cuxhaven draper who emigrated to

Brooklyn.'

'Never heard of it.'

'Not in Germany, you dope. Near Manhattan.'

'She's here?'

'Exactly.'

The jumps are metre high. 'Perfect. We can have Rula, Ursula, Herta…'

'They can't take it on. They're servants. Someone has to be in charge.'

'Tante Martha.'

'She's a trainee teacher. Won't leave her precious studies just to look after us.' Gabby takes a brush and puts it through Doly's hair, stops. 'Unless *you* can persuade her. She dotes on you.'

Doly kicks the bed frame. 'I forgot. Let's go and try. If I stay here a moment longer, I'm going to *die* of boredom. Church every evening *and* all day Sunday drives me nuts.'

'Why Doly, you're so ungrateful. You're allowed Bible Class Sunday afternoons. With Gorgeous Gertie.'

'She really hates me.'

'Because she caught you sneaking out of church with that boy.'

'So what? She knew Moppel took some of the collection money. She only laughed.'

'Told her he was putting some in. She's no idea he'd take the pennies off a dead man's eyes.' Gabby has tidied her side of the room, put away her clothes. 'Anyway, she's sweet on him.'

'What's that supposed to mean?'

'Wants to marry him, dope.'

'Crazy idea even for you, Gabby.' The bed springs begin to squeak again. 'I can't find a friend. The girls dress up and play mothers, and the boys won't let me join in their games.'

Gabby sighs. She came with such great hopes to the country where she was born, the country her father loved, to meet the guardian he chose for them. How could Walter Hudwalker have been Emil Dohlen's best friend? He's so very different from Vater.

She fingers the locket inside her dress. The Hudwalkers don't approve of jewellery, but Gabby wears it, secretly, because she now understands only too well why her mother was so attached to it. A symbol of home, of safety, of belonging—of achievable love.

She's worked out that she doesn't fit into this New World. She isn't a boy who can decide to make his way, substitute work for looks or background. She's a girl who's considered ugly because she has sparse hair. And Grade School has several disadvantages compared to the Cuxhaven schools. The worst is that, being co-ed, she's constantly reminded of how undesirable she is. The boys' reluctance to be seen even talking to her makes that crystal clear. Every single day.

There are none of the compensations of Schwanenbruch. The horizons are bounded by small repetitive houses, there are no dykes to wander, no boats to watch plying up and down the Elbe Estuary. She wasn't any different physically in Germany, but she did live in the best house, and she was cushioned by her father's reputation as Schwanenbruch's most famous son. What's more, Werner Schiffer, the handsomest boy in his class, liked her company in spite of her looks.

What can she do here? The New World is all about being a pioneer, leaving the old, abandoning it. Gabby loves the heritage of the myths and legends she's steeped in, she adores the praise she gets for being well read. And didn't she walk between her uncles at her father's funeral, promise herself that she would help Germany return to her traditions after that terrible War? Isn't she needed there, now that the country is in such trouble? Is it right to desert the place rather than do what she can to bring it back to what it should be?

She isn't needed, or wanted, here. Her background, her culture, her physique—all are against her. All women care about looks, especially about their crowning glory. But Americans seem to care more than Germans. She's heard Ma Huddy pitying her, as well as Doly, to her daughters, to her friends. Hit with the ugly stick, they dub them. Harder to take than snide remarks.

In Germany she has a chance to make something of her life. Not here. 'All Americans are boring,' she announces to Doly. 'It's because they're only interested in looks, or making money or religion; well, making money *is* their religion. They don't *know* anything about the world outside the US of A, and they don't want to. The kids in my class think kangaroos come from Austria, and that that's the same as Germany. They're so damned *ignorant*.'

Doly shakes her head. 'Not about the Bible. The Ugly Sisters quiz me all the time. And make me write out what I get wrong ten times.' She jumps off the bed. 'Why should I learn the Gospels by heart? Vater didn't make us. Even Tante Martha doesn't.'

Gabby squints, short-sighted eyes sizing up her sister. There's no one else she can trust. 'Can you keep a secret?'

Doly throws her books in a heap over her Bible, kicks her clothes. 'You got an idea?'

'We can get Moppel on our side.'

A vicious yank at her sheets which leaves her bed in apple-pie disorder. 'Don't be such a goose. He doesn't want to go back. He's OK because he's part of a gang.'

'That's the point.'

Doly cocks her head, eyes alert. 'What d'you mean?'

Gabby puts fingers on her lips, moves closer. Paper-thin walls. She switches to Plattdeutsch, as broad as she can make it. Hudwalker's German is pretty rusty, the Ugly Sisters aren't even in the know. 'Remember the *Fine Champagne 1811—T. Hine and Co* bottles? The ones Bertrand helped rescue?'

'Moppel downed them all? We can threaten to tell old man Huddy if he doesn't back us up?'

Gabby shakes her head. 'Better than that. He's a bootlegger. He sold them through the gang. It was his initiation.'

'What?' Her mouth hangs open. 'How d'you know?'

'Heard him boasting to Bertie. It's why they let him join.' She walks over to the window, looks across the street at a row of similar houses. All clapboard, all small, all looking more or less the same. Occupied by recent immigrants from Europe. Who, unlike the Hudwalkers, haven't taken the Pledge. And have no plans to. 'Moppel's always after making money. He'll see the point of our taking a little trip back home.'

'Smuggle back booze?' Doly's look of admiration is as unmistakable as it is rare.

'They'd never even suspect.' Gabby's eyes widen as she puts on her special orphan look. 'Just motherless kids. Coming back from their summer holidays spent in a little German village. To rejoin their American guardian, Mr Hudwalker, the highly respected local preacher.' She giggles.

'Whoopee.' Doly prances all round the room, twirls. 'Then we can hide before the boat leaves.'

Gabby grabs hold of her. 'Shut up, you fool. Even the Huddopes'll spot we're up to something.' She knows they'll have to come back for a year or two, until she's old enough to run the villa herself. Meanwhile she can spy out the situation, see how to resolve her problems.

Doly throws herself across her bed. 'OK. Say we fix Moppel. How's he going to persuade Holy Huddy?'

Gabby's pointed little chin shoots skyward. 'Moppel can talk him round.'

'He'll never have the nerve. He's just a scaredy-cat.'

'Not if there's money in it.'

CHAPTER 4

Wyckoff, New Jersey, 1920

Moppel sits truculent, hands in his pockets. Covering some of the rental cash he and Bertrand 'forgot' to give old Huddy. 'I like it here. What's wrong with America?'

'I'm homesick.' Gabby, sitting in the last pew at the back of the church, is holding a bible open on her lap. Camouflaging a *New York Times* article about European immigrants. She's supposed to be with the girls but she's sitting next to Moppel. 'They don't even know where Europe is.'

'Who cares? This is where the action is. Vater said so.'

'Don't you miss Schwanenbruch at all?'

'The house was OK. But I got me some real good buddies here.'

She doesn't bother to explain her brother is so happy in the States because he, too, is boring. He isn't interested in the chaos of post-war Europe; as far as he's concerned, politics is a simple question of practising democracy. In the United States. Republicans or Democrats, you get to vote for the side you want—when you're twenty-one. Meanwhile he never reads anything except the funnies. Behind the Hudwalkers' backs, of course. He has no interest in philosophy, history, architecture: the European tradition. He doesn't think at all as far as she can make out. Except about making a buck.

'That's what I was going to talk to you about.'

'My buddies? What are they to you?'

Gabby smiles at her brother. 'Not much. But Prohibition is law now.'

'You mean they've been suspended from school? Big deal.'

'You're such a dolt, Moppel. I'm talking about the Eighteenth Amendment.'

'The what?'

'The new law. It's now illegal to use or sell alcoholic beverages in every state of the Union.'

His eyes fly open. 'You mean no one can go in a store and buy liquor? Not even adults? That what you're saying?'

'Exactly. If you paid some attention to what's happening instead of going round in that gang, you'd know about it.'

He shrugs. Gabby can tell he's grasped there might be lucrative implications and that she knows how to tap them. 'So? What's it to me?'

'You can work that out all right, Moppel. There are dollar signs attached.'

His eyes have hooded, but he doesn't respond.

'The Schnapps Onkel Wilfred sent over with us. Bertrand hid four bottles in your closet.' No response. 'You do remember?'

'What of it?'

'The two of you drank one. You only let me have one glass.' She puts her head on the side. 'I know you're cowardly, but you weren't even scared when I said I'd split on you. That's because you haven't got any left. Sold it, didn't you? At a good price.'

His face has contorted. 'You mean you want a cut?'

'I'd have asked for it sooner if that's what I was after. Now if we were to go to Schwanenbruch for the summer holidays...'

'You go. I'm just fine here.'

'...we could pick up a few bottles. A whole load. They're worth much more now.'

He stares straight ahead. 'I guess there could be a market. Sure.' Hardly audible.

'Onkel Wilfred would help us.'

Moppel looks very like his uncle. Thinks like him. 'You must be kidding. He never helps anyone.'

'Make a deal, Moppel. Make it worth his while. You sell the stuff to your buddies. Tell them they've got to find the cash to give Wilfred a cut up front. In dollars. He'll go for that. The Mark isn't worth the paper it's printed on.'

Moppel's translucent skin has turned a beetroot colour now he's in a much sunnier climate than North Germany's. No one could call him handsome. 'You mean we could bring bottles back in our luggage.'

'Right. They'll never check our stuff. We're just kids.' She smiles. 'And we can pack some of that Schwanengeschirr on top. Say we brought it as a special present for Ma Huddy. She'll love it.'

'For a girl, you've got possibilities. Waddya want *me* to do?'

'Huddy likes you. The son he never had n'all. Persuade him to let us go back to Schwanenbruch for the summer. Ma Huddy'll go along with it. She's always groaning about how she has to wait on us hand and foot, cook for eight instead of five.'

Moppel narrows his eyes. 'He'll say there's no one to look after us. You and Doly fixed that, whining on and on about Tante Hannah.'

'Not Tante Hannah, dope. She isn't even in Germany any more. Tante Martha. Doly and I wrote to her and asked her to live in the villa with us just for the holidays. She's a trainee teacher, remember. She's got the whole summer.'

'What'd she say?'

'Went for it. Said she'd be so pleased to see us all. 'Course I know she means Doly, but she has to say all of us. Rula and Ursula can take care of the house.'

'And you want *me* to square it with the old man?'

Gabby gives her brother one of her best smiles. 'Right. You're the one who can swing it, Moppel. He thinks you're the cat's pyjamas. Chip off the old block.' She laughs. 'And going to marry one of the Ugly Sisters.'

'Ugly sisters?' This time his batwing ears have reddened. 'What in hell are you on about now?'

'Gertrude and Hildegarde. Even you must have noticed them making sheep's eyes at you. And getting at Doly and me?'

'Don't be such an idiot, Gabby. They're grown-ups. Ancient.'

'So? Maybe Huddy thinks you'll have trouble finding a wife. Because of...' Gabby looks at her brother, at the hair falling out even more quickly than her own. Because the other boys give him a hard time, pulling it. Until he joined the gang. Then Al knocked the bullying out of them.

Moppel sleeks the remaining tufts back on his head. 'I'll marry who I like.'

'Just like Bertrand is thinking about Doly or me. Preferably me, because I come into my money five years ahead of Doly. Thinks I'll have enough dough to burn a wet mule.'

Moppel frowns at Gabby. 'You're on the level about this? Not just one of your crazy stories?'

'You're the one who can make it happen.' She tosses her head. 'Emil Julius Junior.'

'Morning, sir.'

'Emil Junior. Come right on in. You have a problem?'

'No sir, not me. It's about my Onkel Wilfred. We had a letter from our Tante Martha. He isn't well.'

'I'm sorry to hear that, Junior. Is there a financial problem?' Father Hudwalker, sitting benignly behind his principal's desk, smiles across it. 'We need to help out?'

'Oh no, sir. He didn't ask for anything. He always says: "Wer zufrieden ist, hat Überfluss—he who is content has more than enough." I guess he'd appreciate a little physical help from me, is all. He has no son, you see.'

Hudwalker nods. 'Why Junior. That's remarkably high-minded of you. Don't think I haven't noticed you help Bertrand out with the chores.' His eyes are on the papers on his desk. 'Offering to collect your father's Lower East Side rents is a big help. None too savoury a job. Emil Senior would be real proud.'

It's a lucrative little side line. Hudwalker isn't keen on mixing with tenement families. He doesn't check when Bertrand and Moppel bring him the deposit slips for the total rentals. Many are in arrears in any case. Subtracting a few dollars is how the two boys get their pocket money. 'That's what I have in mind, sir.'

Hudwalker looks grave. 'You find the neighbourhood a problem?'

'No, sir. I was talking of my uncle's property in Germany. Maybe I should go over this summer, give Onkel Wilfred a hand with his barns. And I could help him check out the business side of my father's

German properties.' Moppel looks guilelessly at Hudwalker. 'While I'm there.'

'Your Onkel Wilfred's gravely ill?'

Moppel puts on his most beatific smile. He's not good-looking, but he has a certain style, a certain amiability of manner. Uncannily like his uncle. Bonhomie among men. Clubbable.

'He'll be fine if he gets some rest. And we could talk. My uncles Theo and Hinrich are dead; there are no other men left over there from the German side of the family. I think he'd really appreciate my helping out a few weeks. My sisters and I could travel together, come back for school in the fall. That would give Mother Hudwalker a little break as well.'

'You're a good boy, Emil Junior. Maybe you'd like to consider becoming a preacher. A fine career for an upright young man.'

'God bless America, and all the ships at sea.'

CHAPTER 5

Schwanenbruch, Summer 1920

'Tante Martha's got this nutty idea we shouldn't spend time together.'

Doly and Lieselotte are walking on the Schwanenbruch mudflats. From the moment the Dohlen children landed at the Amerika-Hafen a week ago she and Lieselotte have been inseparable. In spite of both families' misgivings. One thing has been made clear. They aren't allowed to ride Flitsi. Or any other horse.

Doly kicks at the Watt, scattering small crabs. She stoops down to try to undo the damage. The little creatures scuttle away from her. 'What d'you want to do when you grow up, Liesi?'

'Become a doctor.'

Doly's eyes widen in surprise. Followed by jealousy, then admiration. She hasn't considered such an ambition. 'Really? What does your father say?'

Lieselotte chuckles. A deep voice, an even deeper laugh. It throbs through Doly. A feeling of tingling in her belly.

'He says it's a crazy idea. Girls don't become doctors. They marry and have children.'

Lieselotte forges ahead, her long legs striding the sand, her athletic form leaving Doly far behind. Admiring her friend's lithe body from afar.

'Hey, wait for me.' Doly sprints to catch up. 'You keep forgetting you've got long legs.'

'Move yours faster then.' She wriggles her toes into the mud, drilling small holes. 'I really want to study medicine. And specialise in paediatrics.'

'What?' The large toe is digging on its own. A deep hole Doly can almost feel inside herself. Oddly gratifying.

'Looking after sick children. Not that it's relevant. My parents are determined. They want me to marry Peter Sondwerk. His father owns the farm next to ours.'

'Lucky old you.' Doly wiggles her own toe beside Lieselotte's, puts her arm around her friend's waist. 'You mean your father won't pay for you to go to medical school?'

'More chance of squaring the circle.'

The girls are close together, kneading toes into the silt. 'He's taking quite a risk. You might run away.'

'I've thought about it. Considered becoming a stowaway on a boat to America. I've heard you can work your way through medical school there.'

'Maybe. Gabby says the American schools aren't any good, all the kids are stupid. She's wrong, of course. Nothing new. You need good grades to get into higher education.'

'I'm always top of my class.'

'You'll need American grades, passed in English. But don't worry. I'll come into my money and pay for you.'

'Will you really?' Lieselotte pulls her toe out. Stamps on the hole. 'That's no good, Doly. You won't come into anything till I'm nearly twenty-two.'

Doly is only floored for a minute. 'Gabby and Moppel will. I'll get them to lend it to me. Until I get my share.'

A massive snort. 'Your sister Gabby will be falling over herself to help me.'

'I'll find a way to get the money, Liesi. You can be sure of that.'

Lieselotte shrugs. 'Let's forget about me. What about you? You can do anything you fancy. What's it going to be?'

'Travel. All over the world. Africa, India, South America. I'm not settling down like a tame little housewife in the States.' Doly fluffs her hair out, feels for bare patches. None so far. She balances on her toe, lifts her other leg in a ballet pose. 'See? I'm a cygnet. When I'm a swan I'm going to marry an English lord and become a member of the aristocracy.'

Schwanenbruch, Summer 1920

'Do I really have to go back, Tante Martha? Can't I live with you?'

Doly watches her aunt carefully. Her gentle eyes are moist. She holds out welcoming arms and gathers her niece in them. 'You know I love you dearly, Doly. Just as if you were my own little girl. But I can't look after you. I'm not married and I live in a single room in an apartment house.'

'You mean you don't have time? Because you have to look after your special friend?'

'Whatever do you mean, child? What friend?'

'Gabby said. An invalid; Herr Doktor Veldun, who lives a few minutes' walk from you.'

'Why, yes, your sister is very well informed. I do visit Doktor Veldun and we have long discussions about the books we both like to read. But that isn't the reason I can't look after you.'

'What, then? You could live in the villa with us, Tante Martha. Take over my parents' room.'

'No, Doly. That isn't right. I have a career; I'm in the middle of my training to be a teacher. I look after you, or I teach. I can't do both.'

'But you don't have to give up teaching. You can take the train to Cuxhaven every day. We could go with you...'

'I'm sorry, my pet. It would be wrong to bring you back to Germany. Even if your guardian allowed it, the authorities wouldn't. Neither the American nor the German ones. Post-war Germany is no place for you and your brother and sister.'

Doly stamps her feet. 'I won't go back.'

Tante Martha strokes the bouncy curls. 'What's wrong, Doly? Aren't the Hudwalkers kind to you?'

'The Ugly Sisters are horrible.'

She hears a gulp; Tante Martha trying not to cry. 'The two daughters? They still live at home? I thought they were in their twenties. Teachers.'

'And don't we know it. They preach from dawn till bedtime.'

'Not all teachers preach.'

'I don't mean you, Tante Martha. But the Huddies do. They say we put on airs, that we expect them to wait on us as though they're servants.'

'I see.' Her aunt looks at her searchingly. 'And do you?'

'Of course not. Sometimes I forget to take my clothes down to the laundry. Making my bed and stuff.' She can see her aunt isn't convinced, she'll have to do better than that. 'They're the ones who tell lies. To fool their father. Who's a pastor.'

'Come along now, child. You're always so immoderate. Your mother was such a gentle lady...'

'She looked after *you* when you were small.'

Tante Martha's face closes up, takes on its schoolmarmy look. 'You can't grow up here, Doly. Apart from the conditions, you have to learn English.'

'I've learnt English. I'm better than the other children in my class already. Huddy Duddy's going to put me in Fifth Grade next year with the ten-year-olds. They're all so stupid.'

'Huddy Daddy? He asked you to call him that?'

Doly screams with laughter. 'Huddy Duddy. Huddy Daddy's even better. He makes us call him Father Hudwalker.'

'And you make fun of him.'

'Behind his back, Tante Martha. He doesn't know.'

'If Herr Hudwalker has put you a year ahead, he's looking after your interests, isn't he? You have to grow up in America, Doly. For your own good.'

'What am I going to do, Liesi? I can't stand it in New Jersey.'

'But I thought America was the Land of the Free...'

'It's like being in prison. The Huddies look glum if I so much as smile, let alone laugh. Their idea of entertainment is family prayers.'

'You have it easy, Doly. I have to fit in my chores before I can even get to my homework. The Sunday service is a chance to relax.' She turns to Doly. 'Stay in your room and read.'

'You imagine I can get away with that? Just encourages the Ugly Sisters to barge in. Start preaching at me.'

'Lock your door.'

'No key.'

215

'What do they preach about?'

'Not straightening the corners of my bottom sheet. Drinking water out of a cup instead of a glass. Earth-shattering events.'

Lieselotte and Doly are in the tree house. Rubbing noses to find out why the Eskimos do it. 'What can you do? Your Tante Martha won't look after you. Can't see your Onkel Wilfred taking you on.'

'Or Minni. Or Rula or Ursula. Onkel Palter would have but he's dead. Now I'm not even allowed to visit Tante Palter any more. Onkel Wilfred's forbidden it. They're all against me now.' She wipes tears from her eyes. 'What about your parents? Could I live with you? I'll pay them back.'

'You're kidding. They don't even like me knowing you.'

Doly's nose jolts away. 'What d'you mean? They're only...' She stops short.

'Only ordinary village people? That's what you were going to say, isn't it?'

'No, it isn't.' Though, really, it was an almost involuntary reaction. A cold fear claws at her. Is she beginning to be snobbish—like Tante Hannah? She was the one who wouldn't let them mix with the villagers. Not even Onkel Palter. Riffraff she called them. 'What precisely am I supposed to have done?'

Lieselotte studies her toe. 'Vater says you're wild. Your family's degenerate. Not really proper German stock.' Eyes blank. 'Says you're diseased, calls you trash. Doesn't want me to have anything to do with you.'

Outrage brings tears. 'Not really German? Both my parents were born in Schwanenbruch.'

Lieselotte's face burns red. 'Maybe it's that illness.'

Doly kicks, stubs her toe against a stone. Stinging pain. 'It's not an illness. I'm very healthy. And everyone knows perfectly well it isn't catching.'

'He thinks it proves you're genetically unsound.'

It is always there. And she can't just marry, even if her hair doesn't start falling out until she's much older. She'll have to tell any would-be husband that she has an errant gene which their children might inherit. 'And you? Is that what you think?'

Lieselotte strides off again. 'I'm going to find the cure, Doly.' She shouts back against the wind. 'I'm going to study medicine and cure all sick children.'

Doly runs after her. 'That's years and years away. We're only nine.' She grabs Lieselotte's arm. 'I could hide in one of your father's barns. You can bring me scraps of food. An egg, half a litre of milk. They'll never know.'

'Goodness, Doly, you're so unrealistic. They notice every crust of bread. None of us has enough to eat.'

'Just for a day or two. Until the *Baden* sails. If they can't find me, I'll have to stay. Couldn't I hide in your barn for two days? I'll bring my own food.'

CHAPTER 6

Schwanenbruch, Summer 1920

Emil Dohlen's leather-bound tomes of Latin and Greek are mouldy building-blocks in the cupboard under the eaves, their long sleep not disturbed until today. They've lain forgotten in the turret room which branded Hannah Bender a servant. A fit punishment for old Emil Dohlen's dereliction.

Exploring birds, ranked by individual enterprise rather than class, have pecked an entrance through the turret roof. That's been neglected for lack of currency rather than revenge. A friendly gathering of dust points bird footprints to cunningly hidden nests in nearby rafters. A spider scurries across a massive web. Repairing clumsy damage.

Doly squeezes forefinger and thumb against her nose. All that dust. She heaves, swallows saliva, air. Her body explodes into a sneeze. Subsides. Has anyone heard? She opens the cupboard door, peeps out. Reflected pinpricks of light watch her anxiously. Dark wings flutter over a peeping brood. Bird's-eye glares warn against approach.

Doly looks beyond them. She sees the giant clock face of the St Nicolaikirche facing her. Nearly ten o'clock. The bell-tower peals the hour. Reverberating sounds wave through colonies of bats hanging from the domed ceiling.

Doly crouches behind the books she's built into a castle wall. Four hours, that's all. The *Baden* sails at six in the evening. Boarding begins at two this afternoon. She should be able to survive that long. It's all

Gabby's fault she's in this mess. Always poking that turned-up nose into other people's business. She must have split on her. The others would never have rumbled she wasn't around until later.

Tante Martha's penetrating voice is calling her. Calm turning to frenzy. Doly has built her barricade of Ovid and Tacitus, Plato and Herodotus jostled by Cicero and fortified by Plutarch and Virgil. Topped by slimmer works by Pythagoras and Horace. Socrates on top. Soft leather declining into dust.

The hollow sounds of treads up the servants' staircase. Knife-edge voices. Doors sobbing against rough treatment. High-climbing boots thump the winding turret stairs.

'Look at this mess.'

Doly holds her breath. Will they notice she drew an old rag through the dust, that the trail leads to her hiding place? Cupboard doors squeal open, shut. A chink in her wall shows rheumy eyes peering into her stronghold.

'Only musty old books in here. No sign of the child.' Rula's voice trapped into relief.

Doly longs to cry out, fall into Tante Martha's arms, hear the sweet words which swear she'll never let her go. Who cares about learning English? How can that make her happy?

'I can't believe she'd be so irresponsible, Rula. She *knows* she has to go back. I explained it all.'

'She's too young to understand, Fräulein Bender.' Rula's deliberate steps retreating. 'And so highly strung. She thought I was rejecting her when I said she couldn't live with me. In my little hut of a house. I can hardly bear it. If she only knew I'd give anything to have her.'

'Pull yourself together, Rula.'

'Listen to that tiny mother bird scolding me, warning me off. What does she think she's doing?'

'We're looking for Doly, Rula.'

'I'm sorry, Fräulein Bender. The poor motherless mite. All she wants is to be loved.'

'Stop making a fool of yourself, woman. We have to find where she's hiding. For her sake. Go back to the kitchen in case she turns up there. I'll cycle over to Lüdingworth. I'm pretty sure Lieselotte Waldeck's behind this.'

Lüdingworth, Summer 1920

'Tag, Fräulein Bender.'

'Have you seen Doly, Waldeck?' Martha is out of breath from cycling to Lüdingworth at top speed. She's used to the exercise but the neighbouring village is nearly six kilometres away. And perhaps it would be wise to use the girl's Christian name.

'Doly?'

'Don't play the innocent. She's here, isn't she?'

Lieselotte looks round. Obviously guilty. 'She left before supper last night, Fräulein Bender. She said goodbye because the liner's leaving Cuxhaven this afternoon.'

'You're not hiding her?'

'No.'

Martha tries to assess the girl. 'We can't find her. Do you know where she might have gone?'

'No.'

'I think you do, Lieselotte. You're her bosom friend.'

'I have no idea.'

'If you don't tell me where she is, I'll have to talk to your father.'

Lieselotte's lower lip juts out. '*He* doesn't know where she is either.'

Martha decides to bring out the big guns. Right away. 'I'll be forced to tell him about the Oxtower fiasco. I can't imagine you'd want that.'

The girl's whole body stiffens. 'I don't know *what* you mean.'

'And a little less insolence if you don't mind. Be good enough to remember I'm a teacher at your school.'

'*Student* teacher…'

'That is pure insolence.' Martha's right hand sweeps across her handlebars. 'Gunther Mettler's sister is one of my pupils.'

'I know, Fräulein Bender.'

'So be a sensible girl.'

'I've no idea where she is.'

'And I suppose you don't know anything about the Oxtower either. That you weren't wearing a stitch…'

'That's just a story.'

'I don't think Mettler has that sort of imagination. He's had it all over the Schleuse Inn. Lucky your father never goes to Schwanenbruch— or drinks.'

'Please, Fräulein Bender. I haven't a clue where she is.'

'You had no idea she was planning to disappear?'

Lieselotte's eyes fill with tears. 'You're all against her. I wish I *had* helped her now. I'm a traitor just like the rest of you.'

'So you do know something, Waldeck.' Martha's voice grates like the barn door when the wind blows. 'It's your bounden duty to tell me. If you don't, you're responsible for the consequences. Which could be very serious.'

'I've told you already. I don't know *anything*.'

'To be precise, you said you wished you *had* helped her.'

'I do.' Lieselotte takes a hay fork and levers hay to the horses. Tosses it.

'I'm speaking to you.'

The hay fork stops. 'She asked me to hide her in our barn. I said no. Worse luck.' She covers her face with her hands.

'Calm down, girl. You must have some idea where she is.'

'D'you really think she'd trust me now, after I failed her?' The girl weeps wildly, noisily.

'All right, all right. Maybe she's at the Oxtower. Minni always did have a soft spot for her.'

'Minni turned her down as well, Fräulein Bender. Like everybody else. She may want to run away but she has nowhere to go. If she's hiding, it'll be in the villa. I'll come back with you and try to find her.'

THE BLESSED WILHELMINA

Wilhelmina was an only child. Her father and mother died of a terrible sickness. They were rich people, and left their daughter a great deal of money. She was brought up by her two uncles, taught to read, educated by the best tutors money could buy.

Wilhelmina lived according to God's word and never ceased to proclaim that, when the great floods came, it was the evildoers who would die. The good would always be saved.

Then the worst Christmas flood for centuries brought devastation. Well over a thousand people lost their lives, and over fifty thousand animals were drowned. And most of the houses were swept away.

Except the tower of the castle in which young Wilhelmina lived. That was able to stand up to wind and rain, lightning and flood. The young girl fled upwards, waited for the winds to calm, the waters to be still.

When the storm's fury had died away she looked down on the waters covering the plains. And realised that the whole village had gone. All she saw on the vast sheet of water were a few survivors in fishing boats piled high with salvaged belongings.

None of the rowers bothered to look up at the tower. The castle ruins told their own story. They simply rowed past. Silently.

That's when Wilhelmina began to sing hymns to the Lord Almighty who looks after the just, thanking Him for her deliverance.

The rowers stopped to look up to the tower. They went to investigate the castle ruins and saw that the stairs had been washed away, that no one could reach Wilhelmina.

'Throw down a rope,' they called to her.

But Wilhelmina had no ropes. 'The Lord will look after me,' she called back to them. Then stood fearlessly on the crenellated tower, spread out her arms - and jumped.

The people below cried out in terror. But instead of plunging to her death Whilhelmina's dress billowed wide. She floated down and landed in the water. Unharmed.

CHAPTER 7

Schwanenbruch, Summer 1920

The cupboard's dank. The dust from the old books is mouldy. It must be safe to come out for a bit. They're looking for her at Lieselotte's.

Doly is very hungry now. Why didn't she bring food? And terribly thirsty. Perhaps she can risk going down to the bathroom, just to have a drink? If Gabby's lurking, she'll run. She's faster than Gabby'll ever be.

Doly creeps down the turret steps, down the second flight to the first floor, into the bathroom. She drinks greedily from the tap, pees but doesn't pull the chain. Climbs back upstairs and looks out of the front turret window.

She sees Liesi and Tante Martha running towards the villa, hears them calling her. With Helga Ketter standing in the street, watching them. Doly ducks at the speed of lightning. Looks from the side. Tante Martha's short-sighted eyes won't have spotted her. But Helga is pointing at the turret window. Those sharp merciless eyes must have seen movement. That harsh jealous tongue will have told all.

And Liesi is there as well; her blood sister Liesi. What can she be thinking of, collaborating with the enemy?

What's left to live for?

Doly opens the window, climbs out on to the ledge, shows herself. She spreads her arms wide. She is ready to trust in God, to jump. If He loves her she will float down, astound everyone. She will be famous, just like the blessed Wilhelmina. Then Tante Martha will be forced to keep her in Schwanenbruch. Because a girl like Doly, singled out by God, will be needed in the village.

And suppose even God forsakes her? Well, she'll be dead. What point is there in staying alive? Not even Liesi on her side. Tears blur her sight.

'No, Doly!' Tante Martha's urgent voice floats up. 'Please, Doly, wait! For my sake.' There are breaks in the voice.

Doly can hear the rush of footsteps echoing on the wooden stairs, Rula's strong voice as she bursts into the room.

'Don't move, Doly! I'll come right out and get you!'

'You come near the window and I'll jump!' Turning on the narrow ledge dislodges part of the masonry. Pieces of brick and stone hit the ground near Helga. Who screams.

'Stay away!' Doly shouts. 'The ledge is crumbling!'

Can she hold on? It's hard to keep her balance when she looks down. Nausea takes hold. She longs for the strong, loving arms which held her when she was a baby. 'I want Herta!'

A crowd has gathered on the pavement outside the villa grounds. People from shops, the pastor, children playing on the streets. A sheet spread out below her billows in the wind. Four men at the corners hold it up. Like a trampoline.

A booming noise sends sound waves as the church bells strike. It's noon. Twelve ghastly booms. The first reverberates through Doly's head, makes it feel as though it's about to burst.

The bell-tower isn't much higher than the turret room. Doly looks across, terrified, as the huge twin towers of the St Nicolaikirche appear to bend down towards her.

The wall behind her shakes. St Nicolaus is the patron saint of travellers. Will he help her fly safely down? She leans back against the wall, hands on ears. Sways. The last boom fades.

'It's me, Doly. Lieselotte. Can I come out and join you?'

Join her? What's she thinking of? Doesn't she know how the story goes? 'No! Wilhelmina jumped by herself!'

'That's just a story, Doly. All I want to do is come out and talk to you.'

'Don't, Liesi! The ledge isn't safe. You'll fall and kill yourself.'

She can see a hand on the window frame, a foot taking hold on the window sill. The window moves.

'Go back!' Doly is sobbing now. 'You'll push me off balance.'

'Then climb in by yourself.' Liesi's voice is calm, matter-of-fact. 'I'll put my hand out to help you.'

'No!'

'Then I'm coming, Doly. We're blood sisters, remember. We took a solemn vow. Whatever you do, I do. I'm coming now.'

'No, Liesi! Wait! I'll come back in.' She edges towards the window.

'Take my hand.'

She creeps nearer. Lieselotte's strong muscular arm is ready for her. She takes her blood sister's hand, clutches her. They step back into the house Doly's father built. The shelter no longer able to cradle Doly.

CHAPTER 8

Wyckoff, New Jersey, Autumn 1920

'You got the goods, bud?'

'Sure thing. Said I would, didn't I?' He's Emil Dohlen's son, a man who keeps his word.

'How many bottles?'

'What I said. Six.' Moppel has smuggled in two extra bottles which he plans to sell on the side.

'OK. Hand 'em over.'

'They're at the house.' Moppel glows hot. And red. Broad-shouldered Alberto Zuccaroni, Bertrand's friend, is standing on the street corner beyond the church. Two older boys with him. His pals.

'You mean the German preacher's place?'

'It's where I live. The stuff's safe enough. Up in my room.'

'You's one hot number from the loony bin. What the hell use is that?'

'I'll get it to you.'

One of Al's companions walks right up to Moppel. Crowding him. 'Don't give me no horseshit. We give you dough to get the stuff afore you left. A big investment. Time to collect.'

Moppel's sweat drenches his clothes. Bertrand's visiting his parents. In Detroit. So he's on his ownsome. 'Sorry. Couldn't get it to you right off because...'

'Cut the crap. You git back there and fetch it down, buster. Or I'll whale the living daylights out on you.'

'Keep your shirt on, Ed. No good paintin' him in a corner. Wait till the old man's out the way.'

Moppel is terrified. All three boys are older, and bigger, than he is. He's heard stories. Which make what coarse tufts of hair he has left stand on end.

He'll have to soft-soap them. 'Old man Hudwalker preaches regular as clockwork. Seven sharp. The whole family's ordered to attend. I'll sneak out the back and get two bottles.'

'Two? What in hell...'

'Is all I can carry without looking suspicious.'

Al struts back and forth. 'Na. Got a better idea. See the door's left open. We'll git the stuff ourseln.' He grins. 'Save you the trouble.'

'Old holy Joe locks up himself. Keeps the key.'

'You joshing me, kid?'

'Give him a break, Ed. They're hefty bottles. You kin wait a coupla days.'

'How come he can git in if the old man pots the key?' Ed twists Moppel's right ear. 'You kin tell *us* which window you crawl through. Then give us the all clear. You got that, sonny boy?'

'Take it easy, Al. If he were born for shootin', he ain't never gonna drown.

'Good morning, Doly.' Gertrude Hudwalker opens the door to the girls' bedroom without knocking. 'I hope you're up bright and early on this beautiful morning. Ready to say your prayers.'

Doly has taken down the small mirror hanging on the wall at adult height. She's propped it against the chest of drawers. She's examining her naked body to see if her breasts have started to grow. Gabby had breasts at ten. She's almost ten and there's no sign.

She snatches up her dress and holds it out in front of her. 'It's polite to knock before coming into a room.'

'Good grief, Doly. You know Father doesn't approve of vanity.' The smug voice is soft.

'He's not *my* father. My father didn't worry about unimportant things. He got on with the important ones.'

'Your father was nothing but an errand boy when he first came.'

'His first job was sweeping floors. Honest toil at a dime a day. There's

227

something wrong with that?'

Gertrude's eyes flounder. Doly can see she's struck home. 'I suppose not *wrong*. Not very grand though, was it?'

Doly remembers some of the sermons preached from the high pulpit in the St Nicolaikirche. 'Just like Jesus swept the floor for Joseph. Carpenters have a lot of sawdust to sweep up.'

Gertrude advances. Hand raised.

'You going to hit me, Gertrude?' Sweet, piping voice. 'Cuff my ears? Like the good Christian lady you are?'

The young woman holds herself back. 'Good golly, I'm trying to help you, Doly. To show you how to tidy your clothes.' Her lips are so stiff she can hardly speak. 'Look at the state of your half of the room. Gabriele's side is all neat and tidy.'

Pangs of fury ride through Doly now. Not a single one of the Huddies can stand her. They dote on Moppel, the boy wonder. They stomach Gabby, the first-class cookie pusher who sucks up all round. Where the hell does she think that'll get her? 'Don't touch my things.'

'I'm doing my best to get the room straightened out.' Gertrude picks up an apron and begins to fold it. 'Since you won't do it. My mother's not your servant, you know.'

'Don't touch my clothes. If I want to tidy my room, I'll do it myself.' She lets go of the dress she's been holding up, grabs pieces of clothing and throws them to the four corners.

Gertrude drops the apron she's folded. Stands and watches.

Doly displays her beautiful lithe body, tosses abundant hair, flashes violet eyes.

'I'll just have to tell Mother what kind of viper she's harbouring in her home. You have no shame, Dorinda Dohlen. You're not fit to live among Christian folk.'

CHAPTER 9

New Jersey, Summer 1922

The advertisement for the school jumps out at Doly.

Riverside Hall

School for Girls
Located in the lovely town of Paradise, Pennsylvania

Junior College and Junior Conservatory of Music
College Preparatory and Academic Courses

Music, Art, Home Economics, Secretarial
and Expression Courses

Rooms in Suites of Two with Private Bath

Golf, Gymnastics, Hockey, Tennis, Basketball,
Horseback Riding and Boating

MODERATE RATES
Illustrated Brochure by return

A school in a town called Paradise! Where the students enjoy horse-back riding. Boating. This is it—the place she's going to go to school. Riverside Hall has everything a girl could ask for. And it's a good long way from New Jersey.

Doly writes for the brochure. Each morning she meets the mailman, determined to get the delivery before the Hudwalkers see it. Each morning she's disappointed.

It's a hot day. Not summer yet, just a hot day in May. Doly feels lethargic, depressed. Why hasn't Riverside Hall sent her the brochure? Because her handwriting is immature, still dogged by that Gothic German script?

She's done her best to rid herself of the spiky lettering. Sometimes her writing still betrays her origins. Is that why they haven't even replied?

'Letter for you, Doly.'

Gabby running up the stairs. Holding a large envelope with RIVERSIDE HALL in cursive lettering emblazoned on the top. 'Who or what is Riverside Hall?'

Doly snatches the envelope from her sister's hand. 'Nothing to do with you.' She makes for their bathroom. Locks both doors.

There's real treasure inside the envelope. The first pictures show Greek columns gracing entrances to architectural gems. The next page shows a tree-lined leafy drive leading up to a complex of school buildings.

There are loads more pictures. A lounge with a blazing fire, students sitting round. Productions by the Dramatic Club. Long shots of exquisite grounds, horse riding, boating, the school's own golf course. All on the Conococheague River below the dam. There are detailed shots of a Regulation Size swimming-pool, archery, make-up tables in the Dramatic Studio, after dinner coffee served in front of an open fire.

Beautiful Environment Makes for Happy Living

Happy Living. Could she ever aspire to that?

'What are you up to in there, Doly?' Gertrude is banging on the cor-

230

ridor bathroom door. 'You've been hours.'

That damned Gabby. She must have split on her again.

'You feeling sick, Doly?' Ma Huddy's voice.

'Just coming.' She pulls the chain, pushes the brochure back into its envelope and under her blouse, rushes past assembled females and plunges into her bedroom.

Gabby's standing in front of the small mirror. Fiddling with the ribbon in her hair. Always where she's not wanted.

'Aren't you kinda old to wear that hairstyle?'

Her sister's shoulders grow tense. 'What's it to you?' Eyes in the mirror focus on the bulge under Doly's blouse. 'Private, is it?'

Doly goes to her chest of drawers, pulls out a sweater, puts it on. She'll swear she's cold.

Gabby grins. 'Even the Huddopes can't be fooled by that trick. I should have known you weren't *washing* yourself.'

'Mind your own damned business.'

'What's it all about? Promise I won't tell.'

There's an application form inside. It's tempting to ask Gabby to help her. She's very good at English.

'I've answered every single question, Mrs Cartwright. All I need is your signature. Would you sign here?

Walter Hudwalker is Principal of the Grade School, but Doly intends to gloss over that. The form says: 'Headmistress or Principal.' Mrs Cartwright is head of the female staff.

'Why, you've done very well with this, Doly.' Her soft brown eyes smile with surprise. 'Did Mr Hudwalker help you?'

A curious question. Doly scuffs her shoes against each other. 'My sister helped me some.'

'Helped me a little.' Mrs Cartwright's brow is creased as she reads through the form. 'Gabriele does so well at her lessons. She's a true inspiration to all you girls.'

Bloody Miss Goody Two-shoes. Does her homework, tidies up, folds her clothes. Sick-making. It's because of Gabby the Ugly Sisters beat up on her.

'And you've discussed this with your guardian?'

Doly opens her eyes wide. 'You think I should? My Aunt Martha in

Germany, the one who teaches grade school there, said she thought I should spend more time with girls my own age.'

'And Gabby is five years your senior.' Mrs Cartwright is reaching for the telephone.

'If I'm not with Gabby, I won't be able to speak German to anyone.'

'That's fine, Doly. We'll make sure Mr Hudwalker is informed at once. I do believe he's still in the building.'

Doly tears the form out of the astonished teacher's hands. 'I'd rather show him myself. Thank you, Mrs Cartwright. Maybe Father Hudwalker can sign it for me.'

'Father Hudwalker, I wonder if I could ask you something?'

'Why, Doly. You know you can talk to me about anything. I'm looking after you in your dear father's place.'

Doly spent time in the bathroom again. Virtuously. Washing her hands and face, brushing her hair, changing into a fresh blouse. 'I came across this brochure.'

'That so? A magazine, you mean?'

'A prospectus. I found it in the school library. It looks real good.'

'Real is an adjective, Doly. You need the adverb. "Really good" would be correct. I would prefer you use "very good".' Hudwalker takes the thin booklet from Doly's hands and flicks through it. The illustrations which looked so entrancing to Doly don't appear to affect him in the same way.

'Advertising literature. Wonder how it got into our library.' He tosses it on the table in the centre of the room. 'That's a school for the daughters of people who can afford it.' The brochure lands on top of the *Daily Christian Monitor.*

Walter Hudwalker is waiting for Bertrand to bring him the *Weekly Christian News.* Which comes every Thursday afternoon.

'My father would have been able to afford it. He was a millionaire.'

'Why yes, child. But I'm only entitled to let you have the income. The capital is tied up until you come of age. I don't know whether...'

'You can pay the fees on his behalf. He'd want you to. Look, they have a Dramatic Club which puts on Shakespeare plays. See? This picture shows them doing the *Merchant of Venice.* That was Vater's

232

favourite.'

'His favourite was *Macbeth*, Doly.' Elsa Hudwalker is darning by the window.

'It's still Shakespeare. And there's a Poetry Club. I bet they read Byron.'

Hudwalker gets up and opens the house door. To check whether Bertrand is coming yet. It's almost time for the evening service.

'I've filled in the application form, Father Hudwalker. All you have to do is sign here...'

'Not so fast, Doly. I shall have to look into the place. To see whether it's suitable.'

'I'm not going to go on living here with you.' Doly screams at him. She rushes through to the kitchen, pulls out the knife drawer. Metal splattering on clay kitchen tiles sounds like screams.

Doly clutches a sharp, honed vegetable parer in her right hand, pushes her blouse sleeve up to uncover her left wrist. Holds it up with the knife touching it.

'If you won't sign, I'll cut my artery. Then I'll bleed to death.'

Hudwalker walks slowly towards her. 'Taking your own life is a sacrilege. A most grievous transgression against God. The sin of despair which can never be forgiven.'

'I don't give a damn about God. He let my parents die.' Doly sweeps the knife across the exposed arteries. Blood spurts. Dramatically.

'Good grief, the child means it.' Hudwalker steps quickly towards Doly. She points the knife at him. Defiant. Threatening.

'Get something wet to stem the flow, Elsa.'

Bertrand opens the front door, takes in what's going on. He runs towards Doly holding the bundle of newspapers in front of him. Then he chucks them at the knife and grabs hold of Doly, quickly winding a dish cloth around her wrist.

'Son of a bitch. What's all this crap about?'

'Don't use that barnyard language here, Bertrand.'

'Sorry, Uncle Walter.' He's holding Doly tight. 'What's wrong, kid? You wanna go back to Germany?'

'I won't stay here. I hate it here. You're stone boring me to death.'

'Well, I can see you're doing your best to bring some drama into our lives.' He winks at his uncle. 'I've seen worse. She'll live. There you are, Aunt Elsa. Let's get a clean bandage on her, shall we?' He holds the struggling child so she can't move.

Doly tries hard to fight him off. More blood spurts.

Hudwalker's face is a frozen mask. 'All right, Doly. Maybe you're right. This isn't the place for you. If you would just stop shrieking and struggling, I'll sign the form.'

'Swear on the Bible,' Doly screams.

He shuts his Bible, puts his hand on it. 'I swear by this holy Bible that I will sign the form for Dorinda Dohlen to go to Riverside Hall.'

'And you'll pay the fees.'

'And that I will make the necessary funds available from the income arising from Emil Dohlen Senior's estate.'

Doly allows Elsa Hudwalker to dress the gaping slashes.

'There are only two more weeks of school left. I'm sure you'd like to spend the summer vacation in Schwanenbruch.' Walter Hudwalker's voice is without expression. 'All three of you. I'll make suitable arrangements for a transatlantic crossing tomorrow morning.'

CHAPTER 10

Wyckoff, New Jersey, Summer 1922

Gabby sees Bertrand slouching by the school railing, his cap pulled low over his eyes.

'Hi, Gabby.'

'Father Hudwalker says nicknames aren't Christian. You're supposed to call me Gabriele.'

'Jeez, Gabby. You don't have to take notice of that sidewinder outa school. No one else gives a damn.'

'I thought you were his special pet. Always helping out. He says you put half the money from the paper round in the collection box, paint the church every year...'

'Hold on right there. Fella has to get dough where he can.'

'He pays you?'

'Some. I do chores he don't have the stomach for.' He looks as though he's about to say more, then changes his mind. 'Say, you wanna soda?'

Gabby stares at the severely crew-cut hair showing pink scalp and making no concession to the large ears standing at right angles to his skull. 'Soda?'

'Ice cream soda. Down at the drugstore. You bin in this country near on three years. Ain't you never had none?'

'No. You know the Hudwalkers don't eat ice cream. Mother Hudwalker says that if the good Lord wanted us to eat frozen food in summer, he'd let it freeze at night.'

'That's real homely wisdom. 'Cept I don't hold with it none.' He kicks the pedals of his bicycle. 'Put your schoolbag on the saddle. You want vanilla or chocolate? Sometimes they have strawberry.'

Gabby smiles uncertainly. Should she pretend to like ice cream for the sake of a 'date'? If she accepts, is she expected to pay something in return? And if so, what?

'I have a lot of homework...'

'C'mon, Gabby. Won't take long.' He takes her arm and guides her along the sidewalk, looks furtively at the Hudwalker house, then crosses over Main Street. 'Coupla blocks from here, is all.'

'What if they miss me?'

'Say you helped Miss Chanter clear the classroom. Nothin' to it.'

Is this boy really interested in her? In spite of...?

'You're kinda studious, right?'

'I like to read. And I'm still learning English...'

He laughs. 'Who ain't?' He parks his bike, pulls her into a small crowded store with a man behind a high counter at the far end. Behind him is the soda fountain, the source of ice-cream sodas. Bar stools are occupied by several teenagers Gabby doesn't know. Bertrand's fellow students from the Senior Class at High School, she presumes.

'Hi, Bert. Who's the doll?' A swarthy-skinned boy with dark, glistening hair and dressed in a fancy suit strolls up to them. 'Ain't seen you with that broad before.'

Bertrand scowls. 'Hi, Al. This here's my uncle's ward. Don't speak English too well so I help her out.'

'That right?'

'She's from Germany.'

'Figures.' Al looks her over without any embarrassment, dwelling on her face. 'Blue eyes, fair hair. And the creamiest skin I ever seed. Lemme get you a soda, doll.'

'She's my date, Al.'

He explodes with laughter. 'Your date? You walk her over from school and she's your date?' He puts an arm round Gabby's shoulder, stares at two boys sitting on the stools by the centre of the counter and flicks his head. They move. 'Sit right here with me, doll. You wan' chocolate or vanilla?'

Gabby is petrified. Is this the gang leader Moppel talked about? His name is Al, too. And he's the one who organised the sale of the bottles of Schnapps. 'Chocolate', she whispers.

'Hey, Mike. A double chocolate soda for the lady and vanilla for me. And a coupla pieces o' pie.'

'What kind?'

'What kind you got?'

'Apple, peach, blueberry.'

'Make it two peach.' He turns to Gabby. 'So you're from Germany. In Europe, right?'

'Yes.'

'My folks are from Europe. Sicily. Know where that is?' His eyes don't leave her face.

'Yes.'

'You do?'

'We learnt that in Geography at my German school.'

'That so?' His eyes are alert. 'So, waddya know 'bout Sicily?'

Gabby swallows. 'It's an island in the Mediterranean Sea. Off the coast of Italy.'

'The largest island in the Med.' He slits his eyes. 'And?'

'It's very mountainous.' She can't remember anything else. Except politics. 'There's a long history of oppression. The last invasion was in 1860. Garibaldi conquered Sicily and Naples and united them with the rest of Italy.'

'If that ain't straight out o' left field.' He twirls round on the stool until he's facing her again. 'Teached you all that in Germany, right?'

'Yes.'

'How long you bin here?'

'Nearly three years. Except we went back to Germany for a couple of summers...'

'Was you there in the War?'

Is he interested in politics? 'Yes.'

'See any action?'

'Fighting, you mean? No. That was in France and Russia.'

'That so.' He looks uncertain now. 'That's somewhere else, right?'

'France was the western front and Russia the eastern front.'

'Did you hear the guns?'

237

This is more like it. 'We heard the guns from the battle of Jutland. That was a big sea battle fought in the North Sea. Our village is on the shoreline of the north of Germany, bordering the North Sea.'

'That was near you?' His eyes are shining now. 'Some guys have all the luck.' He pushes a tall glass towards her. It's filled with brown ice cream swimming in liquid and topped with whipped cream and what looks like chocolate sauce.

Gabby begins to sip. The combination of soda and chocolate is peculiar. Revolting, if she's honest.

'Say, don't you know nothin'? You drink it through a straw, not from the glass.' A loud suck, a burp. 'Use that long spoon to mix with. Eat what don't melt at the finish.'

The well-known proverb comes into her mind: You need a long spoon to sup with the devil. 'I don't really like ice cream,' she says, staring into the mess of soda bubbles and muddy goo. In memory of the time her tonsils were removed. They tried to lessen the swelling by giving her chunks of ice to suck. From her father's wonderful refrigerator. She's never been able to stomach iced food since.

'Some like it hot.' Al grins, grabs Gabby's shoulders and plants a kiss on her lips.

The ribbon slips from her hair. It's pitifully sparse by now. He stares, lets go.

Gabby doesn't hang about. She rushes out of the drug store, down the street, heedless of people, horses, the occasional car. And rushes into the Hudwalkers' house.

Not long to wait now. The *Albert Ballin* sails for Hamburg next week. Gabby rushes up to her bedroom, barricades the door with a chair, flings herself on her bed. Her mother was right: she can't stay in America, they think about nothing but looks. And she's practically bald now; hideous.

PART 4

SWAN SUMMERS

1922–1925

HERCULEAN POWERS

His name was Mait. And he came to be known as the Hercules of Schwanenbruch. Not that he was particularly strong to start with, but he was full of courage. Fearless in fact.

Something Mait proved one cold inky night. He set out to visit his bride who lived on the far side of the Braake. So he had to negotiate the narrow plank which spanned the turgid water and by the time he got round there it was the witching hour. And pitch dark. No moon, no stars. Nothing to guide Mait but his memory and his sense of balance.

'Get out of my way. I want to cross.' The shriek which came across from the other side was high and inhuman.

Mait knew it had to be a ghost. But he wasn't afraid and he intended to stand firm. Why should he give way to spookish demands?

The bells of Schwanenbruch began to ring the carillon which ushered in the end of the witching hour. If the spectre wanted to get back to his graveyard, he'd have to be quick about it.

'Let me cross first.' Mait heard the ghostly voice cry again. This time the tone was lower and more deferential. 'If you do, I'll give you all my strength.'

That sounded like a good bargain to Mait. He turned on the narrow plank, jumped back to his side of the Braake and let the ghost pass.

The unearthly being kept his word. At next morning's threshing Mait not only beat the grain kernels out of their husks with ease, he chopped the straw into small pieces at the same time. Delighting his master.

His jealous fellow workers tried to play a trick on him. They locked the door on him when he wanted to join them at their midday meal. It didn't stop Mait. A simple blow was enough to split the solid wooden door and he walked right through.

After that his fame spread far and wide. When a cart got stuck in mud the farmer didn't send for more horses, he sent for Mait instead. Lesser men watched in awe as he took the left wheel in his left hand, the right wheel in his right, then heaved the whole cart forward to push the horses on to firmer ground.

And so his reputation grew and spread, from his home county of Land Hadeln to neighbouring Land Wursten. That's when the resident Wurster strong man felt the urge to prove his superiority over the upstart Hercules. He decided to provoke him into a contest of strength.

No sooner thought than done. The Wurster challenger set out for Schwanenbruch and saw a man ploughing a field on his way. So he decided to ask for directions.

'Where does the so-called strong man of Land Hadeln live?' he called out in a mocking voice. To show he feared no one.

The ploughman stopped working, looked around. He lifted up his four-metre-long wooden plough and its chassis with his left hand, as though it were some sort of toy. Then he used it to point towards a nearby farm.

'Thar's where 'un lives, and here's where 'un be.'

But the stranger wasn't listening. He turned tail. And hasn't been back since to defy the strong man in a county obviously consisting of strong men.

CHAPTER 1

Cuxhaven, Summer 1922

'What I would really like to do, Tante Martha, is to become a teacher at Berlin University.' Gabby is sure her aunt will applaud this sentiment, support her. An academic education is what she wanted so badly for herself, after all.

'A professor, you mean?' Tante Martha's small eyes blink, then hood away to disguise her true feelings.

Gabby instantly recognises the disdain, can't understand it. She's done spectacularly well in the Wyckoff school, was always top out of a class of thirty-five.

'You're aiming for the Royal Friedrich Wilhelm University? They have the highest standards.'

'That's the whole point. Ein Mensch ohne Bildung ist ein Spiegel ohne Politur—a human being without education is like a mirror without the shine. I'd like to read philosophy, then teach it.'

'You have to be quite clever to get a degree, Gabby.'

'I'm top of my class in Wyckoff...'

'Didn't you tell me the children there are a year younger than you? To give you a chance to learn English?'

'In Grade School, yes. That was in my first year in America. I've finished my second year of High School now. My English is much better than the other children's. As for History and Geography, there's no comparison.'

'But you're an American, Gabby. You need to study in the country you're going to live in.'

'Just because I was born there? I understand now why Mutti begged Vater to bring her back to Schwanenbruch. I can't stand living in America any more than she could.'

'But that was different, Gabby. Your mother was married to a rich man, in peacetime. Post-war Germany is in a terrible state.'

'I'm not going back, Tante Martha. One third of my father's income is available for me. I want to use it to get a decent education. Not in that isolationist backwater, Wyckoff. I want to live in a cosmopolitan city like Berlin. You're just the person to find me the right crammer to help me pass the entrance tests for the Bismarck-Lyzeum. That's the school which will help me catch up the three years I've lost. Then I can pass my exams to get a place at University.' Her whole body feels the glow of enthusiasm, of setting herself a goal she's longing to achieve. 'What I want to do now is to be educated in the most exciting capital in Europe. Luckily for me it's not that far from Schwanenbruch. I can spend my holidays at home.'

'I see you've got it all worked out. But what about meeting the right young men, Gabby? Don't you want to get married? So many of *our* young men are dead. Don't you think...'

'It's going to be hard for me to find a husband wherever I am. I'd rather plan a decent career, something I want to do. I like studying, Tante Martha. Just like you.'

'There are good schools in America as well, Gabby. And excellent universities. Doly has found a fine boarding-school. I believe their senior school could be right for you.'

'Riverside Hall? A swanky finishing school for snobs.'

'Really, Gabby. You make these sweeping statements. Isn't it a Quaker school? I thought that's why Mr Hudwalker agreed to let Doly go.'

'He isn't a Quaker. He's a Fundamentalist. And the connection between Riverside Hall and William Penn is at best tenuous.'

'You're very severe.'

Tante Martha has, as usual, chosen to take Doly's side. She pretends that the moral blackmail Dorinda is such an expert at isn't the real issue.

'I want a proper education, Tante Martha. I've no intention of wasting my time on riding or amateur dramatics. American women may have been given the vote in 1919, but they don't use it. American schools teach nothing about other cultures. Land of the Free, indeed. A nation which makes drinking alcohol illegal is too restrictive for me. I'm going to live here, in Germany. This is where I belong.'

She's put it a little stronger than she wanted to. But Gabby knows she can't allow conventional thinking to cloud her judgement. If she's to amount to anything at all, she has to make the necessary sacrifices, do the work. She wants to make a difference, contribute to the restoration of a decent Germany. As well as escape the dull fate of a bluestocking.

CHAPTER 2

Schwanenbruch, Summer 1922

'Come with me, Doly. I've got something really special for you.' Wilfred's round face is creased sideways, his eyes practically sunk out of sight.

'For me, Onkel Wilfred? Just for me?'

'Nobody else in the whole world. Let's go into the garden and see what we can find.'

He takes Doly's small hand. She's the only one of Emma's children he has time for. Little beauty, for a start. Looks like a Dresden china doll with that fairy-tale complexion. And those pretty curls frame her face like a halo.

He pushes aside the unwelcome image of his daughter Ulrike. How is it she got the dark colouring from her mother, the damned gene from him? Straight horsehair—thinning rapidly—and hanging down in two scrawny plaits. An intellectual forehead without the brains to go with it. And a viper's tongue.

'Put your hand in my pocket, Doly. See what you can find.' His niece's small fingers digging around his trouser pockets make him smile.

'Carrots, Onkel Wilfred?' Her disappointment is only too clear. 'I can't find anything except a bunch of carrots.'

His wife Gerda whines on about his lack of feeling for his family. Is it his fault Ulrike's a shrew? Doly makes him feel good. 'The tenderest

245

young carrots from my own garden. I grow them myself now that Onkel Palter's no longer with us, my little one.'

'Do you really, Onkel Wilfred?'

He can almost feel the way the dainty lips move over the tiny teeth. 'See how delicate they are, Doly? Taste one. Sweet as can be.'

There's grit on the little roots. Doly's a proper country girl. She brushes it off and munches. Nods. He knows she adores crops straight from the soil, offers her one more. 'But they're not for you.'

'No?' She tilts her head up. He sees she's got his drift. 'They're for someone who really loves carrots, that what you mean?'

'For someone who thinks carrots are as good as caviar.'

The dilapidated garden shed was Fritz Palter's kingdom. Gone, like the old man himself. Replaced by a brand new building. Which Wilfred finished only last week.

The door is stiff. He has to use force. 'In you go, Doly. They're all yours.'

'Kaninchen.' She whirls round in a gig of joy. 'You've bought some bunnies for me.'

'Not plain old bunnies, Doly. Angoras. With white fur as soft as down and as pretty as angels' wings. A mother and her six babies. See how she protects them with her body, tries to hide them from us?'

'Will she scratch if I put my hand in?'

'She won't hurt *you*, Doly. She might get frightened and turn cannibal and eat her babies. So give her a carrot first. Slowly now. Be very, very gentle with her.' He pats Doly's head. 'Now, d'you think you're old enough to look after them by yourself?'

'Of course I am.' Doly offers another tiny carrot through the chicken wire. Then stops. 'But I'm going back to America soon, Onkel Wilfred. To a really good school. So who's going to look after them when I've gone?'

'I've brought all three of you together because we have something very important to discuss. About your future. Futures, I suppose.'

Wilfred is sitting in Emil Dohlen's leather chair in the old man's study. Extraordinary that the man still has so much influence six years after his death. Not a single piece of furniture has been moved. The classics have been restored from the turret room, contemporary books catalogued. Gabby's even made an inventory of what she calls the library. Quite a bluestocking she's turned out to be. Just like Martha. Knows there's very little chance of a husband, so what's left? Books.

'Has Herr Hudwalker written to say I can stay in Germany? Go to school in Berlin?'

'All in good time, Gabby.' Wilfred lights a big Havana and puffs at it.

Doly's little body turns rigid. 'I'm going to Riverside Hall. Herr Hudwalker signed the papers and swore on the Bible.' Yesterday's playful little kitten has eyes hard as pebbles, determined chin stuck out.

'Calm down now, Doly. Not so fast. There have been a few... developments.' Where the hell has Martha got to? He told her he wouldn't be able to handle the girls on his own. For all her pretty ways, Doly's as sharp as a whippet. With fangs. She'll tear herself to shreds if she's not careful. 'Come and sit on my lap, sweetheart. Look what I've got in my pocket for you today.'

'He swore on the Bible. Promised God.' Doly stamps her feet. 'He can't go back on his word to God.'

To look at her, who'd ever guess she's so tricky? 'Don't worry, Doly. You'll be going to Riverside Hall. Herr Hudwalker isn't going back on his word, I guarantee it.' Wilfred gets up, gathers her rigid little body in his arms.

She snuggles beside him in the big chair, but her voice is loud. 'The *Albert Ballin* docks three days before the new semester starts. Just in time.'

He strokes her hair. 'There's one thing you forgot to check, Dolikins: Riverside Hall takes young ladies from the age of fourteen. It's a High School. Juniors and up. You're only eleven.'

'Eleven and a half.'

'Not fourteen, my pet. And there's a waiting-list as well.'

She tries to squirm away but he holds her fast. 'That's not fair, Onkel Wilfred.'

'Fair doesn't come into it. That's how it is.'

'He swore to God and he's lying.'

'No, Doly. Tante Martha and I have read the Prospectus ourselves. You were so taken up with the pictures, you didn't look at that part.

247

And Herr Hudwalker wasn't aware until the school wrote to him.' He sees Gabby's nostrils widen, her mouth twitch. 'He couldn't tell you himself because, you see, by then you were already over here.'

'He promised...'

'And he's keeping his promise. He's put your name down for September 1925.'

'1925?' Her jaw is wobbling. She controls it. 'That's years away. And I'll be fourteen. I'm not going back to that stupid Grade School...'

'No, Doly. Herr Hudwalker and I discussed the whole situation.'

'How could you? He isn't here.'

'I telephoned his office at the school. I'm your German guardian, Doly. He is your American one. We think it best if you go to the Cuxhaven Lyzeum. We've engaged an English governess to make sure you keep up your English.'

Doly is calmer now. 'I can live here? Look after Agnes and her babies?'

'And you can keep all six if you want to.' He stands, cigar in mouth, hands in pockets. 'And Herr Waldeck will make one of his ponies available for you to ride. You can stable him at the Waldecks' place.'

'You mean I can ride with Lieselotte? Every day?'

'Lüdingworth's too far on schooldays. You can exercise the horses on Sundays and during the holidays. Yes.'

'Is Tante Martha going to live here with Doly?' Gabby's voice is controlled. Laden with the unsaid.

Wilfred shakes his head. A tactical error. Quickly puts on his best smile. 'Tante Martha lives in Cuxhaven. She's in charge of Doly's and Moppel's German schooling. Miss Jennings will live here.'

'That's the new governess I suppose. And the house? Who's going to manage that?' Gabby's calm voice spells trouble.

'Quite the little Hausfrau, aren't you Gabby?' He puffs again. He takes a gulp from the beer glass on the table beside Emil's chair. 'Rula, Ursula and Minni will see to the domestic duties. I've engaged Frau Reinisch as housekeeper.'

'And what about my education? Is that going to be sacrificed because there isn't enough money to pay for Berlin as well as running the villa?'

That girl's more astute than he realised. Presumably gets her information from the newspapers she devours every day. 'There's far more money if you stay in Germany. Herr Hudwalker and I discussed it. The Mark's been weak against the dollar for some time now...'

'And in August it crashed.'

'You're very well informed, Gabby. But you're right. Relatively few dollars will buy a lot of education over here. It makes good business sense for you to stay.' And good for the man who changes the dollars into Marks. Well, what's wrong with that?

'So I *can* go to Berlin?'

'Martha has looked into it all on your behalf. I'm afraid you're way behind by German standards. We've arranged for you to stay with a family called Meinzer. And to attend a crammer to help you catch up. If you pass their entrance exams, you can go to the Bismarck-Lyzeum next September.' Wilfred puffs a smokescreen. 'Your years in America haven't helped academically as far as Germany is concerned. We're doing our best, Gabby. At least you'll be living in Berlin.'

Moppel has remained silent. His face turns from his sisters to his uncle and back again. '*I* want to go back to the United States. I like it there and High School will be fine by me.'

Wilfred lifts Doly out of the chair. 'Let's all go over to my house now. Tante Gerda has made a splendid Butterkuchen. I'm sure you remember her special cake with the sugar coating. And I know Ulrike is waiting for you.'

He blinks at Moppel, to let him know there'll be a man-to-man talk later.

THE WAGES OF SCORN

Rungholt was a port on the North Sea coast. Hundreds of years ago. Until de groote Mandränke, the greatest flood ever recorded, reclaimed it for the sea.

Rungholt was blessed with fertile fields around its town and populated by clever merchants. It became richer than any town around it. That's when it forgot about God and thought only about Mammon. And brought a terrible catastrophe on itself caused by the sacrilegious behaviour of its benighted citizens.

One night a party of young men sought out the largest sow in the town. They poured beer down her throat until she was drunk. Her moans and groans sounded just like those of a man or woman in their last agony. Then they laid her in a big four-poster bed and covered her with blankets. At that stage they sent for the pastor. To give the dying citizen his last rites.

The pastor came running to do his Christian duty. He was both outraged and dismayed when he found himself praying with a drunk pig. Rightful anger made him turn on the pranksters to tell them the good Lord's opinion of their misdeeds.

They laughed at him, poured beer into his chalice, made him drink until he, too, was drunk.

The pastor called on his Maker to avenge him, to rid the world of the local Sodom and Gomorrah known as Rungholt. As every Christian knows, prayers are always answered. The good Lord appeared to the pastor. He warned him to leave the town that very night.

It was the dark tempestuous night before the greatest North Sea coast flood ever recorded, the one when Rungholt disappeared under the sea for ever. And no living soul except the pastor was saved.

CHAPTER   3

Schwanenbruch, Summer 1922

Wilfred beckons Moppel to join him in his office across the courtyard.
For privacy. There's men's work to be done. Which is why they stride
away from the tea-party with strong virile expressions. Not meeting
Gabby's eager eyes, discouraging her from following them.

'You've certainly made a fine mess of things, young Emil.'

'Mess? What mess?'

Nephew and uncle try to outdo each other in guileless looks. So far
there is no winner.

'Getting in deep with a gang.'

'What gives you that idea?'

'D'you take me for an idiot?' Wilfred's solid right arm, sinewed by
years of hoisting sacks of grain, threatens, flexes into a battering ram.
He swings, an iron fist crashing into Moppel's shoulder as the boy
skips aside to save his face.

His uncle's in no mood for games, clearly intends to take the heavy
line. Jousting is useless when the antagonist refuses to play the game.

'You're talking about the take.'

'What the hell...?'

Moppel, keeping out of arm's way, takes in the folly of prevarication.
His normal weapon of choice. He changes to shifting blame. 'Bertrand's
idea. He's Hudwalker's nephew. He's the one put me up to it.'

'Naturally not your fault. Poor little orphan boy who couldn't help himself. Blackmailed into it by a sixteen-year-old. All of two years older.'

'I had to find an outlet for the Schnapps.'

'Really smart move to get involved with a bootlegging gang in New Jersey. Maybe not quite up to Chicago standards but not a bad start.' Wilfred's snorts are loud enough to scare the housemartins nesting in the eaves of the barn beside his office.

'C'mon Onkel. You know the score. Just a gang of kids.'

Wilfred crashes through to the office, beckons to Moppel to sit, slumps into his chair behind his desk and pours a large measure of Schnapps into one of two small glasses standing on it by his ledger. 'Your tipple too, if I'm not mistaken?' He holds the bottle out.

'Not to drink, no. I prefer beer, if you want to know.'

'That so. So we must try to accommodate your tastes, mustn't we? Mr Bigshot Bootlegger.' Wilfred twists round, takes a beer mug from a shelf behind him, opens the spigot on a small barrel and fills the mug to the brim.

'Rum-runner.'

'What?'

'Bringing alcohol into the country is called rum-running. Bootlegging is selling redistilled industrial alcohol.'

Wilfred's fist shoots out. Moppel is ready for him, ducks out of the way. 'Makes no difference what you damn well call it. Gescheite Hähne frisst der Fuchs auch—the fox gobbles up clever cocks as easily as stupid ones.'

'So I sold a coupla bottles to some buddies.' Moppel drinks some beer, wipes his upper lip. 'It was all agreed. You had your cut. Or is age affecting your memory?'

Wilfred's eyes retreat behind inflamed cheeks. 'No need to worry on my account. I come from a line of long-lived men. It was a business deal as I remember it.'

'Still cash in your pocket.'

'Cash, fine. Blood money is a horse of a different colour.'

'Dammit, Onkel Wilfred. That's melodramatic enough to sound like one of Gabby's trumped-up stories.'

'Not stories. Hoods. Gang members living in the neighbourhood. *Hudwalker's* neighbourhood at that. Poor old saintly duffer could hardly bring himself to talk about it.'

'What in hell are you getting at?'

'The 'buddies' you did business with. Don't know about America, but not my idea of sidekicks; mean murdering hoodlums. Gangsters.'

Moppel refills the mug and begins to sip. 'Gimme a break here.'

'Bertrand is dead.'

The beer pours out of Moppel's mug but misses his mouth and trickles down his shirt front. He stares at it. A dark liquid staining the white material, spreading. 'Dead? What d'you mean, dead?'

'As in buried.'

'He had an accident?'

Wilfred has lit a pipe. He puffs smoke between himself and his nephew. 'No doubt his killers look at it that way. He was told to arrange more imports via you. When he said you weren't coming back, they took it amiss.'

Doesn't figure. Bertrand wasn't in on the liquor deal. 'So what? I told 'em he wasn't in on it. Bert knew the score on that.'

'He was due to fork out protection money for the rents.'

'Yeah?' Moppel steadies his hand. Swallows beer. Looks his uncle in the eye. 'How d'you make that out?'

'Usual way. Interchange of words. Mixture of German and English between Hudwalker and myself. That's becoming quite a habit, though the poor old duffer wasn't in much of a talking mood. His nephew, after all.'

'I mean, how d'you know all that if Bertrand's dead?'

Wilfred nods. 'Young hoodlum by the name of Al. Questioned by the police. Sang a little tune. Seems Bertrand told the gang he was taking your place. In your absence.'

Sweat is pouring off Moppel's face. 'My place?'

'Collecting your father's rents on Herr Hudwalker's behalf. I take it that worthy gentleman isn't keen on visiting the Lower East Side himself. Even though the rents bring in a large slice of the estate's income. Including the guardian's fees.'

'Nothing new. Hudwalker agreed Bert and I should collect together.'

Wilfred draws deep on his pipe. 'I know. But he didn't come up with the protection money because you'd left him high and dry. Where was he going to get it?'

The sweat is now pouring into Moppel's eyes. He fishes out a handkerchief, soaks it with the first wipe across his almost hairless scalp. 'They had nothing on him, he wasn't in on the protection racket. I kept those deals to myself.'

'They didn't buy that. That's how they put it in the jargon Mr Hudwalker passed on to me.'

'Why not? Didn't the chumphead tell 'em to wait till I got back?'

'That was the problem. Seems he told them you weren't coming back and that he was interested in stepping into your shoes. Taking over.'

Motherfucker went out on a limb. Moppel blinks at his uncle. No sense spilling to a civilian that he'd promised Bert a slice of the action. In return for the territory on Long Island where clean-living Bertie did some collecting of his own.

'Without, apparently, your talents.' Wilfred downs his drink, pours more. 'I have to give it to you, young Emil. I never dreamed you had that kind of nerve.'

'Just business, Onkel Wilfred. Things have changed since my father's time. Well, since Prohibition. Let in the gangsters, just like you said.'

'Some business.'

'You gonna let me in on the whole story, or what?' Moppel kicks at chaff clinging to a discarded sack.

'They found him spreadeagled on the floor, his torso covered in small round burns. Cigarettes, cigarillos. Too many for his body to cope with.'

Moppel pulls out the sodden handkerchief, mops more liquid. 'Where?'

'The East Side People's Bath. Where else?'

Moppel frowns. He can't work out a connection. 'East Side People's Bath? What the hell's that have to do with anything?'

Wilfred scans his nephew's face. 'Bertrand held out on *you* on that one, did he?'

'No doubt you'll enlighten me.'

'Your father's most valuable Manhattan property. He built it in the block where most of his tenement houses are. You've been to those places. Seen how it is.'

He's seen the poverty, the brutality. What the hell has that to do with it? 'Seen what?'

'Only a few have running water. A single toilet is shared between ten families. No bathtubs.'

'What's the big deal? The villa's the only place with a plumbed-in bathtub in the whole of Schwanenbruch.'

'But we're not crowded into filthy tenements surrounded by choking traffic fumes.'

'You saying my father built a public bath for people to use?'

Wilfred nods. 'He charged a nominal fee per family. It was one of his charitable enterprises.' His eyes sink out of sight. 'Because of that, Mr Hudwalker collected the monies from there himself, to deposit in the right place. He asked Bertrand to help him out there this summer.'

Moppel wriggles, a mackerel caught on a hook. 'That's where they found Bert? In a public bath?'

'In one of the locker rooms of the East Side People's Bath. No one heard him scream.' He pours another Schnapps. Moppel holds out his mug for some. 'Hudwalker says he can't take the risk of having you back.'

'Sure.' Not just a question of the cops, or the risk; he can hardly expect much of a reception from Bertrand's uncle at any time from now on.

'You have to retire from business for a while, Nephew. Lie low. Give it a couple of years until the police close their file.' He stands. 'Just remember. Eine Katze, die den Kanarienvogel gefressen hat, kann drum noch nicht singen—just because the cat's swallowed the canary doesn't mean it knows how to sing like one.'

Moppel kicks at the floor, sending chaff flying. He's exiled in Germany. Just like Big Daddy during the War.

CHAPTER 4

Berlin, Autumn 1923

'It is morally indefensible for a few people to 'own' enormous assets
while others are dying of starvation. The only decent thing to do is to
embrace Marx.'

'Wonderful theory, Jonah. Except you're leaving out human nature.
The economic organisation of trade depends on ownership.' Gabby's
face flames pink, her eyes shine like sparklers. She's found the kind
of friends she's been searching for all her life. In the unlikely setting
of a Berlin café. Not, as she thought before she got here, a place for
coffee and cakes or somewhere to gorge on many of the hundred or
more newspapers which flourish in this city. Not even just a spot to sip
Schnapps while watching the artistic world go by. A haven for political
dissidents.

'Naturally there has to be social organisation, if that's what's
worrying you. Not an enormous problem. Hold all property in
common. Attribute ownership to the whole community.'

'And that's supposed to work?' Scornful eyes blaze at the seventeen-
year-old sitting opposite Gabby in the Romanisches Café. She
stumbled across the hideous neo-Romantic building with its glaring
lights only a week ago. And it has changed her life. Because it's one
of the Künstlerkneipen—artists' hangouts—in the world of Berlin
where students, writers, painters, artistes and political activists gather.
The unofficial university where the floor is bare boards, the furniture

scuffed and the talk subversive. 'We're talking about human beings. Original sin.'

Jonah Schnatter's small almost feminine hands play with the cutlery. He sets it straight. Dissatisfied, he straightens it again. 'We're all members of the human race. With free will. We can decide whether we wish to do our fellow man down or treat him with dignity.' He stirs the traditional breakfast of two eggs in a glass. It has to last him all day.

The Romanisches Café is divided into three sections. One large room, known as the swimming-pool, is where established artists like George Grosz and Emil Orlik, and writers like Bertold Brecht and Alfred Kerr, hold court at their Stammtisch—a table reserved especially for them. A staircase leads off to the gallery. Gabby is intrigued by the chess tables set up there. She's always wanted to learn to play. She's been told that chess masters of the highest calibre come here to practise their game. The poetess Else Lasker-Schüler, whose onetime brother-in-law Emanuel is a world grandmaster, often plays here. Gabby stands and watches. In awe. She absorbs the rules and dreams of playing.

A second room, the paddling-pool, is the meeting place for budding writers and poets. Some are incapable of working anywhere else. The Café is the first stop for literary hopefuls arriving in Berlin. A place for networking.

'Tut tut, Jonah. You're forgetting Lothrop Stoddard's *The Revolt Against Civilization: The Menace of the Under Man*.'

'Never heard of it.'

'Published last year. Great new scientific theories about the Under Man, what Theodor Fontane called the Untermensch. You know: the congenitally sick, the insane, homosexuals, Slavs. And dirty Jews, it goes without saying.' Friedrich Raufensthal has trouble accommodating his long legs. He stretches them under the little round table and out into the walking space on the other side. He's as tall as Jonah is short. Tall and Small, Gabby has christened them. Her 'Berlin Circle'.

The mixture of genuine writers and dilettantes provides the atmosphere tourists flock to see and Gabby's landlady would abhor. The bearded scribblers in tweed jackets and bow ties, the slinky women with bobbed hair smoking cheroots, the artists sketching ephemeral

257

masterpieces on paper napkins—each one of them gives Gabby an enormous thrill, a sense of belonging she's never had before.

And she's put faces to famous names: T.S. Eliot, Robert Musil, Sinclair Lewis, André Gide.

'What about the Wedekind? The *Erdgeist*'s playing next week. Shall I try for tickets?' A challenge, not an invitation, from Friedrich.

'Matinée or evening?' Gabby prevaricates. 'You know I have to ask my landlady before I'm allowed out at night.'

'You're going to have to talk seriously to the worthy Meinzers, Gabby. Their quaint idea that sexual activity is tied to hours of darkness will have to be dispelled. Somehow. Jonah and I have undertaken your cultural education. We can't have the bourgeoisie interfering. Lesson one is attending the best of Berlin theatre. Lesson two is more advanced. And much more fun. Going to the cabaret at the *Wilde Bühne* and the *Grössenwahn*. The best in the whole world.'

Gabby lifts the empty coffee cup to hide her thoughts.

'If you want more coffee, order some.'

Jonah's damn sharp. But songs about sex? That's Doly's style, not hers. 'Cabaret? I don't think the Meinzers will agree to…'

'Please. No crap. You're chicken.' Friedrich laughs good-naturedly. 'Why choose Berlin, in that case? Think you'll lose your precious mental virginity? We're not talking sex here. We're talking politics.'

'You're telling me that cabaret isn't about sexual innuendo? That it's a hotbed of political discussion? At the forefront of political debate?'

'Exactly. Couldn't have put it better myself.' Friedrich arranges his features to look pompous. 'The University of Free Thought. That's precisely what I'm telling you.'

The young man's long face reminds Gabby of Lieselotte's gelding Flitsi. But the only grey evident in Friedrich is his irises. The rest is vibrant colour. The elder son of an impoverished family which traces its roots to nobility. Which hinders rather than helps in today's world. His father is unemployable, his mother is working as a governess to keep the family from starving.

'Those two are Berlin's jewels.' Jonah raises his cup in a toast. 'Political, cultural *and* sexual. What more can a Gabby ask?'

'Spiritual, Jonah. You're leaving out the spiritual.'

'When your father is one of the most fervent zaddikim, it's what you tend to do.' He sees they have no idea what he's talking about. 'Zaddikim are holy men. Of the pious Jewish kind.'

'We're off to the *Grössenwahn* tonight. Claire Waldoff's performing. The real flowering of the Weimar Republic. Coming?'

'Claire Waldoff's the one who sings *Zieh dich aus, Petronella, zieh dich aus*—Get 'em off, Petronella, strip 'em off?'

'New version on me,' he laughs. 'But you mean you've heard of her?'

'My sister and her friends sing that song all the time. And act it out. They prance around undressing.' Gabby's voice is full of virtuous condemnation.

Jonah looks interested. 'Until they're naked?'

It embarrasses her even to think of it. 'Good as.'

'Well, well. Naughty goings-on in the marshes. I hope you'll introduce us.'

'You wouldn't like my sister.'

'Sounds as though I might really take to her.' Friedrich stalks between the tiny tables. Removing his coat, his shoes, his socks.

Gabby looks round. Furtively. She wonders what Bertolt Brecht and Hugo Lederer will think.

'For God's sake, Gabby. Stop being so damned prim. Live a little.'

Easy for him to say. What man is going to go for her? Her skimpy hair is not just ruining her looks. Unless she wears a hat, she's practically a freak. It's fortunate the fashions favour hats, and that women can wear them indoors. But are they proper dress for the cabaret? 'I'll have to ask the Meinzers.'

'Don't miss out, Gabby.' Friedrich shrugs his coat on again. 'Claire goes in for blatant sex. She's lower class. That's what you've heard, isn't it?'

Her inhibitions aren't due to prudery. She's terrified of being man-handled and—exposed. Even the thought of the possible embarrassment makes her squirm. Is the audience expected to participate? 'So it isn't true?'

'You really are a stupid little prig. What's wrong with sex? The woman is alive. Big, earthy, a bloody genius.' His snort is the clang of an ambulance bell. 'If you think it's only about sex, you're a greater

259

fool than I took you for. Sex is the rim. The hub is about power. In particular, the manipulation of party politics to gain personal power.'

'You're saying cabaret's the place to sharpen up political awareness?' Gabby laughs. 'I know I'm a country girl, but I'm not that naïve.' But the idea does excite her.

'QED. The most subversive statements of our times are made on the cabaret stage. It's the only safe place.'

'Safe?' Little does he know she's thinking about losing her hat, not her virginity.

'If you want to be an accepted member of society. Prevailing beliefs turn into self-evident truths. Remember Galileo supporting the earth revolving round the sun theory?' He sees she may not get the point. 'At a time when the Church maintained the sun revolves around the earth. Poor fool paid for that opinion with house arrest for the rest of his life.' He grins. 'The fact that he was right was neither here nor there. Except posthumously.'

She returns to the attack. 'That was science, not politics.' Triumphant.

'You're kidding. Naïve is right, Gabby. Without its nanny the great majority can't cope with anything contrary to current notions. However obviously nuts. Cabaret pokes sharp instruments into establishment balloons. Anti-Semitism, for example. It's been rife in Europe for centuries.'

She remembers Schwanenbruch's attitude to Samuel Nussbaum. Pork-hater, they called him. She's often wondered what they call the afflicted members of her family behind their backs. Baldies, of course; but she suspects much worse. Degenerates who shouldn't be allowed to breed, probably. 'You mean the odd disturbance.'

'I mean pogroms. Ever since Christianity established itself as the moral order, Jews were, are, the sworn enemies. Killers of Christ.'

'That hardly applies to present-day Jews. And Christ was a Jew himself.'

'That's conveniently lost sight of. He was the Christ. Christian attitudes are responsible for endemic anti-Semitism in the whole Christian world. Have been, from early on.'

'That's quite some statement.' Gabby finds herself fighting for breath. Can that really be true?

Jonah bangs his spoon on the table. 'Only because you're applying logic. Because you're hooked on the premise of common sense. Which is completely beside the point.' His right hand touches his cheek beside his ear. Where curly black hair is cut short. 'Take my family as an example. They are Hasidim, named from the Hebrew word meaning pious. And don't we all know it. They wear black garb adapted from medieval Polish society. So no one can mistake them, presumably.'

'They have every right to wear whatever they like. As long as it's decent.'

Jonah laughs. 'I presume you mean modest. They're that all right.' He stares into his coffee cup. 'They refuse to shake hands with women in public, let alone indulge in the outlandish custom of kissing their hands. The Law Codes forbid such intimate and immodest behaviour.'

'Really? They refuse the usual form of greeting? I suppose that could be taken to be offensive.'

Jonah's palms are curled into balls. 'They go further. We're a hirsute people. Leviticus says "You are not to round off your hair at the edges nor trim your beard." So they sport curly ear locks and long beards. Now, straight up, can you be surprised when they're picked on?'

Gabby has wondered about these strange people. Been irritated herself. Having smooth hairless skin makes hirsute people unattractive to her. She shies away from the sight, and feel, of so much hair. Physically; she knows her feelings are irrational. But she still has them. And if she, who's an outcast, can feel this way what hope is there for 'normal' people? 'I thought Berlin is supposed to be the meeting point of European culture and artistic expression. That it's a refuge for oppressed minorities.'

'So they all say. Be honest. Doesn't their pious zeal put you off? It does me.'

She has to be honest. 'It puts me off personally, yes. But not as far as my behaviour towards them is concerned. Anyway, the bully-boy storm troopers go after other Jews as well, even those who are careful not to make themselves easy targets.'

'Because they can get away with it. Jews are under enormous pressure right now. They're identified with evil, which the colour of their dark hair underlines. They're seen as opposed to fundamental Weimar goals, demonised. Of course it's nothing new for German society to be anti-Semitic. What's changed is the virulence.'

Gabby leans her elbows on the table. Feels sick. Because she too is outside society. A monstrosity, a pariah. For no better reason than that she lacks a woman's crowning glory. What people feel about Jews they could just as easily feel about her. And probably, almost certainly, do.

'I suppose you think *Wilde Bühne* means Wild Stage?' Friedrich asks, nudging her knee with his to draw her attention.

'Well, doesn't it?' She brings her mind back to her friends. Who don't conform. Friedrich does it for the hell of it. Jonah is a Jew. Like her lack of hair, being Jewish is a genetic trait. He cannot escape it, not even by changing his religion.

'Literally, yes. My interpretation is Free Expression.'

'And *Grössenwahn* doesn't mean megalomania, I suppose?'

'It means the lust for power, Gabby. That's what politics is all about. Not saving your fellow man or feeding the poor. Power; naked, ugly power.'

'It is?' Gabby feels dizzy. Punch drunk. Surely the great men of history: Julius Caesar, Napoleon Bonaparte, Alexander the Great, Genghis Khan... Is that what she's thirsting after? Power because she so often feels powerless?

'Believe it or not, that's how it is. Last chance. Are you coming with us or not?'

Politics at the cabaret. Can he be serious? Of course he is. It's why she's having the time of her life with Tall and Small. Small enjoys clowning around. But Tall, it's not his style to kid her. 'I wouldn't miss it for anything.'

'That's our girl. We'll go Dutch. Much as we'd like to, we can't afford to pay your share.'

She knows that's true. And is flattered Tall thinks enough of her to admit it.

'That's the least of my worries. If it helps, I'll be glad to bring extra cash.'

'Absolutely not.'

'But I can't come tonight. I have to introduce you to the Meinzers first. Tell them you're taking me to the theatre.'

'The theatre?'

'Lesson one, remember? Wedekind's *Erdgeist*. Goethe would be better but Wedekind will have to do. I'll talk to them tonight. Let's say tea around four tomorrow. Both of you come.'

'So there is a price, one way or another?' Jonah chortles as he savours the last spoonful of his eggs.

She giggles. 'Only in eating cake.' She watches Jonah sip his eggs, savouring every tiny morsel. 'Wear your most bourgeois clothes. The ones you'd wear applying for a job.'

Jonah brays like a hyena scenting a carcass. 'What d'you take me for? I've just got through telling you. My formal clothes really would upset your keepers.' He wears ordinary clothes and his hair is trimmed. But it is dark and curly. And his long nose has a noticeable bump.

'Don't be so hidebound. Borrow or steal something. Your father's a tailor, didn't you say?'

'My father lend me clothes?' He roars with laughter. 'My family disowned me yonks ago.'

Her foot beats an impatient tattoo. 'A friend.'

'My god, Gabby. What are you trying to do to me? It's a sacrifice I can only make because we're both revolutionaries under the skin.'

CHAPTER 5

Berlin, Autumn 1923

'This is Friedrich Raufensthal, Frau Meinzer. Baron Raufensthal's elder son. The family owned land before the War.' Gabby drops her voice dramatically. 'Their property was in what is now the Polish corridor.' She can see her landlady has no idea what she's talking about. 'The territory which divides East Prussia from the rest of Germany.'

A blank smile.

'Laid down in the Treaty of Versailles.'

'Ah. That terrible War.' Frau Meinzer beams at Tall. 'Herr Baron.'

He clicks his heels. 'My father is still alive, Gnädige Frau.'

'Herr von Raufensthal.'

Gabby can tell Friedrich is about to correct the 'von'. She kicks him. Unobtrusively.

'So that wretched War deprived you of your estates? Let's hope those appalling wrongs will be righted soon. We've lost so much which was rightfully ours.' She beams at Friedrich, the epitome of the blond blue-eyed young Aryan. 'Delighted to meet you.'

'And this is Hans Schnatter, Frau Meinzer. His father is a minister of religion.' Gabby isn't lying. Just putting a helpful angle on things. After all a German form of Jonah is Johann, colloquially Hans. Which sounds so much more—appropriate.

'Herr Schnatter.' Frau Meinzer's expression is guarded. 'A minister of religion? You mean a pastor?' She giggles. 'Well, he can't be a

264

Catholic priest. They aren't allowed to marry.'

What Jonah lacks in Teutonic looks he more than makes up for in manners. 'Küss die Hand, Gnädige Frau.' He presses a wet kiss on the lady's outstretched hand, puts on his best smile. Showing all his teeth. 'A lay preacher, Gnädige Frau. He likes to go his own way.'

Frau Meinzer motions them towards her Biedermeier sofa while surreptitiously wiping the back of her hand. 'Sit down, gentlemen, do. A slice of Butterkuchen, Herr von Raufensthal?'

Her thoughts are clearly grooved in hostess duties. The squeaking voice makes it obvious she's delighted. She takes it Gabby's brought the cream of Berlin society right into her salon.

Gabby knows she can relax because her hostess's butter cake can't be bettered by anyone. Not even by Frau Helland in the apartment below. And she serves it on the finest Meissen. Covered with the dainty doyleys shown in the *Berliner Illustrirte*—her favourite illustrated magazine.

'Wonderful coffee.' Jonah wolfs down a third slice of cake. 'You are a true German Hausfrau, Gnädige Frau. Just like my mother.'

Friedrich's explosive fit of coughing is quite alarming.

'My goodness, Herr von Raufensthal. I'm afraid the cake is quite crumbly. A glass of water, perhaps?'

Berlin, Winter 1923/24

'Good evening, ladies and gentlemen. And children. We always welcome children to our show.'

Children? Gabby looks around. There are no children to be seen. What is the funny little man in the tuxedo talking about?

'And just to keep the little darlings happy, Madame Rosa will sing her special song: *Oh to be a child again.*'

The orchestra bursts into raucous noise. A chorus of girls dressed in Bismarck-Lyzeum school attire dances on to the stage. An elegant red-headed woman, Madame Rosa herself, follows in absurdly high heels.

We brave Germans felt the lust for battle not so long ago. Heil!
Our womenfolk impassioned by the wild courage of our men.Heil!
Thunderbolt and lightning were companions in mortal combat. Heil!
Brave Huns that we are, it is the way we fight.Heil!

Madame Rosa discards her high heels and puts on a pair of children's boots. She sings another verse, after which she throws away her feather boa and replaces it with a scarf. Yet another verse, and she removes her red wig to show two fat blonde plaits.

The audience responds by stomping their feet and clapping at each *Heil*. They push their right arms angled up and held straight out in greeting. As though in a military parade or a political rally. National Socialists in a Beer Hall Putsch.

> *Let's all get back our innocence, turn into kids again.Heil!*
> *Let's gambol on our beautiful green fields again.Heil!*

There's thunderous applause as the chorus leaves the stage in a school column of two by two. Dressed in scout uniform to imitate military uniform. Followed by the singer now dressed as a child. In a black scout's uniform. With a brown shirt. False eyelashes and vivid red nails contrast absurdly with the outfit.

BRAINSTORM

The people of Bramel, noted for their brawn rather than their brains, decided they needed a new well. Which, naturally, involved digging a deep hole. And when they'd finished it they were left with an enormous heap of excavated earth. Which, they felt, did not look good. And it would get in their way.

The assembled villagers stood around scratching their heads, wondering how to get rid of the unsightly pile. Until one of them had a brilliant idea. 'The simplest solution,' he told them earnestly, 'is to dig another hole. Then we can spade the earth into that.'

His companions thought it a wonderful idea. They set to with a will and dug another hole. A deeper one. And then they filled it with the soil from the first hole. The only snag was that they were left with an even bigger heap of earth.

Their brilliant adviser was clear what the problem was. 'You didn't make the second hole big enough,' he told them. 'You should have made it twice as wide as well as twice as deep.'

267

CHAPTER 6

Hamburg, Summer 1925

'How are we supposed to get there? We don't even know where it is.' Lieselotte sits in the First Class compartment in the train from Schwanenbruch to Hamburg, looking forlorn.

'Easy. We'll drive up in style.' Doly signals to a porter. He takes two small cases from the luggage rack and loads them on to his cart.

'Taxi, porter.' The syllables bark. Out of nervousness.

'Yes, Gnädiges Fräulein.' He hails a cab. Resigned eyes lift. 'Where did you want to go?' He's loaded the luggage, waits patiently.

'The Reeperbahn. A small hotel.'

He turns. Slow motion. 'Pardon, Fräulein? I think you've got hold of the wrong street. Got an address, have you?'

'It's where we want to go.' This time the syllables splutter. And spit. Doly tries hard to sound older than her fourteen years.

He nods. 'Of course, Fräulein. And the name of the hotel?'

'Didn't you hear what I said? A small one. *Any* small hotel.' Sweat glistens on Doly's face. Racing blood colours it. She puts on her grande dame voice, a loud and throaty imitation of Tante Hannah at her worst. 'If this driver doesn't know of one, change our luggage over to another cab.'

'Steady on now, Fräulein. He knows the hotels all right. I think you've made a mistake...'

'For God's sake, man.' Doly leans her head towards the driver. 'Take us to a hotel in the Reeperbahn. A small one. Discreet.'

'Certainly, Fräulein. Jump in.'

Doly throws change at the porter. It drops on the pavement with a clang. He's turned on his heel and doesn't look back.

Lieselotte climbs into the cab, motions Doly in. She settles back. 'Told you there's nothing to it.'

The taxi lurches through crowded evening streets and ends up in a cramped one. The driver stops at a dimly-lit hotel entrance.

'This do you?'

'Is this the Reeperbahn?'

'Just round the corner, Fräulein. Here for work, are you?'

Doly hands money through the window. 'The fare.'

He stays in his cab and lets them carry their own cases. Doly puts her hand through his window. 'Take this. A little extra for your trouble.'

He pockets the money without a word, revs the motor hard, accelerates away.

The reception clerk lifts a languid head, jolts back. Round eyes swivel from one girl to the other. 'Can I help you, Fräulein? Looking for someone, are you?'

Doly scans the dingy entrance hall. A pair of worn, stained easy chairs stand guard over a scratched coffee table. 'We'd like a room.' Will there be bed bugs? Doly puts on a bravado she doesn't feel. 'A double. For the two of us. You can manage that, can't you?'

'Certainly, Gnädiges Fräulein. A first floor room?' He looks up from the register. Eyes scan the two girls, their cases. A bell on the desk makes a weak pinging noise. 'The boy will take your luggage and show you to your room.'

A man in his mid-thirties leads them up a small winding staircase. They Indian-file along a narrow corridor. He unlocks a door.

'Your room, ladies.' He puts down the bags. Waits.

'Yes. Thank you.' Doly gives him a tip. Knows it's too large but tries for insurance in case they need a friend.

He stares at it, at her. 'You're in the right place, are you, Fräulein?'

She shuts the door on him. 'At last. You'd think it was the end of the world, our taking a room in a hotel.'

'I suppose we don't exactly fit in, Doly.' Lieselotte's voice quavers her anxiety.

'Fit in? Is there a special kind of human being here? I haven't seen any devil's horns or witches' broomsticks. They all look pretty much the same as everybody else to me.'

'What do we do now?'

'Unpack. Change into Moppel's clothes.'

'Right away?'

'Did you have other plans? Ask them to send up some food, perhaps?'

'Don't be such a goose.'

Doly opens her case, pulls out two pairs of flannel trousers belonging to her brother, two shirts, ties. One sports jacket. A pair of hiking boots, socks, a sailor's cap.

'You have brought some shoes and socks?' She tosses the heavier pair of trousers towards Lieselotte. 'And the right headgear to stow your hair?'

'Yes. You've only brought one jacket.'

'One of us can go without. My stupid brother only owns the two.'

Lieselotte giggles. 'And he's round here wearing one.'

'Worst luck. Thought you were going to borrow your father's?'

'I did try. Miles too big.'

'Right.' Doly puts on Moppel's clothes, stuffs her hair, now shoulder length and still abundant, into the sailor's cap. She narrows her eyes at herself in the small mirror above the chest of drawers. 'Well, what d'you think? Will I do?'

'You look like a boy, not a man.'

'Moppel's a boy.'

'Only a sister could say that. He's nearly eighteen. You're nothing but a fourteen-year-old schoolgirl.'

'So what? He used to come here as soon as the Hudwalkers decided we were too hot to handle and left us to rot in Germany. Moppel was only fourteen then.'

Lieselotte is taller than Doly. And much broader. She manages to squeeze into Moppel's trousers. His shirt is a disaster, the buttonholes straining across her breasts.

Doly bursts into wild laughter. 'Forget about age. You're never going to pass for a man. It's not just your bosom. Your bottom's hardly masculine. It wobbles.'

'You saying I'm fat?'

'Well developed, Liesi. A damned sight too well.' She walks around her friend, trying to adjust the clothes. 'Try the jacket.'

The result is a lumpy female figure in men's clothing. Not a useful disguise.

'I'll go on my own. What d'you reckon? Will I pass for a man?'

It's Lieselotte's turn to show amusement. 'No chance.'

'Boy then.'

'Maybe. Provided you keep well out of the light.'

'That's hardly difficult at this time of night. All I want to do is look more male than female. You come and you'll give the show away. I'm off on my own.'

'You can't, Doly. It's much too dangerous. I hate this crummy place. Let's go and find Josef.'

A pang as Doly realises Lieselotte is still keen on the young man she met through her parents. Not the rejected Peter, but someone else. Someone her friend has chosen herself. 'Josef?'

'I *told* you, Doly. Josef Miessman. He's studying medicine and spending his summer holidays on a boat to get experience. On the *Leander*. She's berthed in Hamburg now. We can tell him we've come to visit him. He's always asking me to.'

'Go creeping off with our tails between our legs? No way. You stay here. I'll be back with all the gen.' A nonchalant wave. 'If I'm not back in three hours, send out a search party.'

Josef is the source of all their knowledge about venereal disease. He spelt out what's involved to Lieselotte. In detail.

'Does Moppel know what he's risking, coming here?' Lieselotte now asks Doly. With a sidelong glance.

'What d'you mean?'

'The clap, Doly. Syphilis. If he goes with prostitutes, he's quite likely to catch it. The cure's worse than the disease, by all accounts. They make you take mercury. A poison which affects you as much as the disease does. It blackens your teeth, can ruin your gums, can even affect the jawbones.'

Doly shrugs. 'His teeth look fine.'

'And it can make your hair fall out.'

Doly giggles. Helplessly. 'A really big deal for Moppel. He's got so much to lose. Anyway, what d'you expect me to do about it?'

Lieselotte doesn't join in. 'Josef said there are other consequences. Moppel's whole personality could change. He could become like your Tante Hannah. You can't have forgotten what she was like, how mean she was, how her temper so often got the better of her.'

Doly's back is turned to her, adjusting clothes made for a man.

'He's your brother, and he hasn't got a father to advise him. You should warn him, you know.'

'That's Onkel Wilfred's job.'

CHAPTER 7

Hamburg, Summer 1925

Doly creaks the hotel room door open, convinces herself the corridor is empty. She walks down, her hips stiff and straight. She remembers reading Mark Twain. Tom Sawyer muffed his disguise as a girl because he pushed his knees together when someone threw an apple into his skirt.

She has to watch her reflexes. Take long strides instead of mincing steps. And remember *not* to lift her cap because her hair would tumble out.

Gawky boots make clumping downstairs easy. She lumbers sideways past an empty reception counter, lowers her head, slinks by.

Mission accomplished. She's on her own, after dark, in the red light district, the most dangerous part of Hamburg. Tingles of excitement quicken her steps, straighten her spine, make her eyes bold. She's as free as a man.

Women are all around her. Leaning against lamp posts, doors, window ledges. Lurid make-up, short skirts, absurdly high heels. Pushing themselves upright as she steps past. Voices soft and come-hitherish.

'Na, Bubi. Komm mit.—Hi, laddie. Come with me.'

Plying their trade. Taking her for a prospect.

She takes long strides, turns her head as soon as she's approached. Fascinated to hear the women at work, to watch them snare their tricks.

Young, old. In-between. Variations on a theme. Some scantily dressed, others immersed in furs. Some bored, some desperate. A side of life she's never seen before.

A young woman, perhaps a girl of about her own age, dressed in a short sleeveless beaded dress approaches her. Teetering on dangerously high heels.

'Erstes Mal, Bubi?—First time, laddie?'

Doly shakes her head.

The girl catches her arm. 'Brauchst keine Angst haben.—Don't be scared.' Her smile is a gargoyle of black teeth. 'That's my speciality.' She pulls the flimsy dress up to expose naked thigh. And a bush of pubic hair.

Doly feels dizzy, almost faint. The shock. Hair in *that* place? It had never occurred to her. Casual games with Lieselotte have never involved seeing her friend's nudity. Not since the Schimmelreiter time, four years ago. When they were both still children. Classical paintings of female nudes show no body hair. Nor does Gabby have it, any more than she does. Because of the gene, presumably. So how long before *her* head looks like Gabby's?

She's seen enough and it isn't funny any more. The thrill of freedom turns to panic. These girls aren't remotely like her. They have hair which they won't lose, a freedom she can't aspire to. Unbidden tears swamp her eyes.

She swivels round, runs, loses all sense of direction. She can't remember the side street the hotel is in or its name. Her breath is getting shorter, she feels sick. Her guardian angel is at her side. A familiar-looking hotel entrance looms up in front of her. She rushes in.

'Hold on there. What do *you* want?'

'I'm just going to my room.' She brushes the wet from her eyes, tries to stop the thumping of her heart, to sound calm.

'Room? You have a room here?'

'Number 22.'

'Out of the question. That room is occupied by two proper young ladies. Now, out of here before I call the police.'

'But I'm one of the young ladies.'

'Out.'

She pulls her cap off, displays still plentiful matted hair turned a darker Titian colour.

The receptionist stares. Turns hostile.

Doly sprints up the stairs, bangs on the door of Room 22. 'It's me, Liesi. Let me in.'

'Is something wrong, Doly? Did someone get at you?'

'We've been found out. We've got to get dressed right away and leave.'

Lieselotte takes Doly's arm. 'But we haven't done anything wrong...'

'Don't argue with me. He's getting the police.' She tears off Moppel's clothes, crams them into the case, changes back into her own things, skirt back to front, not bothering with stockings. 'Don't stand there gaping. Hurry up, we've got to leave.'

She forces Lieselotte to dress, grabs hold of both their cases, rushes down. Hands one to Lieselotte.

Doly throws a wad of notes at the reception clerk. 'This'll pay for the room.' Then rushes ahead with Lieselotte in tow. Their cases, incongruous on the wide gaudy expanse which seemed such fun only a short time ago, feel heavy. Danger growls from the street, the houses, the passing cars. And the prostitutes don't offer a friendly service, they shout abuse.

'Was treibt Ihr hier?—What the hell are you doing here? Get off my beat.'

The women jostle, threaten them with their pimps.

'We've got to find Josef, Doly.' Lieselotte uses her body to ward off grasping hands. 'He said the Reeperbahn goes down to the docks. Look for water.' Her voice ends in gulps.

The Reeperbahn seems to stretch endlessly. They run, their cases banging against their legs, their breath exploding from their lungs.

They've no idea where they are. They stop, stand as close to each other as they can, look around. A tall heavy man is standing in a doorway. Staring at them.

'Ne, komm. Hierblieben.—Come along. Stay here.'

A pimp who uses the local dialect. Who thinks they're servant girls. Will he get his friends, grab hold of them, sell them as white slaves?

Doly clutches Lieselotte's arm again. 'Let's shout for Moppel.' she pants. 'He's here somewhere. Maybe he'll hear us.'

They dash off, their cries of 'Moppel!' re-echoing down the street. Windows open, doorways lighten up. No sign of Doly's brother. Until a rotund figure emerges from a doorway and starts towards them. It is only then they remember that Moppel means tubby. This man is more than tubby, he's fat. And he isn't Moppel.

'Jo, de mag ick lieden—Yes, I like the sound of that,' he shouts.

'My God, Liesi, he thinks we're touting for business.'

Lieselotte is already ahead of her. The man is lumbering across the street as fast as he can. She waits until he's almost within grasping distance, slings her suitcase at his feet, grabs Doly's case and throws it on top of the falling figure.

The shrill blast of a steam whistle coming from their left orients the girls to the harbour. They veer off the Reeperbahn into a side street, see light reflecting off water, the welcome sight of a steamer's hull. And several stacks from other boats beyond it.

'We're going to be all right, Doly.' Lieselotte points to the second boat. 'That's the *Leander*, Josef's boat. Let's go on board. He'll help us back to the station.'

A group of sailors is disembarking, walking towards them. Joking among themselves, nudging each other, spotting sport.

Doly is nervously aware of her bare legs, her relatively short skirt. 'What are we going to do now, Liesi?' She can no longer stop the tears.

Lieselotte spins round. 'Quick, back to the Reeperbahn. Josef will be below deck.'

'I can't run any more.'

'*Doly*. Is that you, Doly?' One of the group of sailors detaches himself. 'It's Werner. Werner Schiffer.' He turns to the other men. 'You lot lay off. These are school friends of mine. They've come to say hello. Carry on. I'll catch you up later.'

'Get lost, Schiffer. Pull the other one.'

He puts his arm around Doly. 'Tell him, Doly. Tell him what you know about me.'

'Werner went to school with me and my brother and sister,' she tells them. 'He's training to be a Lotse now.'

'He's training on the *Leander.* Like my friend, Herr Doktor Josef Miessman. He's your ship's doctor.' Lieselotte's voice

They shuffle aside. 'Let us in on your secret, Schiffer. *Two* girls meeting you when your boat comes in?'

'Just because you can't get yours to do it.'

They walk away, Werner Schiffer taking both girls' arms. 'Keep walking as though we'd planned this. You don't have to be afraid.'

'You saved our honour, Werner. Maybe our lives.' Doly has tears in her eyes.

'What the hell are you two playing at?'

'We just wanted to know why Moppel comes here all the time.'

'A really brilliant idea. You telling me you walked down the Reeperbahn all by yourselves?'

'No one ever tells us anything. We decided the only way we could find out what goes on here is if we dressed up like men.'

'You're dressed more or less as usual. Scruffy.'

Doly tells him what happened. He roars with laughter. 'Some man you turned out to be.' And sobers up. 'Right. I'll see you to the station. This time don't be such idiots. Wait in the Ladies' Waiting Room until the first train to Schwanenbruch. Leaves at 0530 hours.'

Lieselotte giggles. 'I suppose that means half past five in the morning.'

'Never mind the jokes. Just make sure you're on that train.'

CHAPTER 8

Schwanenbruch, Summer 1925

'Let's take a look at the blue salon, Gabby. I've got a super idea.'

The sisters walk along the corridor of the villa's first floor. Doly has taken over the turret room. For privacy. And because she can smoke without being upbraided by the rest of the household.

Gabby enjoys sole occupation of their former bedroom. And Moppel sticks to his old one. Leaving their parents' bedroom unoccupied. In their honour. One thing the Dohlen children are agreed upon is honouring their father and their mother.

'Great room, isn't it?'

'I know that. What are you up to now?'

'Let's bring back the ball, Gabby.'

'Ball? What d'you mean?'

'The annual dance our parents always held on our mother's birthday. You must remember, Gabby. You're so much older than me.'

Doly's been treating Gabby as on the shelf ever since she left for Berlin. An old maid at sixteen. She's not nineteen yet but the fine line down the middle of her forehead is deepening. She relaxes it, smiles through gritted teeth. 'You mean on August 1st?'

'Is that when it was?'

'Yes.'

'August 1st then, Gabby. Well before you go back to that finishing school.' A darting look. 'The latest fashions. That's what you're

278

studying, isn't it?'

'Don't be ridiculous.' Gabby is mesmerised by her sister's display of pointed teeth, knows she's goading her. Still can't resist putting her straight. 'I'm enrolling at Berlin University this autumn. You know perfectly well I passed all my tests for the Abitur with flying colours.'

'Bully for you.' Doly's mocking eyes make Gabby bite her lower lip. 'Well, what d'you say? Moppel agrees.'

'He does?' Gabby doubts whether he's even been asked. His known interests are playing cards, drinking, and frequenting the Reeperbahn. They certainly don't include dancing with village girls desperate to marry an American. And a rich one at that.

'He's not against it.'

Gabby marches into the room which hasn't been used since their mother died. Twelve years ago. It might be a good idea to open the house up. Then she can invite Tall and Small.

Doly minces in right behind her. She grabs her sister, tries to twirl her round the parquet floor.

Gabby pulls away, stiff with anger. 'You know I don't dance.' For the same reason she doesn't go to the beach, let alone bathe. Her usual cover-up, one of those handy cloche hats, is a fashion virtually made for Gabby. Apart from close-covering her skull the cloche states 'new woman', the brim forcing the provocative posture of looking up from under it. Giving Gabby the freedom from hair that she craves.

A ball is a different kettle of fish entirely. You can't wear a cloche to dance in, just as it's usual to take off a bathing cap when you come out of the water, shaking your so-modern, short-cropped hair. Gabby doesn't cut her hair. She holds on to every wisp she can, desperately covering the ever-growing baldness with the remaining strands.

'Of course you don't dance, you're just a stuffy bluestocking.' Doly moves towards the windows facing east. 'That small alcove off centre is great for a live band. I vote for jazz.'

Gabby grins, feeling confidence return. 'Bit passé. I've got these artistic friends in Berlin. They'll know exactly which band to hire.'

'*Your* friends choose the band?' Doly doesn't even bother to subdue her snicker. 'I'm talking about a dance band. Not a middle-aged trio whose best piece is *Eine kleine Nachtmusik*.'

'Naturally we need a dance band.' The assured tone silences Doly, even without the superior smile suddenly dazzling Gabby's mouth. 'What we want is the right music for the Charleston and the turkey trot. Ragtime's much better than jazz to dance to.'

Doly tosses her hair. It's a little less fiery than it used to be, a little darker. The curls have become waves but there's still plenty of volume. 'Yep. Foxtrot, quickstep, even a waltz or two.'

'Trust me. They're experts.' The purr of victory.

'You agree then?'

'Why not?' Gabby has started counting up her Berlin friends.

'Let's make a guest list. We can squeeze in at least a hundred.'

The Villa Dohlen, August 1ˢᵗ, 1925

'Baron Friedrich von Raufensthal? My, how grand.'

Doly's dress was picked out from illustrations in a Berlin magazine where it was described as the latest fashion for 'den Vamp'. It comes with a sequinned layered skirt to just above the knee, a V-neckline plunging almost to the waist and no sleeves. Displayed in a rather muddy shade of orange. Minni was all agog, said she thought it made Doly look much older than she is. Which is exactly what Doly wants. Gunther Mettler merely whistled. Werner Schiffer, still on duty on his boat, hasn't seen it yet.

'Küss die Hand, Gnädiges Fräulein.' Friedrich Raufensthal has come up to ask for the next dance.

'I hope you're going to call me Doly.'

'Delighted. May I present my friend, Johann Schnatter?'

Jonah looks nervous though reasonably presentable in the tuxedo he's borrowed. From one of Friedrich's friends nearer Jonah's size. But his swarthy skin and dark eyes stand out among the throng of blond Teutons. 'Call me Hans.'

Doly turns her back on him. 'Your friend? Really? And his name is Johann?' She twirls the cocktail glass in her hand. 'You look much more like a Jonah. Swallowed up in that whale of a tuxedo.'

The click of Friedrich's heels is louder than the music. 'But still clever enough to escape Moby Dick and find the band for you.'

'And so very short. Tall and Small is brilliant. Gabby's used her imagination for once.' Doly trips precariously on absurd heels. 'The band's terrific, Jonah. Au fait in all the latest hits. Congrats.'

Jonah bows. 'You're too kind, Gnädiges Fräulein.' He catches her arm. 'Careful you don't cut yourself on those spiked stilts of yours.'

'Stilts?'

'Heels, are they?'

She shakes him off. 'I hope you two dance?'

'I think we can manage a step or two.'

'Aren't you going to introduce me, Doly?' Lieselotte's dress isn't in Doly's class. But it's still sensational for Schwanenbruch. A strapless bodice shows off Lieselotte's substantial bosom while the swirling skirt is in a striking shade of emerald green. The cost has been put on a bill which Onkel Wilfred doesn't yet know he's footing.

'My best friend. Lieselotte Waldeck.' Doly sees Lieselotte's really taken with that self-important Friedrich what's-his-name: Mr Tall.

He seems to have spotted that as well. 'Perhaps I might have this dance, Fräulein Waldeck?' And whisks her off. Leaving Doly standing with her mouth open and no sound coming out of it.

Lieselotte doesn't return. Doly retires to the upstairs bathroom to repair her lipstick, and to add more perfume. She notices Gabby sitting in front of the big mirror.

Their eyes meet. 'Oh dear, Gabby. How very sad you look. Don't even your friends bother to ask you for a dance?'

'You know perfectly well I don't dance.' Gabby tries to adjust her hairstyle. Impossible. Her hair has become so scanty that it barely covers her scalp. There's a large bald patch in the centre which seems to Gabby to spread every day. Even the largest bow made of the widest ribbon will not completely cover it. Tears spill on to her cheeks.

Dolly tosses her mane. 'If only I could give you some of mine, I'd gladly do it.'

The tears stop as though turned off. 'Don't worry Doly. I'm sure I'll manage very well with what I've got.'

Doly fluffs her hair fuller, sprays perfume, races back. She spends the rest of the evening dancing with Werner Schiffer. In case he should show signs of talking to Gabby, or even asking her to dance.

Gabby returns, pours more Schnapps, walks from one person to another, talks animatedly.

The evening is almost over. The band announces the last waltz.

'One request before we finish,' Doly calls out as she holds both

281

hands above her head. 'Know *Zieh dich aus, Petronella, zieh dich aus?*'

'Of course, Fräulein. That's all the rage in Berlin.'

'And with my friend and me.' She grabs a chair, stands on it, looks across the dance floor, sees Lieselotte still standing, talking with Friedrich Raufensthal. 'Liesi.'

Lieselotte turns.

'Let's give them a little show. Let's do our version of *Get 'em off, Petronella, strip 'em off*.'

'This isn't the right occasion, Doly.'

'If this isn't, what is? It's a party, isn't it?'

Jonah Schnatter slithers to the front, makes a sign to the band. 'Brilliant idea, girls. Let's go.' He clears the dance floor with waves of his hand, then signals the band to play the introduction.

Doly dances across the empty floor, takes Lieselotte's hand and draws her to the centre.

Jonah grabs a microphone, and sings:

> *Get 'em off, Petronella, strip 'em off*
> *If we're not to bore the audience to death*
> *It's the way to become famous*
> *Even though our deeds may shame us*
> *Beats yawning till we're all completely out of breath.*

Doly and Lieselotte dance to the tune and, as soon as the chorus begins again and the whole assembly sings, Doly takes off the scarf around her own neck, then Lieselotte's. Languorously. The guests cheer. The girls dance together again.

The next chorus sees Doly's pearls coming off. She stands on tiptoe, puts her hands round Lieselotte's neck, kisses her on the lips as she takes her necklace off.

The titters trickle round the room. Some people make for the door.

Each chorus sees another piece of apparel ripped off until, finally, only the girls' dresses are left. Both bow low, show bare thighs. A touch of cheek.

Young voices roar approval. Older ones mutter, or have already left. Gabby runs to her bedroom, shuts the door tight.

THE FETTERED MAIDEN

The Monsilienburg, surrounded by treacherous quicksand, is hard to take by storm. Its walls are twenty-one meters thick and three-hundred and twenty meters high, and it's surrounded by deep ditches which can, when necessary, be flooded to provide wide moats.

The noble family which lived there for generations has long since died out and a family of robber barons has taken over the mighty fortress. But it isn't only the thick high walls and the deep moats which protect the robbers and keep them from being brought to justice. They are also cunning. Their horses are shod so that their shoes point the wrong way. So misleading pursuers and escaping righteous justice.

One day the dastardly thieves stole a young maiden from a nearby farm. They kept her prisoner, refused to let her go even when her father promised a large ransom. Nevertheless, the resilient young woman managed to escape the cruel robbers. She took a chance when her captors were out plundering their neighbours' land and houses. She managed to loosen her shackles, climb over the high wall, jump into the moat and swim to freedom.

Unfortunately, though the maiden was free, her freedom was constrained. For she could never leave her parents' house. The robbers were lying in wait for her outside. Nevertheless, constrained freedom is better than no freedom at all.

CHAPTER 9

Hamburg/Berlin Express, August 1925

'If you want to get the better of that tiresome little bitch of a sister of yours, Gabby, you'll have to do something about it.'

'Such as?'

The three friends are heading back to Berlin. On the train from Hamburg. Gabby is disconsolate. Wrapped in a winter coat though it's summer warm. The big fur collar rides up the back of her head. Covering the skimpy hair.

'I don't want to be indelicate, Gabby.'

'If you've got something to say, say it.'

'You've seen how the cabaret artistes do it.'

'Do what?'

'Change their hairstyles from one number to the next. At lightning speed.'

An image of Claire Waldoff's bushy red hair and bouncy figure comes into Gabby's mind. When she feels like changing to blonde or brunette she simply dons a wig. Could she do something similar? Find a much better style than her mother wore?

'A friend of mine's a hairdresser.' Jonah's voice is low and throbbing. 'I'll be glad to take you to him.' Gabby's sitting across from him. Tense. 'Before you embark on your first semester at the University would be a good idea. Don't you agree?'

She nods. Because she can't speak.

'Why torture yourself, Gabby?' Friedrich's hand is on her knee, pressing hard. 'You're a really beautiful woman, you know.'

She swallows. 'You just say that.' Her blue eyes blaze defiant. 'Neither you nor Jonah have shown any interest in me. Except as a friend.'

'My dear sweet Gabby. Don't you know that has nothing to do with you?'

'Of course, it has. If I were as beautiful as all that you'd have fallen in love with me.' Tears spill, however hard she tries to stop them. 'You danced with Lieselotte all evening, Tall.'

'You turned me down. Said you didn't dance.'

'*Couldn't*, not didn't.' Gabby gulps back the tears. 'Werner Schiffer didn't even greet me. Look at the way he rushed after my sister as soon as she crooked her little finger at him.'

'I guarantee he'll switch to you the moment we've found you the right hairstyle.'

'And you two? It's going to make a difference to you as well?'

'No, Gabby. Not me, nor Jonah. Because no woman is going to have any effect on us. However beautiful she may be. We thought you knew that.'

She stares. It's never occurred to her to think of her friends in that light before. 'But Friedrich. You spent the whole evening with Lieselotte. Except for the last dance.'

Friedrich shrugs. 'She made a beeline for me. What d'you want *me* to do? Tell the whole world? Harmless enough for that one evening, after all. I'm never going to come across her again.' He grins. 'And it annoyed the hell out of the little tramp.'

Can there really be a young man who's rumbled Doly? Gabby can't help herself, she laughs out loud. 'So that's why Jonah encouraged them in that outrageous performance. You sly dog.' Her hands are up to her eyes. 'Schwanenbruch is never going to forget.'

'They're not going to hold it against *you*.'

The smile has gone from Gabby's face. 'They'll hold it against the whole family. For ever.'

'You may well be right. Your sister broke sacred German traditions.' Friedrich's smile is bittersweet. 'Now you know our secret, Gabby. We trust you with it, as you can trust us with yours.'

'Two secrets. You're Communists as well.'

'Touché. Anyway listen, sweetie. Every other woman uses make-up, clothes, perfume and a good hairdresser to make the most of herself.' Jonah appraises her. 'What's supposed to be so different about *you*?'

The conviction which has always nagged at Gabby. Possibly irrational, powerful all the same. She doesn't have proper hair—not on her head, not even on her body. In her innermost being, in the thoughts she'd never express, she worries she isn't a proper, a real, woman. Or even a member of the human race. She's only too aware of the doctrine of the Untermensch shouted from the rooftops by the Brown Shirts of the National Socialist Party on every occasion. Gabby has the feeling that she's precisely what they're talking about. However, it's not a suspicion you express out loud, even to your best friends.

CHAPTER 10

Berlin, August 1925

Gabby takes Tall and Small's joint advice. She pays the "best little dressmaker in the Potsdamer Platz" a visit and orders several new dresses. She learns to apply make-up. And then, gritting her teeth, she makes an appointment with Jonah's hairdresser friend. In his discreet salon. Where many of the assistants are men. The kind of men bold Aryans despise.

The air is heavy with the smell of chemicals Gabby has never come across before. She sees women whose tortured hair is wound into hideous sausage shapes covered by netting, their heads imprisoned under enormous deafening machines blasting hot air. And frequently overheating so that the women scream. Gabby is not clear that the results are justified. Could these people make her look worse?

'I would suggest the new bob, Fräulein Dohlen.' Jonah's friend takes a step back from behind Gabby. Fluttery hands frame her face. Visionary eyes probe possibilities. His high voice speaks out: 'No question at all. Your colour's auburn.' He's at most five centimetres taller than she is but he's quite commanding. 'Sit back and relax. I'll show you what I mean.'

He opens a cupboard, takes a wig from a stand, and shakes it. He turns it inside out and holds it in front of Gabby's face. She sees fine netting with hair knotted through as though it were a filigree carpet. A piece of flesh-coloured silk runs from front to back. It's threaded with single hairs. As though growing from a scalp. 'For the parting. Virtually impossible to spot.'

The whole contraption smells musty. Has oily stains.

'Don't look so horrified. This is a piece we're cleaning and dressing for a client. Won't bite, you know.' He pulls it on her. A greasy skull cap. Not light.

Gabby closes her eyes, breathes through her mouth. Can't bear to look or smell.

'That's right. Don't open your eyes until I've cast my magic spell.'

The wig is pulled back from her forehead, forward again. 'The first thing you have to learn is that every millimetre counts. Too far forward makes you look mentally subnormal. Too far back gives a high forehead, the sign of a bluestocking. Last thing we're after.' He kneads his fingers through the wig.

It's not an unpleasant feeling. Gabby is shocked to find herself enjoying the physical sensation of someone manipulating her head. Is the scalp an erogenous zone? Her mind goes back. Far, far back. To feel her mother's delicate fingers smooth her hair, adjust her ribbon. Gently stroking her.

The fingers are gone. In their place Gabby feels a hard comb, a hand tugging sections of hair. Lifting, combing, twisting them around his finger. A pause. A pat.

'Open your eyes.'

The spasm in her throat brings on a fit of coughing.

'Hold on. A glass of water.'

Has he made her look like a prostitute? Like lamb dressed as mutton? Is there a rigid coiffure sitting on her head? Like her mother's?

Tears blur her sight. She's come all this way, allowed this man to discuss her shortcomings, sat waiting for an hour. Ridiculous to lose her courage now.

She glances in the mirror. Sees a pretty young girl she doesn't know. Is that his assistant? A provocative, triangular face topped by a cap of auburn shingle. If only she... She blots her eyes with a handkerchief, looks up.

The red-rimmed eyes look back. The rest is enchantment. Can that really be *her* reflection? Why, she's... no other word for it. Bewitching.

Gabby looks again. Gasps. That's a pretty woman gazing back at her. With a strong look of Doly. Prettier, actually. She swallows as the tears pour down.

The hairdresser is sizing her up in the mirror. Nodding. 'Superb, my dear. Superb.' A throb in his voice. 'Can't tell you how thrilled I am. Don't think I've ever seen such a transformation. Makes my whole job worthwhile.'

He's smiling as he takes a small comb, pulls tendrils of hair in front of her ears. He takes a little water and smoothes them into place.

'I'll take your measurements. We'll use the finest European hair. Supplied by brides of Christ who give up their tresses. Perfect for you.'

'Brides of Christ?' Her voice is a whisper in the cathedral of beauty.

'Nuns, my dear. One of their sacrifices is to cut off their hair. Very useful from our point of view.'

She should be practical. 'How much will it cost?'

'Some things can't be measured in money. You'll need three wigs. One to wear, one to dress and one for me to clean.' He minces up to her, takes off the wig.

'Dress?'

'Put the bounce back in the curls when the hair goes limp. You attach the wig to a stand I'll get for you, dampen the hair, put these paper curlers in, then let the hair dry. That takes several hours in a warm room. Then you comb out the curls and the wig will look good as new again.'

The old Gabby stares back at her and she knows she can never live with her again. The end of introversion, the beginning of confidence.

'When can you make them for me?'

His eyes meet hers in the mirror. 'It's a very labour-intensive process which usually takes around a month. You need one sooner. I'll pull all the stops out. I'll have one ready for you in a week.'

Gabby relaxes, smiles. 'You're a magician.'

He nods at her. 'If anyone ever tells you it isn't your own hair look 'em straight in the eye. Call them a liar. That hair will be yours. You'll have paid good money for it.'

Herr and Frau Meinzer don't recognise Gabby when she knocks at their living room door. Not until she speaks.

'It's really you, Gabby? You were a beauty in disguise?'

'The ugly duckling turned into a beautiful swan.' She pats the wig nervously. She has to practise being her new self. A visit to Schwanenbruch for a few days should do it. Schwanenbruch—Swan brook. Is the name prophetic?

There's no time to dither. She should go before the University semester starts. Take the next train to Hamburg, change for home. She'll be there in eight hours.

There are unexpected glances from young men on the train, help offered with her luggage. Heady stuff. Gabby sits in a window seat, calms herself by clutching the locket dangling from her throat. Several people, not just young men, have said how pretty it looks. It's never been mentioned before.

Gabby steps off the train at Schwanenbruch, a solitary figure. She walks towards the villa, remembers the hairdresser's words. "Hold your head high."

'Why, Gabby, it's you. I hardly recognised you. What have you done to yourself? You look wonderful.' Rula's round friendly face is framed in her window overlooking the Deichstrasse. 'You're home for a little holiday?'

Gabby waves at her, nods. Floats on as in a dream. Along the Kanalstrasse, round the bend. She's about to go past the Deutsches Haus and across the square just as a front door opens and a familiar figure dashes out. Tall and upright, skin bronzed, the folds under the blue eyes already etched deep from staring out at sea. He leans forward to move as fast as his long legs will carry him. In the direction Gabby is heading.

'Werner. Don't you recognise me?' Will he show a man's interest in her now? Want to do more than take down the heavy tomes in her father's study, listen while she translates Byron and Shakespeare?

He pulls up. Blinks. 'Why, Gabby. Of course I recognise you. You took me by surprise, that's all.' He blinks again. 'You usually write to let me know you're coming.' The blue eyes aren't as open as she remembers them. 'I thought you were far too busy to bother with us. All that studying in Berlin.'

'It was a last minute decision. I've got a couple of weeks before I start at the University. I thought it would be nice to come home for a break.' She tries out a tinkly laugh. 'I've just got off the train.'

His eyes move to the case in her hand. 'Sorry. How slow of me. Do let me carry that.'

Her smile is radiant. 'How very nice of you.' Then the smile fades. Why the hang-dog look?

'You've had a good trip home?' Werner's cheeks pull up, leaving unsmiling eyes and a straight mouth. Just the way Frau Meinzer's cronies look when they feel sorry for the unfortunate young woman renting her rooms. 'My mother often asks after you.'

His *mother*?

His pace has slackened to hers. They're standing by the villa railings.

'That's fine now, Werner. You were in a hurry. Don't let me keep you.'

He stands, arms hanging down, uncertain. Nods. Lifts his sailor cap.

'Your training is going well?'

'Yes, thank you, Gabby.'

'There you are, Werner. Where did you get to? We've been hanging about for ages.' Doly is tumbling out of the villa door.

Looking past Gabby. Not recognising her.

'Hello, Doly.'

Her sister's mouth opens. Stays that way. 'Gabby. What *have* you done to yourself. I hardly recognise you under all that hair.'

Werner turns away. 'I'll come back another time Doly. You'll want to be with your sister now.'

'No way you're sloping off, Werner. Liesi and I've stopped ourselves wolfing down that marvellous cake of Rula's. Sitting here all afternoon, waiting for you.'

'You were coming to tea?' Gabby looks from her sister to the young man whose company she's enjoyed for years. And who had, she thought, enjoyed hers.

His shoulders are hunched, his eyes uncomfortable. 'Well, you see... Lieselotte and Doly...'

Doly's been working up to this one. Pinched the only boyfriend

Gabby's ever had because she can't leave any man alone. And certainly not one who's interested in her unattractive sister. The smile leaves her face. 'I had no idea, Werner. You might have told me.'

He swallows. His face goes red. There's a tear in the corner of his right eye. 'You haven't been around for months, Gabby. I happened to meet Doly...'

'Please don't explain. You're free to spend your time however you wish. I wouldn't dream of getting in your way. So sorry I made you late, getting you to carry my luggage.' She rushes past Doly, through the door, slams it in Werner's face. And storms upstairs to her bedroom.

CHAPTER 11

New York, Autumn 1925

Doly and Moppel have strict instructions to wait for Walter Hudwalker before they disembark. They expected to spot the tall figure waiting on the quay or hurrying his long legs up the gangplank. There's no sign of him.

'Think we should wait by the luggage?'

'Stick 'em up.' A youth with a spotted handkerchief across nose and mouth, and what looks like the muzzle of a gun jutting his right trouser pocket.

Doly moves towards Moppel. He puts his arms around her shoulders and holds her in front of him. Shaking.

'You heerd me.'

Doly spots Hudwalker's tall figure over the railings, ducks out of Moppel's arms and runs towards him.

'Sorry I got held up, Dorinda. Steady does it now.' He grabs her hurtling shoulders and holds her away from him. 'My, my. I hardly recognise you. Such a grown-up young lady.'

'He's got a gun, Father Hudwalker.'

'What's that?' Hudwalker turns towards Moppel who's slumped on the deck. In an expanding puddle. 'Say, Junior, you sea sick? Or did a wave slosh on board?'

The spotted handkerchief is round the youth's neck. A laughing face is topped by a flaxen sheaf of hair covering his forehead. His eyes are squinted tight with amusement.

'He said it was a stick up.' Moppel's eyes bulge out of his podgy face. His hand misses Hudwalker's as his mouth drops open and spittle creeps down the corners. 'I thought you said...'

A Huckleberry grin as two large hands grab Moppel's arms and haul him to his feet.

'Why, Junior. No need to take on so. This here's Bobby, Bertrand's kid brother. I sent him on ahead because I was held up.'

'He pointed a gun at me.'

'C'mon now, Junior. Just his little joke. Surely you remember Bobby? I guess he's the age Bertrand was...' Hudwalker eyes the puddle, looks at Moppel, flares his nostrils.

Doly realises that her brother thought he'd seen a ghost.

Bobby slips nearer Doly. 'You've been holding out on me, Uncle Walter. You never let on you had a ward as gorgeous as this babe.' His eyes twinkle as he pulls Doly to him and plants a kiss on both cheeks. 'I guess that makes us relatives. Kinda.'

She looks at him sidelong. 'Hi there.' He's not bad-looking. In an American kind of way. Muscular body, fly-away ears, freckles which give his nose and cheeks a pointillist skin. 'We never met, Father Hudwalker. Bertrand always said his parents didn't want to be without at least one son at home.'

'That a fact.' The suave face withdraws further. 'I guess mothers hold on as long as they can.'

'Why, I remember...' Moppel stops in mid-sentence as more unhappy memories surface. He flares crimson. The colour spreads into an almost bald scalp.

Hudwalker clears his throat. 'I hope you three young people will be good friends. Maybe Bobby can take the time to show you two some of the sights. A trip to Staten Island, maybe. Before you both start back in school.'

The few days before Doly is due to enrol in Riverside Hall are spent with Bobby Hudwalker. She meant to go shopping for clothes. Instead, she astonishes the Hudwalkers by her fervent desire to explore Washington.

'I've never seen the capital city of my country.' Doly holds a map of the District of Columbia spread out on the kitchen table. 'I've heard there are some wonderful federal buildings. I know Grade School's already started, Father Hudwalker, so you'll be busy. Bobby says he's able to take a few days off. He's offered to show me round.'

'Bobby's helping Father, Dorinda. Besides, he's never been to Washington himself.' Hildegarde's nose is twitching with remembered irritation.

'That's not to the point, Hildegarde, honey. They can't go off by themselves.' Mother Hudwalker bumbles in with chocolate chip cookies and a jug of lemonade.

In the end it's Moppel who's persuaded to play chaperone.

'Guess you know how to make yourself scarce, bud?' Unfriendly freckles jut out belligerently.

Moppel is easily persuaded to leave Doly and Bobby on their own. And Bobby encourages Moppel to look for contacts Hudwalker will never come across.

Doly and Bobby walk hand in hand through the wide avenues of Washington, past the White House, the Capitol, the Supreme Court Building. All built in white or grey stone in the classical style.

'Let's get the Washington Monument and Lincoln Memorial over with. We can't go back to Huddy Daddy without giving an eye-witness account.'

They find benches in nearby parks. Shaded against hot sun as well as onlookers. They neck. Bobby's kisses are as sweet as any Doly can remember.

THE VILLAGE BELL

Every house of God needs at least one good bell to call the faithful to worship. Even the smallest village needs the golden tone of a well-cast bell.

One of the isolated villages on the outer fringes of Land Hadeln was too small for a church. But it boasted a chapel. And the village blacksmith set himself up as the man who could cast a bell with a wonderful tone. One that would call his fellow villagers to prayer. He would make it larger and better than any bell in the whole of Land Hadeln. And Land Wursten too.

The smith worked hard. He saw to it that his apprentice dug an enormous casting-pit. Then he readied the wooden crook—the curved double compass which will trace out the shape—and prepared the core and cope. And he was generous and used plenty of expensive copper for the casting mixture.

The finished bell looked wonderful. But when it was hung in the high tower of the little chapel and the verger rang the virgin toll, the sound was dull.

The smith had the pit cleaned out. He built a new core and cope and used the finest clay. He ordered the faulty bell to be taken down, melted the metal and cast a new bell. And once more the sound was disappointing. Duller, fainter even than before.

With a heavy heart the smith decided to try one last time. He instructed his apprentice to ready everything for the firing of the clay. Then he was called away on important business. He left his apprentice with strict orders to guard the installation and not to allow anyone to even breathe on the preparations.

The apprentice looked at the crook and was filled with the urge to change its shape. Not much. A little bending out round the centre, a little tightening towards the top. And the returning master noticed nothing. He went ahead with firing the clay and on to the casting.

The three-times-cast bell was finished and hung in the tower. It had a glorious shape. And this time the first sublime tone rang with full voice across the land, proclaiming the brilliance of its maker.

The master was the hero of the village. He was fêted everywhere he went and asked to cast another bell by a neighbouring village.

The apprentice could no longer keep the truth to himself. It had to come out. He was sure his master would leap for joy, praise him, and ask his advice for the new bell.

The master heard the apprentice out. His face grew darker with each word. And when the lad stood, smiling, ready for his reward the master flew into a violent rage. He drew his knife and stabbed the unfortunate lad to death.

Since that moment the bell only gives one fundamental tone. Deep, profound and sorrowful, with no nominal or hum-note. And it always sounds four times, however it is struck.

When they hear the funereal tones the villagers fold their hands in pious prayer:

POOR APPRENTICE, POOR APPRENTICE

CHAPTER 12

Riverside Hall, Paradise, September 1925

'And this is our little lass from Germany. Dorinda Dollen.' Miss Phil-land's hand, palm upturned, lifts up the volume of Shakespeare plays while stern eyes are amplified behind pebble glasses. 'She particularly would like to take part in our performance this year because Macbeth was her father's favourite play.'

Hostility covered by duty. Doly runs fingers through her hair and stands. Is it her looks, or is coming from Germany the crime?

'I'd be glad to do anything. Stage hand, prompter, whatever you need.'

'Weird sister?' a soft voice asks, unfriendly eyes concentrated on her hair. Then laughs. It's still abundant, but very coarse. Instead of ginger it has turned to straw: the mouldy kind, left as stubble in the fields. And stands on end unless freshly combed.

A strong arm presses her shoulder. 'No ma'am. She's far too small. Hi there, Dorinda.' A sturdy dark-cropped girl on her right smiles a genuine welcome. The low throb of her voice reminds Doly of Lieselotte. 'That what your folks call you, or d'you go by something special?'

'Just Dorinda.' She's starting a new life with a new name. She crossed the days off her calendar all summer. Which passed slowly. Flirting with boys she didn't care about, striding the Watt alone. Because Josef Miessman, now a houseman in a Berlin hospital, sidelined Lieselotte

298

most of the time. And pursued her with a vigour Doly found distinctly threatening.

'Don't dare to get engaged, Liesi,' she did her best to discourage her friend. 'You're going to be a wonderful doctor.' Doly pointed to her arm. A small scar in memory of a solemn pledge. 'Forget the fees. I'm your blood sister and I'll find the money. Your job's to work for your exams and resist marrying Josef.' She pressed down on Lieselotte's wrist. 'It's just his way of eliminating real competition in the medical profession.'

'Well now, Dorinda.' The English mistress's chalk has spelt out a cursive Dorinda Dollen. 'Why not tell us a little about yourself. Acting experience. Favourite pastimes. What career you have in mind.'

Doly feels the shame of disastrous clothes. Stiff German tailoring which is way too precise for the fluid lines of American fashions. Her haircut, styled in Cuxhaven, looks too like Medusa for comfort. She's ordered *Vogue* and *Harper's Bazaar*. A shopping trip to Lord & Taylor's is a must. She'll schedule an outing to New York next week. That's top priority whatever Huddy fuddies on about. Maybe Bobby can take the Greyhound bus from Detroit and visit at the weekend. So she can check him out again.

'Oh, gee. I saw the Riverside Hall Prospectus years ago. I knew it was a wonderful school right off. Such a wide programme: academic, dramatic, athletic. I'm a keen rider. I'd love to learn to ride Wild West style.'

Miss Philland looks at her notes, changes Dollen to Dohlen.

'As well as study really hard to become a teacher.'

Lukewarm applause.

What *is* she saying? She'd rather scrub floors than teach. She's going to travel. Discover a new plant or animal somewhere exotic and give it her name. Brim her life full before she meets her English prince.

'You wanna learn to ride rodeo style?' The low voice of before, but this time a strong hand stretches out. 'Then I'm your gal. Put it right there, pardner.' The grip is hard and tight. 'Name of Faith Bowler.' Eyes slow and steady. And intense. 'I sure could use the company. These guys are way too tame.'

'And which one of you girls can tell me the capital of Poland?'

Doly puts her hand up before she realises she's made a mistake. Again. The Cuxhaven-Lyzeum has given her an excellent grounding in the fundamentals of most subjects. And, not surprisingly, in European geography and history. Germany in particular, of course.

'So who can tell me some of the clauses of the Treaty of Versailles? The one which ended the War between our country and Germany?'

All eyes are on Doly. She has no choice but to find answers. And the answers she gives, the ones which Gabby has so often dinned into her, are from the German point of view. Her classmates do not actually hiss but no one will talk to her after the lesson.

The only subject Doly lags behind in is English. Not the literature, which she reads avidly, but the way she presents her essays. Her writing still shows that she translates from German rather than thinking in English. And her handwriting still betrays the tell-tale angular Gothic script. Quite unlike the rounded cursive letters Americans use.

Miss Philland loves to point out malapropisms. But Mrs Dartington, the Headmistress, has a better solution. She puts Dorinda up a class.

'You'll easily graduate in three years rather than in four,' she tells her.

If it weren't for the fact that she's now joined Faith Bowler in the second year, Doly might have suspected Riverside Hall didn't want her there any longer than they could help. She isn't even sure she wants to stay.

PART 5

STRAW KNIGHTS

1926–1931

THE CONSTANT TRYSTER

Greta and Enno fell deeply in love. Only one thing marred their bliss: they could not marry. Enno was only a poor cabin boy and Greta's parents were hard put to keep body and soul together. Their only treasure was Greta herself.

Her great beauty attracted suitors from far and wide. Among them was a rich farmer's son who courted Greta with lavish gifts and exaggerated praise. When a rich farmer's son requests the hand of a poor fisherman's daughter, her father doesn't deny him his heart's desire.

The loving father's decision left the two sweethearts no choice but to meet secretly after dark. Enno's boat was anchored near Cuxhaven, off the Alte Liebe promontory. Whenever Greta could creep away from her parents' house she went over to the jutting rocks and hid behind them. From there she flashed a special sequence of lights at Enno. She knew he would be waiting eagerly for her signal. As soon as he recognised their code, he climbed down the ship's ladder to glide into the water and swim ashore to meet his beloved.

All went well until the night Greta's rejected suitor followed her. He spied on the lovers, watched his rival take the girl of his dreams in his arms. And vowed then and there to rid himself of the presumptuous boy.

Maddened by jealousy, Greta's would-be husband made sure she was kept busy at her parents' house the following night while he stole to the Alte Liebe on his own and mimicked her signal to Enno.

The moon shone brightly. The rejected lover hid in the shadow of the rocks. He watched Enno's arms part the water and saw light reflected in silver streaks as his rival swam towards the rock. Finally he waited for the young man's head to bob higher and higher as he climbed the landing steps.

That's when blind fury overcame all other emotion. The impostor grabbed the boat hook and brought it down on poor Enno's head. The young man sank into the sea without a sound, never to be seen again.

Greta returned to her tryst for many nights after that. She saw no sign of her beloved. Nor could she ask questions about him without betraying their secret.

Eventually Enno's ship pulled anchor and sailed away. The cabin boy's murderer returned again to ask for Greta's hand. She still refused him. Undeterred by Enno's absence, she went on sparking the special lights for her sweetheart every single night. She continued with her lonely vigil into old age.

Even death could not end her devotion. To this day, on both stormy winter nights and balmy summer evenings, anyone who takes the trouble to look can still see the ghostly flickerings on the Alte Liebe—Old Flame. An eternal trysting place for true love.

CHAPTER 1

Hamburg/Berlin Express, September 1926

'Allow me, Gnädiges Fräulein.'

The soft sing-song voice Gabby can hear above the chugging of the carriage wheels is coming from the window seat opposite hers. He's not a native German speaker. The words have the lilting rhythm of a Hungarian accent. She's almost sure.

She turns round. Smiling brown eyes are scanning her face, figure, hair. Undoubtedly with approval. Admiration even.

'That's all right. I just wanted to get my book.'

He lifts the small hand-case down from the luggage rack. Sensitive-looking hands. But dark hairs bristle the backs of his fingers which remind her of the legs of a tarantula. She controls her shoulders.

'Why a beautiful young lady like you bother to strain her eyes in readings?'

It's the first time a man has assumed she's too beautiful to be a bluestocking. Her eyes flash as though copying Doly, she wets her lips and lets them part, her breasts tighten her bodice. 'One must do something to pass the time. You travel a lot?'

He clicks his heels in an old-fashioned salute. He's old enough to have served in the War. Something about him—his gallantry, perhaps—suggests a cavalry officer. In the Imperial Austro-Hungarian Army? A Hussar!

'Certainly I do. Over whole world. Turkey, the Balkans, Russia,

Persia, even United States of America. Wherever is needed.'

'Needed? What do you do?'

'I was with Dehomag.' He sees the name means nothing to her. 'Deutsche Hollerith Maschinen Gesellschaft. My profession engineer. Graduate of Technical University of Budapest.'

She got his nationality in one.

He dabs at his forehead with a spotless handkerchief, straightens his tie. A subdued kind of excitement as his eyes merry. 'I become today partner with Büchter and Lebeis. In Berlin.' Perfectly even white teeth beam at her. 'Would you do me great honour and with me celebrate?'

'Celebrate?'

'Becoming partner. Perhaps you allow me to invite you for dinner in dining car? Conductor will come round to take reservations soon.'

It's against all traditional advice to accept an invitation from a stranger she's just met on a train but she can't resist such an adventure. The man can hardly compromise her sexually in the dining car. 'I'd love to. How very kind.'

'Entirely I who am in your debt. Becoming partner is always my ambition. I make the inventions also as the engineerings. Being partner is way to benefit from own work.'

If he's achieved that kind of position the man has to be in his thirties. A good age. And the right one to have fought in the Great War. Gabby revises recent history in her mind. He speaks German fluently, even if his word-sequence is quaint, because all Hungarian schools were required to teach German as the first language under the Habsburgs. When he was still at school, perhaps.

All that changed after the War. Which might account for the less-than-perfect language skills. 'What sort of engineer, exactly?'

'Electrical engineer. I work with business machines. In particular famous Hollerith machines. Is new tool of government and business. Will completely change world in which we live.'

His admiring eyes fire enthusiasm as he holds out the promise of a new world. Is this a line or has she really stumbled across a man with a future?

The compartment door opens and the conductor asks for tickets, wants to know whether the Herrschaften, Gabby smiles at the old-fashioned form of address used for First Class passengers, require reservations for the first dinner sitting.

'You have decided? I may have honour?'

She nods. Why not? An extremely handsome important man who obviously thinks she's beautiful. And he isn't wearing a wedding ring.

'I am called Rolf Ferent. May I have honour knowing your name?'

'Gabriele Dohlen. From Schwanenbruch, near Cuxhaven.'

Rolf opens doors between carriages, guides her to their table in the dining car.

'My family from Baja. Is small town in southern Hungary.'

Gabby is embarrassed that she has no idea where that is.

'South of Budapest. Not far from Pècs.' He sees she's still in the dark. 'East of Zagreb. What is now Yugoslavia. When I was child, before War, was part of Austro-Hungarian Empire.'

'Split off by the Treaty of Saint Germain.'

The surprise in his eyes is followed by understanding. 'You must forgive. I already forgot. You history study.'

'I'm primarily interested in philosophy and politics. I read history to understand the background.' A fresh smell of the best cologne wafts over from the other side of the compartment. He must have shaved this morning but his face already has the dark-blue hue of a fast-growing beard. He has a lot of hair.

'To explain more fully, my sister Olga and her husband live in Zagreb now. Three lovely children have.

'I should tell you something of family. My father was landowner. Wonderful, fertile soil on edge of famous Puzta plain. He interested in two things: horses and grapes.'

'Your father owned a vineyard?'

'We grew only one grape. Special variety. Not for making wine. Is dessert grape. And such a fruit. Keeps longer than any other eating variety. We never have problem to sell whole crop. Customers always to us came.'

'You're speaking in the past tense. You no longer own the land?'

'My father die early. In 1906 when he only forty. I eldest am of six children. Age eighteen then. I leave studies to help my mother raise younger children. My youngest brother ten years junior to me. I remained, looking after the estates, until 1910. By then Andrew twelve, my brother Hugo twenty. I leave responsibility to him. Myself went to train as engineer in Budapest. Always I knew things changing from rural to urban economy. Soon land is not enough to support all family properly. Must find other employment.'

'Really? You sensed a change?'

'Certainly. I leave Hungary as soon as I graduate. First go Germany, then I go Holland. My talent is in computing machines.'

CHAPTER 2

Berlin, Autumn 1926

'You shouldn't speak to strange men, Gabby. It's terribly dangerous.'
Small's eyes twinkle as he assumes the stance his father uses. 'Why,
that almost turns you into a Jezebel. Where did you learn such manners?'

Tall and Small have taught her to ignore Frau Meinzer's convictions.
"Worthy and worthless" Tall pronounced them. Not unkindly. Gabby's
going to be twenty in a couple of weeks. Quite old enough to know her
own mind. If she wants to talk to strange men on trains she's going
to do it. If she wants to continue a relationship started that way she'll
do that, too.

'Gabby. Your whole sitting room has been taken over.'

Gabby hurries in at the end of her first full day of her second year at
the University. The lectures are stimulating, her fellow students bright.
And the pace is tough. She'll have to work hard to keep up with the
others. But she'll do it.

'Taken over?' She can't afford to move rooms at the moment. She
needs all her energy for her studies.

With roses. Huge bunches of red roses from a florist. All bearing
the same card:

To the beautiful Princess I met on the train.

Ornate gold lettering on white cards. All signed Rolf Ferent. That has to be the Hungarian engineer she met on the train between Hamburg and Berlin two days ago.

'Really someone you picked up on a train?' Frau Meinzer is scandalised.

'Hardly picked up. We found ourselves in the same compartment. He invited me to have dinner with him in the dining car. To celebrate the fact that he'd just been made a partner in an engineering firm.'

'As for telling him your name and address, that's completely irresponsible. I'm surprised at you. I do hope you won't be getting in touch with him, Gabby. He doesn't sound right at all.' Frau Meinzer is looking at Gabby's splendid hairdo. Frowning at it. As though somehow it was responsible.

Which, no doubt, it was.

'There's no need to worry on my account, Frau Meinzer. I don't even know where he lives. And I've forgotten the name of the firm he's a partner in.' Forgotten, yes. Unable to find out, no. But the roomful of flowers tells her she doesn't need to. Herr Ferent will come calling. Soon.

His letter arrives two days later. She doesn't have to open it to know who it's from. Typewritten address, white envelope. Postmarked Berlin.

Honoured Fräulein Dohlen
It was great pleasure to meet you, to learn something of you and your family.
Was not sufficient. I hardly can wait to know you better. Perhaps you allow me to call on you and present me to Herr and Frau Meinzer? I am happy to invite everyone to an afternoon tea.
It would be great joy for me to fetch you in my automobile. Please to let me know a convenient day and time.
Yours very sincerely,
Rolf Ferent.

Terribly proper. The man's intentions have to be honourable. And he owns a car. At least two up on Doly.

The note is not the only thing in the post. There's also an enormous box of chocolates which covers the greater part of her coffee table. When she opens the package she sees a beautiful young woman on the cover. Sitting on a swing, eating a chocolate.

Sweets to the sweet
RF

'I think it would be an excellent idea if you were to meet Herr Diplom Ingenieur Ferent, Frau Meinzer.' Gabby adds as many adjectives to Rolf's name as she can think of. 'He's an important man, you know. Not only a partner in Büchter and Lebeis...'

'Really? That's a highly thought of company.'

'...but also an inventor. Herr Ferent says business machines are to the 20th Century what the industrial revolution was to the 19th. And he is at the forefront of the new tabulating machines.' Gabby has no idea what all that means. But she's good at regurgitating information. Like a parrot.

'Of course we have to meet him, Gabby. You are in our charge. We cannot allow you to go out with him unless we see what he's like for ourselves.'

THE TWISTED CROSS

The old women of the village know there's treasure buried in the church: a huge black cauldron full of gold coins. It's buried there, waiting for an intrepid adventurer to dare to unearth the priceless hoard.

But the pot of gold is well-guarded by a jealous devil. He makes sure several conditions are fulfilled before the treasure can be revealed.

Firstly, no treasure seeker is allowed to hunt on his or her own.

Secondly, each one must have the courage to dig during the witching hour.

Thirdly, each male treasure hunter must be called Johann.

And, finally, the fourth condition, the hardest to fulfil, is that not a single word may be uttered during the dig.

It so happens that a clay digger called Johann is living in the village. He's a courageous man, quite without fear of man or devil. His wife is equally brave. The couple decide to try their luck. On a calm dark night they equip themselves with a shovel and a spade and wait for the bell to toll midnight, the start of the witching hour. They go into the church, light their candles, lift the flagstones in the crypt and begin to dig.

To their surprise the treasure isn't difficult to find. It's only a few feet below the surface of the soil. Man and wife grin at each other in the flickering shadows. Their hearts jump for joy. But they don't say a single word to each other. They sign to put both spade and shovel handles through the metal handle of the cauldron. And they begin to heave it out.

It's too heavy to come out first time. They nod at each other, spit on their palms to get a proper grip and are about to try again.

'Hold on there. I'll give you a hand with that.'

The couple's eyes meet, their lips remain shut tight. They're determined not to allow fear to deprive them of their treasure. They look up to see a fine gentleman standing there. Not in the least like the devil they'd feared to see.

He nods at them. He's splendidly dressed in a black suit and

311

wearing the finest white kid gloves. With a white symbol emblazoned on his chest. 'That's much too heavy for a lady,' he says in a soft enticing voice.

The clay digger's wife looks at the splendid gloves. She can't bring herself to let such a fine gentleman help them with their muddy work.

'Oh, sir,' she cries. 'We can't possibly accept your kind offer.' She stops, appalled, as she realises, too late, that she's broken the condition of silence.

The figure vanishes. The wooden handles snap. The cauldron full of gold coins tumbles back into its pit. Deep, deep down. Taking the couple's shovel and spade with it. Leaving them with nothing but the twisted white cross which fell from the devil's black coat. The one known as the swastika.

CHAPTER 3

Berlin, Winter 1926/27

'Too grand for us now?' Friedrich Raufensthal is holding the base of the wooden spine with which the Romanisches Café supports the newspapers it supplies for its patrons. His upper body is completely hidden behind the open pages of the *Berliner Tageblatt*.

'I don't know what you're talking about. We meet every day, just as we used to.' Gabby has her own copy of the paper hiding her face. She's sipping coffee to cover her confusion. Though still as keen as before to read about political events, she's stopped going out with Tall and Small in the evenings. Not that she no longer enjoys their company. They are her whiff of freedom. But she can't mix them with Rolf. 'Have you seen that Reichstag members have been behaving disgracefully? Getting into fights on the floor of the chamber, no less.'

'I read the headlines as well as the articles.' Friedrich puts his paper down.

'There's news from the Chinese front as well,' Gabby goes on, reading avidly. 'Chiang Kai-shek's Kuomintang "Reds" have captured Hankow. In the south the Reds have taken Wuchang and the big arsenal at Hangyang. They'll soon control the whole of China as far as Peking.'

'Stop trying to get out of it. Are you coming with us tonight or not?'

'I'm going to the opera with Herr Ferent.'

'Going to marry him, are you?'

'You don't approve?'

Friedrich's direct gaze is uncomfortable. 'I have no feelings about him one way or the other. What's bothering me is that I don't think you have. You think he's a good catch.'

Far too perceptive. But why is it wrong to think of marriage as a business proposition? 'I'm a woman, Friedrich. If I don't marry, or don't marry the right man, I have a bleak time socially.'

'You don't have to marry a Hungarian engineer who's clueless about anything else. And eighteen years older than you. You can do better than that.'

'You *are* prejudiced against him.' The blue eyes pierce into his. 'Worried about his humble origins, by any chance?'

'Below the belt, Gabby. The last thing I approve of is snobbery. But is he for you? The man was born in the 19th Century. In a Hungarian backwater. He's bound to think women are, at best, playthings for men. At worst they're skivvies.'

Gabby thinks back uneasily to Rolf's words: 'My mother try very hard to find wife for me. Bring girls to house. Daughters of friends. Very beautiful.'

A Hungarian mother-in-law. From a well-to-do country family without pretensions. Gabby imagines a small neat woman. Unassuming but classically beautiful, because all Hungarian women are great beauties and Rolf is a remarkably handsome man. She can't deny that she admires good looks. She imagines his mother is similar to Frau Meinzer but wears stylish clothes because, of course, she has more money. Managing a trio of servants who are devoted to her.

'None of them worked out?'

'I cannot tell. I not in Hungary long enough to get know. Is because I travel so much.'

'What sort of girls did your mother introduce?'

'Hungarian girls brought up to be very good at needleworks. Also excellent cooks.' He has a habit of stroking his left eyebrow with his left forefinger. Whenever he's on uncertain ground. 'Is better for me to marry in Germany.'

Is he ashamed of his Hungarian past?

314

'Is also why I change my name from Rezsö to Rolf. Better for business.'

She can hardly blame him for that. Exactly the way she felt about changing Jonah to Hans.

'He isn't like that at all,' Gabby defends her choice. 'He's a very modern man, right at the forefront of invention.'

'I'm not saying he isn't a superlative engineer. Or inventor. Or even salesman. I don't know or care. What I do know is that he's too timid to tackle the establishment. He wants to do what's right. Poor bugger.'

'You sound as though you think he's a lame duck. That's just not true. He left Hungary as soon as he could. Before the War. He got a job with one of the most up-and-coming companies of the time—Dehomag—and rose right to the top. Then he left to do his war service. He was a Hussar, you know. Survived being a prisoner-of-war in Russia.'

'He's a nice enough chap, Gabby. But you're wasted on him. Just think, he'll expect you to be his hostess, never stray from conventional behaviour. D'you really think he'll let you take an active part in politics? Or study, then lecture at the University? And he'll want you to give him sons, to breed. You'll be bored out of your mind.'

Gabby hears Rolf's words in her head: 'My squad and I parted from regiment by battle. We very hungry. Have to eat horse flesh. Drink blood.'

'You mean the animals you were riding?'

Rolf nods. 'We take own horses to War. I very fond my mount. Special breed from my father. But I wish to live.' He sighs. Large soulful eyes. 'Is often in the past we making hard decisions as Hungarian Huzcár.'

Friedrich is wrong. Rolf's not just a handsome face and a good mind trying to conform, he knows how to make hard decisions. 'That's how the Russians caught you?'

'Yes. We prisoners in camp. Middle of nowhere on Russian steppes. Some men try escape on foot. Was killed. We who remain are also punished to allow them to escape.'

Wartime in Schwanenbruch was uncomfortable. But not life threatening. Rolf has no obvious impediments. 'What punishment?'

'At first they say decimate. It mean they kill every tenth man standing in roll-call lines.'

Gabby is surprised at the laconic tone. It heightens her interest. 'And?'

'I one of them. I not want to die.' He spreads his hands in an expansive gesture she's seen before but can't quite place. His eyes flicker a mixture of modesty and pride. 'Suggest other plan. Say I will find good lorimers among prisoners. I show Russians how fashion better bits and spurs for horses. On condition, naturally. If we allowed to live.' He smiles. 'Better for horses, too. I explain takes highly skilled ironsmiths. My men cannot teach Russians quickly. They need several months. And has to be my men who teach because they expert are.'

Gabby is aware that it takes courage and charm to talk your way out of a death sentence. 'You're here. So they agreed.'

He shakes his head from side to side. 'Russians agree on their terms. We look sun every day as punishment. At high noon. Is why I must wear reading glasses from young age.'

There is another story Rolf told her about the honour of Hungarian Hussars which makes it clear that he may be a nice enough chap but she isn't dealing with just any man. She cannot afford to make him jealous. But then, she doesn't plan to. If she marries, she intends to be faithful to her husband. Just like her mother.

'We highly honourable men, we not tolerating brother officers who betraying us.'

'What d'you mean, not tolerating?' Rolf's eyes are no longer soft, his tone gruff.

'We not countenance. I explain with story. When Hungarian Huzcár accusing his sweetheart of betraying with brother officer punishment very severe.'

'You mean a firing squad?'

Rolf smiles, a kind of sideways knowing smile which makes it clear he is not only proud of his regiment's traditions, he would implement them if required.

'Whole garrison assemble on parade ground. Officers watch from battlements above and bugler blow call to battle. Accused girl, completely naked, brought out. Then she forced to run between two

316

long lines of troopers armed with truncheons.

'At this time girl pushed from man to man. Each time she passing one man he strike blow. She pushed from one end of line to other end, beaten while she staggering from side to side. Then she turned round by rough hands when she reach end of line. Finally she must falter, she only human. This is when men grabbing by plaits to hold upright. Until she no longer able stand, no breath left in body.'

'That's barbaric, Rolf. Have you seen this happen?' She wonders, irreverently, what happens to girls who have no plaits. Like herself.

'Of course, I see. Honour must protected be. But is not end of story. New lover held tight by comrades, forced to watch sweetheart from high above parade ground.'

'His punishment is watching the ghastly scene, but the girl...'

'He not released until girl dead.' Again that mournful smile. 'After this, only honourable course for him is throw himself off battlements. This way he join his treacherous beloved.'

CHAPTER 4

Berlin, January 1927

Gabby has known Rolf for some months now. It's time she offered hospitality in return for all his generosity. She invites him to her rooms. With Frau Meinzer's blessing. The worthy lady agreed, provided the door to Gabby's private living room remains ajar.

Rolf appears on the dot of five. His tailored suit is immaculate, his tie in the best of taste. He is bearing yet another bunch of red roses.

'For the most beautiful girl I have ever known.'

Gabby accepts them without much enthusiasm. She already has the dozen he sent yesterday. He's sent roses every Friday since the day they met.

'And now something else I have for you.' He hands her a small package. She feels the constriction in her throat. A ring box; she's sure he's offering her an engagement ring. Much sooner than she expected. She isn't ready for such a step. 'For me?'

'There is no one else in my life.'

Gabby opens the box. Slowly. Reluctantly. Friedrich's words echo in her mind:

"You may be a woman, Gabby, but you're a rich one. An heiress. Why tie yourself down to some ordinary man? Why not do what you always said you wanted to do? Take up a career at the University. Or become a politician. You can do it. Your father was quite inspired when he called you Gabby. You know how to hold an audience, to captivate them. You have the gift of the gab."

Is she consigning herself to a life of bourgeois boredom? The box is open and she hasn't even taken in its contents. Rolf is standing, watching her. He drops to his knees.

'Will you become my little wife, Gabriele? Sweet girl, you will do me the honour, you marry me?'

The diamond is very large. Set in white gold or perhaps platinum. He isn't being cheap. And he's still kneeling in front of her. Disconcerting. 'Please, Rolf. Do get up. I'm very honoured.'

He stays where he is, kisses her hand. Passionately. 'You say no?'

She gets up, unable to sit still.

He stands as well. Puts her right hand in both of his. 'I think I have much I can offer you, Gabriele.'

'Do call me Gabby. That's what my family call me.'

The handsome face nods. But does not smile. He puts her hand up to his lips, kisses it. 'I think that is a little, how shall I say? Not gracious name? I asking you to become my dear wife. I would like call you my little Grischa.'

'Geisha? Isn't that some sort of Japanese concubine?' She doesn't mean to sound harsh. But really.

He stares at her. 'No, no. Not Geisha. Grischa, with short 'i'. Is Hungarian diminutive for Gabriele.'

Gabby isn't too sure. Her heart hammers discordant jolts. She can't concentrate on trivia so she lets it pass. 'There is something about me that you need to know, Rolf.'

He looks slightly put out, then his face brightens. 'You have unfortunate love affair? You love someone else still?'

'Please, Rolf. You're making me nervous.' He's mistaking Tall and Small for possible past admirers. If only he knew. 'And it's nothing of that sort at all. You are the first man I have ever been courted by.' Should she have told him that?

'Is because you wish study?'

How can a brilliant inventor be so unobservant? She'll have to persuade the Meinzers to spell out her inheritance in detail. Her father's legacy is hardly going to be a hindrance. But the one her mother Emma left her, the one which has haunted her as long as she can remember, the one she still finds hard to live with: how will Rolf react to that?

'Something to do with family?'

Ahh. 'In a way...'

'Your father's will make conditions? You cannot marry until a certain age?'

He thinks it's to do with money, with Vater's will? She's never even seen it. She's assumed he's left her one third of his estate. That she'll come into it at twenty-one. 'I can't discuss it with you, Rolf. I want you to take this ring away...'

He sinks down to his knees again. 'Please not to say 'no' my darling. Say 'maybe'. If it to do money, we not need your father's. I make excellent salary. I will show your guardians...'

'Keep it until you have spoken to the Meinzers, Rolf. My guardian lives in New Jersey, too far away for you to speak to him. And I can't possibly explain.' She holds the exquisite stone up to the light, watches the reflections. They dazzle her. 'I am very touched by your proposal, Rolf. And the ring is really beautiful. But I can't answer you. Not until you have spoken to the Meinzers.'

Gabby is left alone in her private sitting room, fiddling with the locket around her neck. While Rolf Ferent is cloistered with the Meinzers. She was so worried about Rolf's reaction to her inheritance that she's allowing them to decide her future for her. She's even given him the impression that as long as he thinks she's good enough for him, she'll have him. Is she really so afraid that no one else will marry her that she's prepared to be railroaded at the first attempt? Or is it the locket's fault? Does it work its magic so well it snares both the gene carrier and the potential husband?

Tall and Small's warnings come back to her. Why isn't she concentrating on what counts? Is this man really right for *her*? Will he allow her to live the life *she* wants? She's not just a woman who has learned to make herself look attractive. She may be a woman, but she also has talents a man would use to achieve riches, or high office, or both. Is she throwing them away?

Rolf is much older than she is and shows no signs of being autocratic. Will he allow her to fulfil herself as well as be his wife? How can she tell? He's told her what *he's* passionate about. Which must provide her with some kind of clue.

'You would like to know what really important is to me? I greatly admire Herman Hollerith. A statistical engineer. Is a genius. He make machine which can translate data into significant information.'

The one thing which bores Gabby even more than domestic trivia is mechanics. 'What does that mean?'

'Perhaps best illustrated with example. He two things did: first he mechanised recording and reading of numerical data. Then he established a 'unit record', something which contains information relating to particular transaction. He registered this in form of punched holes. Punch-card machine.'

Completely stultifying. She must try to grasp what he's talking about. 'I still don't understand.'

Rolf looks to see if she's really listening. Decides she is. 'Hollerith punch-card machines make it possible to analyse data as never before. Laborious, time-consuming tasks of enumeration and computation can now be done by machine.'

Gabby has no idea why this should be important. 'What tasks?'

'Collating data from census information is excellent example. Hollerith's first success was when he applied his methods to United States census. His idea was to use one card for each individual, with salient points of each person punched into the edges in form of notches.' He smiles. 'Along the lines of railway ticket. Hollerith noticed collectors punch tickets to show identifying features: male, light hair, dark eyes, etc. Known as punch photograph.

'Cut long story short, such method mean same characteristic for many people you can pick out very quick. If you use complete card, punch holes instead notches, one card able contain enormous amount information. Then, if it possible to put tool like knitting needle through same hole for whole set of cards, you now having cards showing all people with such characteristic.'

Knitting needles are not Gabby's forte. Needlework has always been a problem. But Rolf's language has improved dramatically.

'For example, Caucasians. Then male Caucasians. Then male Caucasians living in Kentucky, say. Working in office. And so on.'

At last a point she can understand. Politicians are interested because they're after power through information. 'The US Government used the census to establish more than just the number of people in the country?'

'Exactly. I discover because Vienna used to be big scientific capital of world. Then came Hollerith from America. He bring machines over from United States to England, then Germany. In 1911 he install in Berlin.

'Then man called Heidinger formed his own company—Deutsche Hollerith Maschinen Gesellschaft—now Dehomag, as I already told. He need money. I join him in 1913, give small amount money. I make lots improvements in machines.

'War broke out. As I told, I join my regiment, spend four years as Huzcár, many months leading my men from central Russia back home to Hungary.

'After War I return immediately to Dehomag. In 1920 I nominated best tabulating man in Europe.'

'Really?'

'Is long time ago. My world never still stands. I must new inventions make. I sure I have exciting and important career. I like you join me. You are beautiful, well educated and come from background which understands investment. I need you as partner as well as wife. You like join me?'

He invited her to be his partner. So it's not all to do with breeding and hostessing. Rolf is really quite like her father. From a humble background, but with vision. Striding out into the world to make his mark. Not simply motivated by money, any more than her father was. Rolf wants to better the world, to forge it to a new design. An exciting prospect. And he is prepared to include her in his plans. How can Friedrich misjudge him so?

The knock on the door is discreet, but emphatic.

They're through already? It's only been fifteen minutes. He's decided it's a lost cause, he can't possibly marry her...

'May I come in, my sweet little Grischa?'

'Rolf. Of course.'

His face is beaming. 'I think we don't let small detail of hair upset us. Not need worry, my dear. I enough for two have.'

322

Her mother's story comes back to Gabby, the one which carilloned like a set of joyful bells from generation to generation.

"I have enough for two."

She fingers the locket she's wearing inside her dress. Rolf Ferent used the exact same words Great-grandfather Hinrich used. The fates have spoken. This will be a marriage made in heaven.

CHAPTER 5

Berlin, February 1927

'Is very small, Rezsö. She will able to have the childrens?'

Josephine Ferent is enthroned in the centre of her son's sofa. She cradles Gabby's outstretched hand in both of hers. Holds on. Forcing even Gabby's diminutive form to bend down. Her daughter Elisabeth, an unusually tall woman, has stood to greet Gabby and glowers above her.

'Is not heights is of importance, Mother. Is pelvic bones.' Rolf's lateral thinking is not confined to machines. 'Gabriele cannot make grow taller than God wish.'

A hissing intake of breath. 'Why you don't call me Mama. Always you calls me Mama.'

A small embarrassed smile curls round Rolf's lips. Tentatively. 'Mama...'

Frau Ferent is examining the engagement ring. Worn on Gabby's left ring finger, to be transferred to her right hand at the wedding ceremony. Mama compares it with her own smaller one. Which is also worn on the left hand, as befits a widow. 'Is fine diamond, Rezsö. Good colour.'

'I buy in Budapest,' Rolf says. Proudly.

Gabby reclaims her hand. She settles in the chair furthest from her future mother-in-law and sits demure, ankles crossed.

Josephine Ferent is shrouded in black. As is only proper. 'I give up the colourings,' she tells Gabby. Evaluating the emerald satin which slips seductively round Gabby's slender figure. 'On day my dear Paul left us. So young.'

Gabby's mental arithmetic tends to the patchy. Rolf's is reliable. He told her his father died twenty years ago. Do Hungarian widows wear weeds for life?

Black silk moulds the grieving widow's body into a pillar shape, disguising curves. Her footwear bears unexpected tribute to fashion. Patent leather, strap sandals with a heel. To display small feet and enviable ankles. Clad in the finest silk. In suitable black.

She draws up millimetres of skirt to display more leg. 'You have the problems with the legs? I tell good exercises.'

Gabby pushes her feet further under her chair. Emma's inheritance did not confine itself to the errant gene. Both her daughters have her delicate bone structure. Swan necks, tapering fingers, tiny waists and fashionably slim hips. Small breasts to go with them. Perfect flappers. Except for the heavy legs. With ankles which have an annoying tendency to swell.

The black sable Rolf gave his mother is draped around her shoulders. Clutched tightly around her body, despite the warmth of the apartment. A tribute to filial devotion, a token of worldly success.

'I think we no need worry, Mama. Gabriele no shorter is than you, and you three sons and three daughters give my father.' Rolf walks up to Gabby and hands her a slim rectangular golden box. 'Open.'

A present while his mother's watching? An advance for six children? Gabby opens the little box. Irritation makes her clumsy. The contents fall into her lap. She gasps. A string of opulent pearls.

'Is deep sea.' He picks the necklace up. Undoes the clasp, tries to put the string around her neck.

'Just one minute, Rolf. I'll have to take the locket off.'

'I this can do.'

Her mother refused a pearl necklace, chose to wear only the locket. Gabby thinks hard, decides that's not required of her. She twists away, unfastens the locket. Rolf catches her arms, turns her back, slips the pearls around her neck, begins to busy himself at her nape.

That's much too intimate for Gabby's comfort. He could easily draw attention to... her thoughts shy away from the word wig. Her hairdo.

Show it up. Something his lynx-eyed female relatives will spot at once. She stands. The necklace stays in place.

'I almost not finish,' Rolf says, standing himself, hands cupping her shoulders.

Disarming smiles are the mainstay of Gabby's fight against detection. 'I can't wait to look in the mirror.' She walks over to the mantelpiece, looks into the gilded mirror above it. Assesses Mama's sharp eyes behind her. Too busy calculating the value of the pearls to notice the tell-tale bunching of lifeless hair at the base of Gabby's neck. She pretends to check the clasp to finger her hair into a more natural shape.

'They are beautiful, Rolf.'

'Oi yoi yoi. So small she is.'

'What she shall do, Mama? Eat magic mushroom make herself grow?'

'Just I worry about the childrens.' Frau Ferent stands, walks over to Gabby. A finger is swept along the mantelpiece. She examines the tip, discovers a white hair, holds it up. Accusingly.

'Is white. Is yours.' Rolf's laconic tone is practised. The apartment is spacious, immaculate. His mother and sister are well taken care of by an excellent housekeeper who bosses a maid and a cook.

Mama's extravagant hat hides most of her hair. Escaping strands are completely white. But they look irritatingly abundant.

She notices Gabby look. 'Is latest fashion,' she tells her. Lips pursed at Gabby's hairdo. 'Is own colour, or you dye?'

Rolf's sister Elisabeth, called Bözsi by her family, has been mesmerised by the attractive shingle-cut since the moment she met her future sister-in-law. She's not just taller than Gabby, she's taller than her brother Rezsö. Somewhat angular and thin, with a full head of straight jet-black hair. Quite unlike her feminine mother. She uses her height to inspect the roots of Gabby's hair. Which, unsurprisingly, pass the test.

The midday meal is served by a maid dressed in black. With a white apron and cap. The first course is asparagus. Thick juicy asparagus raised in a greenhouse. At a high price.

'Why you don't have proper food, Rezsö? Is not good for important man to live on rabbit food.' Mama nods her head like a wise owl. The chandelier lights up the face under the hat.

Gabby can see that she must once have been beautiful. Large eyes which, presumably, were not always mournful. An oval face with still attractive skin. And her figure, if one can guess at it under the mass of black which protects Mama from the prying gaze of dangerous men, is still trim. The woman has to be getting on for sixty. Her eldest child is thirty-eight.

'Is not good to wear so much powder, Gabriele. You spoil the skin.'

Gabby smiles and nods her head. She assumed that Rolf was like her own father, abandoning his native land for greener shores. It's possible there were other, even more pressing, reasons. They shouldn't affect her. The female members of Rolf's family will remain in Hungary. Or Yugoslavia, where Olga and her husband have made their home. Whichever part of old Austro-Hungary they live in, Gabby intends to make sure they stay there.

'You have sampler for show me? Or finished pieces?'

A small rapier thrust Gabby isn't expecting. What, exactly, is a sampler, anyway?

'Our girls so good are with embroidery. Bözsi bring you blouse for special present.'

Her daughter disappears from the dining room on what may have been a pre-arranged signal. Invisible to non-Hungarian perceptions. She returns with an enormous box done up with ribbons. Patriotically green, red and white.

'Is for you. I make myself.'

'How kind.' Gabby's voice is a little high with nervousness. A valiant effort holds the box above her plate. She opens it. Clouds of tissue paper take up space. She stands and takes the whole thing to the sideboard.

The diaphanous Magyar blouse with billowing sleeves and red, green and black embroidery is eventually disembowelled from the box. The cross stitch is exquisitely worked. Covering what would otherwise show indelicate parts of anatomy. The dense embroidery is what keeps the garment decent. Assuming the right size.

This blouse is enormous. Gabby's slight frame could be wrapped twice in it.

'How lovely, Frau Ferent. And you, Bözsi. Thank you both so very much.'

Consternation in Mama's eyes. She turns to her son, arms lifted in supplication. 'Why she call me Frau Ferent?'

Surely even Hungarians don't expect fiancées to call their future mothers-in-law... Gabby balks at the very thought. She'll avoid all names.

'Because that is your name, Mama. You remember your name.'

An odd reaction. Coupled by a remarkably firm tone. Almost a warning. Gabby leaves this interesting development for later thought and holds the blouse up. An image of Tall and Small appears. Unbidden. Jonah's sharp eyes examine the gaudy patterns, Friedrich's aristocratic nose points down. She can only hope her involuntary grin will be taken as an expression of delight.

'Why you don't put on.'

'It is quite beautiful. What do you think, Rolf? The sleeves may be a little too long for me. I will ask my dressmaker...'

'Dressmaker? You not your clothings make?'

Ludicrous thought. Gabby finds it impossible to sew on a button, let alone use a needle for more demanding work. 'I'm a student.' Gabby feels confident that even Hungarian mothers will see the value of an education.

'You study? At such old age?'

Gabby's skilled tongue is silenced for several seconds. Senility applied to twenty is a new concept. 'I attend the Royal Friedrich Wilhelm University.' It's been tough to get in, the standards are very high. She's a year older than most of the other students in her year; American grade school took its toll. At least it's unlikely that Rolf's family will question that.

'Oi yoi yoi. I took you for some years younger.' A frowning reassessment. 'Fifteen, sixteen. Is your height is deceiving.'

Gabby fingers the hair by her ear. Easing it into her smooth creamy cheek. A flawless silky complexion is one of the compensations of her inheritance.

'I you told Gabriele study, Mama.'

Mama brushes irrelevancies aside. 'Our girls marries often at twelve.'

Gabby readjusts Mama's age. She may be only just over fifty. Likely to live another twenty years. Or even more.

Mama stands, clasps Rolf, enveloping arms choking him to her maternal bosom. 'We have such young girls in Budapest, so beautiful. Oi yoi yoi.'

Gabby keeps her eyes firmly on the blouse. Bözsi is Rolf's youngest sister, but she is not the youngest sibling. She must be thirty. And unmarried.

'We not in Hungary, Mama. Things different in Berlin. Gabriele also beautiful is, and well-educated. How you think she welcome my important guests if she talk only of needleworks and cookings?'

The arms leave her son and fly upwards. For heavenly succour. 'If your dear father were alive, what he would think?'

It crosses Gabby's mind that he might have viewed death as his only means of escape.

CHAPTER 6

Berlin, February 1927

'And this my brother Andrew, Grischa. We call Bandi. He with Remington Typewriter Company now, soon to merge with Rand Kardex and become Remington Rand. They want Bandi join new company. Is great honour.'

Gabby has heard of the Remington Typewriter Company. A rival firm to Rolf's, she thought. Are the brothers competitors? Her outstretched hand is taken and reverently kissed. Andrew Ferent, the youngest Ferent, ten years Rolf's junior, is about twelve centimetres taller than his brother. And very dashing. With the most inviting lips she has ever seen. Not exactly more handsome than his brother, Rolf is a very handsome man, but reasonably good-looking. Oozing sex appeal. A trait Doly is always going on about and Gabby has never noticed before.

'Should I call you Andrew or Bandi?'

'Bandi, naturally.' He grins. 'As long as you don't use the English 'a', and stick with the German 'aah'. Being bandy is not an attractive attribute.'

Gabby laughs. 'I promise, Baahndi.'

'I hope we will become the best of friends.'

A lilt of Hungarian accent. No trace of Hungarian word sequence. The very touch of his hand sends tremors of electricity through Gabby. Her breasts feel as though they are on fire, about to swell out of her clothes. Her thighs tremble. She sits down.

'You're not feeling well, Grischa?'

'It's a little close in here.'

Rolf opens a window. Bandi goes to his brother's drinks cupboard, takes out exquisitely-cut Venetian glass and a matching decanter filled with brandy, pours Gabby some. 'Allow me.'

Gabby drinks gratefully. Though the desire to sing is hard to subdue. 'You're also an engineer?' Surely this demi-god does something more interesting?

'Never bothered to qualify. My talents lie in sales. I have introduced more typewriters into European offices than any other salesman east of the Rhine. Now I am to become European manager for the new Remington Rand. An American company.'

'You're visiting Berlin?'

'For the moment I am working out of Berlin. I have just taken an apartment.'

'And your wife? She's with you now or she's coming later?'

'I'm a bachelor gay.' He laughs. 'Not for want of trying on my mother's part. Every time I visit Budapest I'm subjected to a string of potential brides.'

Budapest, March 1927

The Ferent vineyard was abandoned after the last of Mama's three sons left home. To go abroad. First Rolf in 1910. The 1914 call to arms claimed Hugo. He was taken prisoner early in 1915 and sent to England. Where he married an English girl before the War was over. He has not returned.

Andrew was sixteen when War broke out. A tall boy who lied about his age and enlisted. Leaving Mama and two unmarried daughters to run the vineyard. The eldest daughter, Ankara, married within six months. Mama sold up and moved to an apartment in Budapest. Her opulent rooms, proudly detailed to Gabby by Rolf, house Persian carpets on the walls, the floor. Crystal chandeliers are suspended from the ceiling at two-metre intervals, plush velvet easy chairs invite comfortable seating.

The furniture is heavy Biedermeier. Holitsch tureens, two magnificent examples in the shape of peacocks, stand on the dresser.

331

Several Dresden figure groups are scattered around the room. When Frau Ferent took Bözsi to Budapest she moved into a new style of life. In which they conspire together.

'This very dear friend, Frau Blumenthal, Bandi. Her daughter, Irene. Made all these cakes we have for tea.'

Bandi smiles. A well-practised sideways smile which tells his mother he knows quite well that the girl's mother baked the cakes. And that he has no intention of marrying a Hungarian girl. Or any other girl. He isn't looking for a wife. Mistresses can be changed with the decorations. And his location.

'And also the tablecloth. Irene embroidered herself. Is wonderful workmanship.'

He recognises his sister Bözsi's work. She's had a lot of practice. 'Workwomanship would be a better description.'

Blank stares show the witticism has misfired. As usual. 'You don't eat cake?' Frau Ferent asks. Solicitous for her son's health.

Bandi dutifully bites into his favourite poppy seed strudel. The pastry is exquisite, the filling perfect. He needs a trim figure. 'It is superb,' he tells the young girl. Nodding and smiling. Eyes dull.

She knows something is wrong and wants to prove her honesty. 'Mama helped me.'

Her mama bridles so that her pearls oscillate in protest. 'Hardly at all, my pretty one.'

Frau Ferent remembers that domestic talents are not enough. 'Irene is skilled musician, Bandi. You like hear her play?' The piano stands in a corner of the enormous living room. A vast ornament. No one in his family plays.

'I am so sorry, everyone. I do have a very important business meeting.'

'On Sunday?'

He doesn't even take an extra breath. 'An American colleague is over from New York. His boat is leaving from Hamburg tomorrow. He's taking the early train from Prague. Changing in Vienna. I meet him there today or not at all.'

CHAPTER 7

Berlin, March 1927

'Grischa. I am so sorry.' The enormous bouquet of red roses is held like a shield.

Gabby swallows, forces her features into a smile. His mother didn't approve of her. He's decided to break off the engagement. Doly will dance with glee.

'Hello, Rolf.' The words sound husky.

'There is nothing I can do. I cannot go.'

Gabby frowns. 'Go where?'

'The Berliner Staatstheater. You wanted specially go to the première of *The Merchant of Venice*.'

What's all this about? He's nervous about being seen with her? 'You weren't able to get tickets?'

'I am meeting Mr Thomas J Watson. The head of remarkable company: International Business Machines. We call IBM for short. He interested in offering me important position. Director of company. And maybe, in due course, Eastern European manager for whole firm.'

'But I thought you were a partner?'

'IBM is going to be most important business machine company. Not just Europe and America, in whole world. Mr Watson has rare gift. He new technology understand, and know how to sell. You know I inventor am. Also salesman. I want my work be part of new energetic company. So is noticed.'

The man is more ambitious than she realised. 'That is a wonderful opportunity, Rolf. Of course you must meet Mr Watson. He wants to see you in the evening?'

'Because he returns to United States tomorrow.' He pulls his wallet out, extracts two tickets. 'You can go, Grischa. Maybe with Frau Meinzer.'

Both Jonah and Friedrich would give their eye teeth to go to that performance. 'Well...'

His face is suddenly transformed by a beatific smile. 'Why I didn't think myself? Bandi. Bandi will you escort, my place take.'

The brother with the enormous sex appeal.

'What did you think?'

Gabby and Bandi are walking out of the theatre after the première. Tall and Small were right in their assumptions. Fritz Kortner, himself a Jew, played the title role as Shakespeare wrote it. No compromises. He played Shylock as a tragic, but also as a mean and hate-filled character.

'Some friends of mine are quite knowledgeable about the theatre. They said the director wanted Kortner to make Shylock more sympathetic.'

Bandi hails a cab. 'A little supper?'

'Lovely.'

'Why more sympathetic?'

'So as not to inflame even more anti-Semitic feelings.'

He stands tall. Eyes levelled above her head are fixed in a stare. Is he, by any chance, anti-Semitic? 'You think there's a risk of that?' Dispassionate tone.

'Kortner is a brilliant actor. He played the role under Berthold Viertel in 1923, and under Max Reinhardt in 1924. I read he was excellent then. Now he's magnificent. It's bound to affect people's perceptions.'

Bandi's eyes are on her now. Contemplative. 'You're very politically astute. Particularly for a young lady.'

Is that a compliment or a condemnation?

His special enigmatic smile. 'Now let's forget such problems. Enjoy the evening.' He pulls her fur around her. Berlin can be bitingly cold, even in March. 'I hope you're hungry.'

'Were you a Huzcár like Rolf, Bandi? In the same regiment?'

There is a reptile quality to his eyes. A tortoise ready to submerge under its carapace at the first hint of domestic problems. 'I would not consider anything else. But the cavalry was not easy to serve in. I was sent to Russia as soon as I was trained. I was seventeen in early 1916.'

'So you were thrown in at the deep end?'

'The older officers were already exhausted. I rose quickly from lieutenant to captain. Then there was something of a set-back.'

'You were wounded?'

'Nothing so exciting. My large toe froze during the winter offensive.'

'But you were on a horse?'

A condescending smile. 'That was the reason. I couldn't get much circulation in my feet.'

'So you were sent to hospital?'

'They wanted me to have the toe amputated. I refused.'

'Really?' The young man is not only handsome. He's very sure of himself, determined. 'And was that wise?'

He inclines his head, lids his eyes. 'As it turned out, yes. I took sick leave, and massaged the toe with calendula oil. My mother always swore by it.'

'That worked?'

'A miraculous cure. Within five days I was back in the saddle.'

The feeling of excitement, of not being able to take her eyes off this strong, handsome, commanding man, makes Gabby less talkative than usual.

'You're very silent, Gabriele. Aren't you feeling well? Or simply tired?' Bandi is scanning the menu. 'Perhaps a cocktail to revive you? Or a Bucks Fizz to applaud Kortner's triumph.'

Gabby smiles gratefully. Rolf does not stop her drinking. But he doesn't encourage her. His brother seems to understand her needs. 'What I'd really like is a Brandy Fizz.'

'Of course.' Bandi snaps his fingers at the waiter.

'And for you, sir?'

'A glass of fresh orange juice.' One of the strangest characteristics of the Ferents is that none of them drink wine, or any alcohol. They are not against it, they merely do not themselves enjoy it.

The waiter is blissfully prompt. Gabby gulps eagerly, enjoys the brandy, speeded by the fizzy soda water, firing it through her veins. She feels herself relax, her tongue begins to loosen. 'You've never been tempted to get married, Bandi?'

'Tempted, of course. The endless stream of would-be brides my mother introduces includes many beautiful girls.'

'But you resisted?'

'I need a special kind of wife. One who looks good, is a superlative hostess, can hold her own in any company, speaks English. Someone I can talk to.'

Gabby takes a deep breath, remembers Friedrich's constant lectures about not marrying the wrong man. She has to be brave. She looks challengingly at Bandi. 'Like me, for instance.'

He puts his right hand out to cover hers, draws back. 'Exactly like you, Gabriele. But you are engaged to my brother Rolf. It is a matter of honour. A Huzcár officer would never steal his brother officer's lady. Nor would any Hungarian steal his brother's betrothed.' A wan smile.

So deliciously old-fashioned. Another of Bandi's attractions. But it left nothing further to be said. For the present.

Berlin, April 1927

'Why we don't marry now? Why we wait?' Rolf's approach is always direct, without finesse.

'I would like finish my studies properly, Rolf. Graduate.'

He nods. 'You can finish also when we married. I don't stop.'

Gabby looks down and blushes. 'There are other aspects to marriage. Which have consequences.'

'I engage more servants.'

'Personal consequences.' The hint of tears. 'I'm not sure that it is right for me to have children.'

'You worry about the inheritance. Is not necessary.'

Why would he worry? He doesn't have to live with it, only beside it.

And she has learned to conceal it very well. Her mother's pain-filled eyes come back to her. Bad to cope for oneself, but there's no option. Entirely different to watch one's children begin to comprehend what their inheritance means, how other people react to it. That must be torture, producing a pain which has to be hidden to stop the children feeling worse. Particularly if they're girls.

'I prefer not to have children at this point.'

He kisses her hand. Smiles down at her. 'Womens always the childrens want. I wait.'

Insufferable male arrogance. A blast of fury sweeps through Gabby. She subdues it. Is he saying he's prepared to marry and not have children? She can have her cake and eat it?

'You mean you know how to arrange...' Her voice trails off.

'Certainly. If you so wish.'

'So you would have no objection to my continuing with my studies at the University?'

'I think Mr Watson very impressed.'

'My guardian won't give permission for me to marry without elaborate provisions about my inheritance. Money, I mean.'

'Is understandable.' He nods his head. 'We wait till you twenty-one, Grischa. Is not long, is end September. For this we plan big wedding in Schwanenbruch, invite all family.'

CHAPTER 8

Riverside Hall, May 1927

'Dorinda. Show a leg there, Dorinda Dohlen. Call for you.'

Doly opens the door to her room. She keeps in weekly touch with Tante Martha. Writes to Bobby Hudwalker, Lieselotte and Gabby at regular intervals. But a phone call? Virtually unheard of unless it's local. Has someone died?

'You are a dark horse. So you do have a secret beau apart from boy Bobby. I always guessed.' Faith's solid laugh chuckles around the corridor.

She has a barrelful of beaux besides Bobby. In Schwanenbruch. Werner even writes now and then. But Bobby's letters come daily. He wrote and asked her to marry him two weeks after they met.

Faith dismisses him as wet behind the ears. Tante Martha wrote disparagingly. "He doesn't sound at all right for you, Doly. You can't marry a car-factory worker's son." Seems even when a boy has honourable intentions he isn't good enough.

'A man's voice?'

'Sure thing. My *John* doesn't he sound cute. Like I imagine Rudi.'

Doly and Faith have seen every Valentino movie playing in town. He was better looking than any other man they know, but the real attraction is the display of his horsemanship. They ride together in his style. Faith is Rudi, Doly his latest love.

Doly picks up the dangling receiver. Shuts the booth door. 'Hello?'

'You Dorinda Dohlen are?'

A lilting foreign voice. Not German. 'Yes. Who is this?'

'My name Rolf Ferent. Fiancé to your sister, Gabriele. She speaks often of you. I have in Pennsylvania business, and I promise her I visit you. Relate her how you are.'

Rolf Ferent. Gabby's big lover number. Hallelujah. 'How very nice.'

'I hire car. You like, I can drive your school and fetch you tomorrow. We go out and have tea. Maybe see film.'

Sounds unbelievably boring. Tea. Where would one drink tea in Pennsylvania except in the Tea Room in Riverside Hall? 'That would be divine. I guess you know I have to check with my house-teacher. Sign out and all that.'

'But can be arranged?'

'Lessons aren't a problem. I have a soccer practice scheduled. But I'm only the second substitute. I guess they'll let me off.'

Faith is pacing up and down outside the phone booth. 'OK? Who was it?'

Doly hooks her arm through faithful Faith's. 'You got it in one. My sister's fiancé wants to say hello. He's Hungarian. And he was a Hussar. I guess you'll understand if I break our riding date.'

'As long as he's your *sister's* fiancé, that's just fine.'

Doly doesn't get to bed till one o'clock in the morning. Too busy trying on what clothes she has. She settles for a tight-fitting, royal blue silk. Which makes her look older. And seductive.

She oversleeps, misses breakfast. By the time she's dressed she's half an hour later than the time Rolf said he'd call for her.

She saunters down. A dark handsome man is waiting in the hall. Studying photographs of old alumni of Riverside Hall. Which are the only decoration.

He recognises her at once. 'You so like Grischa look. Is what I call your sister. Both beautiful.' Bows. Hands her a small box. 'For you.'

A present from a man she's never met? Doly opens it carefully, pulls out a bracelet. In silver and gold.

'Is three types gold,' he tells her. 'White, blond and gold colour. You like?'

She certainly likes. She puts it across her slender wrist and holds it out for Rolf to fasten. He does so, raises the hand to his lips, kisses it. 'I hope give you great pleasure.'

'Perhaps you'd like to see my room. Then you can tell Gabby all about it.'

Dear Diary,

Gabby's beau is not at all what I expected. So easy to talk to. Not remotely like my idea of a boring businessman. He's interested in discussing questions of morality, the emancipation of women, what I'm studying. Even the sports I enjoy.

I've never talked to a veteran before. So exciting about his war experiences. The way the Russians ruined his eyesight. The way he led his own men back after the War. Across the boundless Russian steppes and through large parts of Eastern Europe.

And such exciting plans for the house they're going to rent and furnish in Berlin. A really big house, with large rooms for entertaining. Gabby's so lucky.

We talked for hours. As though we knew each other really well. Then he drove me to Paradise, took me out to lunch in a fancy place.

We went to see a stupid cowboy film which we had fun pulling to shreds. He's got a wonderful sense of humour. And we walked for hours afterwards.

I saw a huge box of chocolates in a store window. Made a joke about hardly being able to carry it. Can't believe he charged right in to buy it for me. Absolutely enormous. Must have cost a fortune.

I've never met anyone like Rolf. No idea such wonderful men exist. A charming decent handsome man. Clever as well. Told me about the inventions he's patented. How on earth did Gabby get her claws into him?

We finished off a wonderful day by going out to a splendid meal. Then he rushed me back to Riverside Hall for ten o'clock curfew. Said he'd promised my teacher. Just like Cinderella and the glass coach.

I think he adored me from the start. He took me right up to my *room. Held both my hands in his. To warm them, he said. Though they weren't in the least bit cold. Then he kissed each fingertip.*

He behaved just like Rudi, and in the way I'm always hoping Bobby will treat me. Not that he doesn't try to be a gentleman. But he grips my head when he kisses me. Quite hard sometimes. As for bringing flowers, the best he's managed so far is stealing a bloom from someone's window box.

Riverside Hall, Summer 1927

'Dorinda! Phone call for Dorinda Dohlen.'

Doly runs along the corridor to the phone booth reserved for Riverside Hall students.

'Hi, Bobby. How d'you get to a phone?'

'This is Dorinda Dohlen?'

That lilting Hungarian rhythm. Rolf Ferent in the US again so soon? Gabby wrote nothing about it in her last letter.

'Is that you, Rolf?'

'This is Andrew Ferent. Rolf's brother. I heard so much about you from Gabriele I thought I'd look you up. I'm in Pittsburgh on business.'

'Why, hello. I didn't even know Rolf has a brother.'

'He has two. Hugo lives in England.'

Is Gabby match-making? Or is Rolf's brother so taken with Gabby that he wants to meet her sister? 'And you? Where do you live?'

'In Berlin.'

Maybe it's Rolf who's match-making.

'Perhaps I could pick you up and take you out? A film, perhaps? Followed by dinner?'

'Do you see a lot of Gabby, Andrew?' The man seems obsessed with similarities between her and Gabby.

'Do call me Bandi. Spelt B a n d i, but pronounced Baahndi. More or less. And, before you ask, my legs are not in the least bit bent.'

'Right. Baahndi. D'you get together with Rolf and Gabby all the time, living in the same town?'

A curious tucking of his neck suggests an assessing tortoise. Distant and reserved. 'Not really. I travel a great deal.'

341

Doly has no intention of being steered into marriage yet. She's very young and beautiful. And her hair is still abundant. Why would she tie herself to such a cool customer, a man who's not exactly going to lose his reason over her? Or perhaps any woman.

'But Gabby gave you my address?'

Elegantly coated shoulders shrug. 'My brother suggested I might look you up. He says he visited you himself. That you are a very charming young lady.'

So it was Rolf, not Gabby. Figures. 'I don't know about charming. I think maybe I shocked him.'

A slow, slow flicker. 'I don't think my brother is easily shocked.'

'Your brother's such a sweetie. Of the old-fashioned kind.' Bandi's expression is very different from Rolf's. Whose honest open eyes are tinged with melancholy. Bandi's bold gaze is shadowed behind hooded lids. A reptile basking in the sun.

'And you are a modern young lady. I see.'

Is he taking the Mickey? Doly shakes her American-style bob. Invitingly. Bandi's brown irises widen. With pleasure, she's pretty sure.

'It's quite remarkable how similar you sisters look. Both with fiery red hair, both petite, both slender as reeds. Gabriele's eyes are cerulean blue. Yours are nearer violet.'

Doly has hennaed her hair successfully, almost back to its vivid red. And Bandi has noticed Gabby as a woman. Damn her for stealing Doly's hair colour. Why couldn't she stay blonde? 'We may look alike. But we're completely different in temperament.' Doly takes out a cigarette holder, inserts a Lucky Strike.

Enlarged irises retreat to spots as Bandi looks on impassively. No motion towards striking a match for her.

Doly whips a lighter out of her handbag, clicks it into flame.

'In what way different?' Slow somnolent eyes watch as she pulls at the cigarette, inhales, exhales. With deliberation.

His eyes focus without widening, his lips purse.

What's going on? It affects all the other guys she's met. No reaction of any kind.

Damned nerve. What the hell, she's not going to know this man anyway. 'Gabby's the one who does everything the way it should be done. Never kicks over the traces, never breaks the rules.'

'That's how you see her?'

Doly blows a stream of smoke at the calm collected face. 'Gabby doesn't gamble, doesn't flirt, doesn't smoke.'

He waves the smoke away. 'I can't comment on the first two. But for cigarettes you can substitute Schnapps.' He walks over to the window, ostentatiously opens it to breathe fresh air. 'And what else is so different?'

Doly has the uncomfortable feeling that this man has got her measure. To the millimetre. 'What? Oh, well. I like to live a little more dangerously, that's all.'

CHAPTER 9

Berlin, July 1927

This time there are no flowers from Rolf. A long letter. Typed, but not by an expert. His talents are obviously confined to improving the design of machines. Their practical use he leaves to Typfräulein—girl typists. Scorned at first, their nimble fingers won out over the men's.

July 10th, 1927

My dearest Grischa,

Is soon to be your birthday. I know is not yet, and we wait to marry until you twenty-one. But is important event in my family. My brother Hugo and his wife have London house. You know I told he made prisoner of war in early 1915 and not return. He marry English girl August 15th, 1917. Now they celebrate tenth anniversary. We all invited.

Would be great honour and pleasure for me if you come with me to England. If you wish we take train from Berlin to Hamburg and change to liner for Hamburg/ Southampton.

You prefer we take train to Ostend and ferry to England. Is for you to decide. Is coming my mother and sister Bözsi you already met, my sister Ankara and family. Also my sister Olga and family. And is coming Bandi you also already met.

I write so you can consider. I so much like you to meet whole family. Naturally you stays as guest of my brother Hugo.

With all my love

Rolf

A tenth wedding anniversary celebration with the Ferents? In Gabby's experience, confined to Schwanenbruch and New Jersey, such family events are shatteringly dull. She must remember to pack a bottle of Schnapps. The upside is she'd meet the whole Ferent clan. No need to travel to Hungary and Yugoslavia, and she would not be under particular scrutiny. The happy couple would be taking pride of place.

She remembers Bandi will be there. She hasn't been able to get him out of her mind. Has she fallen in love? With a man she can't marry? Meeting him again might dispel the magic. She has to quench the fire. One way or another.

Dear Rolf

Your brother Hugo's tenth wedding anniversary sounds like a wonderful occasion. I would love to come along. Also, I have never been to London and it would be very exciting to visit the Houses of Parliament and other historic sights.

Please make all the arrangements as you see fit. I will go along with your choices which, I am sure, will be excellent.

As always

Gabriele

She cannot bring herself to sign Grischa, and he has turned down using Gabby. Which puts another spoke in the wheel of their relationship.

LORD OF THE HUNT

The last six days of the old year and the first six days of the new are the twelve nights reserved for the Lord of the Hunt. That's when He flies through the air and expects certain rules to be kept. No laundry may be hung out to dry and get in His way, no wheel may leave the house and no hunter may look for game. Whoever disobeys these rules must reckon with the Great Deer Hunter himself.

In spite of all these warnings a young hunter decided to try his luck. After all, he'd have the whole place to himself. Even so, as he strode purposefully through the winter landscape, his gun in his hand and his holster round his waist, his heart thumped pitter pat. He knew that the mighty Deer Hunter was entitled to the twelve days for himself.

He hadn't gone far when he heard shots followed by loud barks. The Deer Hunter's hounds were baying for his blood, and the great figure himself was coming towards him.

The young man chucked his gun away and rushed back home. He could hear the dogs following on his heels, the Deer Hunter shouting that the wretched miscreant would get his just reward. On this occasion the young man escaped. But he's never going to mess with the Lord of the Hunt again.

CHAPTER 10

London, August 1927

Hugo Ferent isn't driving his own car. Nor has he brought his wife to Victoria Station to welcome Rolf and his future bride. But he tries to please. The taxi is asked to cross Vauxhall Bridge and drive along Millbank, past the Houses of Parliament and Westminster Abbey, and to return to Buckingham Palace Road so that Gabby can glimpse the palace. Pall Mall, Trafalgar Square, Piccadilly Circus and Regent Street are all pointed out to her.

'And Dorothy. She well, I hope?' Rolf asks. At last.

Hugo's enthusiasm seems to flicker. 'As well as can be expected, thank you, Rezső. Dorothy is a delicate lady. She has a slight headache due to all the excitement. She's resting. Which is why she couldn't come to meet you.' He turns to Gabby, points. 'Just rounding Oxford Circus. We'll go down Oxford Street so you can see Marble Arch.'

'We don't disturb her.'

'I know you won't, Rezső. It's a little difficult with Mama. She talks about the sadness of marriages without children. And she expects poor Dorothy to cook like a Hungarian housewife.' An embarrassed shrug. 'It doesn't help when Bözsi takes over the kitchen.'

'Is only for few days.' Rolf points to Lord's cricket ground now appearing on the left. 'Is where they play famous English game. Cricket match.'

The city has become less impressive. Gabby sees they're driving

347

along Finchley Road. Winding out of central London. She knows Hampstead is a suburb. A garden suburb, Hugo explains. A wonderful place to live.

Rows of semi-detached houses in identical streets do nothing for Gabby. Though it is August the day is cold and grey, with a keen wind blowing drizzle. Very English, though the legendary fog is absent.

'Well, here we are.' Rolf pays the cabby while Hugo helps Gabby out, takes her bag.

They are standing in front of the bedraggled-looking garden of a Victorian semi. 'My mother-in-law lives right next door. She has prepared two rooms. One for Gabriele. You and Bandi will have to share, Rezsö. We've found rooms nearby for Ankara and Olga and their families.'

Net curtains move at an upstairs window. Hugo looks up, waves. Cheerily, his whole face a broad grin. There is no answering wave. But the face at the window is joined by that of a dog. White, with black spots.

The Dalmatian is enthusiastic about welcoming Gabby. He spurts out of the opened front door and signifies his pleasure by placing muddy paws on Gabby's skirt, then sniffing at her crotch. She suppresses the instinct to kick the animal. It could turn nasty.

'Pluto. Behave yourself.' Dorothy Ferent stands just inside her front door. Watching proceedings. With pride.

Hugo takes the dog by his collar and hauls him off.

'Hugo. You're not to be rough with him. He's only a puppy, remember. It's just his way of being friendly.' She turns away from the door and walks inside. The dog, unable to get at Gabby, struggles frantically.

Hugo beckons her through his front door. She goes ahead, Rolf following with both bags. The smell of dog is overpowering. Gabby can't stop her sneeze.

'The little Gabriele is not so small as the little Dorothy.' Mama, Bözsi at her side, stands guard at the entrance to the living room. 'We sit,' she says firmly. To the dog. Who dutifully obeys, his tail between his legs.

'So, you had good journey, yes?'

'Very nice, thank you.' Gabby smiles sweetly.

'Come, sit. Here there is space.' Josephine Ferent sweeps aside some cushions from a dog-marked settee standing forlornly in the centre of the small front room. The only other seating is a pair of Windsor chairs. 'Is not much space. The men they stand.'

Gabby is making elaborate mental arrangements for urgent telegrams to call her back to Berlin. This is an emergency, the astronomic cost of international phone calls justified. The Meinzers are no use for such a stratagem, and Tall and Small are not on the telephone. She may have to enlist Doly, who's spending her holidays in Schwanenbruch.

The unexpected entry of a large tray followed by tiny Dorothy is greeted with silence.

'I made tea.' The tray is dumped on the small table in front of the settee. 'Milk and sugar?' It seems to be a question addressed in general

'I take the lemons.' Mama Ferent's face is a study in restraint.

'We don't drink tea with lemon in England. That's a Russian habit. I don't hold with Communism. You want milk *and* sugar, or just milk?'

A stream of dark brown liquid emerges from the teapot which is covered by a sort of cap. 'My mum knitted the cosy for me,' Dorothy explains, seeing Gabby's stare. 'Pretty, don't you think?'

It is a notch or two down from the embroidered Hungarian blouse.

Gabby accepts a cup of the brown liquid and holds it on her lap. She's longing for a Schnapps. Well, any alcohol would do. She never drinks tea unless laced with rum. She's heard the British take sherry before dinner. She's not going to fuss; any kind of alcohol will do.

There's nothing but the sound of slurping from earthenware cups. Mama is sitting without one.

'Do you knit as well as embroider, Bözsi?' Gabby enquires. She's been told of such activities. They sound safer than political topics.

'I crochet.'

Gabby's never heard of anything like that. It can't possibly be as indelicate as it sounds. Surely there has to be some topic they can all discuss. Inspiration strikes. 'Have you had a good summer this year?'

Smiles all round. Long treatises on the state of the weather. Indulged with relish. The dog knocks over a teacup in his attempt to steal a Rich Tea biscuit. He is severely reprimanded. By Mama. Dorothy bursts into tears, stalks out of the room (followed by the dog) and doesn't return.

'Rolf and Hugo are talking business, Bandi. I need to stretch my legs after all that travelling. What about you and me going for a walk?'

Gabby has noticed that Bandi doesn't join in with his family. He has turned down the offer to share a room with Rolf with bland references to important business meetings. He's staying at the Piccadilly Hotel. He takes no part in the discussions surrounding Hugo's abortive attempts to found an engineering firm. Nor does he offer to lend Hugo money. And he has already announced he will be leaving tomorrow. Right after the celebratory meal. And he's clearly happy to escape from Hugo's house right now.

'Excellent idea.'

Even the dog doesn't notice their escape.

'Have you met Dorothy before?'

He shakes his head. Catches sight of Gabby's expression. Laughs out loud. 'Love me, love my dog. I think that we won't meet often.'

'You don't go for Pluto?'

'I wouldn't describe him as attractive. Except for the delivery of a very good kick to the right part of his anatomy. But for the sake of my mother and you young ladies, I have restrained myself.'

'Please don't worry on my account. On the contrary.'

'I'll bear that in mind.'

'I want to ask you something personal, Bandi. You're a man of the world, you will have an opinion.'

Bandi has a trick of pulling his eyelids down. Giving him an impassive look. No doubt an excellent business device. 'Delighted to help in any way I can.'

Gabby *knows* Bandi is the right man for her. And she can tell he's definitely attracted. If she doesn't even try to persuade him to admit his interest in her, she'll never be able to forgive herself. 'D'you think I should marry Rolf?' The words come out in a rush.

He stops as though a thunderbolt has riveted him to the spot. She sees the heavy lids lift rapidly, then return to their habitual half-mast position. Bandi's inhaled breath expands his chest so much that his coat buttons threaten to pop off. He puts an arm around Gabby's shoulders and steers her to a park bench surrounded by rose bushes. He takes out a pristine handkerchief, wipes the seat, motions her to sit down and cups both her hands in his.

'You are a quite unusual woman, Gabriele. I wish very much I had met you before you met my brother. But I cannot change the past.'

Gabby swallows. Her throat is dry. 'Rolf is an extremely nice man.'

Bandi drops her hand. He takes a stick and draws a heart with an arrow through it on the sandy footpath. 'Indeed he is. And very much in love with you.'

'But he has no social graces. And a disturbing lack of talent for languages.'

He uses the stick to obliterate the heart. 'That's why he's picked you to be his wife. It's clear he worships the ground you walk on. But he's also aware that you complement him. You are gifted in languages, you're an outstanding hostess. And I've seen your touch transform a room from the banal to the sublime. You'll make him a wonderful wife. For the first time in my whole life I envy Rolf.'

'Do you see all that much of your family?'

He draws an aeroplane. 'No more than I can help.'

One last try for what she knows they both want. 'Then marrying me wouldn't be...'

He draws a zeppelin.

'...wouldn't actually make much difference.'

He drops the stick, puts both hands behind his back. 'I am not like my brother, Gabriele. I'm neither noble nor heroic. But I can't betray him. Rezsö took on our father's responsibilities the day he died. He rushed home from his engineering course at the Technical University of Budapest to look after his younger brothers and sisters.' His eyes are moist. 'I am the youngest, he treated me like a son. He didn't go back to his studies until Hugo was old enough to cope. Without him we would all, except Ankara, have been thrown to the wolves. Rezsö is a fine man, Gabriele. A good man. To paraphrase the Bible: a prize greater than diamonds. And that is rare. Believe me, very rare.'

'You think I should marry him because he's *good*?'

Bandi's eyes are suddenly Rolf's. Soft velvet chocolate innocence. A polished toecap scrapes the dust. 'Much more than that. Ethical,

351

inventive, able to earn an impressive living. Even good-looking. Take him while you have the chance.'

Rolf's the important one? That's what he's saying? Is it because he's told Bandi about her genetic inheritance, that she isn't a complete woman? Is that why Bandi is turning her down? Her mouth tightens into a white line. 'You think I won't have many chances?'

'Not at all.' His voice is quiet and assured. He's being honest. 'Many men will wish to marry you, my dear. Not many will be able to offer what my brother can. He's an important cog in the world of business machines. He's made momentous contributions to these new devices. I'm sure you already know that office machines are going to transform the commercial world. Rezsö will always be a key man in that field.' He gets up, takes her arm, walks her out of the park. 'And now I think I'd better leave. Tell them I contacted my office and had an urgent call. I will send a telegram.'

He clicks his heels, bows. And is gone.

THE FIDDLER'S LAST TUNE

Towards the end of the 18ᵗʰ Century, around the time Hinrich Bender and his bride were conceived, Schwanenbruch was home to a young fiddler by the name of Hans Blank. The young man played so soulfully that his fellow villagers said he could charm the crows off the trees and make millstones weep.

One day Hans was, as so often, invited to play at a wedding. A rich merchant was getting married, and Hans was offered a fat purse to play for him. The young fiddler was in great demand for such occasions because, it was said, when Hans plays at your wedding he blesses it with everlasting love and many strong children.

The bridegroom was not only rich, he was a worthy man. When his parents died, he took his young sister Katharina under his wing, and brought her up as though she were his own daughter. While Hans was playing, young Katharina danced, enchantingly and gracefully, with the young nobleman her brother had chosen for her to marry.

Hans watched Katharina as he played and his heart leaped with each step and soared with each note. Without knowing what was happening to him, Hans lost his heart to the beautiful maiden.

But it was too late. Katharina's brother had already given her fiancé 200 Reichstaler for her dowry, so she was pledged to him. Which didn't stop Hans feeling as though he'd been born again when he looked into the graceful maiden's eyes, and when he watched her twinkling feet. So he used his faithful fiddle to play as he'd never played before.

The dancers twirled, the music became sweeter and faster. Everyone clapped, delighted that Hans's playing had reached heights even he had never managed before. No one guessed that he played only for Katharina, and that he played himself right into her heart that day.

Katharina's wedding was already set to take place at Michaelmas. Nevertheless, the young girl slipped secretly out of her brother's house to meet Hans. They found a quiet trysting place under the big tree by the schoolhouse, sheltered from curious onlookers by the dark shadow cast by the St Nicolaikirche. Only St Nicolaus himself knew of their love.

Michaelmas drew inevitably nearer. Katharina's relatives prepared her for her wedding day. The night before Michaelmas, Katharina arranged to meet her beloved for the last time before her marriage.

Hans had no words to change her mind, no money to carry her off. So he took his fiddle and played the most moving melodies ever heard for the lovely girl he could not win for himself. And Katharina sighed, but said her farewells and left him as he played.

The fiddle sang on until the sky turned rosy with the light which brought his sweetheart's wedding day. The Nicolaikirche bells rang joyful carillons for the wedding, drowning the softer tones of Hans's fiddle. He walked across the road to the tavern, put his fiddle on the landlord's table, exchanged it for a bottle of Schnapps and tossed the fiery liquid down his throat. Then he took himself down to the turbulent waters of the Elbe Estuary and waded in.

The bells were still carolling their joy as Hans waded deeper and deeper, right out into the tempestuous North Sea. At precisely the time Katharina vowed to forsake all others in favour of her new husband, Hans felt the waters closing in around him. But he went on, oblivious of the waves, until he disappeared.

Now, each time the storms whip the North Sea high and foamy, the villagers say "der Blanke Hans" is the one who plays the tune the waves dance to.

CHAPTER 11

London, August 1927

Gabby and Rolf are riding in a cab, on their way to the Old Bailey. Gabby is ridiculously disappointed that Parliament isn't in session. She'd have loved to visit the Public Gallery, to listen to the debates. The Old Bailey is a poor second. But it's definitely better than nothing.

The only way Gabby is going to be able to survive Bandi's rejection is to change her life. Radically. Now. It's absurd to wait for her twenty-first birthday, to plan the wedding then. What the hell does she want with a big wedding? She isn't interested in folderol. She's interesting in getting married right away. Before she loses her nerve.

'Your whole family is assembled, Rolf. All except Bandi. That's quite hard to organise. Why don't we get a special licence and marry here, in London? As soon as it can be arranged.' A practised, disarming smile. 'Then they can all be witnesses.'

At first Rolf looks startled, then his face creases into a radiant smile. It's obvious he's delighted.

'You wish this? You wish we marry in Registry Office? Not in St Nicolaikirche?' The lines from nose to mouth are deep, his eyes look mournful. He must know something isn't quite right. 'And what about brother and sister? You no wish them present?'

'I must speak honestly, Rolf.'

He nods. 'Is not right to marry without honesty.'

355

'I think you are a really good man, Rolf. Honourable, hard-working, devoted to your family. No one could ask for a better husband.'

His eyes, large and soft-brown, are watchful. 'But?' Hardly above a whisper.

'I'm not in love with you.'

The pain shows though he tries to hide it. 'You very young, Grischa. Will come.'

'Perhaps. But you are not young. You'll be forty soon. And you're on the brink of the most important step in your career. You need the right wife, and I fit that bill. I'd like to propose a trial marriage. We marry here, in London, in a Registry Office. Let's give it two years without having children. If it doesn't work out, we get divorced.'

'Is not so easy to arrange, Grischa. Is not good position for woman.'

'I've heard it's easier if you marry in England. Let's make a deal, and promise no hard feelings whichever way it goes. What d'you say?'

His head is nodding. 'I take risk. You will childrens want. Then we happy family.' He takes her hands in his. Bandi's hands are not hairy. 'Is before your birthday.'

'What's Hudwalker going to do? Refuse me my rightful inheritance?' She looks out of the cab window at rain-sodden London streets. 'He doesn't have to know, Rolf. He'll never find out in a month. I'll let him know before he signs everything over. So that he gets the name right.'

Rolf takes her in his arms, plants a wet kiss on her lips. 'You make me so happy, my little Grischa. So very happy. We go tell Mama, yes? Old Bailey you can see any time.'

The questions on the marriage licence form are detailed. They ask not only the time, date and location of birth, and parents' names, but also the applicant's religion.

The registrar is impatient. He has another wedding after the Ferents'. Gabby tries to look at Rolf's answers before they're whisked away. She manages to see that he's a Lutheran. Surprising. He's never mentioned it.

'Your family are Lutherans, Rolf?'

He doesn't look at her. 'My family not religious. We nothing. I convert after I leave home.'

She tries to work it out. There were Protestants in Hungary, but only until the beginning of the 17th Century. Then Jesuit Peter Pazmany converted his country to Catholicism with cruel zeal. 'Converted from being a Catholic, you mean?'

'Throw bouquet, Grischa. My sister Bözsi catch. Then she marry soon. Is last of my sisters to marry.'

CHAPTER   12

Berlin, November 1927

Rolf's new-found enthusiasm for Sunday morning service is some-what startling. Gabby can't help wondering why, if he's so devout, he settled for a Registry Office marriage. And the duties of a bourgeois housewife—planning the meals, taking the maid to the market every day, overseeing the cleaning of the dinner service, organising parties, buying the right wine—already lie heavy.

As for the marriage bed, Gabby finds it a chore of the most boring kind. Her husband is ardent, tries to please, is considerate. But his hairy arms and stubbled chest are distasteful, his eager caresses, wet kisses and sentimental declarations leave her icy. She wonders why any woman is remotely interested in sex, has become expert at side-stepping the whole caboodle. When she can't escape she lies unmoving, willing her hairdo to stay in place, while Rolf cavorts around her, huffs and puffs. Embarrassing and uncomfortable. What luck he travels so much. It crosses her mind that one way out of sex would be to become pregnant. They can afford a full-time nursery maid, a baby need not cramp her style—only Rolf's. And she does want to be a mother, to have a child she can cherish. Not right away, perhaps; but worth considering.

Gabby sees Tall and Small socially as often as she can. But only when Rolf is abroad on one of his frequent trips. They don't come to her house, except to pick her up. Friedrich knows how to drive and is teaching Gabby. On occasion he takes Rolf's car and chauffeurs Gabby and Jonah. Only to the theatre. It's no longer suitable for her to be seen at the *Wilde Bühne*. Or any cabaret. She is Herr Diplom Ingenieur Ferent's wife. And he is an executive at International Business Machines, a US company with an important relationship with the German government.

She's meeting Tall and Small near their rooms in the Breitenbachplatz today. As soon as they're together they saunter over to the Romanisches Café. A sense of freedom makes Gabby feel heady.

'Your husband was brought up in southern Hungary, you said? And Baja is almost as near to Zagreb as to Budapest?' Jonah's nostrils widen. A bloodhound on the trail.

Gabby's upturned nose scents trouble. 'He lived there until he left to study in Budapest. He left Hungary to join a German firm as soon as he graduated.'

Friedrich's eyebrows form wings. 'How old was he?'

Why this interrogation? 'Twenty-five. What of it?'

'And now? How old is he now?'

'He'll be forty this coming summer.'

'So he was thirty-eight when you met. And still a bachelor.'

'I've always wondered why you waited until your late thirties to marry, Rolf. Is that usual for Hungarian men?' Gabby asked her husband as soon as she felt she could. 'Your mother mentioned girls often marry as young as twelve.'

'I engaged to be married before leave Hungary. A wonderful girl. Lovely, gifted in all household skills. So charming.'

'What happened?'

'She always delicate. Her complexion translucent. Remarkable. Very beautiful. But was sign of disease. She tuberculous was. We could not find doctor help her. She suffer long time and die.'

'How terrible.'

'One of reasons I leave Hungary as soon as possible. Get away from sad memory. Then came War. I not have opportunity to meet young ladies.'

'But you were back in 1918.'

'Took till 1919 to return, remember I walking from Russia with comrades. And I not settled in my mind where I live. I worked and so have no time for emotional involvements. Also I travel great deal.'

She can vouch for that. 'Which is how we met. A pick-up on a train between Hamburg and Berlin. Was I the only girl you met in that way?'

Rolf looks down. Blinks modestly. 'Not exactly only one. But only one I fall in love with.'

Gabby understands what her friends are getting at. How wrong can they be? Rolf definitely likes women. Though she's pretty sure he's the faithful type. He admires from afar. 'He had a fiancée who died. Of consumption.'

Friedrich grins. 'Well, that's a relief.'

Jonah hunches his shoulders. 'There's still something weird about the set-up. Hungary isn't exactly overrun with Lutherans, Gabby. In a place like Baja they must be as rare as the dodo.' Jonah pats his head. Where his long hair used to annoy him.

'What of it? His family aren't religious. He didn't even think about it until he left home.' Gabby's conviction that she's done the right thing is beginning to ebb. Though she doesn't know why.

Jonah tightens his lips, draws them back. 'Won't wash, my girl. Hungary's a Catholic country. And country people always belong to some organised religion, whether they believe in it or not. I'm amazed you haven't worked it out for yourself, Gabby. Well, I'll enlighten you, because you need to know. Your husband comes from a Jewish background.'

'Nonsense, Jonah. He hasn't even got a Jewish name...'

'Exactly my point. You said the old lady thought it odd you called her Frau Ferent? I'm willing to bet the poor old sod changed it from something damaging.'

She tries to remember the names on the marriage certificate. Too busy thinking about the religion to notice them. 'Don't be ridiculous.'

'I'm deadly serious.'

A stab of recollection as she hears Rolf say: "Because it is your *name*, Mama."

'What's more, I think he got himself christened to hide the fact that he's Jewish.'

'You're going too far, Jonah. You disproved it yourself. How could he have become a Lutheran in Baja?'

'Thought he told you it was after he'd left his family behind?' The crow of triumph.

'Budapest, then. Still very few Lutherans there.' Then she remembers. Rolf told her he'd become a Lutheran after he came to Germany.

The mournful look in Jonah's eyes is uncannily reminiscent of that in Frau Ferent's. 'Obvious. He converted to *Christianity* when he moved to Germany. And became a Lutheran because that's the majority religion.'

Gabby is not devout. But she remembers her maternal grandfather, Pastor Bender, thundering hell and damnation from the pulpit in the St Nicolaikirche. 'I don't believe you.' Sacrilege, she remembers, is a serious matter. The unforgivable sin.

'Not obligatory.' Jonah stares at his shoes. 'And I know enough about the New Testament not to chuck the first stone.' He looks up, his eyes bright. 'The only difference between your husband and me is that I elected for Communism instead of Christianity.'

'But that's entirely different, Jonah. Communism is a political system. Christianity is a religion.'

She's never seen Jonah look so depressed. 'That's relevant, is it? So why did I let you introduce me as Johann to the Meinzers? Ask your sister to call me Hans?' His eyes look more mournful than Gabby remembers, and so like Rolf's. 'No better than another Jew you've heard of. Denying my identity to save myself while judging others.

Amen, I say to thee, the cock shall not crow, till thou deny me thrice.

Gabby giggles. 'If we're quoting:

And upon this rock I will build my church.

Just remember that Peter became the first pope.'

'Aren't you making rather a lot of assumptions, Jonah?' Friedrich is frowning. Heavily. 'Talking behind the man's back?'

'I have no wish to upset Gabby. She's made a 'good' marriage in the eyes of the world. But I'm supposed to be her friend. Rolf Ferent was a bachelor at thirty-eight. He comes from southern Hungary and has a name which is not overtly Magyar. He's already admitted to changing Rezsö to Rolf. And he's a Lutheran from a Catholic country. All you have to do is ask him, Gabby.'

Friedrich stands and puts his arm around his friend. 'In this life we have to survive as best we can.' He turns to Gabby. 'Jonah could be wrong. Even if he isn't, don't hold it against your husband. If he's Semitic and not religious, why should he broadcast his past? Jews have been persecuted by Christians for centuries. That's hardly a Christian attitude. What's worse, if they offer to become Christians they're persecuted for their race instead.'

'Not always. In the days of the Spanish Inquisition they were allowed to convert.'

Jonah throws his head back. 'You're living in cloud cuckoo land, Gabby. The truth is that in our time a Jew is branded a Jew because of his genetic heritage, not because of his religion. As you say, even the notorious Inquisitors allowed a change of heart. Now we're concerned with genes, and a change of genes just isn't within the realms of the possible.' He touches his nose. 'All you can do is hope to cheat. I changed my Hebrew name to a Christian name. No pun intended. And I do what I can to hide my Jewish nose.'

CHAPTER 13

Berlin, Spring 1928

'My sister is in Germany for the summer, Rolf.'

'You want invite her? Of course we do.'

Gabby can't complain that Rolf isn't hospitable. He's always glad to welcome her family and her friends. And, now that she's safely married and Doly is no longer a threat, she'd like to show off to her.

She's been looking forward to showing her sister how wonderful married life can be. She is, she tells herself every day, blissfully happy. Rolf has kept his word. He's even encouraged her continued attendance at the University. Where she's reading Philosophy and Politics. And is subjected to the anti-Semitic opinions of the day. Which she tries to refute, amidst shouts which are not seemly in a lecture hall.

Gabby and Rolf have rented an unfurnished apartment in a large house on the Kaiserdamm, the swankiest part of Berlin. Rolf finds it a little extravagant, even on his salary, but Gabby has persuaded him that she will make good any shortfall.

She looks round her reception rooms. Large and high-ceilinged, they are furnished with the finest antiques, the parquet floors covered with exquisite carpets Rolf has brought back from Persia. Several vitrines display glass and porcelain Gabby bought or imported from the Villa Dohlen. Chandeliers give excellent light, and expensive clocks ensure Rolf always knows the time.

'We have my money as well as your salary, Rolf. Why shouldn't we

363

live in decent style?'

'And Mr Watson was very pleased we invite him.'

'Exactly. Your business interests need this sort of thing.'

Gabby is clear that Watson couldn't have cared less about the place Rolf lives in provided it's in the right district of Berlin. What he enjoys is Rolf's wife's talent for running a salon. Her fluent English, her vivacity, the way she tells stories. And that she's safely married to one of his executives.

Gabby knows Watson only tolerates her fondness for alcohol. She presumes he's a supporter of Prohibition. So she's made sure she's knowledgeable about wine. She chooses the right vintage for the dinner parties she gives for his business associates. And she's managed to find a couple of bottles of *Hine's Fine Champagne 1811* which she offers instead of the ordinary Schnapps she's so fond of. She knows that that will impress Watson's German colleagues. Which he recognises as an invaluable business asset in his top European executive's wife.

Watson is also the clue to Rolf's sudden enthusiasm for Sunday worship. IBM's president tells everyone he's a devout churchgoer. And makes sure he knows which church his top people attend.

Which is why Jonah's guesswork has been preying on Gabby's mind.

'There's something I need to know, Rolf.' She's not anti-Semitic. Not in the least; she's proved that at University, voicing her opinions at almost every political lecture she attends. Anti-semitism is totally against her principles. But she has to know.

His face is in profile. No sign of a hooked nose. His features are regular, handsome. Dark hair and skin which have a definite Magyar cast. He could easily be descended from the dark-skinned Ugric and Turkic stock which settled beside the Danube in the 9th Century.

'Ask.' The resemblance to his brother Bandi is striking. Proud. Resolute. Unflinching. He seems to sense what's coming.

'You told me you became a Lutheran after you left home. Were your family Catholics?'

A second or two passes before he answers. 'Were not religious.'

'You said. What irreligious background was it, then?'

Those deep lines between nose and mouth come into focus. Not Magyar. 'You wish I answer you?'

'Not wish. I should know.'

A deep, long sigh. 'Maybe I should tell before. Is Jewish.' The mournful eyes stare at her. 'You did not guess?'

She shrugs. 'Not really. You don't look Jewish.'

'You well educated, Grischa. You understand political situation. But you will forgive if I say I understand better German attitude to "Jewish Problem". Is not just vague anti-Semitism. Was always in Christian society. Is much more widespread in Germany since beginning of 19th Century. Now very bad. Really they having obsession against Jew.

'Jews always in past considered malevolent and powerful. You know from studies were many pogroms in Poland and Russia. Only five percent Jews in Hungary compared to rest population, yet all educated. Make others angry. Now also Jew considered cause of all is wrong with Germany. Therefore dangerous to German Volk. I still remember ritual murder accusations. Happen frequently in past. Even I remember such a trial in old Austro-Hungary.' He pauses, takes a deep breath. 'You must also have heard. Present German anti-Semites say no peace in whole world until Jews destroyed.'

He looks at her sadly. She could almost swear there's a tear in the corner of each eye.

'Logically, this mean elimination of Jews. I mean by this they must leave country, live in ghetto, maybe new pogroms will kill many.' His voice is heavy with gloom. 'Is not good to be known as Jew. This I cannot help. But I should tell you before we marry. Is wrong I did not. Especially as you told me about problem of hair in your family. I sorry, Grischa.'

She remembers Bandi's reaction to her comments about the Shylock they went to see. And she still didn't guess. 'I hope you know I'm not anti-Semitic, Rolf.'

No smile on the normally eager face. 'I glad to hear.'

'It would not have made any difference to my decision to marry you. But your name sounds Magyar. You have some Magyar blood?'

'Maybe. Jews not often intermarry. Even Jews who not religious seldom this do.'

But Rolf has done precisely that. Which proves his acumen. And explains why he didn't marry any of the girls his mother introduced.

'My father's name Paul Krausz. Not good name for business. I search long time. Ferent sound Magyar, still is easy to say in English, German. Rest family follow me and also change.'

She nods. Another secret. A much more dangerous one than hers, or that of Tall and Small. Or so she thought. At that time even Gabby, for all her political acumen, had no idea how wrong she was.

THE SNAKE CHARMER

An unusually lovely young girl with a willowy figure was the pride of Land Hadeln. She lived in a cottage between the marsh and the heather. Her greatest beauty was her hair. It rippled down her back in shining glistening waves. Not flaxen, nor nut-brown, nor raven black. The young girl's hair was a most unusual colour. A bright golden-yellow which could be seen from far away, standing out against the green fields and the tawny heather.

Young men came from both town and country to bid for her hand. But she would have none of them. She preferred to live by herself. Until she heard that two of her suitors had decided to take her by force. She knew her little cottage wouldn't provide a hiding place, and the land was flat with a wide horizon and no bushes to hide in. Then she remembered the field of rape blooming behind her cottage. So she ran into the flowers and sank to her knees. And stayed safe, camouflaged among the golden blooms.

She heard the two men knock on the cottage door, saw them burst in, heard them rampage from room to room, then rage around her garden. Eventually they gave up. But they didn't leave the cottage; they went back in presumably to wait for her.

By now the sun was setting, the rape flowers closing their blooms. The young girl had to find a safer hiding place. She remembered the heather. And the adders who love to bask in the dry earth between the woody stems.

The evening glow set fire to the girl's golden hair, turned it a tawny brown. So that it blended in with the heather fronds touched by the setting sun.

The snakes were curled up under the heather bushes, to keep them warm against the cold of night. Disturbed in their resting place one rose up to bite her.

But the young girl knew how to speak to snakes. She made the sign of the snake and chanted:

367

Mother Mary walked over the fields
When she met a bad worm
The bad worm wants to bite
Mother Mary said: Bite and you'll die.

The snake slithered away, the sun sank below the horizon, the heather turned from red to black. Only the young girl's golden hair, touched by moonlight, stood out in the darkening plain.

The young men looked across from the cottage. They recognised the glorious hair, shouted with glee and made a beeline for the heather.

No sooner had they entered the kingdom of the snakes than they were set upon and bitten. They writhed in agony.

The young girl was free to go back to her cottage. Where she lived without further disturbance.

CHAPTER 14

Schwanenbruch, Summer 1928

Doly's bare legs are dangling from a branch of the large beech behind the Villa Dohlen. Her skirt is hitched up at the waist. She's blowing smoke rings in the still summer air.

'Letter from Huddy Daddy this morning. He won't send cash for a holiday. Even Tante Martha thought that a good idea.'

'Thought your aunt considers me a bad influence.'

'Not any more; she thinks you're steady. Best of all, of course, you're not a boy.'

Lieselotte's heavier body is threatening their equilibrium. 'So what's your guardian's objection?'

'A whole page of longwinded rubbish about learning to cope with money. God, he's boring.'

'Your father did put him in charge, Doly. He's just trying to do his duty.'

Doly's eyes sharpen to pinpoints, glint. 'Apparently you're the big bad wolverine. He thinks you're sponging on me.' She tears the letter into shreds. 'I'm not saying some of our worthy neighbours haven't tried it on. Why the hell does he pick on the only one who doesn't begin to?'

'There's plenty to do around here. We can ride, swim, walk...'

'Let's get Josef and Werner to take us away for a couple of weeks. At their expense.'

Lieselotte swings her heavy legs. The branch creaks. 'You mean go away on holiday with them?'

'Why not? We'll chaperone each other.' Doly lights a new cigarette from the butt of the old one. Inhales deeply.

'Must you smoke non-stop like that?'

'I'll write the answer in fire.' The cigarette tip draws a large N. 'Naturally I mustn't. But I enjoy it. Anything wrong with that?'

'Not very ladylike.'

'Damn it, Liesi. What the hell's all this 'ladylike' crap? I got enough of that at Riverside Hall to last me a lifetime.'

'That why you're not going back?'

'I graduated, Liesi. There's nothing for me to go back to.'

'You two boys game for a couple of weeks' holiday?'

Doly watches Josef Miessman's face. It doesn't take Freud to interpret the downturned mouth and sidelong glance at Werner. He's miffed at being forced into spending his holiday with Doly. She heard his overbearing voice telling Liesi: "Eine goldene Wiege ist nicht immer eine gute Kinderstube—A golden cradle doesn't always make a good nursery". He thinks she's nothing but a spoilt rich brat, and that's bad enough. But he'll also have to put up with Werner Schiffer. A ship's pilot. Not an officer. Doly knows Josef's stint on board the *Leander* is nothing more than a cheap way for the ship-owner to get medical staff but he does eat in the officers' mess. Werner Schiffer eats on his own. Might seem like neither fish nor fowl nor good red herring to Josef, but to Doly he's a free spirit, the sort of human being she likes to be with.

Good old Liesi comes through trumps. 'I think the four of us going is brilliant.'

Josef's face is easy to read. He'll do almost anything to be with Lieselotte. Ein Gründling ist besser auf dem Tisch als in dem See ein grosser Fisch—A sprat on the table is better than a big fish in the sea. He nods his head through scowling eyes.

'You mean the four of us?' Werner's skin is tanned to a pleasing brown. White crow's feet radiate from his eyes. Invisible when he smiles.

'Liesi and I thought it would be fun. We can take photographs. I bought a movie camera in New York before I left. It's hard to lug around, so you may have to lend a hand.' Doly's smile is mischievous. 'Let's make a film. I've already written the script.'

'You're the big director, naturally.' Josef's hostility manages to surpass Doly's enthusiasm, spurs her on.

Showing her little fangs makes Doly's face look impish. 'And producer. And investor. You're the actors. The only setting we need is a cottage in the country. Near water. So we can bathe.'

'You're offering to do the cooking?'

'Don't be an idiot. We'll share the chores. A little place with two bedrooms; one for Liesi and me, the other for you two. Primitive as you like.'

'The heather's nice and soft, Doly. And fragrant.' Werner sits at her feet. Strokes them, fondles her toes.

Idyllic surroundings. Life is wonderful. The two couples have found a small cottage beside a warm tranquil river banked with reeds and bulrushes. Teeming with kingfishers, storks, herons. Lüneburg Heath is within cycling distance of Schwanenbruch.

The summer night is warm and balmy. Doly is wearing a skimpy sleeveless dress. A pair of knickers. Nothing else. Not even sandals.

The heather is still warm from the sun's rays. Which have only just disappeared. A long drowsy summer night is ahead. Nightingales sing. Owls hoot.

Werner moves to lie beside Doly. His left arm circles her slender shoulders. He leans towards her, finds her lips. He kisses her with long drawn-out kisses and an exploring tongue. Musk fills her nostrils. She stops his hands wandering further than her thighs.

His kisses become harder, more pressing. His touch hardens as well. And she can feel him large and eager against her groin.

He undoes her dress, pulls it down. Cups her breasts while kissing her. Sweet caressing kisses she returns. A sudden change as his teeth tear at her lips, draw blood. An oddly exciting feeling.

His head lowers. His mouth finds her left nipple, sucks. His hand has found the leg in her knickers, groped past. Fingers in her opening move up and down. Her back arches in delight.

He slips out, grabs the elastic, pulls. And breaks the spell. She slaps

371

his hand away, lunges at his head. 'Stop, Werner.'

His mouth clamps over hers. The kisses are no longer sweet. Intrusive. Demanding. Her lips tighten, retreat. She bares her teeth. 'I said stop.'

He tries to wrap her whole body in his arms. She ducks, slithers below him, rolls away into the reeds. Dips out of sight.

'Doly? Where have you got to?' Werner's voice is husky.

She keeps completely still. Holds her breath.

'I didn't mean to force you, Doly. It's just that I love you so. I want to marry you.'

She slips her body into the water. Softly, silently. Werner Schiffer is not the man she has in mind. Women are judged by the men they marry. She's going to marry an Englishman. From an aristocratic family.

'Come out, Doly. I promise not to do anything you don't want me to.'

He sounds so mournful. So sad. But he's roused. They're in an isolated part of the country. Liesi and Josef have cycled away on their own.

Doly riffles her fingers through her hair. The colour of the reeds. They'll hide her, deep within them. She slides further into the swampy water and waits for Lieselotte to return. They sleep in a double bed. Clasped in each other's arms. For safety.

CHAPTER 15

Cuxhaven, August 1928

'I have to talk to you seriously, Doly.' Martha Bender is walking briskly along the top of the Cuxhaven dyke. A glorious day in mid August. The grass is already turning yellow, and the falling willow leaves betray the first signs of autumn.

A tight lower lip juts out as Doly trudges along with her aunt. 'More Schwanenbruch gossip?' The sun is shining, warming her back and the top of her head. But the chill of Martha's condemnation puckers bronzed arms and legs into gooseflesh.

'If it were just gossip, I wouldn't be so worried.' Martha strides ahead, forcing the pace. 'It's rather more than that. And not idle chatter from Schwanenbruch. A serious report from Cuxhaven. Frau Sparr has been in touch with me. As a friend of the family.'

'Sparr? Who's Frau Sparr?'

'Do remember, Doly. Cuxhaven is a small town. And I teach their daughters.'

'I've never heard of anyone called Sparr.'

'Heinz Sparr. Where you have your photographs developed. Stills *and* movies.'

Doly, having moved a step ahead, whirls round. Nearly tripping Martha up. 'You're telling me these people looked at my pictures? Then went behind my back and whinged to you about them?'

Martha backs away. 'They didn't say a word. They showed me, Doly.

The stills, that is. There isn't a projector there to view the movies.' Stocky legs planted square against gusts from the sea, eyes round. 'You really took those pictures?'

Doly's hands push wind-swept hair out of her eyes, hold it against her scalp. 'Hardly all of them. Some of them are pictures of me.'

'Don't be flippant. I mean the ones of naked men.'

'One man. His body is as splendid as that of Michelangelo's David.'

'They're photographs, Doly. Not works of art.'

'That doesn't mean they can't be.' Doly focuses on floodtide waves reclaiming their territory. 'Anyway, how would I know, Tante Martha? Apparently I'm the last to see my own pictures. But I set out to be artistic, not pornographic. And that's what I think these photos are: works of art.'

'Realistic is the correct description. And we don't need that.'

'What's wrong with nudity? It's how God made us.'

'Stop trying to evade the issue, Diern. If you took pictures of a naked man it means you were *with* him. And that has implications far exceeding nudity itself.' Martha's shoulders droop. 'Sexual ones.'

Doly feels for her. She's thinking of Helmut Veldun. Apparently, in spite of being tied to a wheelchair, unable to do more than raise his face and hold her hands, he's the most exciting, most stimulating man her aunt has ever known. Though Doly isn't sure that that amounts to a number greater than one.

Martha has given Doly long lectures on the joys of celibacy. She and Helmut have that sort of relationship thrust on them as a result of his polio. If anything, it has enriched their friendship, made it special.

'I've mentioned it to you before. It is possible to have relationships with men which don't involve the body.' She smiles. 'There is another advantage. That tiresome genetic problem is neither here nor there.'

'So why don't you get married, then? Much easier to talk if you live in the same house.'

Martha's eyes drop, a red flush creeps over her cheeks. 'A marriage has to be consummated to be valid, Doly. Otherwise it is just a hollow sham.'

'I see. Things are different for me, are they? You think a few pictures prove I had relations with the man in the photograph?'

'It's my job to look after your moral welfare.'

'You mean you want me to tell you who he is. That's really what is bothering you, isn't it?'

A sharp squall cuts Martha's words to disjointed syllables. 'Tha... would... approp... behaviour.'

'I never thought you'd get it so wrong, Tante Martha. You're all so set on my being a trollop you don't think past that.' She spreads her hands wide. 'All right, I'll prove it to you. Take me to your doctor and ask him to examine me. You'll find I'm virgo intacta, if that's what's so important to you.'

Martha stops, frowns at her niece. Doly can see she's nervous her words will damage their relationship for good.

'Always such a dramatic pose, Doly. If you say so, I believe you. But you must see that your reputation is at an all-time low. I've lost count of the young men you've been seen around with. I can name six without even trying: Dieter Kroner, Fritz Schnecke, Albert Mackter, Julius Vendt, Harland Drucker. And even an older man. Josef Miessman should know better.'

Doly cradles her mass of hair, tosses it back. Fairly impressive. Until she sees the admiration turn to pity in Martha's eyes, feels a stab in her heart. How long before she loses her looks?

'Wrong again, Tante Martha. Miessman is Lieselotte's friend. A jumped-up peasant who thinks he's God because he's a doctor. I despise him.'

'That still doesn't explain all those boys, Doly.'

'You think we're all horsing around and worse. Not true. Werner asked me to marry him.'

Tante Martha is obviously taken aback. 'You mean Werner Schiffer? The pilot's son? He's the one in the pictures?' She frowns. 'There's nothing loose or giddy about that young man.'

'What's so surprising about that?'

'I thought he was a friend of Gabby's. A platonic friend, I mean. He's a steady lad. Quite different from the other village boys.'

'Have you remembered Gabby's married, Tante Martha? To an extremely nice man called Rolf Ferent.'

'You've met Herr Ferent?' Martha's blue eyes shine bright, then cloud.

'Yes. A real gentleman. Far better than she deserves.'

'You haven't been quarrelling with your sister again, have you? Or is this just the usual snipe? Do remember everyone needs as many loving relatives as they can muster.' Her eyes flick over Doly's hair. 'Particularly in your case.'

The top buttons of Doly's dress are undone. Showing swelling cleavage. 'He came to see me in Riverside Hall. Look, he gave me this bracelet.' She shows off the triple-coloured gold. 'He took me out for a whole day. We had some very interesting discussions.' That self-destructive glint. 'But don't worry. I didn't take pictures of *him*. He's much too old for that.'

CHAPTER   16

Schwanenbruch, August 1928

'I've got something exciting to tell you.' Gabby has arrived in Schwanenbruch. Eyes bright with news, skin gleaming health.

'You've done well at your University? Passed all your exams?'
Everything seems to be going Gabby's way. Adoring husband,
transformed looks, academic success. All Doly gets is brickbats from
Tante Martha.

A distracted blink. 'Well, yes. My professor was very pleased with
me. But it's not what I mean...'

'Rolf's been promoted again, I suppose. He's incredibly gifted.' Doly
overfills her lungs, coughs out smoke.

She can see Gabby's glow subside into routine irritation. 'What on
earth do *you* know about it? You've only met him once.'

'When people understand each other, once is enough.' She practises
her haughty Janet Gaynor smile in *Seventh Heaven*. 'We spent the whole
day together, Gabby. Talked for hours in my room in Riverside Hall.'
She won't mention the soulful looks, the taking of her hand in his to
warm it, the slow kiss on each finger as he left. But she does remember
it. She relives the romance. Through a smouldering languid tone of
voice.

'You mean you and he were in your room? Alone?'

Gabby sounds outraged. What an idiotic schoolmarm attitude. 'With
about eighty other girls playing chaperones. Even you can't think that

improper.'

'Don't they have a visitors' room? I would have thought that was much more suitable.'

Doly relapses into a grin, swings her hair. Gabby's not the only Schwanenbruch swan. 'If it's not Rolf, what is it?'

'I'm going to have a baby.' A tender, gentle smile. Quite uncharacteristic.

'You are?' Her voice sounds winded. Flat. A hard blow. Has Gabby noticed? Not just a marvellous husband. Baby as well. How Doly would love to have a little baby. A sweet little thing which would truly love her. 'When?'

'Early next spring.' No excitement now. Just matter-of-fact. 'End of February, beginning of March.' Gabby's face pinches white. 'I've been feeling sick for weeks.'

'That's marvellous news, Gabby. Congratulations.'

'Is wonderful see you again, Doly. You very beautiful look. Just like sister.' Rolf's soft smile criss-crosses the skin around his eyes. From constant use. 'I bring you present from Hungary.'

'Why, Rolf. That's so sweet of you.' Doly opens the beautifully wrapped gift. Soft smooth material surrounded by long fringes. In heavy brilliantly-coloured shot silk. The blue of the dress she wore in Pennsylvania, blended with the autumn hues of her hair. Must have cost a fortune, even in Hungary. 'How exquisite.'

'Why you not put on?'

Doly stands and twirls the shawl around.

'This how is worn.' Rolf puts his hands around her shoulders, folds the shawl over once, allows its ends to cover Doly's breasts. 'Now you need brooch.' He pulls a box out of his jacket pocket, hands it to her.

The brooch is round and solid. In three shades of gold. Matching the bracelet. Is Rolf tied to Gabby, but in love with her younger sister?

Hovering fingers take the brooch and fasten it on her bosom. She feels the warmth, the flow of adrenaline. Her breasts, small and pointed under the thin dress she's wearing, heave with excitement.

'You don't move or I stick into you.'

A quick reflex motion away. What is he saying?

'I told. You don't move, Doly. Is very sharp pin.'

378

She relaxes. Allows hands skilled at pinning brooches on to female bosoms to secure the shawl around her. She snuggles into it.

'Rolf. I didn't even know you'd arrived.' Gabby by the open veranda door. Eyes cold.

Rolf moves away from Doly. 'Maid let me in. She say you out on walk. I meet Doly here in veranda.' He walks up to his wife. Tries to embrace her.

She side-steps him as she stares at him with irritable eyes. Followed by a determined smile, a nod.

'For you I bring something special, Grischa.' He pulls another box out of his pocket. 'For beautiful mother-to-be.'

Colour returns to forget-me-not blue irises as Gabby's shoulders relax. Slim fingers fumble with the box fastening.

'Allow me help you.' Rolf presses the button and the lid springs open. He hands the box back.

Meaningful silence as Gabby looks at the brooch. A circlet of diamonds set in platinum. Perhaps white gold. Ten large diamonds set in a round, with smaller ones connecting them. Breathtaking. 'That's lovely, Rolf. Thank you.'

'For mother of our baby. For start of our little family.' His eyes caress her as he puts his arm around her. 'I help put on?'

'Not now, Rolf.' Braced shoulders ward him off. 'Rula has cooked a special meal in your honour. Let's go through to the dining room before it spoils.'

'I want you to come to the family conference with me, Rolf.'

'Is problem?'

'A big problem. Though most men can't see it. Not even Onkel Wilfred.'

'So? Is female problem?'

Gabby's annoyance barks into laughter. 'She's certainly female. My sister Doly is virtually out of control. Now she's left Riverside Hall, she's at a loose end. She chases after every pair of trousers she comes across. Regardless of suitability. Uncles, guardians, every unmarried boy in the village. Even Tante Martha's friend in the wheelchair.' Gabby empties her glass. 'Any male friends of mine before I was married. Now, of course, my husband is fair game as well.' She hates the way she sounds so hard. Her mother's dying words come back to her: "Be good to your brother and sister, Gabby." It's her duty to steer her sister away from self-destruction.

'You have good imagination, Grischa. She like show feelings. Sister feelings for new brother-in-law.'

Rolf is such an innocent. 'Onkel Wilfred and Tante Martha will be there. Even Tante Leni is coming.'

'Who she is?'

'My uncle Theo's widow. The one who's most exposed to village gossip. Doly spends virtually every night in the churchyard. Necking with one boy or another.'

'She seventeen, Grischa. Is normal.'

Isn't the difference between Doly's behaviour and that of an ordinary young girl only too obvious? Gabby really wants to be friends with her sister. But how can she be, if the girl insists on flirting with her husband? Positively nymphomanic. 'It's normal to fall in love. To go out with one boy at a time.'

Wilfred and Gerda Bender have prepared a feast of cold-cuts for the family. With plenty of beer and Schnapps, together with a liberal supply of the cigars Wilfred favours. Gabby is keen to try one. In spite of Rolf's unhappy looks.

'Before we discuss Doly we need to discuss some money matters. Not that they don't coincide.' Gabby looks round the room at her assembled relatives. 'Doly seems to think she's made of money. She spends it everywhere, invites everyone. Mr Hudwalker is worried about using capital as well as income. He sees it as his brief to hand on the capital complete. As he has for me. And as, no doubt, he will for Moppel.'

Wilfred buries his face in his beer. Which isn't lost on Gabby.

'Moppel tells me Hudwalker's hopelessly conservative. That he could do much better if he were allowed to control the money.'

Wilfred's face emerges. Turned a darker puce. 'Emil Junior thinks he's his father. Wrong. Let me remind you that Emil Dohlen didn't manipulate money. Or spend it. He made it.'

'Grischa say he spend huge sum money on Villa Dohlen. He using Goldmark.'

Stolid family faces stare at the outsider. Rolf helps himself to a slice of sausage which has a vague resemblance to the look of Hungarian salami. Tastes it. Leaves the rest.

'I think Moppel's got a point. Old Huddy's pretty unadventurous.' Gabby's eyes stray to Rolf sitting unhappily with a mug of beer in his hand. He has no idea what to do with it. 'As soon as he's of age, I'm letting Moppel handle my American properties. I've tried to get Doly to agree to switch from Hudwalker but she refuses to discuss it. She says she finds the constant talk about money distasteful.'

'Constant talk? Well, well.' Wilfred takes a long draught of beer. 'I've tried to get her to see sense, Gabby. She's interested in spending it, all right. Simply can't seem to grasp there's a limit. That doesn't suit her, so she brushes it aside.'

Gabby knows how much her uncle has prospered. At the Dohlen orphans' expense. His girth has spread with the bulging and proliferating barns. Face as round as a millstone, his sainted father cloned. It's time to cut him out and save some of Doly's money for her in spite of herself. Then anchor responsibility for Doly's moral welfare on Tante Martha, for the finances on Emil Junior. As soon as possible.

Martha sighs. 'Doly has no sense of reality. To her everything is part of a fairy tale. When she was a child, she took refuge with her pets. Now she tries to substitute young men. Dozens of young men. Literally. She doesn't even bother to deny it.'

Gabby smiles. The mere suggestion of sex embarrasses Martha. 'You mean she has relations with them?' Unlikely. Doly isn't that much of a fool. Gabby thinks back to the times she enjoyed so much, is wistful about her friendship with Tall and Small, remembers their carefree visits to the cabaret performances with pleasure. She downs the brandy in her glass, pours more.

'Nothing like full-blown affairs, no. She walks blindly into dozens of relationships and can't see the danger to her. But there is one redeeming feature. She enjoys Lieselotte's company. Even more than the boys'. Now there's a really sensible girl. I thought maybe they could spend a long holiday together. Take an educational trip along the Rhine for a couple of months. That is, if the money can be found for Lieselotte to go.'

'Lieselotte? I thought you felt she was the wrong kind of influence?'

Gabby has often been irritated by the strong attachments her sister attracts, apparently without even trying. And her extraordinary hold over Tante Martha. To the extent that their aunt rejects virtually all other friendships to concentrate on Doly.

'She's turned into a sensible young woman. I think she'll be the right travelling companion for Doly.'

'That's not a solution, Martha. Lieselotte is working for her exams. Anyway, travelling would only fill in a month or two at most. Somehow Doly has to settle down. The girl keeps saying she wants to study.' Wilfred waves his cigar. Precipitating smoke into Rolf's nose. Making him sneeze.

Gabby's shrill laugh would threaten the glasses if they weren't quite so coarse. 'She wants to study in Berlin. You mean at the University?' She pulls herself together. She has no right to be jealous that Doly is still free. Without responsibilities. She *chose* to give up studying to have a baby. Bandi is for ever out of her reach, and she longs to channel that love. That's why she finally allowed Rolf to discontinue the contraceptive he always used. And she is content. Happy, even, waiting for the baby to be born.

'It's not out of the question that they take Doly, actually. Her grades from Riverside Hall are quite good.' To Martha's evident surprise. 'Excellent, in fact.'

Doly in Berlin? A disquieting thought, even if she should be looking after her sister. That might be a little too close. 'She's mentioned Barnard College. In Manhattan. Why not let her go there?'

Wilfred beams. 'Because, my dear Gabby, the Hudwalkers refuse to take her on. Too hot to handle, he said.'

'Can't she live in a sorority house?'

'Not until she's eighteen.'

Rolf stands and walks to the window. Out of the smoke. 'Why Grischa and I don't have her stay with us? She can attend University. Poor child need to live with family.'

Gabby's involuntary response is indignation. Then she nods, ashamed of herself. Rolf looked after his younger brothers and sisters when they needed him. He's simply applying that attitude to his young sister-in-law. And he's right. What Doly needs is a real home. She and Rolf can supply just that. Doly might even be good company when

Rolf's away on his frequent trips. So, however tiresome she finds Doly on occasion, she'll offer her warm hospitality. Somewhere to live until she's of age.

CHAPTER 17

Schwanenbruch, August 1928

'So, Doly. You accompany Grischa to Berlin when she return in September?' Rolf is sitting in Emil Dohlen's chair at the head of the dining table. He nods at Herta as he helps himself to a tiny piece of fish. None of the Ferents can stand seafood. Hungary is a land-locked country.

'I'd love to. You're sure I won't be a nuisance?'

'We happy you have as guest.'

Gabby finishes the wine in her glass. Eyes dart from husband to sister and back again. She has to encourage Doly to be part of their Berlin lives. 'I read about the most marvellous piece by a new artistic team: music by Kurt Weill, lyrics by Berthold Brecht.'

'You mean *Mahagonny*?'

'You've heard of it?'

'I saw an article in a Hamburg paper. At Herr Doktor Veldun's. Tante Martha's friend. He's invited me to coffee a couple of times.'

Tante Martha sounded distressed when she told Gabby that Doly flirts with a man old enough to be her grandfather. 'So you know what a brilliant work it is. I can tell you right now that that partnership is going to be quite something.'

'According to the critic I read, there's no real cohesion in Brecht's lyrics. Nothing but fantastic mishmash without any logic or psychological meaning...'

Gabby thumps the table with her right fist. Imitating her professors.

Making the wine glasses shudder. 'Brecht is one of the shrewdest political commentators we have. His brilliant insight into the worst excesses of the NSDAP party...'

'The what?'

'The Nationalsozialistische Deutsche Arbeiterpartei, Nazi party for short, had its third rally in Nuremberg three days ago. They're right-wing maniacs. Fascists. Who won't just go away, as everyone seems to think. I don't suppose you even noticed.'

Doly's eyes have glazed over. 'That jumped-up little man with the moustache? I thought he'd been stopped from public speaking.'

'My God, Doly, you never know anything. The ban was lifted in March. He was at it again in Munich just a few days later. Spreading his revolting anti-Weimar, and anti-Semitic, doctrine.'

'He's just a clown. Nothing to get worked up about.'

'Exactly what I'd expect you to think. You're such a political simpleton, Doly. That man is dangerous. Twenty thousand people at the Nuremberg rally were putty in his hands. He had them cheering against the occupation of the Saar. He preached about Germans being the Herrenvolk—master race. He not only wants Germans to control their own country, he wants them to forge a new Reich.'

Doly draws a cigarette out of a packet. Sees Rolf's reaction. Puts it back. 'Actually, Gabby, I also want Germany to be independent again. What's wrong with that?'

'Nothing. Versailles was a disaster and it should have been seen to properly a long time ago. Now it's much harder, perhaps even too late. Because Nazi policies will lead to extending Germany's boundaries, and so to another war. That speech was a rabble-rousing attack if ever I heard one.'

'You exaggerate always, Grischa. Let silly man talk. Is not dangerous to talk, is good to let explode.'

'Please don't try to lecture me about politics, Rolf. You may be an important inventor, but you understand nothing about political ambitions.' Ice-blue eyes assess her sister and husband. 'Or about human nature, either.'

'And you know everything, do you, Gabby? You're the oracle that will put us all to rights?' Doly's voice is soft.

If she can't get the message across, maybe theatre can. 'I'll take you to a Brecht/Weill opera, and you'll see what I mean. Never mind the lack of logic and psychological insights. What we need is *political* insights. Even the critics understood the power of the *Mahagonny* performance. They admitted they didn't know why. But they instinctively felt the truth of it.'

'God, Gabby. Every time you're around we have to have these homilies about politics. You sound like a rabble-rouser yourself. Why can't we talk about the beauty around us? Enjoy the natural world. Listen to birdsong...'

However hard she tries she can't communicate with the fatuous girl. 'I don't know what it is about you, Doly. I've no idea whether other people feel the way I do or not. All I know is that when someone gets you into a philosophical corner you escape into twittering about the birds and the bees. You're not a child any more. It's time one could have an adult conversation with you without getting infuriated by your rubbish.'

Doly pushes her plate away from her, grabs the napkin to her streaming eyes and rushes out.

'Is not necessary upset your sister, Grischa.'

She isn't proud of herself. She'll make it up to Doly. But that nitwit would tax an angel's patience. 'She didn't have to take it all so literally, Rolf. I do get a little carried away by politics. But only because I care.'

'Politics for men is. Women look after home.'

Fury overwhelms all reason. Her chair tips backwards as her body uncoils. How can a man who is so brilliant at his job be such a complete idiot?

THE PRICE OF PEACE

A long time ago, when Land Wursten was still untamed and virtually uninhabited, two brothers lived in the area. They could not get on with each other at any price. They quarrelled bitterly every time they so much as caught sight of each other.

Finally the younger one had had enough. He decided to leave the family home they shared and arranged to build himself a separate place to live. As far away from his older brother as possible, but still within the confines of their inheritance.

He chose a site in Land Wursten, in the middle of the wetlands. He shipped in good heavy loam to make solid foundations for the very first house to be built on the marshy soil of Land Wursten.

When the house was ready, the younger brother thought he had achieved his goal. He could now live in peace. So he cried out for joy: 'Hier schall he sück wol betämen.—Here I can live in peace and tranquillity.'

Since that day the place has been known as Tämen, now written as Themeln. The strange thing is that when the foundations were ploughed up recently, the drained land now proving an excellent medium for growing grain, the ploughman maintained he could hear an odd rumbling noise. As though someone was angry at being disturbed. He insisted that he'd come across the cellar of the oldest house in the county.

CHAPTER 18

Berlin, September 1928

Doly can't sleep in her sister's Berlin apartment. Its hothouse atmosphere. She gets up at first light intending to go out for some air. As she's about to leave, a gangling man saunters up to her.

'Well, well. You're up bright and early. Abandoned Old Dykeland to wallow in the pleasures of gay Berlin?'

'If it isn't Mr Tall himself.' Lieselotte's dancing partner at the ball. Whose name she has forgotten. Handsome as ever, though his attitude is strange. Does he mean a double entendre, or is he just being jocular? And how can he know she's come to stay?

'You look ridiculously young after your marshland stint.'

What's he talking about? If she were any younger, she'd still be at school. 'Come on in.' Doly leads him into Gabby's salon, draws the curtains, opens the shutters. 'D'you study philosophy at the University as well?'

He blinks. As though he's only just realised who she is. Surely he didn't mistake her for Gabby? Then he bows. Gravely. As befits a student of philosophy. 'Your sister and I attended virtually the same classes. I also study logic. Not a topic she finds too interesting. She prefers the political aspects of philosophy.'

'Do sit down.' Analytic thought is not, indeed, one of Gabby's greater talents. Perhaps, if she's honest with herself, not Doly's either. They are a pair in that they live by emotions. Though not the same ones. 'And your friend? Is he a student too?'

'Jon... Johann? His father died. He's with his mother at the moment.'

'They don't live in Berlin?'

He smiles, his eyes focusing on a spot behind Doly's head. 'Perhaps you and Gabby and I might go to the theatre together. Tolstoy's *Resurrection* is on.'

'Tolstoy?' She doesn't mean to sound so affronted. The man died yonks ago. His stuff must be thirty years out of date. Utterly boring.

The door opens and Gabby walks in in her dressing gown. 'I thought I heard the door. Friedrich. To what do we owe this pleasure?' Her eyes dart from Friedrich to Doly and back again.

He stands, his towering form stooped as he studies the Persian carpet. 'I just dropped in for a moment, Gabby. I thought, as your husband's away, you might like to see the Tolstoy our professor recommended. Tonight. We can get another ticket for your sister.'

'Rolf's trip was called off. I'm sorry, Friedrich. I'd have loved it. But you know how it is. Important business dinner tonight.' A yearning quality in her voice. 'But if you and Doly would like to go...'

Doly shakes her head. 'No Tolstoy for me, thanks all the same.'

Friedrich retreats towards the door. 'Sorry to call so early. I was on my way to the library. Another time then, Gabby. Don't disturb yourself, I'll let myself out.'

Doly submits to outings. The Berliner Schloss, described by Gabby as the Italian Baroque imperial residence which grew out of a 15th Century castle. Grotesque, to Doly's perceptions.

Gabby's unstoppable. Subjecting Doly to sightseeing marches through Berlin streets. Adding historic patter.

'The Deutscher Dom is the cathedral the Lutherans built.' Voice brimming with the penetrating tones of the dedicated mentor. 'Right at the beginning of the 18th Century. The broad steps were used to display the coffins of martyred revolutionaries. From the March 1848 uprising.'

Doly's feet hurt. Town shoes aren't meant for walking. She's hopeful this is the last of to-day's exhibits, and wants to sound grateful. 'So this is Berlin's main cathedral?'

'No, no, Doly. That's called the Berliner Dom. It's only a short step from here, built on the banks of the Spree. We'll walk over if we have time.' A brisk trot Doly has trouble keeping up with. 'The Rotes Rathaus is called the Red City Hall because of its red brick construction. In the 1860s. Built on the site of the medieval town hall.'

There's a ghastly tiled frieze running round along its façade. Doly doesn't ask what it represents. In case she's given more history lessons. Or walked right round it.

'And this is my alma mater: the Royal Friedrich Wilhelm University. It repudiates all attachments to any particular creed or school of thought. And professes subservience only to the interests of science and learning.'

'Just up your street then.'

The irony is completely lost on Gabby. Who strides on. Masses of public buildings. Each more hideous than the next. Doly thinks nostalgically of the day she spent with Bobby in Washington. The city's clean lines. The unobtrusive architecture of the White House. Painted that colour to hide the smoke stains which were left after the British burned it down. Much more exciting than crenellated medieval walls.

'It's very kind of you to take me sightseeing, Gabby.'

'It's my job to see to your education, Doly.'

'Very kind, but unnecessary. I can perfectly well go round by myself.'

Gabby stops long enough to frown. 'Nonsense. You'll get lost.'

'I wouldn't go, Gabby. To be honest, I don't think Berlin's a patch on Washington.'

Her sister's mouth opens wide, clamps shut. She swallows, coughs, gapes at Doly. 'What on earth are you talking about?'

'Bobby showed me the sights.'

Gabby tries to keep her face still, cannot stop her voice from rising to a high shrill. 'Bobby? Who's that?'

'Bobby Hudwalker. Bertrand's younger brother. He was staying with the Hudwalkers when I visited them on my way to Riverside Hall. I saw quite a bit of him in the holidays.'

All the energy has left Gabby's face. She stares at her sister, then along Berlin's magnificent streets. 'I see.'

'We still write to each other.'

'And his presence transformed the sights of Washington into greater architectural achievements than the beauties of Berlin. That's what you're saying?' How is she ever going to get on with this woman, so like her and yet so unlike?

'I prefer Washington. I have a right to my own opinion.'

'Which doesn't automatically make it worth anything.'

'And doesn't automatically make it worthless, either.'

Gabby stops. Suddenly. On the street. 'I'm not going to exhaust myself to bore you. Why don't we go to a film, instead? Buster Keaton's on. A sharp-witted comedy.'

'You saw good film, Doly?' Rolf is presiding over his dinner table. He pours wine for the sisters and only takes a token drop for himself. 'What you think?'

Doly turns bright, provocative eyes on him. 'You want my honest opinion?'

'Of course honest. Is not I make film.' A guileless smile.

Doly watches her sister eat. Food is propelled into her mouth at speed and swallowed almost immediately, apparently without mastication. More like a snake than a human being. 'I thought it infantile.' Delivery quiet. Nonchalant.

Gabby's next forkful hangs between plate and mouth. '*You* thought it infantile?' Her lips form into an O. 'At least you can't blame that on Berlin. It was made in Hollywood. Nothing here seems to be good enough for you.'

Doly notes she's scored a bull's-eye, decides to try for more. 'Why shouldn't I say what I think?'

'Because it's good manners to at least pretend to enjoy your hostess's attempts to entertain you. Hard to achieve, in your particular case.'

'You don't have to play the older sister all the time, you know.'

'Come now. You sisters are. Is not good all time quarrel.' Rolf holds the bottle of wine up high and Gabby nods at him. He pours her another glassful. Smiles at Doly who also holds her glass out. His hand brushes hers as he stands to take it. 'Remember, Grischa. Tomorrow is important exhibition of business machines. Is included IBM and I must go.

'You understand. Establishing use of tabulating machines in business world is difficult. Governments bought for census, but to sell new machines in offices is much harder.'

Doly suppresses a yawn. Another boring convention of businessmen. Last night's dinner conversation was bad enough. She can't remember another time when she was so bored while surrounded by men. She's inclined to cry off. After all, Rolf is Gabby's husband. It's *her* duty to go with him.

'You can count me out. Doly and I are off to Potsdam after lunch. I'll try to impress her with the Versailles of Berlin. Even if we can't rival Washington.'

Rolf's eyes show his disappointment. 'You not come? Mr Watson very disappointed.'

'Really, Rolf. I can't get up at the crack of dawn for the exhibition *and* then show Doly round.'

'But Grischa...'

'I'm sure Mr Watson will understand I'm not quite up to it. And be much too busy to notice my absence.'

'I'll go with you, Rolf.' Doly can't resist peeking. Her winning thrust has glazed her sister's eyes. Doly tells herself she offered because she feels sorry for the poor man. He tries so hard to please his wife. Occasionally he has to fulfil his business duties.

Her second reward is Rolf's quite intense smile. 'Is good, Doly. I think you like. Is very interesting machines. We must explain to visitors how new devices cut down tabulating work, replace manual data sorting.' In his excitement he drinks some of his wine. 'Salesmen work very hard, but always people say: "We don't need tabulating machine. We already have tabulator on our typewriter." They not understand is entirely new concept we try to sell. Tabulating machine nothing to do with tabulator.'

'Grischa. We back.'

There's only the echo from the high-ceilinged hall, the tinkle of crystal from the chandelier drops fluttering in the draught.

'Gabby? You there? We're back.'

No sound of any kind.

'I look in bedroom. Maybe she need to rest. Is having baby.'

392

Gabby is not in the apartment. No note, no sign. The table is laid for the midday meal in the dining room, the maid waiting in the kitchen. Who has no idea that Frau Ferent has gone out.

'Where she can be? She never do this before. She always here when I come home.' Rolf can't stand still. He rushes from room to room. Although he's already checked that Gabby isn't in any of them.

He returns to the living room. Frowns at his fob watch, shakes it. 'Is stopped. I told you fetch me, Doly. I say we leave latest by eleven o'clock. What is time?'

'We aren't late, are we?' Doly was bored enough to know the time. She chose not to draw Rolf's attention to it. Preferring to let Gabby wait.

He walks over to an ornate mantel clock. With double-basket top, cherub spandrels and a face with large Roman numerals. Gabby's latest exuberant buy. 'What I do? Is already twelve-thirty. She await us noon. I very worried, Doly. You think she go out and herself harm?'

Her heart misses a beat, then steadies. Not bloody likely. Peeved, more like. Because Doly sacrificed herself to help poor Rolf. Taking the limelight, so Gabby felt left out. 'She'd never do a thing like that.'

His hands twist back and forth inside each other. 'She told she never jealous. Has no reason, I look no other woman since I marry.' Empty eyes stare at Doly. 'She told she only jealous of one person in whole world. Of sister. I see she think we have rendezvous. I call police.'

Doly is pleasantly aware that Rolf finds her attractive. Is attentive. Gives her presents. The way he held her hands in Riverside Hall, lowered his voice. The jewellery, the Hungarian shawl. Does Gabby have real grounds for jealousy?

She takes the twisting sweaty hands in hers. 'I'm sure she's fine, Rolf. She'll be back in no time.'

His eyes beseech the door, shift restlessly. The lines from nose to mouth are deeper. White. He looks his age.

'You don't take personally, Doly. When Grischa come in, you go out, please? Leave us for hour. Let simmer down. Go for long walk before you return.' He removes his hands from hers. Pecks a kiss on her cheek.

The door bursts open. Gabby stops short enough to be in danger of tripping. Rolf rushes over. A furious arm keeps him at bay. He tries to embrace her as she twists away. 'We sorry we a little late, Grischa. My watch...'

'Late? You've ruined the whole day. I got up at dawn to do the shopping, chivvied Gerda so she'd produce lunch at noon. The outing was planned for Doly's sake.'

Gabby's nostrils are broad. Like a dragon's. Doly is sure she can see smoke writhing out of them.

'We make excursion another day.' Rolf looks meaningfully at Doly who starts towards the door.

Gabby catches the look, clearly misinterprets it. 'And where d'you think you're going?' Her voice spits like the hailstones on Schwanenbruch beach. 'The meal is ready.' She pulls at the bell cord by the fireplace. Loud jangles reverberate.

Doly's feeling of smug uninvolved superiority turns to unease. She and Rolf exchange furtive glances.

Gabby's nostrils quiver, sweat beads her face. 'Legally you're still a child, Doly. In my care. You do exactly as I say. When I say it.' Clipped, hard, furious.

'Is plenty time to go to Pots...'

She throws her handbag at a glass ornament. It shatters on the parquet floor. 'See what you've done?'

Rolf stoops to pick the pieces up.

'For God's sake, leave that to the maid. It just won't do, Rolf. She's not staying here.' Gabby whirls to face Doly. 'Pack your bags. You're taking the first train to Hamburg tomorrow morning. Then back to Schwanenbruch. Tante Martha will have to take over for the time being.'

Her sister's voice is almost back to normal. No doubt in the blessed knowledge that Doly is about to remove her evil presence and not contaminate Gabby's delicate susceptibilities any further.

'I accompany to station.' Rolf carries Doly's bags to the waiting taxi.

Gabby goes with them. As a chaperone. 'I shall be writing to Mr Hudwalker. We have to work out what's to be done with you.'

'He's my guardian. *You* needn't do anything.' Did she go too far? Deliberately try to make Gabby jealous? Her sister is, after all, in a delicate condition.

'It goes without saying that we shall never see each other again. But I can't just abdicate my responsibilities.'

Rolf buys several magazines, finds Doly a seat in a compartment in which another woman is already seated. He kisses her hand. In a brotherly way. 'We remain friends, Doly? In spite of everything.'

The train ride back to Hamburg, and on to Schwanenbruch, is uneventful. Rain mingled with soot trickles down the carriage window. Crooked rivulets in sympathy with the tears trickling down Doly's cheeks. Gabby hates her.

What's the point of her life? She needs love and nobody cares a damn. Tante Martha is kind because Vater's money paid for her teacher training. The Hudwalkers get paid to do their duty. Onkel Wilfred holds her to him, pulls her on to his leering lap. Werner no longer even greets her since she turned him down, and the other boys are just after one thing. Bobby is far away and hasn't written lately. Even Lieselotte prefers Josef's company.

It's possible she's been a little thoughtless as far as Gabby is concerned. She did invite Doly to live in her home. And she's pregnant, overwrought.

Exasperation overcomes regret. Her sister plays dirty. Uses her clever tongue to get at Doly, stab her in the back. At least Doly fights with open weapons.

No question about one thing, though. Gabby is flexing her muscles. She has money, a husband, will soon be a mother. Queen bee. If Doly lives anywhere near her, she'll be in her power.

Doly makes herself a promise. Never to cross paths with Gabby again. Berlin University, *Royal* Friedrich Wilhelm University, is off her list.

'Na, Doly. Back so soon. Decided not to study in Berlin?' Onkel Wilfred's fat fingers are on her shoulders. Slip down over her breasts. She twists away.

'Gabby doesn't want me there.' Doly tells the dismal story of her abrupt dismissal.

Tante Gerda is listening as well. She nods her head. She's not a fan of Gabby's. Who has subverted substantial sums from Onkel Wilfred's control. 'That husband of hers has straying eyes.'

No reproaches. No condemnations. An unusual turn of events.

'How would you like to stay in Cuxhaven for a while, Doly? Tante Martha has moved into a bigger flat. With a guest room. She's willing to have you.'

'Willing?'

Tante Gerda's eyes look up from her darning. So soft. So full of love for her daughter Ulrike. Whatever she does. 'I mean she's really keen to have you.'

'She doesn't know about Berlin.'

'Gabby rang her up. At the school. Martha came over right away. We talked it over. You two can plan your future, Doly. As a team. We don't think it right other people should tell you what to do. Think about it. Take your time.'

'Will Herr Hudwalker approve?'

'He's hardly going to turn down something your Tante Martha recommends, now is he?'

PART 6

FREEDOM FIGHTERS

1928–1930

THE MERMAID'S CURSE

Wolderich, Knight of Lappe and Lord of Castle Ritzebüttel, was a headstrong man who often sailed alone, braving the tempestuous North Sea, going as far as the island of Oe.

One soft summer night a golden sun was setting behind Oe's tower. The tide was out, the mudflats lay exposed. Gulls shrieked, a seal barked. An uncanny silence followed. Wolderich's sails hung limp and, sandbanked, he couldn't even use his oars. Gentle ineffectual breezes teased his locks, tickled his beard. And held him captive, waiting for the returning tide.

As the sun set, Wolderich was astonished to see a female figure lying on the sand. Her face was turned away, her body on fire with the last golden rays of the dying sun. Her hair was festooned with seaweed and shells and, instead of legs, she had a shimmering glittering fishtail.

Wolderich was entranced. He clicked his tongue and whistled to lure the mermaid to him. She turned her head and he felt her steady gaze, sensed fire flashing through his veins.

'Come to me, come to me,' he called out. Softly. Seductively.

She slipped into a creek and swam towards him. He helped her into the boat. She sat down beside him, placed her cool hands in his. Her eyes were as clear as the sea, a film of salt spray coated the lips he kissed passionately.

The tide came in, the boat rose in the water. The wind began to quicken and fill his sails. Wolderich grabbed his tiller with his left hand and held on to the mermaid with his right. When he was in sight of his castle, he strapped the mermaid's arms to her sides.

She didn't resist. But he saw the green of her irises turn to grey, and he heard her sweet sighs change to sobs.

'Why have you trussed me up so I can't move?' she cried out.

He felt neither pity nor love, only the conqueror's triumph. 'Because you belong to me.' he crowed. 'You're mine, like the seas around me and the tower of Castle Ritzebüttel.'

'The land and waters around your castle may be yours,' she said. 'And so may the castle tower. But the North Sea and the tower on Oe, those are mine. You'll never keep what you've taken by force. They will avenge me.'

'We'll see about that.' Wolderich heard her cries of pain, so like the mournful calling of gulls circling the sea. He watched her throw herself at the rim of the boat, trying to escape, laughed at her efforts to free herself. Wolderich anchored his boat, lifted the trussed mermaid out and carried her up to his castle tower. That's when she laid her curse:

As you hold me by force today,

Another's sword shall here hold sway

He paid no attention, simply left her there. By morning his mermaid had disappeared.

Wolderich worked hard for many years, amassed great wealth. But, anxious for his castle and his lands, he could never forget the mermaid's curse. He made sure his dykes were braced against the turbulent North Sea, stood and watched the great breakers crash on his shore.

'I don't fear you,' he shouted at der Blanke Hans. 'I've protected myself against you.' And he was right. The floods did not break through his dykes.

Then one day, as the noble knight Wolderich Lappe stood on the ramparts of his tower and scanned the wide horizon of his flat lands, he saw an enormous dust cloud rolling towards him. He soon realised that it was a troop of armed Frisians marching on Ritzebüttel, carrying a proud standard.

Wolderich shuddered. The picture on the flag was the face of a beautiful mermaid, and one he recognised. It was the very one he had deprived of her freedom so many years ago. The mermaid's friends had come at last to avenge her wrong and to carry out her curse.

Castle Ritzebüttel surrendered after a few weeks' siege, when Wolderich lay dead. The victor's flag was carried past his corpse and hoisted high to fly from Ritzebüttel's tower.

As you hold me by force today,

Another's sword shall here hold sway

Since then the Knights of Lappe have been deprived of all their lands, their castle taken over by the victorious Frisians who carried out the mermaid's revenge.

CHAPTER 1

Berlin, Winter 1928/9

'I know you don't like talking about politics, Rolf.'

'Is nothing ordinary peoples can do. Is waste of time.'

'Politics depends on ordinary people. Even you must have grasped what happened with the Russian uprising.'

'Is not from people. Is from revolutionaries.'

'I can agree with you there. And we have one right here in Germany. His name is Adolf Hitler.'

'Grischa, you exaggerate always. Is small party. Is nothing.'

'Don't be so gullible. In the March elections the National Socialists, the Nazis, were the largest party in Bavaria.'

'Is only one region, Grischa.'

'The war reparations required from the German people are absurd. Germany can't pay, and that rankles with people. What's happening in Bavaria is the writing on the wall; there'll be another war within twenty years.'

'Grischa. You just young woman. How you know?'

Her eyes are sparkling. 'Because I read the papers, follow what's going on. We're having a child, Rolf. It's due in spring. If it's born in Berlin, it will be German or Hungarian. Those will be our only choices and not, in my view, happy ones. I want to go to the States. If it's born there, it will be an American citizen.'

'Grischa, Liebling. Is not sensible. You wish go America you must sail already in early February. When could be stormy weather. And come back soon after birth may also be bad weather. And you must go on own. I cannot leave work one/two months.'

'We aren't children, Rolf. If we have a son and there is another war, he may have to fight for Germany. Against the Americans.' Gabby has thought it through. He'd be half Jewish. The Nazis aren't just volubly anti-Semitic. The Brownshirts beat up known Jews in full daylight. Dare she voice that, or will Rolf's aversion to such a reminder of his origins turn determination into resolve?

'IBM main office in New York. Watson will us to America take.'

'Put not your trust in company presidents, Rolf. Remember war means the breakdown of old values. You went through all that yourself not so very long ago.'

He's sitting at his desk. Paying bills. His left temple is resting on his left-hand thumb. The index finger moves back and forth across his eyebrow. A habit which shows concentration. Worry.

'We compromise. If boy you sail America. If girl you here stay.'

Gabby stares. 'And how are we going to know whether it's a boy or a girl?' She's longing for a son. She even prays for one. But it's in the lap of the gods.

'Is new method. Go see Dr Frischmeister. He distinguished medical man and also inventor of new technique. He hold needle over belly. Goes clockwise is boy, anticlockwise is girl. Is accurate ninety-five percent.'

A prominent Jewish practitioner the Nazis have pilloried recently. 'But... '

'You only go if boy.'

The bills are large. Rolf's in charge of her finances, and she has no idea how to manage on her own. It wouldn't be easy to disobey him. She'll talk to Tall and Small. Small—well, his Hasidic family—is bound to know someone who can get her out of this hole.

Jewish traditions are quite clear. Brides must be virgins. That's easy to achieve within orthodox Jewish communities. Because no woman may ever be alone in a room with a man who isn't her husband. And Jewish bridegrooms know how to tell a virgin from a scarlet woman.

But every loving Jewish Mama knows that traditions can be bent.

Her daughter understands that the lifting of the wedding veil to receive her bridegroom's kiss is symbolic of the rending of the maidenhead. Which may no longer be there.

In such a case Mama has good advice. Voice low so no one else can hear. 'Make sure the lights are dimmed,' she whispers to her daughter. 'No bridegroom will ask his blushing bride to put up with unromantic lights.'

The girl's hand is taken, a tiny vial pressed into it.

'Not perfume,' the mother whispers. 'Chicken blood. Sprinkle it discreetly on the sheets. He'll be too taken up to notice.

'Make sure you practise well. A little is better than a lot. Just a few drops. He'll never suspect a thing.'

Unless, of course, his father has warned him to inspect the tip of his circumcised penis. As well as the sheets.

Jonah's mother's considerable store of Jewish folklore is unable to shed light on the circular direction of needles held over pregnant abdomens. Jonah himself comes up with a scientific approach. A magnet concealed in Gabby's underwear. On the right side.

How is he to know that the practitioner uses a gold needle suspended on one of Gabby's hairs? A double travesty.

The needle circles anticlockwise. Rolf is convinced the baby is a girl.

'Girl not asked to join military. You stay for birth in Augusta-Viktoria Krankenhaus. Is safer.'

Rolf is ecstatic about the imminent birth. He longs to be a father. He's determined to see his daughter as soon as she is born.

Berlin, February 1929

'What we call her, Grischa?'

'You don't have any special wishes?' Gabby can see that Rolf hoped their child would be one of the mistaken five percent of predicted gender. A sentiment she shares.

'Is girl. You choose.'

'What about Gemma? That's easy to pronounce in both German and English. A simple and not too common name in any language.'

'What language matter other than German?'

Gabby's instinct is to scream her frustration. Rolf's latest invention has resulted in promotion. He's to be Eastern European Manager for IBM, with special duties in Iraq and Persia. 'She will have to learn to speak English, Rolf. There's obviously going to be another war. We won't be here, in Germany.' Hasn't he read Hitler's diatribes against Jews? That he wants to cleanse Germany of them? Rolf himself said that that could mean severe measures, possibly even some deaths. Has he forgotten? 'We'll be in England or the United States.'

'Always this obsession you have. I never heard this Gemma.'

'My mother's name was Emma. Mine is Gabriele. I thought perhaps combine the two in Gemma.'

The midwife brings the baby over to Gabby. 'A perfect little girl, Frau Ferent.'

Gabby accepts her child. Not perfect. The blank face without eyebrows or lashes. The genetic line has not been broken. Gabby's hands tighten into fists. Rolf has black curly hair on his chest, his arms, his legs, the backs of his hands. He has to shave twice a day. Yet his daughter will end up bald.

'I take.' Rolf puts a finger in the baby's hand. She grips him like a vice. He draws her up with the strength of it. 'You see? She very forceful.'

'You'll have your hands full there,' the midwife laughs. 'Determined little package.'

Rolf scoops the baby on to his arm, motions the woman to leave. He stares at his daughter. 'She has it. I not think I have child without the hair. I so much have.'

Rolf's long lines from nose to mouth deepen, but not because the baby is a girl. He can't spot political dangers written in huge headlines on Berlin walls, but he's devastated by a blemish which won't be obvious for years. How can such a clever man be so short-sighted?

'Call her as you like. Daughters for mothers are.'

Gabby touches the locket at her throat. She wore it throughout her pregnancy—an amulet to ward off the evil gene. It hasn't worked. Like her own mother she has to face the reality, one she longed to escape, one which is worse than having to cope with her own lack of a woman's crowning glory. Her daughter has the gene, and she cannot prevent the dawning despondency this will engender in her child. She blinks away tears.

The baby turns her head, opens her eyes and stares at Gabby. She feels a sudden rush of love, a surge of wonder. Gemma may not be perfect but she's her baby. She will protect her against all comers. And she will teach her daughter how to cope—as she herself has done.

Rolf hands the baby back to Gabby as the doctor who delivered her walks in. 'Ah, Herr Ferent. Heartiest congratulations. You've got a winner there. The healthiest pair of lungs I've ever heard. And who'd have thought a little woman like your wife could produce such a whopper?'

An almighty explosion drowns whatever else the worthy doctor might have uttered. He throws himself on the floor while Rolf swoops across his wife and child.

'Is bomb. We call police...'

'Those bloody Brownshirt thugs bombing hospitals now?'

Gabby pushes Rolf away from her. Tries not to laugh. 'I'm sorry, gentlemen. It's not a bomb. Just champagne.'

'Champagne?'

Gabby can't stop herself. She laughs until the tears run down her cheeks. 'My friends,' she gasps. 'Two fellow students at the University. They brought me a bottle of champagne. I thought the hospital would frown on that. They put it in the airing-cupboard.' She giggles. 'We were going to wet the baby's head after you'd gone.'

'My dear lady. What a misapprehension. We welcome celebrating the birth of such a lovely little girl. What's her name?'

'Gemma Elisabeth,' Rolf pronounces. 'For grandmother and aunt.'

The doctor opens the cupboard door, pulls out the lower part of the exploded bottle. He trickles foaming liquid over the baby's bare scalp. 'Let's do the honours with what's left. Gemma Elisabeth Ferent: May she follow in her beautiful mother's footsteps.'

Beautiful. The doctor thinks she's beautiful. Because he doesn't know, didn't even notice throughout the birth. Because she's become expert at wearing her wigs, dresses them to look part of her. That is, perhaps, the strangest part of her inheritance. A blemish no one need know about—a secret she's become expert at guarding.

Gabby puts a finger into the liquid, into her mouth. Raises her thoughts to a fitting toast: She'll never allow Gemma to be mocked—

not by her father, not by anyone. She'll see to it that her child has the best hairpieces as soon as she needs them, won't let her suffer the way she did. Her daughter will never have to face the world without sufficient hair.

It suddenly occurs to her that the toast is right for both daughter *and* mother. And that she has, at last, come to terms with her inheritance.

CHAPTER 2

Cuxhaven, Winter 1928/9

'Your eighteenth birthday is coming up in April, Doly. We really must try to find out what you would like to do until you go to university. Whichever one you decide on.'

Doly knows exactly what she wants. To meet Prince Charming. From England. 'I could study at Oxford or Cambridge University.'

'Their Matriculation requirements are very strict. Latin or Greek to School Certificate level, as well as English and Mathematics. I'm afraid you haven't a hope in England.'

'What about Barnard College. That's in New York City.'

Tante Martha nods. Her hair has remained brown, though all her contemporaries are showing grey. 'An excellent idea for autumn 1929. They'll accept you in a sorority house by then.'

'Meanwhile I can stay with you?'

'Why not use the time to round out your education, Doly? I've been given a splendid prospectus by Herr Doktor Veldun. An academy just outside Vienna. The Foxburg Academy. The syllabus includes art appreciation, attending the Vienna Opera House, dancing...'

'You mean they teach you ballet?'

Tante Martha's smile is a little lop-sided. 'If you enjoy that. Also ballroom dancing. The Viennese waltz, the polka, and modern dances like the quickstep. As well as the dance forms of Isadora Duncan. And painting classes. Art appreciation and history. That sort of thing.'

'May I read the prospectus?'

'That's what I got it for.'

'Will Herr Hudwalker send the necessary funds?'

The brown head nods. 'With Herr Doktor Veldun's backing, and the wide academic and cultural programme, I think he will agree.'

'He wouldn't even pay for my holiday with Liesi.'

Tante Martha's expression is bland. Like a teacher's. 'He's afraid people are trying to cash in on your money, Doly.'

Teachers stick together. 'But Liesi...'

'He doesn't know her the way you and I do.' The small eyes flutter to conceal their thoughts. 'Gabby wrote a letter to Onkel Wilfred. Suggesting that it isn't wise to let you go so far away from the family. But Herr Doktor Veldun agrees with me. Foxburg is just the sort of place which could be absolutely right for you. It will give you the chance to show your guardian that you're serious about improving yourself. Learning as much as you can.'

Very gratifying. And Gabby's clearly furious that she has a choice. Of course she'll go to Foxburg. The sooner the better.

Foxburg Academy, Winter 1928/9

Dear Diary,

Four men have managed to kiss me since I left America, and four more tried it on. Werner was the most persistent, the most handsome, the closest to my secret dreams. And his intentions were honourable. But he never came near me again after my escape on Lüneburg Heath.

And the three others? Fritz took advantage when I was witless with drink. It wouldn't have mattered who he was with. Dieter was the one who forced himself on me. The one I couldn't stop. I still shudder when I think of it. I cannot bear to be forced, dominated by a man.

Harland is the one I really went for. He was gentle and unassertive. That's why I was able to give myself to him of my own free will.

And the four who didn't make it? I was tactful with Peter. Because he allowed me to be. I simply pretended I didn't understand what he was after. I actually had to fight Albert Mackter off. That left

407

something of a bad taste

Harland was the one who rescued me from Markus. And Julius Vendt got a slap for his pains when he tried it on in the train.

Tante Martha says I'm lecherous. That it's a characteristic tied up with temperament. If so, it's hardly under my control. I've always expected high standards of myself. I don't know whether I'm trying to whitewash my shortcomings or not, but Tante Martha's words hit me like a thunderbolt.

I pretended her judgement was fact. Gave reasons for and against my so-called randy behaviour. Do I disagree with her because I don't like the accusation, or am I just kidding myself?

Tante Martha's an old maid. The truth is I'm eighteen and I also have a healthy sex drive. That's nothing out of the ordinary. What is difficult to understand is that, when it comes to the point, I don't really want to go ahead. Something is stopping me, and I don't believe it's just stuffiness, or that I'm being coy. It's more than that. I wish I knew what's wrong.

CHAPTER 3

Berlin, March 1929

'Vienna? You want us to move to Vienna?' Gabby can hardly believe her ears. Leave Berlin? The lively fascinating city she's come to adore, the shows, the University; and Tall and Small? Move to a city which produced the Johann Strausses at roughly the time Germany produced Richard Wagner? Schmaltz with a big S hardly compares with the brilliant Saxon.

'Not I, Grischa. I very happy in Berlin. Mr Watson ask me to go.'

The furrow down the centre of her forehead is deepening. Underlining her frustration. She blinks, relaxes facial muscles. 'Why? Isn't the new job working out?'

'Is working very well. Mr Watson arrange IBM Headquarters for Eastern European market in Vienna. Is right place. Manager must from Headquarters work. I cannot help.'

'But Rolf, Vienna is even more dangerous than Berlin.' And Doly has recently enrolled in the Foxburg Academy. Just outside Vienna. Of all the places she could have chosen, did she *have* to plump for Vienna?

'What you mean, dangerous?'

'Politically. I suppose you've forgotten the riots of 1927.'

'You mean Communists. Is already two years. Almost.'

She's talking to a half-wit. 'The problem hasn't gone away. They called for the deaths of all judges and the middle class. That's people like us.'

Rolf nods. 'What I do? Is bad all over central Europe. And Germany with Austria wants annex. Soon all is one. Make no difference.'

'You want to expose your wife and child to such a place?'

'You said self. National Socialists becoming very popular. Hitler is wanting power in Germany. Austria safer at present.'

She tries another tack. 'What about my studies at the University? You know I was going back.'

'You mother now. How you can study? Who look after little one?' He takes Gemma out of her crib, rocks her. The baby has thrived, grown some blonde hair. 'She look she could be pretty after all. Maybe not taking too long.' His fingers curl soft tendrils as he kisses Gemma. 'We find first-class house in Vienna, Grischa. We buy. You furnish as you like. I can't help what Mr Watson say. Is my job to move.' He pushes the baby's palms together. 'Or you wish we emigrate to America? I can arrange.'

Has he forgotten she's a citizen? That she chose to return to Europe? 'You know I prefer living in Germany, Rolf. It's my cultural heritage, one I enjoy. And I want to contribute, to stop that maniac before he takes over.'

'Grischa, you nonsense talk. You just young mother. Is job you can do anywhere.'

In spite of the errant gene, Rolf is infatuated with his daughter. Because she is, after all, his child. He makes the most disgusting ga-ga noises. The only good omen is that Gemma seems unimpressed. 'You will Vienna like, Gemma. You learn dance Blue Danube. I teach.'

Dancing the Viennese waltz has to be worse than taking part in the idiotic ritual for any other dance. Except, perhaps, the csárdás.

The baby blows a raspberry. Gabby can see she has to say goodbye to Berlin for the present. At least Vienna is a capital city. 'When do we have to move?'

'I go two weeks. Buy house. Come fetch you when all settled and you ready. You stay till summer if convenient.'

Foxburg Academy, March 1929

Foxburg Academy for Young Ladies is set in a delightful little village only a tram ride from the centre of Vienna. Park-like surroundings, woodlands, a sheltered grove. And all very above board.

Lessons are highbrow. Art, theatre, discussions about Tolstoy and Thomas Mann, readings from Goethe and Grillparzer. And dancing, both traditional and modern. As promised in the prospectus.

Today there's an excursion to Vienna. Tours round the Staatsoper and the Baroque finery of the National Library. Followed by a walk through the gardens of the Belvedere Palace. Monumentally boring.

Margarete shares a room with Doly. She's from Yugoslavia. Tall and dark. She reminds Doly of Lieselotte. Most of the girls are from abroad. When the others climb into the bus back to school, Margarete says she'll take the tram back later. She wants to do a little shopping. Doly catches on and stays with her.

'I know a great place to flirt.'

Such candour. Doly is thrilled. Margarete is a wonderful new friend. They hurry to the Hotel Sacher. The Thé Dansant starts at five o'clock. She has a rendezvous with her boyfriend there.

Good music, lively dancing. A dark-haired man asks Doly for a dance. Bright button eyes look into hers. 'Have you been in Vienna long?'

'A few weeks. I'm studying at the Foxburg Academy.'

Small buttons become larger. Darker. 'What a coincidence. I've met another pupil from there. D'you know Greta Sindheim?'

'No.'

'Well, if you come across her, give her my best regards. I'm Doktor Wolfgang Seffert, incidentally.'

The man leads her expertly round the floor. The fox trot, the waltz, the tango. He's a brilliant dancer.

'Are you planning on coming into town often?' A caressing hand rubs Doly's back.

'If I can get away.'

'Good. Will you have some time to yourself?'

'I hope so.'

The music stops. He bows, clicks his heels, leads her back to her table. 'Perhaps we might meet up?'

That sounds like an exciting adventure. What could go wrong in a town full of people? 'Why not?'

'Shall we say in front of the Hotel Bristol next Wednesday afternoon?

411

Around three o'clock?'

'Why not? I'll be there.'

Vienna, Wednesday, 7th March, 1929

Herr Doktor Seffert is waiting when Doly's tram drops her off outside the Bristol. Punctuality is a good sign. She's wearing her red winter coat, like last time. So he can't miss her.

He spots her right away. Hands her down from the tram. 'It's Ash Wednesday. One of Vienna's many religious holidays. We're supposed to be living in a Catholic country. So the beginning of Lent is meant to signal the start of forty days' self-denial. But we won't find a place in a coffee house, they'll all be jam-packed with gluttons who have no intention of denying themselves anything. Never mind. I'll show you the sights.'

He takes Doly on a tour of the city, pointing out past glories. Does everyone in Austria live in the time of the Habsburgs? One ancient building after another. This isn't what Doly's here for.

'I live near the University. Just past the Rathaus.' The arm through hers has become insistent.

'Please.' Doly detaches herself. 'I can hardly walk.'

'Sorry. Why not come up to my room? It's warm and comfortable. It's still so chilly out.'

Is this the come-on Tante Martha warned her about? Well, if he becomes too pressing, she'll just leave. But he looks like a decent human being.

The smile is all teeth. 'Let me take off your hat and coat, Schatzie.'

Why is Seffert using endearments when he talks to her? She hardly knows the man. But she allows him to put her outdoor things over a chair.

He locks his door and dims the lights. Arms spread out, he swoops towards her. Begins to kiss her.

'Stop that.'

He takes no notice, bends her backwards.

She loses her balance, falls on to the sofa.

He holds her tight, kisses her again.

Doly twists her head away. 'If you don't stop, I'll scream. At the top of my voice, so all the other students will hear.'

412

'My goodness, little girl. Whatever's wrong with you? You don't really think I'd do anything against your wishes, do you?'

She fights him off in earnest now. Kicks him in the groin, snatches up her hat and coat, unlocks the door and rushes out.

Foxburg Academy, March 8th, 1929

Dear Diary,

Yesterday was a terrible disappointment. I ran away before the adventure even started. Am I just like the rest of the sheep? Old-fashioned, stuck in ways more suited to the past than the present? Why call Tante Martha a fussy old maid when my behaviour is exactly like hers? Will I ever get out of this stupid rut?

I've written a little story to make me feel better, less of a freak. Fairy tales are true, truer than facts.

Foxburg Academy, March 12th, 1929

Dear Diary,

Maybe I'm not such a freak. I think what puts me off is male aggression. No tenderness, no thought of love. No innocence. Oh Bobby, Bobby. You were so sweet. Do you still remember me? Remember our pure unsullied kisses on the bench in Washington? Or have you found another love?

Strange that I hardly remember Harland now. I thought I loved him so much, and now I can't even bring to mind what he looks like. I can no longer feel his lips on mine. And yet we kissed until my lips were bruised and still something was missing. Is all love a fantasy, a passing fancy with no real basis?

I dream of the man I want to love, to marry. Tall, Nordic, strong. Like Werner, but not so set in his passion for following in his father's footsteps. I want a man who can control his animal urges because of his love for me. Who thinks of me rather than himself, someone who longs to be with me. Someone who wants to make love, but also wants a friend. Who talks with me, not at me. The way Liesi and I discuss philosophy, religion, psychology. An artist, perhaps. A poet or a painter. How I long for my one true love.

I will find him, and find him soon.

413

Today was the first real day of spring. The woods are balmy with that soft green patina which heralds the bursting leaf-buds. The sun was warm on my back, the birds singing their love songs.

I adored the little clearing by the brook. It felt good to be part of nature. To be alive.

LITTLE REDCOAT

When Little Redcoat entered the Viennese forest of buildings she was met by big, dark-haired Dr Wolfgang Seffert.

'Look at the wonderful old buildings around you, beautiful maiden. The Oper, the Rathaus, the Stephansdom, the Karlskirche. We have an example of whatever great architecture your heart desires. Your family will be so pleased if you learn all about our glorious past.'

And Little Redcoat listened to all the historic names and all the significant dates. And tried not to be bored by all the special monuments, the towering statues of conquering heroes.

Herr Doktor Wolfgang Seffert was dressed in the robes of a medical man. He told Little Redcoat how cold it was in the big city and invited her to his warm lodgings. Then he drew the curtains against prying neighbours.

'What big eyes you've got, Dr Wolfgang Seffert.'

'All the better to see you with, my beauty.'

'What big ears you've got, Dr Wolfgang.'

'All the better to hear you with, my pretty one.'

'What big teeth you've got, Dr Wolf.'

'All the better to gobble you up with, my little princess.'

No sooner had Wolfgang Seffert said the last words than he jumped at Little Redcoat and tried to eat her up.

CHAPTER 4

Foxburg Academy, Spring 1929

Doly is in her back-to-nature mood. She leaves the school buildings behind her, walks deep into the woods and gazes at the trees around with glistening eyes. They are so very beautiful, their branches heavy with drops of early-morning dew. Weeping, she feels, for her loneliness. If only she were a poet and could write it all down.

She meanders on, looking for the idyllic grove she came across yesterday. She finds herself on the same mossy path, basks in the slanting rays of early-morning light, sinks down on cushioning leaf-mould. A broad tree-trunk seems eager to give her back the support it needs. She watches water splashing diamonds of light over moss-covered stones, breathes deep as she listens to the brook playing the music of the spheres. Birds twitter communion with her feelings.

Her idyll is shattered by an approaching figure, an inchoate form which she sees as a threat to her privacy. She watches the form take shape, then turn into a tall young man. As he comes nearer, she makes out wavy blond hair and gentle blue eyes which smile a shy greeting.

Long legs stop in front of her. She stands, responds with a smile of her own. Wordlessly they wander together along the primrose paths, beside the bubbling brook, treading soft grass and spring-born plants. In silent fellowship.

He stops, turns towards her, takes her hand in both of his, lifts it to his lips. 'Where have you come from, angelic vision?'

A gentle laugh. 'I'm from the Academy.'

A radiant smile. 'My mother's school? I'm Bruno Flendeier. You must be one of the new girls.'

'Dorinda Dohlen. I've been here a little while.'

He bows. 'Mother is having one of her evenings next month. We'd have met at that.' He kisses her hand again. 'But this is so much more romantic.'

Words and thoughts mingle as they tell each other of their pasts, their hopes, their longings. He writes. And paints. Theirs is a clear communion of two souls, a meeting of like spirits.

'I've never met a girl like you before. How will I ever be able to think of other women now that I've met you?'

He's a poet. She's come across the man of her dreams at long last. 'You don't need to.' Can he hear her heart pounding? A hammer of joy. 'We are meant for each other.'

He interlaces his fingers with hers. That kindles a fire in her arm which spreads throughout her body. 'We can't putter around all day. Shall we go to my private quarters? I live in the right wing of the castle.'

'Taboo territory,' Doly giggles. 'I'm longing to see your paintings. And your room.'

They amble towards the school, skirt stone walls, go in by the back entrance forbidden to the girls.

He studies architecture for his career, and he writes poetry to express his emotions. But his true love is painting. Vivid sketches, a glowing still-life, broody landscapes fill his walls.

Doly stares, entranced, at the vibrant colours. 'I love your work.'

'I'd like to show you these as well.' He pulls out a shallow wide drawer. 'This is my special hobby. Small arms of all kinds.'

Knives, pistols, revolvers. All small, all ornate. They don't look as though they could hurt anyone.

'Just feel this.' He hands her a small dagger with a jewelled shaft. Sunlight refracts tinted lights against white walls. A mosaic of colour.

'It's beautiful.'

'And this.' A lady's handgun. With mother-of-pearl handle nestling in satin. He takes it out, strokes the barrel, hands it to her. 'Isn't the workmanship wonderful?'

Doly accepts it gingerly. 'Is it loaded?'

'Of course not.' He shows her the six silver bullets lying in a row above the imprint of the gun. 'These aren't weapons. They're jewels in the form of weapons.'

His room reflects his personality. A desk overflowing with architectural plans, books piled high in a profusion of enchanting disorder, a piano with music open on a Chopin sonata, pieces of paper with odd bits of verse.

'Sorry there isn't much furniture. Do sit down.'

The sofa is a mattress piled high with cushions. Ornate satin shines a palette of crimson and gold. Perhaps this does duty as his bed as well.

'Would you like some tea?'

The kettle is at the ready on the Kachelofen set in a corner. China tea. Cracked china cups. The taste is nectar.

All that is forgotten as the liquid spills because the mattress is soft and squelchy, and they're kissing. Long deep kisses. Tongues searching each other's mouths. Darting to unexpected places. Tasting.

He's only the third man Doly has really wanted to kiss back. Bobby, Harland and now Bruno. Beautiful wonderful Bruno. The man she's longed for all her life. Fresh, magnetic, fascinating. And so very sweet.

His hands find her breasts, pull at her blouse. Her nipples harden, her back arches as she feels her body push itself at him, feels her blood hot in her veins. She's longing to open herself up to him.

His grip tightens. She feels him hard on top of her. His fingers no longer caress, his kisses no longer brush her lips. Instead there's the threat of a shafting barrel about to penetrate her secret place. Her temple.

Her body stiffens. She isn't willing. She has no idea why not, but a gag of distaste makes her draw back, edge her body away. 'We have to stop, Bruno. My love, my true love. We can't go on.' She has no wish to titillate or hurt. But she cannot allow him to go further. It doesn't feel right.

He stops at once. Strokes her hair, her cheek, her neck. 'We are free beings, my sweet. You are free, I am free. Why are you trying to tie me up in knots?'

He moans, and his lower body jerks, just the way Bobby's did that one time. She feels herself shaken as he comes.

Doly makes herself stay with him while he shudders, holds her tight. 'Oh, darling. I'm so sorry. Can't you control yourself?'

He smiles at her. Sad eyes. 'Only up to a point.'

How to excuse herself? 'What we want to do, we can't, and what we can do isn't enough.' She loathes the way she has to deny him what he wants. Is longing to fall around his neck and let her body take over.

Some feeling she can't control, some sense of revulsion which is not to do with Bruno but with her reactions to Bruno, freezes her into tight muscles. She can't allow him to enter her. She even has to deny him the sweet kisses. Because she can't trust herself any more than she can trust him. She stands to leave.

'You want to part like this?'

'I have no choice.' What made her say that? Is she afraid? It isn't fear. What is it? Something is wrong with her. Who can she talk to?

He stands, takes a bottle of brandy, uncorks it. Offers it to her. She shakes her head. He guzzles. She wants to bash it out of his hands but holds herself back.

'Will you come back tomorrow?'

'No. We need to give each other space.' Her eyes fill with tears, her mouth opens one more time for an overwhelming kiss. 'I'll write to you.'

He shakes his head. 'My mother might find out. Leave a message at the grove. In the big split in the bark.'

He's very sure how to set it up. 'You've had this sort of liaison before?'

'That was in the past. As long as I live, I'll never so much as glance at another girl. I give you my solemn promise I'll always be true to you. May my precious collection crumble into rust if I break my word.'

CHAPTER 5

Foxburg Academy, May 5th, 1929

Dear Tante Martha,

I'm so terribly excited, I had to write and tell you right away. I've met the man I'm going to marry. At long last. I am so in love—really in love. And this time I'm sure you'll approve. I know you'll like him as much as I do.

His name is Bruno Flendeier, and he is Frau Flendeier's only son. He's studying architecture, but there's much more to him than that. He is a poet and a painter. His paintings are marvels of colour. So exciting and unusual.

We meet in the school grounds and have long philosophical discussions about all kinds of things. He's very well educated and able to talk on any subject. He and Herr Doktor Veldun would get on so well together.

We are not in a hurry to marry, of course. He still has his studies to finish, and I my education. But I will write to you again as soon as there is any more news.

In great excitement, and with lots of love,

Your Doly

Dear Diary,

I want to write him a letter:

My darling Don Juan. I'm afraid you'll conquer me as you conquer all women. I don't ever want to be parted from you. I love you too much. Goodbye.

I can't settle to anything. I pace my room like a caged animal, torn between heaven and hell. I'd no idea life could be so

420

wonderful. And yet such torture.

I've known Bruno a whole month. We meet and talk and kiss. But I still cannot give myself to him. Why? What's wrong with me?

'What's the matter, Doly? Don't you love me enough?' Bruno is patient and gentle. But evidently sad.

'Nothing like that. You don't know how much I love you.' And yet she simply cannot bring herself to allow him to go inside her.

He kisses her eyes, her neck. His hands move across her naked breasts, down to her thighs. She trembles as he goes higher. He puts his fingers inside her, uses her own wetness to move his fingers in and out. First one, then two, then three...

'Stop.'

He moves his hands beneath her. A finger touches her anus, circles round.

Sensations she's never felt before. The urge to pull him inside her. She feels her legs move apart, feels herself thrust. He is on top of her.

Then suddenly that gagging she can't control. Her legs go rigid. She finds it hard to breathe. 'No, Bruno. No.'

His lips are on her ear, pull at the lobe. 'Why not, my darling little Doly?'

'Because I can't.'

'It's safe. I swear to you...'

What can she say to stop him? 'I have a sweetheart in America. I left a virgin and I will return a virgin.' The words, meaningless, tumble out. Sentiments she's read in women's magazines. Tripe. But better than the fact that thinking of him inside her revolts her to her inner being.

He stops at once. Withdraws. 'You should have told me sooner, Doly. That puts a completely different light on everything.' He stands. Dresses. 'There's another man between us and it is only honourable to finish now.'

Doly gulps. She expected him to soothe her, to woo her, to try again. What has she done?

'You're the most beautiful girl I've ever met. Fragile, a woodland nymph. I'll never, ever, forget you.' He opens the wide drawer, takes out a little box. 'This has to be goodbye. I want you to have this in memory of me.'

She takes the box, tears wetting the lid. 'D'you have the book I lent you?'

He hands her James Barrie's *Peter Pan*. Her hand trembles so much she finds it hard to write: 'I loved you so much. Dorinda.'

THE BROKEN PROMISE

A dashing landowner swore unending love for the young woman he was courting. He promised her that he'd look at no other until the day he died. 'If I ever stop loving you, my house will burst into flames,' he vowed solemnly. Sealing his pledge with a kiss.

Not many weeks later the young man met another girl. He promptly forgot his first sweetheart and prepared to marry his new love.

The wedding day dawned. The bridegroom's kitchen was teeming with servants preparing a sumptuous wedding feast. A searing log fire burned briskly in the hearth, huge pots held bubbling soup, the aroma of roasting meat filled the whole house.

Suddenly the sound of galloping horses' hooves and rumbling wagon wheels was heard above the sizzling fire and the simmering soup. The bridegroom's helpers were taken by surprise. They weren't expecting the bridal pair for some time yet.

The women preparing the nuptial feast left the kitchen while they rushed outside to see whether the approaching wagon really was their master's. And when they recognised his colours they knew they had to hurry to be ready for the bridal pair.

In all the excitement one of the women toppled a pot of rich fatty soup on to the blazing logs. Flames leapt high and menacing. Panicking, she poured a second pot of soup on top of them, hoping to quench the fire. All that did was to feed the scorching flames until they leapt so high that the whole house caught fire.

The servants rushed out to safety. They ran to the well for water. All in vain. The fire burned hard and bright. A glowing cinder from a window was carried on the wind and fell on to the bridegroom's barn, kindled that. Now both house and barn were in flames.

The wagon, lavishly decorated with festive ribbons and colourful flowers, drew up nearby. The bridegroom stood, silent and bowed, as he watched his worldly goods go up in smoke. Both his house and his barn were turning to smoky ruins. On this, his wedding day.

CHAPTER 6

Foxburg Academy, Spring 1929

Doly creeps stealthily out of Bruno's room. Out of his wing of the castle. Listens to the night noises. Owls hooting in the woods, bats swooping in the dark shadows of the converted castle. She puts the key she's purloined from a maid into a side door. Already unlocked.

She feels her hot body cool. Rapidly. Feels nauseous. Takes off her shoes. Climbs noiselessly up the small twisting staircase towards the room she and Margarete share.

She sees the door is wide open and the lights are on. She creeps out on to the hall balcony and takes off her clothes. If she's caught, she'll pretend she went out to get some air. She shivers against the wall, wrapped only in her coat. But she's prepared to wait until the lights go out. While she nearly freezes to death.

Darkness at last. She waits a few minutes, then flits into her room and trembles herself under the bedclothes.

Margarete sits up. Whispers. 'Frau Flendeier came looking for you. I told her you'd gone to the toilet. She went to check and saw you weren't there. She waited in here for ages. Then she gave up and left.'

Doly is shivering under her blankets. Teeth chattering. 'Thanks, Margarete. You're a true friend.'

Slow rhythmic breathing from Margarete. Doly tosses back and forth. Still cold. Because there can only be two reasons why Frau Flendeier came to check. Betrayal in either case. Bruno? Impossible.

So it was Tante Martha. The letters Doly wrote. Confiding her true love. And its innocent nature.

Morning dawns grey and cold. Frau Flendeier is waiting for her in the dining room.

'So you did finally steal back in.'

'I...'

'Don't bother to lie. I know you were out last night. How often have you sneaked out without permission?'

Half-truths are more convincing than lies. 'Three times.'

'There's no need to ask you why. What kind of relationships do you have with men?'

'Platonic ones.'

Frau Flendeier all but snarls. 'I knew you were trouble as soon as I laid eyes on you. I'm very sorry.'

'So am I.' The words are lost on the back striding out of the room.

Doly nibbles at food. Goes to the Amalienbad with Margarete for a refreshing swim. Tells her the whole story about Bruno. How much she'd love a sister to confide in. How Gabby doesn't fit the bill. That she wrote to Tante Martha instead, and what a mistake that turned out to be.

They return to change their clothes before the midday meal.

'Margarete, look! My bed's been stripped.'

'Naturally. Didn't you know you were supposed to be packed by late morning? That the taxi's ordered for after lunch?'

'I suppose I hoped she'd forgive me.' When Frau Flendeier said "I'm very sorry," Doly assumed it was a ticking off, a warning. Not an expulsion.

Margarete shakes her head. 'Bruno's her only child. She has no intention of his marrying anyone, let alone a foreigner. He might sneak off abroad. See you in the dining room.'

Doly opens the wardrobe, pulls out a shiny white satin dress and tumbles the rest of her clothes into a case. She empties the chest of drawers, goes to her desk to pile her books on top of clothes. And sees the little box Bruno gave her.

Is it a piece of jewellery? Too large. A miniature? She opens it up.

The tiny revolver glints at her. A silver barrel inlaid with abalone shell. Intricately carved, beautifully polished. Six silver bullets lie beside it in the white satin lining. She sees a distorted image of a face in one of them. Sees Gabby's wide nostrils; she can't face the way her sister will crow when she hears she's been expelled. She opens the chamber, slips the offending bullet in.

She spins the chamber. Even Tante Martha no longer believes in her. One bullet in six chambers. Russian roulette. That's it. Use Bruno's present to end her life—if the fates wish it. She spins the chamber again, returns the little pistol to its case. Puts that inside her handbag. Feels the weight of it.

She tosses her head and marches to the dining room. The chatter stops as she sits down. A maid offers coffee, brings a piled plate. Doly pushes the food around because she can't swallow. She leaves within minutes, hears the low hum of young female voices. Discussing her.

She needs the wind to sweep away her hurt, the sun to warm her body, the birds to sing her praises. Her footsteps plod heavily along the woodland path. Memories crowd the little grove where she and Bruno met so often. She drinks in the cool air, listens to the birdsong, feasts her eyes on the trees in their young finery. They seemed so glorious only yesterday.

Doly's tears dim the sunshine, cloud the trees. Where is her life leading her? Two hours ago she still had hope and purpose. Now there is nothing. She and Bruno did nothing wrong, yet they have been betrayed by the one person she thought she could trust. Has he heard? Put a note in their secret letter box? Suggested they run away together?

The handbag is heavy. She drags it over leaf mould. To the gnarled oak where she and Bruno first found each other, as though pre-destined. Where they communed. Kissed. She slips sweaty fingers into the crack of bark, feels only tree. Scrabbles with her nails in case thin paper has slipped right down. Nothing. No letter, no sign.

'I've tasted life and found it wanting,' she whispers to the brook which sparkled crystals and now splashes shoes. It gabbles gobbledegook instead of sweet nothings. 'Better to have a beautiful death than an awful life.'

She upends her bag, grabs Bruno's parting gift. She cradles her head against the trunk she leant against when she first caught sight of him, watches the glints of sunlight her tears have turned to daggers. She unwraps the pistol and holds the muzzle against her beating heart, finger poised on the trigger. One squeeze will determine her fate.

The scene plays out for her. Like a movie. Janet Gaynor's face is a study in conflicting emotions. Love, anger, pride. The beautiful, proud woman who prefers dignity to humiliation. A quick death is a noble destiny.

Janet's finger applies dainty pressure. The sound of a small muffled bang. Janet's beautiful body slides gracefully along the mossy bank. Scarlet spreads across the glinting white of satin. The rush of running feet. A young man eases a cushion under her head, embraces her shoulders. Another's cupped palm offers crystal brook water to Janet's parched, still beautiful lips.

An ethereal hand stretches out in a last gesture of love. 'I'm dying. Fetch Bruno Flendeier. I want to say goodbye.'

Bruno's running footsteps rumble through the tinkling of the brook. He arrives and kneels by Janet, surrounds her face with gentle hands. 'How will I live without you?' His voice breaks. 'I'll never marry now.'

'My darling Bruno…'

'Don't talk. Don't move.'

'It is too late to save me.'

Dimming eyes see his tears streaming down. A waterfall of grief.

Doly's left hand strokes the barrel of the gun. The way Bruno did. If God wants her to die, He shall have His wish.

She squeezes the trigger. No movement. A toy which doesn't work. She holds the gun in both hands, points the barrel at the oak, pulls hard. The spring engages, there is a click. She swings the barrel back to her chest again, and squeezes.

The shot explodes noise. It shocks her ears, invades her chest. No pain. Her body loses its balance, topples into a heap. A gush of sticky liquid surprises her.

She becomes aware of two men standing over her. They shout, grab her shoulders and legs, manhandle her.

She has to make them understand 'Listen to me.' she mouths, pain spreading through her ribcage. 'Fetch Bruno Flendeier.' Have they heard?

She comes to in the school's sickroom. There is no Bruno; no one she knows. Only the matron she hasn't met before. Who pushes her down when she tries to move. 'Keep still, you little idiot.'

'Pen and paper,' Doly whispers. The pain is excruciating, but the matron merely turns her back.

Doly's finger traces letters on her sheet:

Oh Bruno, Bruno, my one true love. I am dying.
I lived like a tramp. I shall die like a tramp. I can't play the jester any more.

She's heaved into an ambulance by two men. Driven to hospital.

'Such a young girl. Breaking the law like that. If she survives, will they really put her in jail?' The two attendants don't speak to her, only to each other. As though she didn't exist.

'Where are you taking me?'

No answer. She's untouchable, laid on an operating table in a bleak empty room. Like a sacrificial lamb. Quite alone.

'Is this how I'm going to die?' Scrubbed clean, tiled walls echo back. '...going to die...to die.'

CHAPTER 7

Hotel Bristol, Vienna

May 10th, 1929

Dear Gabby,

You will have been informed of the shocking news about Doly. I dropped everything to come to Vienna. She has lost litres of blood and is very weak. The doctors have given me hope that she is holding her own.

I know you have a new baby, and that moving from Berlin to Vienna will be difficult enough. But Rolf—you have such a very kind husband—has put me up in the Bristol Hotel while I am in Vienna. Now I can be with Doly. She needs someone to trust, someone she can rely on utterly. Someone to hold her hand. To talk to her.

Doly must also have the support of the rest of her family, particularly her older sister. May I tell her she can stay with you when she's discharged from hospital? Assure her you'll be there for her as long as she needs a sister by her side?

Your loving

Tante Martha

Berlin

May 14th, 1929

Dear Tante Martha,

Of course Doly can rely on me. She is welcome as soon as she is able to leave the hospital. Rolf has now found us a house and I shall be in Vienna within two weeks.

Naturally you are welcome as our guest as soon as the house is habitable. Give my love to Doly.

Yours,

GDF

St Elisabeth Krankenhaus, Vienna, May 1929

'Doly.'

Ache in her chest. Pressing down hard. 'Wh...?' Pain stops her speaking. Tears cloud her eyes. Not pain. Agony.

'I'm here, Doly.'

Tante Martha's voice. Is she at home? In the turret room?

'Don't talk, child. You're still very weak. You're in hospital, in the St Elisabeth Krankenhaus. In Vienna.'

Vienna. Her mind tries to make sense of that. Vienna Woods. She was in woods, alone. With Bruno's little gun. But no Bruno.

'You did a terrible thing, Doly.'

A lecture? Now?

'But we won't talk about that. Try to get well. There are some excellent doctors here.'

Tante Martha's hands hold hers. She sits at the side of the bed. And stays. For hours.

Doly drifts in and out of consciousness. Dreams. About the promises Bruno swore he'd keep. "As long as I live, I'll never so much as glance at another girl. I give you my solemn oath I'll always be true to you. May my wonderful collection succumb to rust if I break my word." He didn't come. Not even when she was dying. Is there such a thing as true love? Will she ever find it? What is the point of living without love?

Tears run unchecked down Doly's cheeks. She remembers Bruno swore undying love, yet he hasn't even come to visit her. 'Why has everyone deserted me?'

'The young man made promises? He broke them, betrayed you?'

'You, Tante Martha. You were the one who betrayed me. You wrote and told Frau Flendeier that Bruno and I were meeting.'

'I only tried to save you from yourself, Doly. Because I care. You know I'd never harm you.'

CHAPTER 8

Vienna, June 1929

'This is the house?' Gabby stands in front of a town house. A poky unimpressive monstrosity in one of the less fashionable sectors of Vienna. Gabby looks up and down the street. A tram putters along, dings. The house is on the fringes of a working-class district. Not suitable for what she has in mind.

'Is good house, Grischa. Good rooms for baby and nursemaid. And where you stay if we don't take?'

'Cancel the contract, Rolf. We can stay at the Bristol until I've found us a decent place.' Can't the man be trusted with anything but business machines?

'But, Grischa. You not even have been inside...'

'I'm not living in Hernals. We need to be further out. Somewhere like Grinzing or Neuwaldegg. On the fringe of the vineyards or the Vienna Woods. That should appeal to your romantic nature, Rolf.' She's angry, but that sounds too sharp. 'That will also be the right sort of place for entertaining Thomas J Watson.'

She's back inside the car. With a black mood on her face.

'Is not necessary go hotel. Bandi apartment has. Also he in Vienna for six months. He rent. He give us rooms.'

'Bandi? Bandi is in Vienna?'

'Remington Rand bring here. For few months. He transfer to Basle soon.'

431

The move from Berlin may, perhaps, be providing mitigating circumstances.

'Where we put Doly if you not take house?'

'She isn't out of hospital yet.'

'Is soon. I visit yesterday before you arrive.'

Is he expecting her to take on a house she can't stand because her suicidal sister needs somewhere to stay? She'll do what she can for her sister. Naturally. But there are limits. She's intending to stick to them. 'She can stay at the Bristol with Tante Martha. I'll write to Hudwalker for the necessary funds.'

'You not know? Your aunt gone back to Germany, Grischa. To school. She away too long already.'

Gabby tenses. Leaving the nursemaid and Gemma in the hotel is one thing. Leaving them there when Doly is on the prowl again is quite another. She has to face the fact that her sister is unstable. She might snatch the baby.

Odd how a little being who can't even speak can stir such protective feelings. 'Gemma is beginning to fret, Rolf. If Bandi will really put us up, we'd better go to his apartment.' She looks over her shoulder at the nursemaid. 'You've brought a bottle with you, Maria?'

'It isn't warm, Gnädige Frau.'

'Then give it to her cold.' Even if Bandi has enough room, and offers to put Doly up, she'll be preoccupied making a play for him. So Gemma should be safe.

'I've found the perfect house, Rolf. Literally minutes from the Vienna Woods. Bandi and I went to see it this afternoon.'

Bandi greets his brother affably. 'Grischa is right, Rolf. Hard work isn't enough. You will wish to entertain. So you will need an impressive place in the right location. Watson will see the point of it.'

'Where is?'

'In Neuwaldegg. Artariastrasse 10 is the last-but-one house before the woods. It's only just come on to the market.' Gabby walks up to Rolf, shows him a photograph. 'Wittgenstein lived around there. In the house next door to this one.'

'Who this Wittgenstein?'

'The famous philosopher.'

Rolf glances at the photograph, holds out his hand for the details. 'What is price?'

'It's not a question of money, Rolf. You're buying status.'

'I not able afford this.'

'I knew you'd say that. Sell some of my shares and we'll own half each.' Gabby's eyes are shining. The place is smaller than the Villa Dohlen, but it is comparable. An imposing entrance hall, a sweeping staircase to an enormous first-floor living room, adjoining dining room, a veranda, the master bedroom with bath and dressing-room on the same floor, nursery and guest accommodation on the floor above. Garage, servants' quarters, domestic offices on the ground floor. Even an annexe for a housekeeper or gardener. A perfect set-up.

'Why don't we all go out and look at it?' Bandi is watching his brother's reactions. 'I'll drive you.'

Rolf is silent as they walk around the splendid house. 'You know how run such place, Grischa?'

'I was brought up in the Villa Dohlen. I'll turn it into a famous salon, Rolf. Before I've finished you'll be Managing Director of IBM.'

He laughs. 'What Watson will be?'

'What he is now. President, as the Americans call it. That should continue to satisfy him. And he'll *love* bringing important people here.'

'Maybe we should sell New York property. Pity sell shares. They doing very well.'

Gabby is walking round the house, eyes everywhere. 'I leave all that to you, Rolf. Just bear in mind that I have to put in central heating, modernise the kitchen and redecorate. Oh, and a marble fireplace in the living room. White marble.' She assesses the large space. 'The Berlin furniture won't be enough. Allow for extra furnishing as well.'

'But Grischa...'

'D'you want a decent house for entertaining, or don't you?' She's no longer the shy, self-effacing orphan maltreated by Tante Hannah, looked down on by the villagers, persecuted at school. She's the good-looking, well-dressed, highly-educated wife of Rolf Ferent, the man who heads IBM East of Vienna. And she's going to be the most popular hostess in this city. For that she has to have the right house.

Bandi comes to her rescue. 'It's an investment, Rolf. Just think of it

433

as an investment.'

St Elisabeth Krankenhaus, June 1929

'My name is Guido Gallo, Fräulein Dohlen. I'm one of the doctors assigned to you.'

A posse of doctors poked at Doly minutes ago. None of them amiable. Two nurses changed her bandages so clumsily that she cried out.

She flutters her eyelids. A butterfly caught in a spider's web. 'My wound has just been seen to.' What possessed her to trust to a toy gun?

'I'm not part of the surgical team. I'm a psychoanalyst.'

Her eyes open wider. He's very young, the skin on his face still soft. He doesn't sport the blank impersonal glare of the practised doctor. He shows concern.

'I studied under Herr Professor Sigmund Freud. At Vienna University. Perhaps you've heard of his work?' A shy glance as he drops his eyes. 'I was told you're a student of philosophy. Maybe you've read some Freud? His *Ego and Id* is quite brilliant.'

A doctor who's actually interested in what she thinks? 'One of my teachers did refer to him. *Three Essays on the Theory of Sexuality.*'

No shyness now. Excitement. 'His most controversial work. The old guard are set against him. And my position here.'

A fellow outsider. Doly can feel the balm of empathy relax her whole body.

'It's part of my official duties to explain the law as it affects your case. I'm sure you already know that attempted suicide is a serious crime, or a prognosis of mental illness.'

Harsh words, soft voice. 'You think I'm mad.'

He stiffens. 'I'm not in a position to say anything at the moment. I'd like to talk to you at length. I'll make my assessment after that.' The inflection of a Latin tongue makes his German sound soothing. An aria.

'So my future depends on you?'

Dark tender eyes caress her face. Uplifted mouth corners promise sympathy. 'On your answers to my questions, Fräulein Dohlen.'

Easy to tell he's on her side. 'On your interpretation of my answers.'

Impetuous, no doubt. But it proves she's not an idiot. She makes a huge effort at a smile. 'If we're going to have long cosy chats just call me Doly.' She raises herself up. 'Which part of Italy are you from, Herr Doktor?'

'Trieste. The battle zone between Italy and old Austria-Hungary.' A boyish grin. 'An excellent preparation for dissension. May I sit down?'

'Can I stop you?'

'You're not obliged to talk to me. I'm tolerated here because I'm doing my thesis. It's up to you.'

She's to be a footnote in an academic work? 'You'll use my name?'

He looks horrified. 'Psychoanalysis works on mutual trust between patient and analyst. Everything you tell me, however trivial, is confidential.'

'We just talk?'

He nods. 'You talk. I listen. Call me Guido when we're alone. That will help to break down unhelpful barriers.'

'What d'you want to know, Guido? Why I committed this terrible crime?'

'No, Doly. Why you didn't succeed.'

The tears are genuine. What is there left? He doesn't even believe she meant it.

'Analysis is as painful as physical medicine, Doly.' He pats her shoulder. 'I can help you. In depth. But only if you want me to.'

She gropes for a handkerchief. He hands her his. 'You think I'm a common criminal.' She's never going to forgive him.

'I've stated the law. I didn't say I agree with it. Allow me.' He gathers pillows, places them behind Doly. Very carefully. 'You're still in a lot of pain?'

'It's getting better.' The accent isn't soothing any more. Irritating. She's had enough of it.

'Will it exhaust you to speak to me?' The young doctor sounds almost beseeching.

'I'll let you know.'

Tante Martha's daily visits, her obvious concern, boosted Doly's self-esteem. Not that her aunt could grasp that it was her betrayal, not the parting from Bruno, which led to the shooting. She was hooked

435

on Doly being a victim of unrequited love. Compared it to her own strong, and presumably unrequited, feelings for Helmut Veldun.

The visits were consoling. Doly has begun to grasp that her aunt has problems of her own. She, like Doly, lost her mother when only a toddler. She suffers from the family curse and, like Gabby, lost her hair at an early age. She considers herself ugly, has given up on ordinary men. Even her friendship with Herr Doktor Veldun is frustrating. Not because he's twenty-five years her senior and in a wheelchair. What upsets Tante Martha is that he's given up on life, simply waits for death. Which isn't a true romance in Doly's book. And so can't be classified as the same problem as her own.

Gallo clears his throat. 'Tell me about yourself. What you enjoy. What you can't stand.'

She talks. That day, for a whole week. Words flow like a mighty river which cannot be dammed. Her feelings of despair because no one in the whole wide world gives two hoots about her. Tante Martha betrayed her, Bruno was only too happy to see the back of her, the Hudwalkers are afraid of her. Her fights with, and jealousy of, her sister. Her disappointments with herself. Her inhibitions when faced with physical love, and her failure to understand this. Her loathing of establishment values. Her love of nature, poetry, all the arts. The travelling she would enjoy.

'Teenage turbulence. It all sounds entirely sane to me.'

How tritely doctorial. But he has fallen for her. It's obvious in the liquid eyes which follow every move, the low voice which trembles with emotion. 'And they'll take your word for that? Leave me in peace?'

He looks away. She could swear his eyes are moist. 'They're a lot of preaching jackasses who can't let well alone. If I tell them what I think, they'll arrest you.'

'And if you say I'm mad? Then what?'

'Medical intervention.' Guido's head jerks back, eyes fever bright. 'Tell me, once you leave here; can you stay with your aunt in Germany?'

'Ye...es.' Not precisely what Doly has in mind. Not because she carries a grudge. But for tempestuous untidy Doly to live with neat prim Tante Martha would be purgatory, if not hell, for them both.

'You don't sound sure.'

'My aunt lives in a small apartment in Cuxhaven, where she teaches.

Our family house is in a village about ten kilometres from there. There's a resident housekeeper. I can convalesce there.'

The bobbing head shocks hair into his eyes. 'Excellent. I'll smuggle you out of here and on to a train. Make your escape to Germany before those meddlers can get at you.'

He's prepared to risk his career, even his freedom for her? 'Won't you get into trouble?' He's offering true undemanding love. How tiresome that she's not remotely interested in him.

'I wasn't planning on advertising my role. I take it I can rely on your discretion?' A conspiratorial wink.

She laughs. Stops short because of the pain. Can't afford laughter yet, but she feels better about herself than in ages. Even if she isn't happy.

St Elisabeth Krankenhaus

June 12th, 1929

Dear Gabby,

You'll be delighted to get this after I've gone. That's right. Out of your hair, if that were an appropriate metaphor. You may not be so delighted by the aftermath of my departure, which will make waves. Not my fault you came to Vienna. Remember I was here first.

Sorry I never saw the new bunny-bun. Don't suppose there's much chance I ever will.

Doly

CHAPTER 9

Schwanenbruch, Summer 1929

'You really have to be such a poophead, Doly? How 'bout throwing out the odd apple core or two. Don't look great spread over the furniture.'

'And hello to you as well, Moppel.'

'And those damned ciggies reek. The smoke in the hall's thick enough to cut with a knife. You got the turret room to yourself. Must you smoke down here?'

Moppel is paying a rare visit to Schwanenbruch. Prudent absence from New York and summer vacation from Columbia University. And he's come to inspect what remains of his German inheritance. Now that he's twenty-one.

'How was I to know you were coming?'

'I sent a postcard to Onkel Wilfred.' He moves wads of newspapers from the sofa in the red living room. 'Normally you don't know from nothin'. What's the news to you all of a sudden?'

'Just checking whether my breakout gets a mention.' The blank stare tells her he has no idea what she's talking about. Least said soonest mended.

Doly's flight from the Austrian authorities was not spectacular. Guido Gallo brought her a nurse's uniform, helped her dress, explained the best time to leave her room and meet him outside the hospital. Conveniently situated on the Landstrasse, the busiest route in and out

438

of Vienna.

Doly sat on her bed feeling weak. She had to make the effort to escape, so she grabbed at furniture to steady herself, used willpower to manoeuvre out of the room, crept along endless corridors. Guido was waiting in a taxi. He helped her into it, whisked her off to the Westbahnhof, gave her the train ticket he'd already bought and saw her on to a sleeper.

'You'll be all right?'

'All I have to do is lie here. Tante Martha's meeting me in Hamburg. I'll never forget you, Guido. You are the greatest gentleman I ever met.'

He hugged her, produced a bouquet of carnations. Red. Never even tried to kiss her. Though she was ready to respond.

Her brother's voice cuts through the reminiscences.

'You mean you're on the lam?'

'Not here. In Austria.'

'What in hell for?'

'Attempted suicide is a crime.'

'Dopes; what's it to them?'

Doly, her face whitening, puts a hand on her wound.

'Say, you OK kiddo?'

'As you can see, Moppel.'

He stares, nods. 'Great. Well, now you know I'm here, don't futz around, maybe even try for a trash-free zone?'

'Keep your hair on, Moppel.'

He scowls.

'Jeepers creepers. Anything to please. Lieselotte and I were putting on the ritz last night, so it's a little messy. Guess what? She's passed her Medical School exams. For Berlin. Quite some triumph for a girl.'

Moppel scowls round the room, heaves newspapers into a corner. 'What for? Thought her old man wouldn't foot the bill.'

What luck. Her lead in. 'You've put your finger right on the problem, Mops. I wrote to our revered guardian for funds in a good cause. Typical Huddy. Turned me down flat.'

Moppel is wearing a baseball cap to cover his bald scalp. '*Your* guardian. I don't have none no more.' The cap is lifted, put back. 'His reaction's not unreasonable. Rubes attract spongers. Be nothing left if

Onkel Wilfred'd been in charge.'

Accelerating blood reddens her face and makes her wound ache. 'Sponge? Liesi? Never taken a dime from me. More like the other way around.'

'You come up with the dough to ride her father's horses, splurge on party frocks, take her on trips. Mounts up, kiddo.'

'Never asked for a nickel, Moppel. Came on trips with me because I invited her. She's my buddy.'

'So what's the deal on her university fees?'

'I offered. Her father's a pill and Huddy secretly can't stomach women being doctors. That's the real reason he turned us down.' Doly knows she can't ask Gabby for money. Or Rolf. And Moppel's as tight-fisted as they come. 'I have a business proposition for you, Moppel.'

'A business proposition? You?' Moppel pushes the cap back to front. Clown buffoonery.

Doly feels a steady pounding of pain which she ignores. Then suddenly feels faint, leans an arm behind herself, sinks down into a chair.

Her brother frowns. 'Say, you OK, kid? That bullet-hole still bothering you?'

'I'm fine.'

'Yeah? You don't look it.'

'You want to hear the deal or not?'

'Sure. Go right ahead.'

'You're of age. You can do what the hell you want with your money now. Right?'

He twists the cap round again, taps the peak. 'In a manner of speaking.'

'Huddy's in charge of all my stuff in the US. Not here. I could sell you my share of the Villa Dohlen.'

Round eyes show dollar signs. He tears the cap off, mops his scalp with a handkerchief. 'No can do. Not legal. You're a minor.'

'Damn the legality. Let me have the cash and I give you my solemn pledge: my share is yours.'

'C'mon, Doly. You said business?'

'I'll sign anything you like. Post-date it to April 4th 1932. All tied-up and legal after that.'

'That a fact?' He pulls at his collar as he shuffles over to the window, looks out. 'Reckon I know where the problem's at.'

'What problem?'

'Not sure I can raise enough dough.' His eyes narrow, disappear into his face. So very like Onkel Wilfred. 'How much you figure the place is worth?' He walks to the window with a determined tread.

'I don't care what it's worth, Moppel. I want $3,000. $2,000 to cover Liesi's fees, and $1,000 for the two of us to buy a car and go on a grand tour. Soon as I'm up to it.'

'You're talking about a lot of nickles and dimes.' Moppel looks out of the window. For several minutes. '$3,000? That's your actual selling price?'

Doly is holding out for that. It's what she needs. 'I can't take less.'

He's motionless. 'You'll stick to it? No going back on it?'

'My word is my bond. Write out the contract, date it April 4th 1932, and I'll sign it.' She suddenly remembers Moppel's reputation. 'When you hand over the 3,000 bucks.'

'I don't have that kinda dough hanging about, Doly. I'll have to raise it.'

'Sell some shares or something.'

'I did. Ploughed that into real estate.'

'You're in business already?'

Thumb and forefinger grip his nose. 'Kinda. Slow turnover. Could take a while to get 3,000 in greenbacks. What's your deadline?'

'August, say?'

'Coupla months?' He's clearly thinking dollars, not health. 'Where you heading?'

'Switzerland, France, Italy. Then skiing in the Alps when there's some snow. Maybe head over to North Africa if the winter's very cold. What I need right now is enough to buy a car. And the trip expenses. Can you raise that?'

'I'll do my level best, work on it. Late fall OK?'

Doly rips a piece of paper out of her diary. '$1,000 by mid September 1929, $2,000 by August 1930. That's when Lieselotte has to pay her Berlin fees. I'll write my share of the villa over to you then and there.'

Something's still bothering him. He shifts from one foot to the other. 'Where you headin' when Lieselotte's in Berlin?'

Already worried about her using the villa when she no longer owns part of it. 'Barnard College,' she reassures him. 'Even Huddy approves my enrolling there.'

His eyes have reappeared, are shining. 'I got to hand it to you, kid sister. You're quite a trouper. Let's drink to our big business deal.'

CHAPTER   10

Schwanenbruch, August 1929

'Guido. What a surprise. Have you come up all the way from Vienna just to say hello?'

'I've left the hospital, Doly. I've taken a job as a houseman in Bremerhaven. It's wonderful to see you again.'

Doly's conscience pricks. Momentarily. She didn't even write to him. 'Someone saw you helping me?'

'No. I resigned. I've ditched psychoanalysis. That's only practised in Vienna. And I have some good news for you.'

She's not socialising with anyone except Liesi at the moment. But it's churlish to be unkind. 'How nice. My friend Lieselotte is turning up any minute. You must meet her.'

'Perhaps we could go for a walk?' His hands cup hers, his lips cover them with kisses. 'You're looking so much better. Blooming, really. All back to normal?'

'Pretty much. I get a little tired sometimes.'

'Smoking doesn't help with a punctured lung, you know.'

'If you've come to preach at me...'

'No, no. Entirely your business. What I really want to tell you about is that I've come across a cure for your—condition.'

She jerks her head back, slits her eyes. Even though he's a doctor, even though he has her best interests at heart, she feels imposed on, violated, by the mere reference to her future lack of hair. 'I'm perfectly well.'

'I realise it's painful, but it's useful for you to know. The impulse which led to your trying to take your life is not due to mental illness. It is what we call a personality disorder.'

He's not talking about her hair. A stab goes through her as she grasps he thinks she's not quite normal mentally. What a nerve.

'I would describe your personality type as dependent.'

Doly starts up from the sofa, turns towards the window. 'That's nonsense, Guido. Actually, I'm very independent. I...'

'Let me explain. A dependent personality is characterized by a need to be taken care of, tends to cling to friends and relatives and fears losing them.' He takes her hand which she immediately withdraws impatiently. 'Such a personality may become suicidal when a break-up is imminent.'

'You really have a high opinion of me.'

He tries to take her hand again but she shies away. 'We all have tendencies to self-destruction. Once you know yours, you'll be forewarned, can adjust your behaviour.'

'I'm perfectly capable of making my own decisions.' How dare he judge her? Does he think helping her escape gives him the right to moralise, tell her what to do? All she wants now is for him to go. Stop the odious preaching and leave.

'Please listen, Doly. The reason I'm telling you all this is so that you can be prepared. You're intelligent enough to control these tendencies.'

'*Something* to be said for me then.'

'So much, my dear. You're a wonderful young woman.' Puppy-dog eyes bring on more fury on Doly's part but she turns away, suppresses it. 'The problem is that you might be inclined to let others make important decisions for you, jump from relationship to relationship.' Expressive brown eyes caress her. 'You can avoid that once you know the danger you're in.'

She feels the urge to run. The pain of her physical wound makes her wince. She'll just have to change the subject, wait for Liesi to rescue her. 'Lieselotte and I are about to go on a trip. The Grand European Tour. We're just waiting for some funds to come through.'

Guido appears to be aware of his surroundings for the first time. 'I can see your father left you well-provided for. You'll be travelling in style.'

'In theory. My guardian thinks I should keep my head down. Study.'

'A long holiday is just what this doctor would order.'

'I've promised to enrol at Barnard next autumn.'

'That's a university?'

'Part of Columbia University. In New York City. For now I just want to get back on my feet.' She can't resist it. 'My own two feet.'

He nods, the sage physician. 'Quite right.'

His intense look drives her over to the window. She opens it wide and takes great breaths of squalling air.

'Could I come along?'

'You mean take an American degree?' She sits on the window sill, leans out. 'It's a college for women.' He's obviously sweet on her, but she doesn't want to know. With any luck they won't allow men into the sorority house.

'Just women? You think that would suit you?' Voice sickly-sweet.

She's off young men for the time being. Into education. Just like Gabby. Because it brings lifelong benefits whatever the future holds. 'You're underestimating my choice. Barnard was founded by Frederick August Porter Barnard, President of Columbia. He believed in equal opportunity for both genders.'

'I didn't mean to imply...'

'Now Barnard's one of the best colleges in the whole of the United States.'

Guido puts his arms around Doly, embraces her again. 'I'm sure any college you choose is excellent. All I was asking was whether I could join you on the tour, Doly.'

She slips away from him. 'What about your job? We'll be gone for as long as the money lasts. That could be months.' He knows too much about her, thinks of her as a victim of mental disease. She'll never be able to forgive him for that.

'My Bremerhaven appointment starts on January 1st, 1930. I'll leave you to it after that.'

There could be one advantage in his joining them. 'Know how to drive?'

His eyes shine. 'Drive? You're taking a car?'

'I'm hoping to buy one. I've already applied for my German driving licence.'

'Really? That's wonderful. I'm crazy about cars. The Mercedes sports model K with a supercharged 6.25 litre 24/110/160PS engine is the fastest touring car in the world. If you're buying a car, why not get that?'

'I've never even heard of a Mercedes.'

'You've heard of Daimler, I'm sure. One of his customers, a man called Jellinek, was so taken with his first Daimler that he recommended it to all his wealthy friends. Then he persuaded Daimler to produce a really high-performance car he called Mercédès after his eldest daughter. That's how the marque was born. The new sports model is a fantastic car. I know because my father owns one.'

Doly has never seen him so excited. Perhaps cars are the true love of his life.

'I'll be happy to teach you to drive, Doly.'

'No need. It was part of the school curriculum in the States. But a second driver would be great. You can teach Lieselotte.'

He blinks. 'It would be a good thing if I go touring with you. If you should have a relapse, I'll be on the spot. Make sure you get the right treatment and all that.'

God. Trying to take over her life. 'Lieselotte is going to be a doctor too.'

'If she's your age, she can't even be a medical student yet. And it does take a few years to complete the basic training.' Dry. Unamused.

'She's looked after her father's horses for years. But come if you want to. As long as you and Lieselotte hit if off OK.'

'Where shall we head first?'

The beautiful tourer, bought second-hand, is being driven by Guido. To start with. Doly takes the wheel as soon as they're on a macadamised empty road.

'You're a natural, Doly. Who'd have thought a little thing like you could drive?'

Lieselotte is sitting in the passenger seat, Guido in the back. 'The whole point of machinery is that women can use it as easily as men.'

'Women have no talent for mechanics.'

Lieselotte prides herself on hers. She's had experience with her father's farm machinery. 'Real mechanical genius is a rarity. Most men aren't Daimler or even Ford. They can't mend cars when they go wrong any better than women can. Steering and changing gears is all driving is about.'

'Women have no sense of direction.'

She's holding the map. 'We heading for Bremen? Turn right here.' She leans back. Complacently. 'Typical example. When typewriters first came out, they said women wouldn't be able to type. Turns out they're better than men. Smaller nimbler fingers.'

'You predicting women will make better drivers than men?' Guido laughs. Good-naturedly.

'Not so keen on speed, perhaps. Safer.'

'Get into the *side*, Doly,' Guido shouts. 'There are other cars on the road as well as ours.'

'Well, some of them.' Lieselotte's voice no longer sounds quite as confident.

'And better doctors?'

'In time, yes. Before the century's out women will be better than men at everything.'

'Now that we've settled the distant future, where are we heading after lunch in Bremen?'

'Let's make for Switzerland eventually.' Doly is now keeping to the right side of the road.

'So let's go via Frankfurt, Munich, Zurich, then down to Italy. By the time we come back up to Zurich there might be snow. There's a nice little skiing resort at Grindelwald.'

CHAPTER 11

Vienna, Autumn 1929

'You gave Doly money for a car? You must be out of your mind.'

'Give the kid sister a run for her money,' Moppel says, his usual deceptive grin covering his thoughts.

Gabby knows he's been up to something; she also knows he's not about to tell her what. And she's not exactly going to find out from Doly. She's invited her brother to stay with her in the Neuwaldegg villa. She's refurbishing the whole place. Installing central heating. Ahead of the times, just like her father.

'Great house, Gabby. As elegant as the Villa Dohlen. A heck of a sight better lay-out.'

'It's a real hit with the IBM, both Watson and his executives. A constant stream of hopefuls traipses through the place. The opera's obligatory once a week. One hell of a bore after Berlin cabaret, I can tell you that.'

'You bet. Say, can we get some action around here?'

'Action?'

'Girls, Gabby. Know any?'

'Ah. Yes.' Sexual activity isn't one of Gabby's entertainments. Which is why Rolf takes a benign interest in pretty women he comes across on his travels. That's how he met Viktoria.

'There is one young woman I've recently come across, Moppel. Her name's Viktoria. Jolly little thing. Viennese.'

'Yeah?'

'Tell you what. I'll give a dinner party tonight, invite her and seat her next to you.' What is it about sex which so turns on her brother and her sister, but not her? Will she ever know? 'I'm sure you'll love her, Moppel. She'll show you all the sights.'

He raises his eyes to heaven. 'God, Gabby. I'm not talking sight-seeing here.'

Does he really think she doesn't know what he's after? His interests run to money and sex. Fifty-fifty, Gabby reckons. 'You Americans are so crass. I'm talking about Parisian sights.'

Viktoria Scheiderbauer called unannounced a few weeks ago. A curvaceous young woman in her early twenties. Pretty, in a chocolate-box way. Viennese. A minor actress with beguiling skills which make men feel comfortable, at ease. A true daughter of her native city.

'I met your husband on the train,' she confided to Gabby. 'Returning from Budapest. Such a gentleman. He found me a seat in his compartment.'

Gabby nodded. Without rancour. Rolf has an eye for pretty women, but she doubts he'll ever give a wife concern. 'Really?'

'He insisted you'd be glad to see me.' A razzle-dazzle smile. 'Said you might have a job for me, Gnädige Frau. Helping with arrangements.' A pause, while Gabby wondered what 'arrangements' was supposed to mean. 'Social get-togethers, parties, outings. I understand you frequently entertain gentlemen from America.'

Gabby knows very well that Rolf talks to young women on trains. And what follows. This girl is clearly looking for a husband. Could that be fruitful for all of them?

Mr and Mrs Watson were announced unexpectedly. They stayed to tea. Viktoria turned out to be a hit with IBM's chief executive. She was vivacious, charming, and spoke enough English to please the Watsons. Who were content because they were introduced to her by Rolf Ferent's wife. And very keen to ask her to join them at the opera that night.

She smiled prettily. Assured them she'd be delighted.

Gabby seized her opportunity. Made her own excuses. Viktoria would take them under her wing in Gabby's stead, would make sure they knew where to dine after the performance.

The two young women understood one another. Without an exchange of words or looks. Viktoria was happy to take over bookings for all visitors. The Staatsoper, the Burgtheater, the Volksoper. She knows them all. And she's willing to tour museums, the castle of Schönbrunn. Play the guide in general.

Then she brings guests back to Gabby in Neuwaldegg. She stays around to help serve drinks. All very fortunate. All round.

CHAPTER 12

Vienna, October 28th, 1929

'Is very bad news, Grischa.'

'You've lost your job?'

Rolf laughs. A barking, bitter laugh. Nothing like his submissive smile. That mournful quiet smile which indicates heavy responsibilities weighing him down. He's never been young and now he sounds defeated. 'No. I not lose job. Watson need me. Other firms me want recruit. I speaking of you, Grischa. You lose much money.'

'What on earth are you talking about?' The long ageing line down her forehead is deepening. The rest of her could pass for late teens.

'Was very bad last few days on New York Stock Exchange. All shares lost ground. We should discuss you sell or no.'

For God's sake. She reads the papers, she's seen the headlines. Exaggerated rubbish. And only a small proportion of her money is in equities. The bulk is in Manhattan real estate. Not buoyant at present, but safe enough. Rolf's always fussing about money. 'I've told you, Rolf. You're in charge. I have complete trust in you.' A wicked grin. 'Lucky I spent all that money, isn't it? Better than paper losses.'

'Is little more complicated. We not yet paid all bills, Grischa. Is not so easy now.'

Does she have to spell the finances out to him? 'So sell one of the Manhattan properties.'

He's stroking his left eyebrow, the sign of deep anxiety. 'Naturally I consider. Is owned by all you three together. We need conference with Emil and Dorinda.'

'Emil and Hudwalker.' A very good point. Best to act before Doly comes of age. 'How fortunate Emil's on the spot. I'll give him power of attorney. He'll talk Hudwalker round and sell one of the houses.'

Rolf looks uncomfortable. 'Emil very young, Grischa. You not think...'

The man's ridiculously over-cautious, and has the middle-aged man's prejudice against the young. 'We can hardly wait till he's your age, Rolf.'

Vienna, November 1929

Gabby's boredom threshold is getting dangerously low. Vienna is just as she expected: stuffy, dull, bourgeois and antiquated. The capital city of a country reduced from a great empire to a tiny insignificant republic. On paper. In real life Austrians still behave as though they were living in imperial times. Pomp, circumstance, putting outward show before inward talent, that infuriating assumption that they own the world, their central European world, because nothing else counts.

Not content with that, the heart of the Viennese world is 'die Oper'. It's right in the centre of the Inner City, it's a fine building and no doubt the acoustics are all they're cracked up to be. But Gabby's interest in music, let alone the caterwauling of singers rendering famous arias at top pitch, doesn't just leave her cold. It leaves her yawning, longing for a Schnapps and the rapid-fire exchange at Berlin's Romanisches Café. How is she ever going to survive if she has to listen one more time to Mrs Perkins, wife of some American executive kow-towing to Rolf, drone on about children and running a house in a country which doesn't have modern plumbing. It's driving Gabby nuts. She has to find some outside entertainment. At least she has to have the excitement of owning a decent car. The house in Neuwaldegg is fine and the Vienna Woods, though a poor substitute for the Schwanenbruch marshes, do have wine bars called Heurigens—places serving the new wine of the season. She and Viktoria can take ambitious protégés of Watson's out there to 'show them the real Vienna'. Gabby's convinced that even Americans must be able to talk about something other than baseball or money under the influence of wine. And Viktoria can take them on to the bloody opera or concerts at the Musikverein.

'We can't live out in Neuwaldegg without a larger car, Rolf.'

'Is good idea, Grischa. I go look...'

'I know the car I want. Bandi's latest Minerva is absolutely stunning. A wonderful car. Except it's a convertible. I want the new saloon.' What reason can she give? 'That's much more suitable for taking a small child around. Even with the hood down, the cabriolet's too cold for Viennese winters.' She chooses to forget that Gemma spends hours in her pram in the garden.

'You mean 22CV AP? Cost enormous amount money, Grischa. I look already. Is possible buy good car for half this price.'

You can rely on Rolf to know all the latest models. He adores anything mechanical. Naturally it's possible to buy a cheaper car, but that's not what she's after. If Doly can prance round in the latest Mercedes without even having come into her money, Gabby isn't going to settle for less than the best Minerva.

'We'll buy the car together, Rolf. Like the house. Then you'll only pay what you expected to.'

He tries to reason. Every which way. Fails. And he has to leave on his crucial trip to Baghdad within the hour. As Gabby knew when she brought the matter up.

She doesn't know everything. It's a surprise that Bandi arrives in his splendid vehicle to pick Rolf up to take him to the station.

'Why you not also come, Grischa? Then we can all discuss.'

An even greater surprise that Rolf not only asks his brother to adjudicate on matters between his wife and himself: he suggests the two of them go on discussing it when he leans out of the First-class carriage window to wave goodbye. 'Go for ride in horse sleigh through Vienna Woods,' he suggests. 'Gemma also will enjoy. Is lovely afternoon.'

Bandi hands Gabby into his splendid vehicle. He heads the car towards his apartment rather than the villa in Neuwaldegg. He doesn't try to change her mind, just her location. Away from Rolf's house. 'I have some business people coming to dinner. Why not join us?' His excellent chef is known for his Hungarian cuisine.

Gabby's mind races through possibilities. Spurting blood tingles warmth through hands and feet grown icy waiting on the draughty

453

platform. 'What a good idea.'

'Times are rather difficult, Gabriele. There's a recession. Wall Street has plunged and shows no sign of recovery.'

He's going to talk about money? Gabby draws her furs around herself. Viennese winters are freezing cold. 'Rolf has an excellent job. The only way to further his career is to live in the right style. How can we offer Mr Watson a ride in anything less than a prestige car?' Her small face peeps up from under a large becoming hat. She batters eyelashless eyes. 'You drive an expensive Minerva, Bandi.'

'For business reasons.' His eyes half-lidded.

He is tall and handsome, and earns even more than Rolf. Because he's good at deals, including his own salary. She can hear the rumble in his voice, can feel the blood pounding in his veins as his hands touch hers. But his words are commonplace, his political insight only slightly more aware than Rolf's. Which she's very willing to put aside, if properly courted. 'Exactly, Bandi. Would you expect your brother to settle for less?'

Bandi agrees the Minerva would be a good investment. Gabby accompanies him to his apartment. Entertains him. Prettily. An inviting smile on her face, in her eyes, even her gestures point to a heaving bosom. She accepts alcohol which he doesn't share. Not a good omen.

Even so, the time Gabby spends in her brother-in-law's company is pleasurable. Her body thrills to his pat on her shoulder, to the sound of his voice lowering to a sexy timbre, to the sight of his tall body bending to fill her glass again and again. But he does not sit beside her. Perhaps because it could be awkward if one of his guests were to arrive early.

Frustrated, Gabby hears herself launch into politics, sees dullness in Bandi's eyes.

The guests arrive. Gabby's mind strays from the tedious dinner conversation about the latest business machines, the lack of sales. She daydreams herself back to the Romanisches Café, Friedrich's caustic remarks, Jonah's more prosaic but very pertinent ones.

The Nazi party is gaining more supporters. She wonders whether part of Hitler's success lies in his effect on large numbers of women. Is it possible they get a sexual thrill from the way he opens his speeches by staring at his audience without uttering a single word, allowing silence to increase tension? He starts off softly, caressing his syllables, following with the crescendo of a lion's roar as he makes a major point. Sexual foreplay disguised as oratory?

She waits, impatient, for Bandi's guests to leave. For him to pay court. Why else has he asked her here? Never mind bloody Wall Street. What does he feel about her personal assets? Her sinuous figure, her elegant clothes, her sex appeal?

Bandi nods amiably as the last guest leaves. Smiles at her as he picks up her coat. 'I'll run you back.'

The turbulent blood in her veins will not cool down. But he will never make love to her, however hard she tries. She refills her glass with Schnapps, gulps it down and walks away from him. It takes all her will power not to kick his shins.

WILLA O'THE WISP

When the sun dives into the glittering sea, and the gold-tipped marshes turn to grey, the countryside is peopled with all kinds of wonderful beings. Not flesh and blood as we know them, but ethereal bodies in human form.

They are of a rare beauty. Like the ravishing young girl who could be seen at dusk on still summer nights, gliding in and out of the ruins of an old castle. She rises up from the misty meadows carrying a basket of flowers on her arm. She sweeps gracefully through marsh and meadow, over moor and heather. Then she evaporates, lost to human sight as gently as she made herself visible.

Local people enjoyed the enchanting apparition for many a year. Until the night a few lummox youths, louts from a neighbouring village, wanted to test what kind of being the translucent figure was. They armed themselves with flails, stalked the shape, ran up to her.

But the foolish young men remained none the wiser. The enchanted form simply swept away from them. And from all men's gaze for ever more.

CHAPTER 13

Grindelwald, December 1929

'Listen, Liesi. It's damned cold here. And foggy. This isn't what I want to do. What about you?' Doly and Lieselotte share a room. A double bed. Not just for reasons of economy. Comfort. Warmth.

She watches Lieselotte stare out of the window. Idyllic alpine scenery, crisp white snow, mist-hazed morning sun which turns to brilliance later in the day, perfect pistes. Her first attempt at skiing proved her natural ability, leaving Doly struggling, undignified, on the nursery slopes.

'You don't like the skiing here? Real shame. You got on so much better yesterday.' Lieselotte is already dressed to go, waiting for her since God knows what hour of the morning. 'You'd learn in no time if you put your mind to it.'

Doly inhales; a deep, long drag. She's the one who's paying the piper, and a fairly hefty tune at that; she'll be the one to decide how and where they spend their holiday. 'I don't like Guido following us around like a little dog. He's getting on my nerves.'

'His determination to prostrate himself before you *is* irritating. I quite agree.' Lieselotte's mouth sets in a resolute line. 'The skiing's too hard, and Guido's too easy.'

'Exactly. I think we should find something else to do. Without Guido following us around.' Apparently part of her problem personality is she can't stand a man who makes himself too available. He's the brilliant psychoanalyst. Can't he see he's inviting nothing but scorn?

'Bit keen, I agree. You mean ditch him? He has been sweet, you know.'

'Has been.'

'He'll be terribly upset; he's due in his new post on the first of January. Want me to break it to him?'

Lieselotte is willing to see him off, though Doly suspects her friend's been looking forward to Guido keeping Doly company while she enjoys herself with the advanced skiers. That would be really boring.

She lights up again. Getting through a pack a day, beginning to stain her teeth. She must try to cut down. 'Why don't we just take off? Guido's from Trieste, his family's still living there. That isn't all that far from Grindelwald. I'm sure there'll be a train from Zurich. He can go home for the rest of his holiday.'

'Just like that, eh?'

'I don't owe him anything.'

'You owe him your escape from the Austrian authorities, Doly.' Lieselotte opens their bedroom window. Overnight falls of snow lie virgin, dazzling a welcome in the strengthening sun. 'Where shall we go? There are sunnier ski resorts if this one isn't good enough.'

'Let's skip winter by taking a boat to Morocco. Tangier is nice and cheap. And warm.'

Lieselotte flicks through the touring guide she's brought along. 'As long as you realise Tangier is simply a convenient escape. And that you're ditching Guido because he reminds you of Vienna and Bruno.'

'Thought you were going to go in for paediatrics? Or have you decided on psychoanalysis instead?'

'Don't be such a bloody prig.' Lieselotte's head jerks up from the guide book. 'Hold on a minute. It's not that simple. We'll have to travel via France and apply for a visa.'

'You have a genius for fabricating problems. Tangier's an international zone.'

'I know. But I thought while we were there we might explore Morocco itself. So we'll need a reason for going. Which is?'

Doly grins as she blows her umpteenth smoke ring and puts a finger through it. 'We'll enrol at the University of Tangier. No one can force us to attend classes.'

Morocco, December 1929

'This is more like it, Liesi. Loads of sun.'

The temperature is warmer than spring in Schwanenbruch. And Doly is giving Lieselotte the chance of a lifetime. Touring Europe in a luxurious car, learning to drive, discovering a talent and delight in skiing. And the chance to experience ways of life school geography lessons can't even hint at. 'It does feel good. So what shall we do first? Find a guide for the kasbah?'

'Why not join a nunnery while we're at it? Let's explore the desert. On our own.'

'You mean get camels and ride them?'

'I looked into that. They won't let us go without a bloody caravan. I wasn't planning on an expedition. Let's take the car and drive. See everything from there.'

'We were warned about bandits, Doly.'

'For goodness sake, Liesi. If you're too chicken to explore, wait for me here. Sit in on yawn-making lectures, get cheated in the souk.'

Can Lieselotte understand her hunger for love, adventure, risk? She's young and attractive. But for how long? Her hair is starting to thin, a grim reminder of her inheritance. Once it starts falling out, she'll have lost the freedom of wind blowing through, a lover's quickening hand. A wig will make her a prisoner to constant pressure: does it show, do people talk behind her back, will it stay on in the wind, how will she bathe? Can Liesi see these problems, empathise? Understand Doly's need to grab life while she can? There are compensations, after all. Doly is generous enough to share everything.

'I'm not chicken, Doly. I was thinking of being around for my next birthday. The desert's a dangerous place. We'll have to plan ahead. Take water, petrol, provisions. Sandstorms and all that.'

'Sometimes I think I should re-christen you Fuddyliesi. We're a bit low on funds already. How much d'you think we'll need?'

The two girls leave Tangier behind them, drive on roads leading to the desert proper. Spend nights in the car, sleeping on the seats with the soft-top shut against the elements, don their skiing outfits against the cold of the desert night, cover themselves with rugs. Lieselotte insists on frequent drinks from ample bottles of water to ensure against dehydration.

The fresh air of morning is their favourite time. They drive ever further into the interior. Along tracks, with wide vistas of shades of beige around them. No other people in sight, as though they were the only inhabitants on the planet.

'I often think you're over the top, Doly, but I have to admit I admire your spunk. Without you I'd spend my whole youth in safe worthy excursions riding a prosaic bicycle into the flat landscape of middle age.'

Doly smiles her love for her friend, is surprised by the sudden poetic turn. Then sees something which puts everything else out of her mind. 'Blast. Look over there, Liesi.'

Four horsemen on the horizon. In Arab clothing. Riding Indian file, jellabas billowing behind them as they advance, arrow-like, towards the Mercedes.

Doly's eyes slit. 'Who d'you think they are?'

'It wasn't just the people at the hotel. The man at the garage talked of bandits.'

'Let's get out of here.' Doly puts her foot down. Sand pours a deluge over the windscreen, coats the girls' hair, their clothes. The desert is no place for speeding.

'You can't see, Doly. Slow down or you'll get us killed.'

She slows. The four horsemen divide, there are two abreast along both sides of the car within minutes. One of each pair of riders mounts the running board while his companion holds his horse's reins.

The men shout words the girls do not understand, gesture by pointing towards the far horizon. The one on the left grabs the steering wheel.

Both girls shake their heads. Doly bashes the brown hand holding the wheel. Without effect.

The men shout louder, urge them on. A huddle of stone buildings comes into view.

'I'm not going to be a white slave,' Doly shouts above the noise of the excited men. 'Are you?'

'Death before dishonour.' Lieselotte shouts back. Clearly means it.

Doly presses down on the accelerator as hard as she can. The car surges, speeds, moves from side to side. The men bellow. The buildings approach. Rapidly.

'Looks like a sheer drop in front of us,' Lieselotte screams. 'Quick way to end it all.'

'I'm going over. Now.'

'Stop, Doly. Stop.' Lieselotte pulls at the handbrake, the car shudders from side to side.

A majestic unswerving man dressed in the flowing red cape and fez of a Camel Corps officer steps forward several metres ahead, arms outspread. He jumps aside seconds before Doly skids the car down a gentle ramp on to a sunken garden, a hidden jewel in the desert. The Mercedes comes to rest in a blaze of colour.

'Bonjour, Mesdemoiselles.' The officer lifts his fez. 'Capitaine Malraux.' Sweeps his headgear in front of him. A clear invitation to his quarters.

The men jump off the running boards, salute their superior.

'Don't let on we're from Germany,' Doly hisses at Lieselotte. 'I'll show him my American passport.' She grabs her bag, flourishes the small green booklet. 'Ne parle pas Français,' she simpers.

He speaks in English. 'Your throat must be very dry, M'amzelle. Yours and your friend's. Travelling at such speed in the desert is unwise. May I invite you to have some tea or coffee?'

A Captain in an outpost. Whose scouts were checking on possible bandit activity. Who hasn't seen a European for months. He spends his time reading, learning languages. He can hardly contain his delight at the chance to talk. 'Do stay for a meal. My cook is very good...'

'We have to get back before dark.'

'I can put you up.'

Doly sees a rerun of another brush with death. Not long ago. And involving another young man who smiled as amiably as this one. All she wants is a safe haven. She smiles back and shakes her head. 'Some friends of ours are waiting for us. So nice to meet you.'

Their car is low on petrol, they have no reserves left. The Captain offers some from his meagre store. They accept, get into the Mercedes, drive off.

Lieselotte's nerves cannot cope with more strain. 'Enough adventures for a while, Doly. Let's sail back to Europe. Do something really tame in Spain.'

461

CHAPTER 14

Tangier, January 1930

'I'm so dusty, Liesi. Let's stop and take a swim.'

The girls are out of the desert. Waiting for a ferry to take them to Gibraltar. With two hours to kill.

'Must you? They don't like women showing their bodies in this country.'

'We're not their women.'

'I'm all for a swim. But I'm keeping my clothes on. You do what you like.' Lieselotte has changed into a dress. She walks down the beach and into the cooling waters of the Mediterranean.

Doly sits on a log. Smoking a cigarette while she contemplates how to take off her slacks without causing a riot. She sees a man coming towards her. Crabwise approach, furtive body language. She watches him under cover of the smoke rings she's expert at.

A brown hand is about to snatch Liesi's bag. Doly flash grabs the handle. Sunrays reflect light from a naked blade. Arrogant male eyes demand surrender.

Doly's peripheral vision is good. She spies Lieselotte walking up the beach dripping water. 'Keep away, Liesi,' she says in German. Blessing the clipped syllables which carry across the shore. 'Walk over to those fishermen.' She keeps her voice low, even. As though she's pleading for her life. Betting the man can't understand her words.

Lieselotte's voice sounds irritated. 'What's going on?'

She can be slow to grasp the obvious. 'Take my word for it. Get over there.' Voice level as before.

The blade glitters up and down. Doly makes placatory gestures. He comes nearer. She takes a deep breath, fills her lungs with smoke. Turns. Puffs into the man's face. Streaks away with the two handbags.

Lieselotte runs towards her, brandishing an oar she's grabbed. The two fishermen run after her. Armed with the second oar. The two girls are between two devils and the sea.

The fishermen run beyond them, curse at the man with the knife. Who takes to his heels.

The girls clasp each other. Smile at the fishermen. Offer money.

They shake their heads. Real men do not take money for protecting women in their territory. They are proud to be of help.

Lieselotte searches in her bag. She finds her bible and ceremoniously hands it to the fishermen. A present from Germany.

They salaam their thanks.

Gibraltar, January 1930

The man in the uniform which threatens to unbutton any moment doesn't look at Doly or Lieselotte. He examines the car. Walks to the front. Looks under the bonnet. Lieselotte's dress is draped over the radiator where she put it to dry. And forgot about it.

He spits, aims at the front wheel of the passenger side. 'Passports. Driving licence.'

Lieselotte has all the documents in a special wallet. She gets out of the car, hands it over. Smiling submissively. The man examines her. Minutely. His eyes slit at her trouser-clad legs. Her instincts were right. Mediterranean women keep to traditional female garb. She and Doly should have stuck to local custom.

Beer Belly's hands flick through their papers, suspicious eyes examine the visa to Morocco. 'You are students at Tangier University?'

'We were. Now we're travelling to Madrid.'

Doly's hands brush over the steering wheel. Ready to drive on. Gibraltar is a staging post.

The belly behind the buttons protrudes further. Followed by a podgy hand which strokes the bonnet. 'A very fine car for students. What did you study? Digging gold?' The smile is expansive.

463

The French captain's scouts were less threatening than this official. And easier to deal with. 'Philosophy and psychology.'

'How long will you remain in Gibraltar?'

'A few hours. We're passing through.'

'Mercedes Model K. Very fine car. For this you pay 50 pounds. Sterling. Then you can go.' Implacable.

Doly's hands leave the steering wheel. She digs her purse out of her handbag.

'How much have you got left, Doly?' Lieselotte pulls out her own purse, counts 50 Reichsmark. A little change.

'200 dollars.'

'How many English pounds is that?'

'No idea.' Doly holds the wad of dollars out to the customs official. 'How many of these?'

He stares at the notes. Doesn't take them. 'You come inside to pay.' He points at the customs house.

The two girls leave the safety of the Mercedes behind. Self-conscious as they walk towards the customs shed in their slacks.

'I told you we should have worn skirts.' Lieselotte's voice is low.

Doly doesn't even hesitate. 'Why should we pander to their stupid prejudices? Wouldn't have been practical for travelling.'

Pot-belly pulls a small notebook from a drawer, licks his fingers, turns the pages. Slowly. Laboriously. '$4.69 to the pound sterling.'

The contempt is harder to take than the actual figures. Though those are hard enough.

'That's more than I've got.' Doly hands over the dollars. 'Will you take these? The only other money we have are Reichsmark.'

'You pay or your car stay.'

Liesi draws her German money out of her purse. Blinks at Doly. 'We'll have to give him some of these.'

It takes a good hour of arduous calculations to sort it out. And leaves them barely enough cash to tank up, buy a loaf of bread and a little fruit. They won't be able to get more money before they reach Madrid. Can't do it in a day. They'll have to sleep in the car again.

THE EVERLASTING HAM

It was around noon that the tattered starved-looking girl came up to the farm. Just as the farmer and his family were seated at their table and about to start their midday meal. An enormous platter stood on the sideboard, weighed down by a huge ham. Only one or two slices had been cut, and it was clear that there would be enough meat for the whole of the coming week.

'I wonder whether I might have a small piece of ham?' the stranger asked. She held her thin hands out expectantly. There was, she could see, more than enough ham to feed a much larger family.

'Certainly not,' the farmer yelled at her. 'If I were to give every Mary, Jane and Lizzie a slice of my ham, I wouldn't have anything left for myself. As it is, there's only just enough for us.'

'If you're that hard up I can only wish one thing for you,' a surprisingly loud voice shouted out. 'May you never see the back of that ham.' And with those words the girl was gone.

Her wish became reality. However much the farmer and his family cut off the ham, it didn't get any smaller. And things were never quite the same again on the farm. The next day the farmer's wife helped herself liberally to the ham, eating with gusto. She sickened and died within the week.

This was too much for the farmer. He took the wretched ham, dug a pit near the house and buried it. That didn't help at all. The dogs unearthed it before he even got back to the house.

Not willing to be defeated, the farmer made more elaborate attempts to rid himself of the damnable meat. He took a long trip all the way to the Elbe. There he threw the ham as far as he could, right out into the water.

That didn't help either. When he got home the ham was already back on the kitchen table.

The farmer could see that he had to do better than that. So he went out into the streets and invited the poor, the halt and the lame to feast

465

at his table. Hoping the girl who had laid the curse would reappear and lift the curse. But she did not.

After the feast the farmer took the ham, still almost whole, down to his cellar. He dug an enormous pit, laid the ham inside it, and bricked it up.

And that's where it finally stayed. Except on bright moonlit nights, when it can't stand its narrow confines any longer. That's when it leaps out of its prison and sets itself on the top of the roof. Where it can be seen far and wide. And doesn't disappear till dawn.

CHAPTER 15

Spain, January 1930

The journey to Madrid is exhausting, dry and dusty. Hunger is making the girls feel faint. The needle on the tank shows ominously low as they reach the centre of the capital. Passing Spaniards show no interest in two sweaty foreign girls dressed in trousers. They turn their backs.

Their petrol runs out in the middle of a busy Madrid street. No one cares. Nothing for it but to abandon the car, grab a small bag each and search for rooms which will allow them to pay when they leave. Then they'll have to look for the American consulate and borrow money from the Consul.

The search for rooms is more difficult here than in any other country they've passed through. Cheery exchanges dry up. With their throats. They croak in monosyllables. And Lieselotte wonders why she thought Spain would be easier than Morocco. Perhaps Doly's recklessness pays dividends.

They stumble on a willing landlady at last, in the poorer part of town. No bathroom. They wash from a bowl, change into clean blouses, set out for the consulate. It's mid afternoon.

'I'd like to see the Consul.' Doly hands her passport over to a young Spanish man sitting at the desk. A supercilious look is meant to quell her. She stares straight back.

'Wait, please.'

The young man returns, left eyebrow raised. He flicks through

Doly's passport, pointing to several coffee-stained pages. It seems the Consul is not in a hurry to meet Dorinda Dohlen. Whose name is unknown to him.

When the Consul finally appears, his reaction is not friendly. His eyes flick over two girls with matted unwashed hair. Wearing trousers, dusty shoes, blouses stained with sweat. Tramps who have no business in the American Consulate. 'I'm afraid we can't help you here.'

'But I'm an American.' Doly is outraged. Ashamed of such behaviour in front of Lieselotte.

'The United States Consulate is not a source of credit for impecunious citizens. Please leave before I call Security.'

'Would you at least cable my brother-in-law? Herr Diplom Ingenieur Rolf Ferent.' So fortunate she can quote such impressive-sounding titles. 'He's the head of the whole of IBM in Europe,' Doly exaggerates, with a dazzling smile.

The Consul has already turned to leave the room.

'I'm going to make sure your superiors in Washington know about this.' Doly's voice carries well. 'Perhaps you will, at least, find me the number of the local office? I don't think International Business Machines will be quite as unhelpful as the representative of the United States Government.'

He nods at the reception clerk. Who finds the number of the Madrid IBM office. Dials, holds the receiver out to Doly. Lips curled.

'Hello? My name is Dorinda Dohlen. I'm Rolf Ferent's sister-in-law. Could you please get in touch with him for me? I'm stranded in Madrid. I need his help urgently.'

'*The* Herr Ferent? The one in Vienna?'

'Yes.'

'Of course, Señorita Dohlen. Delighted. I will cable him at once. Would you like me to contact you at the Consulate?'

'My friend and I are staying in la Casa dos Torres. Please get in touch with us there.'

Doly hands the receiver back to the reception clerk, turns on her heel, walks out. Followed by Lieselotte.

Rolf's return cable is received by his office in Madrid within the hour. It instructs them to do anything necessary for Fräulein Dohlen and her friend, and to make funds available immediately. The Manager drives over to la Casa dos Torres to pass the news on. Because there is no telephone.

Doly and Lieselotte give a loud whoop of joy. They accept pesetas, treat themselves to an enormous meal. Then they rescue their car, park it outside the modest boarding house and invite their landlady to share a bottle of champagne.

The American Consul calls at la Casa dos Torres. In person. The Madrid office of IBM, an outpost of the United States, has been in touch. They told him that Dorinda is a rich young woman connected with an important man. He's come to tender his apologies.

Doly, a glass of champagne in one hand, a cigarette in the other, waves the landlady bearing messages away.

'He's far too late. I've had all the help I need.'

PART 7

THE SWITCHING HOUR

1931–1932

CHAPTER 1

Vienna, August 1931

Rolf travels extensively. To Baghdad, Istanbul, Bucharest, Budapest, Helsinki, even Moscow. Romantic names, long trips away from home. And IBM thrives on it.

He brings his wife beautiful hand-loomed carpets from Persia, his daughter Gemma hand-made dolls from every country he visits. A disappointing child. She prefers the paper aeroplanes her Onkel Emil makes and flies for her. And she's as reluctant about Rolf's kisses as her mother.

Bandi visits when his brother is at home, and also when he is away. Gabby finds herself physically roused in a way she can't explain. Because, though Bandi is excruciatingly polite and evidently enjoys her company, he does not approach her sexually. And his conversation is hardly scintillating. Not in the least like Tall and Small. So far Gabby has not met any heterosexual men who are willing to talk to her on an equal footing. Does it mean that the only males willing to take her seriously as a human being are homosexuals? In other words, are most men so obsessed with their superiority over women they cannot grasp that gender has nothing to do with brains? Gabby is beginning to understand that gay men, labelled deviants and worse by society at large, know only too well that characteristics attributed to them are simply projections of others' prejudices. The ones she's met have learned the lesson. It's the clue to why they can see women as people rather than as objects.

Gabby realises that she, too, sees life through her own lenses. When she was young she assumed she was ugly. It took Tall and Small to point out that other people won't see her in that light if she chooses to make herself beautiful. Because they see her brilliantly crafted, elegantly worn wigs as signs of a beauty she doesn't actually possess. Has her personal history opened her eyes to the meaning of the electioneering around her? Is that why she can see what's happening in Europe, politically, better than Rolf or Bandi? Both laugh at her prophecies, seeing her as a young mother afraid for her child. Incapable of holding civic views, let alone contrarian ones.

The locket around her neck begins to chafe. She holds it away impatiently. She may fool other people, but deep down she knows she's ugly, cannot make her hair grow. A vision of her child comes into her mind. Gemma harbours the gene but for the moment she has pretty blonde hair and hazel eyes. Her governess comes back from trips in the park and boasts about the compliments heaped on her. Gemma *is* beautiful. Perhaps it's time she thought of herself that way as well.

Was that the secret of her father's success? He saw beyond himself as an impoverished immigrant, saw way beyond. He swept away the trivial and concentrated on the core. That's why he abandoned the backward-looking society he lived in, that's how he changed his life, that's why he succeeded, why he made his fortune.

She sees more clearly now. Her lack of hair could be taken to be as much good fortune as bad. As far as personal relationships are concerned, it sorts them out nicely. Into the traditional sheep and goats, she grins to herself.

Gabby slaps her fist down on the table in front of her, pours herself a stiff Schnapps. What she makes of her life is up to her, on how she chooses to view, and use, her inheritance. Inheritances; she does, after all, have more than one: her father's fortune, her mother's gene and the one that really counts: her father's spirit and courage.

It's a strange situation. Unfulfilled passion for Bandi stirs the marriage bed. In spite of herself, Gabby welcomes Rolf back from his trips, allows him to approach her sexually more frequently. She's startled because she's actually broody. Astonished to find she's keen to bear another child. She's wearied of trips to the Heurigen, fitting out the house, buying an exciting wardrobe. And the dashing stalwart figure of Bandi is never far from her loins. He makes her womb ache. But he'll never father a child on her. And he's about to move to Switzerland.

'Why don't we have another child, Rolf?' Gabby knows he's longing for a son. As she is. And Gemma needs a companion. Of course she's well aware that each child she bears stands the same fifty-fifty chance of inheriting the gene as her first. Is she willing to risk it? Why not? She's managed. So will any of her children who need to. Because she'll pass on more than a lack of hair. She'll show them how to embrace life in spite of it.

Rolf has just come home from the office, is already sitting at his desk. The room beyond the bathroom adjoining their bedroom has been turned into a study. Where he's closeted for long hours. Totting up figures, making sketches, rubbing his left eyebrow with his left index finger.

He looks up and his face breaks into a broad delighted smile. 'We have son.' he says. 'Is wonderful news.'

'Just one thing, Rolf. This time I have to go to America for the birth. Whether it's a boy or a girl. The political climate in Germany is highly suspect. And Austria isn't immune. Remember the Nazi demonstrations in Berlin in December, and here in January, against the showing of the film *All Quiet on the Western Front*.'

'Is not dangerous, Grischa.'

'They barred the film in Germany. Can't you see what that implies?'

'I not argue. What you wish I agree.' Another broad grin. 'We go to Prater talk to gypsy. She tell us boy or girl.'

'But I just said...'

'Still go to America for birth. But she tell what we will have.'

Vienna, August 1931

The Prater district originally provided hunting grounds for the Habsburg royals. This is the only part of Vienna actually bordering the Danube. It's the unromantic Donaukanal which flows through the city centre.

Joseph II put the royal hunting grounds at the public's disposal.

474

His generosity did not find whole-hearted acclaim. His courtiers complained that they no longer had anywhere to walk with their peers.

'Think yourselves lucky,' the emperor told them coldly, 'If I wanted to be with *my* peers I'd have to join my forebears in the Kapuzinergruft.'

Vienna's entertainment centre isn't reserved for innocent pleasures. Connoisseurs of the fiery Yugoslavian Cevapcici enjoy their favourite tipple in special bars. More intimate pleasures are also catered for. And there are plenty of clients for the Pratersprizzi. Who are delighted to provide a variety of accommodating young women. And boys.

The city is an exciting mixture of east and west, the Prater more like a scene from *A Thousand and One Nights* than the playground of a European city. The Turks brought coffee, the Magyars rowed up the Danube with their meaty Gulyás and Paprikahuhn, the Poles contributed fat geese, the Bohemians Topfenknödel, Palatschinken, Buchteln and Mohnstrudeln—substantial flour-based dishes to fuel hefty appetites. Even the famous Wienerschnitzel started out as a Byzantine method of cooking meat. East meets West in the Prater. And enjoys the experience.

This fairground district of Vienna isn't Gabby's natural stamping ground, but it is the Vienna Rolf has fallen in love with. He admires the technical achievement of the world's largest ferris wheel, the Riesenrad. He treasures the romantic connotations. He adores the simple tales hammered out in the Punch and Judy booths, shows off his marksmanship at the shooting galleries, enjoys the thrill of the Hutschen-Schleuderer and can't get enough of sitting Gemma on the horses of the Ringelspiele.

The gypsy is Hungarian. She understands Rolf in the language he is most at home in. She takes his hand, turns it palm up and examines it.

Her face is smiling, benign. He's crossed her hand with many Schillings. 'Three children.' Her dark eyes widen, then she murmurs something in Hungarian which Gabby can't understand.

'What did she say?'

He blinks, hesitates for a second. 'All healthy. Two boys, one girl.'

'I see very important career ahead for you. You rise will in your profession very high for several more years.' The shawl, so like the one Rolf gave Doly, slips from her shoulders. Her eyes grow dark, veil.

'You something bad see?' He's speaking German.

She looks beyond him. 'Bad times are coming for us all. The world soon will be at war. Big war, involve whole Europe.' Her eyes meet his. 'Beware the Ides of March.' She puts his hand away. Picks up Gabby's.

'Three children,' she tells her. 'You mother will be for three children. Second will be fine, healthy son. Born in the pink.' Her eyes widen. She drops Gabby's hand.

'And the son born after him?' The gypsy just told Rolf his third child would be a boy. He did react oddly, looking sideways at Gabby. Did he hesitate because the gypsy foretold a sickly second son? Gabby gasps as she remembers her own mother died in childbirth. Did the gypsy foresee her death? Is she destined to die in childbirth?

The old woman hunches her shawl around her shoulders. She refuses to say another word even when Rolf offers her more money, speaks to her in Hungarian.

A shudder goes through Gabby. For no reason. What has the gypsy seen she isn't telling them?

THE BRAMEL BELL

The people of Bramel have always had a certain reputation. Lacking in grey matter is the general opinion. When they want to pasture eager cattle they put ropes around their necks and drag them to the fields. And a builder hailing from Bramel finds it hard to figure out how to get a girder into a new house, because he carries the beam sideways.

During the Thirty Years' War even the Bramelers became aware that their neighbours buried their valuables. Until such time as the foe would have left their country. The Bramelers copied their neighbours and hid everything of value. The only precious thing left was their beautiful church bell. The question now was, where could they best hide that?

One man spoke up: 'Sink it in the Sellstedter Lake.'

His idea was greeted with acclaim. The bell was taken down from the tower, loaded on to a wagon, transported to the lake and jammed into a boat. Several of the town worthies climbed into the boat as well. They all rowed into the centre of the lake and carefully lowered their bell into the water.

'Hold on.' one of them cried out as the others were about to row back. 'We've got to mark the spot.'

They all nodded, and scratched their heads to help them think.

'I've got it.' another cried out. 'Let's make a really big nick in the boat to show where we dropped it from.'

His companions cheered him and duly carved a notch in the boat. Then they rowed happily back.

Peace came, and the villagers wanted their bell back. The notch in the side of the boat was still there. Unfortunately the place where they'd sunk the bell was not so easily found. Their bell still lies at the bottom of that lake, waiting for someone to haul it out.

CHAPTER 2

New York City, June 1931

Doly is feeling restless. Again. She enjoyed her Freshman year at Barnard, managed a decent number of credits in spite of missing most of the first semester, ploughed through the Sophomore semesters, is at the start of her Junior year. She can muster forty credits, needs ninety if she's to graduate. A lot of work to get through. Does she really want to continue, in the company of serious young ladies hell-bent on graduating summa cum laude? Damned bore, actually. Even Faith Bowler, majoring in Chemistry to Doly's Philosophy, is determined on academia. And chickens out of double dates.

As far as Doly is concerned, she's had enough dry-as-dust lectures to last a lifetime. Dates with Columbia students, dutiful, snoring-boring sons of New York's well-to-do, can't be the best the US has to offer. She craves Lieselotte's company, longs for the bare-back horse rides over the Watt, is wistful about their double dates with local boys, their Mercedes tour through Europe and Morocco.

The truth is she's in a hurry to live life to the full. When she washes her hair, the drain is blocked, when she combs it, too many strands clog the teeth. No telltale bald spot yet. But she can't help wondering how long her auburn mop will last. The colour, already changed to dingy brown, has to be hennaed to look good. She has to fit in life before she's scalp-cuffed to a wig, straitjacketed like Tante Martha and Gabby.

New Jersey

July 12ᵗʰ, 1931

> *Dear Liesi,*
>
> *Fuddy's come across with a return ticket to Cuxhaven on the SS Hamburg. Onkel Wilfred's supposed to provide the cash. Why not have a go at changing the ticket to your name; you know the shipping office people in Cuxhaven, don't you? Come and spend some time here, for as long as you can get away. We can have a ball together.*
>
> *Your blood-sister Doly*

New York City, August 1931

'Can we go and see the Empire State Building?'

Doly watches as her friend scans her list of starred excursions. A long one.

'America is such a vast country. Full of modern buildings and extraordinary scenery. I want to cram in what I can.'

'You really want to see all those boring sights, Liesi? When we've only got two weeks?' Doly's small face is pinched. 'We could go riding in Connecticut.' She pouts disappointed lips.

'You live here, Doly. I may never have the chance to see New York City again.'

'You sound like bloody Gabby.' And it is, after all, Doly's invite. And involved her guardian's wrath at the change of ticket to Lieselotte.

She can see Lieselotte sneak looks at the latest skyscrapers. The Chrysler Building completed last year, the Empire State just finished. Over four hundred metres high. Blood sister maybe, but Doly can see she's longing to walk slowly down Fifth Avenue, along Broadway, end up in downtown Manhattan.

'Could we go up to the top of the Empire State Building? A hundred and two storeys, Doly. The tallest building in the world.'

'Must we, Liesi? It only opened in May. It'll be crowded as hell.'

'Oh, right. What about downtown, then? Isn't that where your father started out? Selling sandwiches on Wall Street?'

'OK, OK. We'll go downtown.'

Lieselotte puts on her best smile, one which doesn't fool Doly. Humouring her best friend just because she's given her the money for her studies. Does the whole world gravitate round that unsavoury stuff?

Doly is bored here. Even with her friend for company. She's no longer the same: just another stuffy adult who's lost the knack of living for the moment, enjoying her youth. If Doly had known it would turn her into an early fuddy, she'd never have given her the means.

'Don't you want to live a little, Liesi? Before that hospital and Josef turn you into a complete bore.'

'Studying medicine isn't an entertaining option. I see too much of sadness to go gallivanting around. But I do enjoy it, I feel the privilege of helping people, of real achievement. Aren't you enjoying your studies?'

Doly kicks at the litter which Lieselotte has commented on several times. She finds it such a surprising feature of Manhattan streets. Even on prestigious Fifth Avenue. Schwanenbruch streets are swept clean every day.

'Not all that much. I thought Philosophy was going to be really fascinating. All the professors do is drone on. Plato. Socrates. Kant with a capital C.'

Lieselotte's dark eyebrows gather storm clouds. 'For me New York's a welcome escape from daily ward rounds, the sickly-sweet odour of disease and death. Immersion in pure thought sounds like heaven.' She tries to arrange her features in a smile. 'Why not change to another subject? How about German Literature?'

'Everything's such a drag, Liesi. I wish I was like you, doing something practical. All this book work, holed up on sunny days in that stuffy library. Stuck in Manhattan when I could be in New England. It's such a great country. New York City's only one tiny bit of it.'

'Actually, Doly, the fumes of the city are heady compared to the acrid stench of disinfectant.' She kicks at paper tumbling along the street. 'If you're so set on fresh air, why not take a round-the-world cruise?'

'With bloody what? I'm stuck with Fuddy Duddy's tender mercies until next April.'

Lieselotte, evidently infuriated, grabs a *New York Times* from a news stand, turns to the small ads. 'Want a sea trip? How about this, then? It might just suit you.'

Crew wanted. Privately-owned sailing yacht, the Alamyth, *destination West Indies. Must be willing to try his hand at all chores. Allow a year for return trip.*

Doly snatches the paper away from her. 'You're brilliant, Liesi. That looks great.'

'Hold on a minute.' Lieselotte tries to retrieve the paper. 'They want a man, not a girl.'

But Doly's already headed into the nearest hotel lobby, is on the phone.

'It was just a silly joke to stop you moaning.' Lieselotte straightens her clothes, squares her shoulders. 'Not a chance in hell they'll take you, Doly. Who's going to employ a slight girl like you instead of a man as crew?'

New York City, August 1931

There's a phone call at the Hudwalkers' from the captain of the *Alamyth* two days after Doly sent in her letter of application. She arranges to go for an interview.

'What experience of ocean-sailing have you had?'

'I was brought up by the North Sea. I'm used to heavy weather.'

'Can you cook?'

You only have to look at her to know she's never used her hands. 'As well as anyone.'

'We'll get back to you.'

The owners, two brothers whose rum-running has not yet been discovered, are in need of funds. They make enquiries and find out Doly is well-heeled. They'll take a chance. There's always the option of holding her hostage.

Another phone call two days later. 'We'll take you on as cabin girl.'

'As a Moses girl,' Doly breathes. Voice full of pride.

'Moses girl?'

'That's what we call a cabin boy in North Germany. A Moses.'

This'll show Lieselotte, and everybody else, that she isn't just a poor little rich girl with no spunk for the ordinary life.

'They're not really taking you on, are they?'

'Why shouldn't they? My father always said "Holy Moses" when he was shocked or surprised. He started as a cabin boy, you know.'

'It's not the same thing, Doly. He came from a poor background, he had nothing to lose...'

'And he'd be proud of me now. He'd admire my pluck.'

The look in Doly's eyes makes Lieselotte wince. 'You really want to go?'

'I thought you'd be congratulating me on my first job.'

'You're joking, aren't you?' Lieselotte looks at her sceptically. 'You can't really want to wait on two men you've met just once?' She's so upset she literally wrings her hands. 'It was only meant as a joke, Doly. To show you how well-off you are.'

'Misfired, I guess. I'm deadly serious. Just one tiny problem.'

'They can't afford to pay you, they want you to pay them.'

Doly turns away. 'Close. They want me to pay my share of the victuals, yes. OK by me. The real problem is they're sailing the day after tomorrow. Your boat doesn't leave for two days after that. I can't just leave you to it.'

'No need to worry on my account.' The strong jaw is set tight, the wide shoulders firm. 'I'll be happy sightseeing. I'm sure the Hudwalkers won't mind my staying on with them.'

Liesi thinks she's play acting. As usual. Even her best friend doesn't know what she's made of. 'That's what you've been wanting all along.'

'Not true. But I'll make sure to see you off. I'll take you to the docks. A few days working at sea will do you good, show you starboard from port.' Lieselotte laughs, irritatingly. 'You'll disembark at the next port on some pretext or other. No harm done.'

'How wrong you are. Expect to see me with muscles twice the size of yours.'

Doly allows Lieselotte to see her on board, to check out the boat's in good fettle, the galley stocked.

It's a fine sunny day. The wind fills the sails and Doly waves goodbye, hair streaming in the wind, delicate arms hauling at a rope.

Two days later the weather is so bad that the SS *Hamburg* puts off her departure for Germany. Lieselotte stays on in New Jersey. Unhappily. She reads the *New York Times*. The shipping news.

The lump in her throat is huge and tight. She has to rush to the toilet, is terribly sick. The *Alamyth* is reported sunk in the gale. All hands swept overboard, presumed dead.

It's all her fault. How could she have been so stupid, so irresponsible, as to encourage Doly's recklessness? And then to make sure the girl actually went?

She returns to the Hudwalkers with the news. Spends several hours in a daze. Pulls herself together. There's one last thing she can do for her friend Doly. She offers to cable Rolf Ferent at IBM in Vienna, Wilfred Bender in Schwanenbruch. And to contact Barnard College. She even pushes herself to ring Faith Bowler up. Someone to talk to. Faith rants abuse until Lieselotte is so overcome she slams the phone down.

Barnard College arranges for an obituary to be read by Professor Mattler, head of the Philosophy Department. The subject Doly majored in.

CHAPTER 3

Vienna, September 1931

Rolf returns early from the office and arrives in the nursery with a telegram in his hand. Instead of taking Gemma from the nursemaid, playing with her, he puts his arm around Gabby's shoulder and steers her towards the door. 'Is best you come downstairs with me, Grischa. I something have to tell.'

His eyes are wet as he ushers her into their drawing room. 'I want you sit down, Grischa. Drink this glass of Schnapps.'

'What on earth's the matter, Rolf? You look as though you've seen a ghost.'

He pulls out a handkerchief. 'Is about ghost. Is about little sister.'

Not another suicide attempt. 'She's had an accident?' Her voice quavers as she realises that, this time, her sister might have succeeded.

'Is telegram from Lieselotte from New York. Doly take trip on small boat. There was terrible storm and boat sank.'

'You mean she went out on her own? Without Lieselotte?' That doesn't sound right even for Doly. Surely, in spite of her foolishness, her sister wouldn't be idiotic enough to go on a small boat by herself?

'Is not clear from telegram. What Lieselotte say was terrible storm, which we already saw in newspaper. Weather so bad even liners don't leave. Somehow Doly caught on boat.'

'But there were lifeboats? She's all right?' A terrible tightening in her chest.

'I very sorry to tell you this, Grischa. Your sister drown.'

Gabby allows Rolf to pour her another drink. It can't be possible. Doly is only twenty and seemed to be settled at last. She wrote she was enjoying Barnard. Even maintained she was having a wonderful time. That she'd met a splendid set of young women, and they had fascinating philosophical discussions late into the night. All that energy, all that life... How could she possibly be dead?

'She so young. Is terrible tragedy.'

Gabby is taken aback at the strength of her reactions. 'I can't believe it, Rolf. Her guardian angel always looked after her.' She's upset enough to welcome Rolf's embrace. Doly was a pest but she was her sister. Why did she always allow her irritation to get the better of her? Why couldn't she have tried to understand the girl? The poor child was always so desperate for love, always so terrified of the ghastly fate she felt hanging over her. Gabby slings back another glass of Schnapps as she tries to dull the knifing pain.

'Maybe her angel not on guard this time. Bandi in New York on business. We contact him. He represent us, Grischa. Boat take at least five days, we must first take train to Hamburg, and not always possible to get passage. So we cannot go in time for funeral ourselfs. I send cable to my brother now.'

Gabby feels a tightening in her chest she did not expect—compassion for her wayward sister. She's always known Doly's Achilles heel: her terror of how she will look when she loses her hair. Has Doly lost her life because she was determined to cram dangers into the years before she lost her looks? Was she actually trying to die, hiding from a future she couldn't face?

So is her own passion to conceal her baldness at all costs the same reaction expressed in a different way? Is Doly's example a grim pointer to how Gabby should change her own attitude to her inheritance? Accept, rather than fight it? She is healthy, she is intelligent, she has several excellent traits, and she can make herself attractive to men when she wishes. There's no excuse to whinge about her gene.

New York City, September 1931

Bandi scans his brother's telegram:

DORINDA DOHLEN PRESUMED DROWNED IN SHIPWRECK
OFF EAST COAST UNITED STATES OBITUARY SPEECH NEXT
WEDNESDAY TEN AM BARNARD COLLEGE PLEASE SELF AND
GABRIELE REPRESENT IF BODY FOUND ARRANGEMENTS
MAKE RETURN TO SCHWANENBRUCH FOR INTERMENT IN
DOHLEN MAUSOLEUM.

Andrew Ferent arrives at Barnard College minutes before the scheduled eulogy. The lecture room is large and packed with weeping young
women. Standing room only. Was Dorinda really so very popular? Or
is it just the romance of a young girl, a fellow student, lost at sea? He
stays at the back beside a tall young woman leaning against the wall.
She's barely able to stand.

'Are you a relative?'

The swaying girl's sobs increase. 'She was my best friend. My most
treasured friend. I don't know how I'm going to live without her.' She
looks up over a sodden handkerchief. 'Who are you?'

'Her sister is married to my brother. They're both in Europe. I'm
representing the family.'

'Andrew Ferent?'

Surprise widens his eyes. 'How do you know that? Are you related
to Mr Hudwalker?'

She puts her face against her hands. 'I'm Lieselotte Waldeck. From
Germany. Doly's best...' Bandi hands her his handkerchief for the
overflow from hers. 'I'm staying with the Hudwalkers. They're too
upset to be here.'

'Understandable. I've only met Dorinda once. Some years ago. At
Riverside Hall.'

Lieselotte swallows hard. 'She always spoke affectionately of your
brother Rolf. I was stranded with her in Madrid. Your brother rescued
us. By transferring funds.'

'So I heard. Dorinda was a spirited girl. I'm sorry I never got to
know her properly.'

'She was wonderful. So generous, so loving, so full of life. Very
different from her sister. Do you know Gabriele?'

Bandi lifts his head towards the lecture dais. No one there yet.
'Quite well. I worked in Vienna until recently. From what I've heard

486

Dorinda could be a little wild.'

'She was terribly misunderstood. She was a child of nature. A free spirit.'

The professor arrives. The snuffling dies down. He's dressed in black from top to toe. He lifts his hand for silence.

'The death of a fellow student is always a sad occasion to those who remain behind. The cutting down of a young girl at the dawn of womanhood is a tragedy. When that girl was a promising student, the tragedy is that much greater.' Loud clearing of his throat. 'You may wonder why I, rather than one of her many devoted fellow students, am giving this panegyric. The answer is quite simple and prosaic. I come from the same part of North Germany Dorinda was brought up in, from Hamburg, the big city along the coast of the river Elbe. Dorinda was brought up right by the mouth of the Elbe, in a small village by the name of Schwanenbruch—near Cuxhaven. A wonderful mystic part of old Germany.

'The only words of comfort I can think of are: Whom the gods love, die young.

'We, who knew Dorinda Dohlen and enjoyed her company, mourn her passing. She was an unusual student: eager, full of promise, but with a restlessness which drove her to choose adventure over entering her Junior year with us.'

The smile is slow and mournful. 'Perhaps she has something to teach us all. She enjoyed her studies here. But, as she explained to me at the end of last semester, she needed to experience life, not to read about it. That is why she chose the unusual path she did.

So I would like you to hear a poem Dorinda wrote. It was brought to my attention by her friend and fellow student, Faith Bowler.

THE SPRING OF LOVE

I'll be no scholar any more
For spring has come and nature sings
No mannered cloth to cover naked limbs
But burgeoning leaves which will turn mellow gold
And opening flowers ripening into fruit
I long for life and love, not printed words

Poems of love can't quench my thirst or feed my heart
I want no studies to dull my eyes
Out of my sight, each preaching book
I'm sick of paper, pen and ink
I want to hug, I want to kiss
I long for life and love, not printed words.

'I don't think I could have found a more fitting epitaph.' The professor trumpets his nose. 'Sad indeed to lose such promising talent. But I can only applaud a young woman courageous enough to break loose from the constraints that bind most of us to tradition, to living our lives in the ruts made for us.'

There is a stirring at the back of the hall. A curious buzzing as an odd unkempt person slouches in from the back. The professor is reminded of Bohemian friends his one-time pupil loved to spend her time with. The stranger is surrounded by a cluster of students. Professor Mattler frowns. He hasn't finished yet. He takes his reading glasses off. Focuses on a short slight figure swamped in too-big clothes. Topped by a mop of hair he remembers—recognises. Surely there's no one else with that shock of thick, oddly coarse hair?

The buzz grows louder, swells to cries, to sobs, to laughter. And finally loud applause as Faith Bowler hurtles towards it. The crowd pushes a young woman forward. She's pallid, dishevelled, obviously exhausted. But she is undeniably Dorinda Dohlen. How could she possibly be here?

Faith grabs her, pushes her towards the dais, up the steps to the professor.

She shakes his hand, says a few words to him. He asks some questions through the din of people chanting: 'Doh*len*. Doh*len*.'

At last the professor holds up his hand for silence.

'It's not a resurrection that you're seeing, ladies and gentlemen. Dorinda Dohlen is safe and well. It seems the august *New York Times* got it wrong when it reported the loss of all hands on the *Alamyth*. Apparently a passing ship picked everyone up. You all know our stringent Prohibition Laws. Foreign boats are not allowed within a 12-mile limit of our shores until they've been inspected. That's why

488

no one realised the crew had been picked up, how the mistake was made.'

A crescendo of applause as Doly stands and waves.

'We're all delighted to see you, Doly. This time the old German proverb won't be true: Der Horcher an der Wand hört seine eigene Schand—eavesdroppers will hear about their own misdeeds. On the contrary.'

More applause, the stomping of energetic feet.

'We hope to see you back in class, Dorinda. We can make an exception for your being late. Why not enrol for the new semester now?'

THE HEDGEHOG AND THE HARE

The race between the hedgehog and the hare, on Buxtehude Heath not far from Schwanenbruch, is often told. Hedgehogs of a quill avert all ill. As the saying goes.

Mr Hedgehog is out walking one fine morning before breakfast. He meets Mr Hare. Arrogant bragging Mr Hare who maintains he can run faster than anything else on four legs.

'Taking a walk, Mr Hedgehog? Aren't those squat legs of yours more suitable for other things?' A high-pitched laugh. 'Running, perhaps?'

The blood in Mr Hedgehog's veins courses fast. Which doesn't show under the quills. Nor do his thoughts. Fast legs, harebrained, is how Mr Hedgehog thinks of Mr Hare.

'I'll bet you I can run against you and win,' Mr Hedgehog says. Quietly. Nonchalantly.

'You? With those miserable stumps? You'll win a footrace against me?' Mr Hare laughs out loud. Clearly not worried about hurting Mr Hedgehog's feelings. 'What will you bet?'

'A Goldmark and a bottle of Schnapps.'

'Racing on foot? That's the deal?'

'On Buxtehude Heath. First, I'll have to have some breakfast. I'll meet you there in half an hour. We both deposit our bets there before we start.'

'You bet.'

Once home, the hedgehog tells his wife he needs her help. 'I want you to hunch down in the second furrow at the far end of the Heath,' he tells her. 'When the hare arrives in the furrow next to you, just say: "I'm here already."'

'That's it? That's all I have to do?'

'Do exactly as I say.' And Mr Hedgehog eats his breakfast while his wife goes to the Heath, waddles to the far end and makes herself comfortable in the furrow.

Mr Hedgehog walks back to meet Mr Hare who is already at the

490

starting post, thumping impatience.

'Ready to start?' Mr Hare cries. His long ears are alert, his long legs poised to spring.

'Here I am. Ready to go.'

'One, two, three, go.' the hare shouts over his shoulder. He sprints off as though the devil's on his tail, arrives breathless at the other end. In record time even for him.

Mrs Hedgehog always does exactly as her husband says. 'I'm here already,' she says. Quietly, without making any kind of move. And, as everyone knows, all hedgehogs sound the same. So the hare could not know she wasn't Mr Hedgehog.

The hare is baffled. Upset. How can this be? 'The race was from the starting point and back again,' he yells. And bounds away towards the starting post.

He arrives winded but triumphant. He can't believe his long ears when Mr Hedgehog says: 'I'm here already.'

'Let's race again.' the hare cries out. 'Do the whole course again.'

'You can race as often as you like,' Mr Hedgehog says. Smugly. Because it is well known that Mr and Mrs Hedgehog are as alike as— two quills. And the hare will never know the difference.

Mr Hare cannot believe he's slower than a hedgehog. He races back and forth. And each time the hedgehog is there before him.

At last the hare's body gives out. He collapses in mid-furrow. Blood pours from his paws, from his throat. He breathes his last.

Mr Hedgehog is unperturbed. He claims his winnings, drinks his bottle of Schnapps, and shares his Goldmark with his faithful wife.

CHAPTER 4

New York Harbour, September 1931

Doly and Bandi take Lieselotte to her liner, see her on board. Leave when the bell rings for visitors to go ashore. Stand beside each other on the wharf as they wave goodbye.

Doly's body trembles as the liner churns harbour water. She can't forget the shock of wind boxing her ears, grabbing her body. She fingers the bruises on her arms where she wound them around ropes to save herself from flying overboard. Waves knocked breath from her body, punched her against the deck rail. She clung on until the boat itself was swallowed up. Remembers the long slow rise, her fight for air. The ecstasy of clinging to floating wood, the gratitude for rescue, the warmth of dry clothes.

She survived through pluck, through holding on. And the grace of hope. Meaningful life, she now knows, means being true to her own values, her own standards. It means not seeing herself through others' eyes.

'How marvellous to meet up with you again, Doly. Even if the circumstances are a little unusual.'

Doly keeps her head turned away. She feels Bandi's eyes on her face, her neck, her bosom. And moves swiftly before he reaches her legs. 'And I'm with the dashing Bandi. Gabby is always going on about you.' She can sense that's where his true love lies. Gabby, she knows, is never affected by anything as physical as sex.

His eyelids lower. A silent leopard. 'Gabriele is a beautiful young woman. What is extraordinary is how alike you are.'

Obsessed with Gabby. Must know her beauty is fake, while she herself still has a good head of hair. Would he care? Apparently Rolf doesn't, which is something of a surprise. Well, same old story their mother Emma always told. 'Only in outward looks. Inside we're as different as oak and ash.'

Again that stillness. Has he heard?

'If you think about Aesop's story, Gabby is the tortoise, I'm the hare.' He moves back into a shell of silence. 'Well, actually in Schwanenbruch we have the hedgehog and the hare. Gabby is much more like a hedgehog.'

He stares at the hull of the liner, no sign of having heard.

'You don't agree?'

He doesn't smile, flourishes his right arm at the cluster of passengers on the rails still waving their goodbyes. 'I hope you haven't forgotten that the tortoise wins.' Measured. Unemotional.

'Perhaps I used the wrong analogy. She's the conventional one. I'm the outsider.'

'She's the eldest sibling in a family left without a father, you're the youngest. A little like my brother Rolf and myself.'

'I like your brother.'

Slow, slow blink. 'So do I. He is a fine man.' He lifts his hat to the departing boat. 'Time to go. Now we have such a golden opportunity, why not make use of it?'

So different from Rolf. No kissing of hands, no flowers or chocolates. He makes no allowances for the difference in their heights to shorten his stride. She's forced to take rapid steps to keep up.

But he's a man, so he's vulnerable. Perhaps he'll change allegiance from Gabby to her. An older man who dotes on her? It's an appealing thought.

'Dinner at the Stork Club, perhaps?'

'I could eat an elephant.'

'I don't think even the Stork Club can manage that. They do excellent steak, American style. Quite filling.'

'I'll settle for that.'

He smiles. 'Exotic food, and sunshine, will be available in South

America. I'm about to find out what kind. I'm off to Curaçao on a business trip. With the Royal Netherlands Steamship Company. Outbound on the *SS Cottica,* returning to New York via Port au Prince on the *SS Oranje Nassau.* Then back to New York on the *SS Stuyvesant.* Two weeks altogether.' The tiniest uplift of the corners of his mouth. 'My little excursion to the West Indies. Staid in comparison to your recent expedition.' He inclines his head.

His hair is thinning. Fancy that. 'Really? You haven't been before?'

'Never.' Lowered lids immobile. 'I think of the boat trip as a little holiday. It would be good to have stimulating company on board. Want to come along?' He takes her arm. 'As my guest, naturally.'

He's fallen for her? 'A sort of cruise, you mean?'

'Couldn't have put it better myself.'

'How long to buy some glad rags?'

'Three days.'

'Deal. Wouldn't miss it for the world.'

SS Cottica, September 1931

'Well, Doly. Is your stateroom comfortable?'

'Wonderful.'

Shipboard dancing in First Class is to a live band. In the main dining room with a small parquet square in the centre of the floor. Cramming the dancers into each other's arms. Unexpected swells allow the men to steady their partners by holding them tight.

Bandi has natural rhythm, twinkling feet. Like Rolf. He can foxtrot, waltz, tango and rumba. He offers to do the polka and the csárdás which the band can't play. He settles for a versatile version of the Charleston. Outdoing Doly.

'Shall we go on deck to cool off?' Sounds like a question. Is a statement. He ushers Doly ahead of him.

Champagne cocktails before dinner, a vintage wine, liqueurs. Her gait is unsteady. She lets herself lean back. Bandi grabs her, puts comforting arms around her, holds her to him. Fraternal. Affectionate. And, she can sense, warming to her.

The sea is glassy calm, Indian summer is back. They watch the boat's wake reflected back in shattered moonlight. Twinkling like diamonds.

His aftershave is spicy, sharp. He suggests she's tired, offers to take her to her cabin.

Doly feels repercussions from the shipwreck which didn't kill her. Disembodiment, instability. She basks in the attentions of a trustworthy, older man. A gentle elder brother-in-law. Dependable. Safe. She invites him in.

'You're quite ravishing. Perhaps one bottle of delicious Hungarian wine before you go to sleep?' He rings the bell for the steward. Orders Tokay.

'A tawny liquid for a tawny girl.' He raises his glass to hers. Strokes the hair back from her forehead. Smiles into her eyes.

Doly sees him take a sip or two while he replenishes her glass. Unlike Bruno and his bottle of Schnapps. She feels his arms around her, his kisses moving from forehead to lips. Becomes aware he's stroking her face, her hair, her neck, her arms. Drawing her to him.

The alcohol makes her too languid to parry the soft fluttering kisses on her lips. Until she puckers them, eager to turn the flutters into something stronger. She barely notices Bandi's hands unzip her dress, unclasp her bra.

His lips leave hers, tremble down her neck, find her bosom. Draw on her nipples, making them hard. He sucks until she thinks she can feel liquid going through.

Delicious. Doly leans back, allows Bandi's hands to glide back and forth on both breasts while his lips go lower, find her navel, the space between her legs now opening up to him.

He licks her bare mound of Venus, doesn't hesitate. Her flesh takes over as she feels her legs want to spread. One deft movement and his tongue hardens, finds her clitoris. Sucks the sweet nectar.

Sensations she's never dreamed of fire her blood. She should stop him now. Can't. He's smooth, sure, expert. Utterly unlike the youths and young men she's known. He's Gabby's brother-in-law. Unthinkable he'd take advantage of her.

He grasps her buttocks, moves himself up and down. A feeling of hardness inside her. Sweet, dangerous.

She gasps. Wants to shout no. His lips cover her mouth. His movements rock her body. His hands are on her nipples, pressing hard. She feels him slide in and out. Engorges, presses into him. He climaxes, makes sure she climaxes as well.

He stands. Puts on his clothes. Kisses the top of her head. 'Sleep well. See you tomorrow.'

And he's gone.

SS Cottica, September 1931

'Good morning, Doly. Did you need a lie-in, or are you seasick?'

She's furious about last night. She planned to make him fall for her and forget Gabby. Instead he tricked her, stole her virginity. She'll never forgive him. 'Thought I'd get up late. Then I played quoits and table-tennis on deck. Great against the heaving of the sea. We played Upper Deck cabins against Lower Deck.'

Half-closed eyes assess her. 'Of course.'

'I'm off to play in the semi-finals now.'

'How energetic.' The slow blink. 'Perhaps you shower afterwards. Dinner is at the Captain's table tonight. Put on your best frock.'

Doly is late, dressed in the short white skirt used for playing quoits on deck. With young people who consider Bandi in his dotage.

Bandi's eyes open wide, lower. He stands, holds a chair out for her. Doesn't speak.

The ship's officers stand as well. Doly is one of three women at the table. The wife of an important banker, bejewelled and begowned, an opera singer in blazing sequins, and Doly in her sportswear. A little soiled by sweat and the stain where she fell on deck when the boat lurched.

Conversation is desultory, polite. Doly stays silent. After the meal Bandi suggests they go and see a movie before dancing. 'You might like to change into something more comfortable?'

'This is fine with me.'

Large numbers of very young men greet Doly. She met them playing deck games. They vie to dance with her. Bandi retires early from the competition.

He's not available himself after that evening. He's found a new companion. Fräulein Glasser is from Switzerland, originally from Vienna. The banker's secretary. Doly watches her from the table next to the Captain's. She wears just the right dresses for the august honour.

Nods her head and smiles. Contributes precisely the right number of words required. Without stopping the men from having their say.

And she retires discreetly when it's clear the men wish to talk business.

Curaçao, October 1931

'Well, Doly. I hope you enjoyed the trip out?'

'A great experience.'

'You'll be travelling back on the *Oranje Nassau* with me? She sails in three days' time.' Bandi's impassive face shows no sign of anger. 'You can explore Curaçao while you wait.'

'No thanks. Cancel my booking. I'm trekking round for a while. I've always wanted to do that.'

Slow, slow blinks. 'Trekking? On your own?'

'To Venezuela with the Bauers. By train. Then back to New York on the *Cottica* with Rainer. He's got a couple of months before the next semester. He's studying at Columbia.' Rainer Bauer was the most persistent of her admirers on board. Younger than she is, very sweet. And travelling with his parents.

'And then?'

'I'll be all right, Bandi. I'm an old hand at travelling. Lieselotte and I toured North Africa.'

'Which isn't South America. And there were two of you. And you ended up needing Rolf's help.'

'It's not your business.'

'You're under age, Doly. But I'm not your guardian. I can't exactly force you.' He hands her his business card. 'Use this if you have a problem. I'm with Underwood now. They'll see you're all right.'

It's some days later she finds out he talked to Rainer's parents. That he's arranged with them that they will keep an eye on her. The nerve of it.

497

CHAPTER 5

Berlin, February 1932

'I'm in a spot of trouble, Liesi.'

Lieselotte meets Doly's train from Hamburg. Reluctantly. She should be spending her day following her professor's team on a ward round. Attending lectures. Watching a major operation. A heavy and demanding schedule. Examinations are only weeks away.

Doly's cable sounded urgent. Lieselotte is very fond of her, beholden to her. And not keen on precipitating another suicide attempt. Or even an escapade disguised as a job. Why can't the wretched girl sort out her life? She has so many advantages. Looks, money, brains, hordes of suitors. But no loving parents to steady her, no sense of purpose. And a sword of Damocles hanging over her beauty. Which must be harder to bear than Gabriele's early loss of hair. Gabriele *had* to deal with it. And did so triumphantly.

'Not again, Doly.' She sighs. She's surprised her friend's put on weight. Not like her to eat herself out of trouble...

Doly pats her stomach. 'I'm pregnant.'

'Arrh.' Vocal cords paralysed as her jaw drops. Hot surges of fury at such stupidity. She blinks hard to quell hot tears. How could even Doly be such a fool? After all the warnings, details of birth control she's given her?

'Aren't you going to say *anything?*'

Doly is in real trouble. She needs her best friend, her blood-sister.

Lieselotte gulps traffic-choked air. Again and again. 'God, Doly. Are you determined to wreck your life?'

Characteristic shrug. 'These things happen.'

Lieselotte knows that if Doly were going to marry the father she wouldn't be here. 'Only if you allow them to. Know who the father is?'

Doly's face is puffy. Breath whistles through small teeth. 'Are you my friend, or a reincarnation of my sister?'

Recriminations are beside the point. 'Sorry. Of course you do. Just don't want to marry him.'

'Out of the question.'

Lieselotte comes across unmarried mothers in her work. Often. She's seen German attitudes to "fallen women". Harsh, no sign of empathy, not to be recommended. The doctors she's come across are determined upholders of establishment values, approve punitive policies for social miscasts. Prison is probably the least immoderate policy, being locked up in a mental institution a frequent consequence. Doly should get out of Germany as soon as possible.

Lieselotte feels her belly bloat with swallowed air. Belches discreetly. 'You're not expecting me to do anything about it, are you?' Voice grating with conflict. Friendship insists she help Doly by any means at hand, reason tells her that finding someone to abort the foetus, however medically sound, would be a death knell to anyone of Doly's temperament. She escapes into attack. 'Because I won't. Abortion is extremely dangerous. It's also against the law. I refuse to commit murder. Even for you.' Loud snap of lips. Finality.

Doly's small figure wobbles, sinks down on her suitcase. 'Such a solution never occurred to me, Liesi. I simply wanted to talk decent options through with a true friend.' She rubs swollen ankles.

Lieselotte bends, helps Doly up, grabs the case. 'We'd better get you something to drink.'

'Think I should have it in Schwanenbruch or in a big city?'

No time for sentimentality. True friendship now means persuading Doly to leave. Quickly. Lieselotte's acquaintance with modern German medicine makes one thing clear: it isn't always a healing profession. 'Those aren't options. Forget the village. You'd never live it down.'

Black-circled eyes look haunted. 'Difficult in any case. Moppel is asking me for rent every time I show my face there.'

'God. What a heel that man is.'

'Says the place no longer belongs to me, so it's only reasonable I pay rent when I stay.' She grins. 'Not that I take any notice. What's he going to do? Bring a case against me?'

'You saw him, then? Signed over the house?'

Was it wrong to allow Doly to sell her stake in that house just so she could get her medical education? Not that she knew about it at the time. Now she's hoping Emil Junior isn't actually heel enough to enforce the sale.

'I signed it over when he gave me the money for your fees. I'll make it all square and legal when I'm twenty-one, in April. I'll keep my word. Of course.'

'I see.' It's entirely because of her that Doly is out on that particular limb. But, however much it hurts, however much Doly misunderstands, she has to be firm for her friend, can't allow her to make things worse. She cannot—can *not*—stay in Germany. She could—would—lose a lot more than money.

'Go back to America, Doly. Put the child up for adoption when it's born. Then re-enrol at Barnard and finish your degree.' She spots a café, leads Doly in. 'You'll need somewhere to live meanwhile. The Hudwalkers are hardly going to welcome you with open arms. What about that Barnard College friend?'

'Which particular one?'

'The one you introduced me to when I was over. Dark, rather tall and masculine. A cowgirl, she said.' Lieselotte remembered her well. She was the one who knew the shipwreck was Doly's friend's fault. And said so. Vociferously.

'Faith Bowler? I've known her since Riverside Hall.'

'Wonderful. She seems genuinely fond of you. Will she stand by you?'

Doly shrugs. 'She's a year ahead of me. She graduated this summer and moved all the way out to Oklahoma.'

'So she's kept in touch?'

Doly nods, contrasting the palomino mustangs she rode with Faith to Flitsi, the white gelding she and Lieselotte so often shared. 'We rode the prairie together. It's made us close.' The tears come, wiped off but coming fast and unstoppable.

Playing at ghost rider is all Lieselotte can offer Doly. Who won't realise her blood-sister is doing all she can because the only kindness she can offer Doly is to reject her, to get her the hell out of Germany. Doly will see it as betrayal; it's the price Lieselotte has to pay. A searing bitter price which chokes her.

She clears her throat. 'Sounds perfect—if she's willing to help you out.' Her voice breaks again at the thought of sending Doly away.

'Who knows, Liesi? She graduated summa cum laude and landed a brilliant job with the Seismograph Service Corporation. Another high-flying career girl, just like you.'

'Married?'

'Faith?' Doly giggles. 'She doesn't date. She's living in digs with a pleasant-sounding landlady. Maybe there's a spare room.' Her eyes search Lieselotte's across a tiny marble table. 'Or I could stay with you. In Berlin.'

The hungry look in Doly's eyes is hard to take. True friendship means she has to seem ruthless. Lieselotte turns to the waitress. 'Two large white coffees. And a selection of cakes.'

'I want bread, not cakes.'

'Do the child a favour, Doly. Give birth in America so it's an American citizen. And can find the right parents.'

CHAPTER 6

Wyckoff, New Jersey, June 1932

'Emil Junior. Real surprise to have you dropping by. Guess you kept in mind our evening service is in half an hour. You here to join us?'

Moppel's head is watermelon red, his teeth pips along a broad grin. 'Be glad to, Father Hudwalker.'

Walter Hudwalker extends his hand, shakes Moppel's gingerly. 'Say, what brings you to lil' old New Jersey? Fella who's living all the way in uptown Manhattan. How you doin' there?'

He's managed to scrape through his drawn-out degree course at Columbia with the minimum of credits. 'Just fine. Graduation Day coming up right soon, Father Hudwalker.'

'Why Junior. Haven't seen you in a good long while.' Elsa Hudwalker walks through from the kitchen, bearing a jug of lemonade. 'Thought I heard your voice.'

'Great to see you, Mother Hudwalker. I sure hope you all can make it to my graduation ceremony. Gertrude and Hildegarde too, right?'

'Well, now, Junior. That's mighty thoughtful of you. Wouldn't miss it for the world.'

Unlike his Onkel Wilfred, Moppel has decided to brave the world without artificial hair. Weighing pros and cons convinced him he was better off the way he is. Not handsome, with hair or without. A toupee requires a constant mental check to avoid disaster. What's more, being bald is not the turn-off with women he expected.

From a business point of view, bald presents the image of a bluff honest man. What you see is what you get. He covers the sparse pickings with a hat he only reluctantly takes off. 'That's great. My aunt Hannah's coming.'

'The good lady who looked after you when your father died, right? In Germany?'

'Sure thing.' Moppel has chosen to forget the horrors of his early childhood. What good does it do to harbour resentments? Fate is already dealing with Tante Hannah.

'Say, that reminds me. Is your aunt's husband better now?'

'The news is none too good, I guess.' The Hudwalkers' house hasn't changed since the day Moppel first walked into it. Though the curtains are a little shabbier. 'Sad to say he passed away. Didn't leave her nothing. And she never had no kids.'

'Never had any...'

'All on her lonesome without no dough. Working as a housekeeper for a family in Brooklyn. They're giving her the day off.'

'I sure am sorry to hear that. Sometimes the Good Shepherd tests his lambs.'

Moppel has never expounded on Tante Hannah's credentials for being the blackest of sheep.

Hudwalker's lugubrious face lengthens further. 'Well now, Junior. What kind of job you looking out for?'

Moppel's small eyes almost close as his smile widens. 'That's partly what I came to talk to you about. Guess I'll set up an office for real estate and insurance. Kinda winning combination.'

Hudwalker allows himself a smile. 'Why, that's a fine idea. Your father would be proud of you.'

Moppel nods, opening his eyes and fixing Hudwalker with intense blue. 'I guess you know Gabby's arriving next week. She wants her new kid born in the States.'

'Yes, indeedy. Wonderful news she's having another baby.'

'Sure.' Moppel takes off his hat and scratches his head. 'She kinda hinted she'd like me to look after her Manhattan properties. Maybe Castle Bath as well."

'That so?' The smile goes abruptly. Hudwalker looks down at the hands twisting in his lap. 'Her husband doesn't feel he can handle that?'

Moppel is keen to combine his and Gabby's interests. That way he just might persuade Hudwalker to go along with his schemes. Though Doly came of age in April she wrote the old man, begged him to carry on looking out for her. 'Reckon Gabby feels she's better off with someone on the spot. Someone she can trust.'

Hudwalker looks over his glasses at Moppel. His wife looks from one man to the other and decides to fill the long silence. 'Makes good sense.'

Moppel picks up a copy of *The Christian Monitor* and turns to the property section. 'Sure would get me off to a good start. See that? My advertising copy.'

Hudwalker nods. Unenthusiastically.

'Thought it might be useful to get your angle on what to do right now. I can't do nothing without Doly's part of the estate, all our properties being bound together.' His ears stand away from his head, giving him a clownish childlike look. Innocuous. 'I guess that's where you come in. Seeing as how you act for her when she's out of town.'

'Right.'

Moppel folds the paper in half, his advertisement prominent on the table. 'I reckon now's a real good time to sell the East Side People's Bath. Castle Bath as well. The market's slipping.'

'Hold on now, Junior. Your father built the People's Bath from the highest motives. That block houses more than forty tenement buildings, over three thousand people. They have no running hot water, no permanent bathtubs. He built it to help them out.'

'Sure thing. A terrific business venture.' The old man sure knew how to make a buck.

'That wasn't the reason; no sirree. It was an act of pure charity. But those two properties bring in the major part of the income. And now you want me to agree a sale?' Hudwalker always sounds gloomy. This time he excels even himself.

'That's about the size of it.' He sees Hudwalker's frown. 'People are installing their own bathrooms, Father Hudwalker. Even on the Lower East side.'

'Well now, Emil Junior. You know I like you. Think highly of you. But there was that little business with Bertrand.'

Moppel's hat is back on his head. Shading his eyes. 'Sure thing. But I was a kid then. Led astray.'

'Real estate is all your younger sister has to live on now her stocks have lost their value. She hasn't gone back to her studies, isn't married yet. There's no one to look out for her.'

Moppel shrugs. Hudwalker doesn't know Doly has sold her brother her part of the Villa Dohlen. He never will if Moppel can prevent him finding out. 'Plumb right. But she's a looker. She'll get hitched real soon, for sure.'

Mother Hudwalker nods her grey head. 'She has a great many admirers, that's a fact. Including Bobby. You remember Bertrand's brother, don't you, Junior?'

'Sure do.' Not exactly a recommendation as far as he's concerned. Too keen on practical jokes which made Moppel look a sure-fire duffer. All the more reason to get on with the deal.

'Never got over her, poor boy.'

Moppel nods while opening his briefcase. He pulls out some papers.

Once started, Mother Hudwalker finds it hard to stop talking. As though she's been wound up. 'She wouldn't see him on her way out West, wouldn't even write to him.'

'Yeah. I didn't see her neither.' No way he'll say so, but he was only too relieved that Doly avoided him. Until her twenty-first birthday, when he'd have been glad to wish her well. Get her to sign a new document, make it law tight. 'She wrote to say she'd finally holed up in Oklahoma somewhere. Sounded happy. Cowboy country. She always was a keen rider.'

'We've had a letter or two from Tulsa. She asked me to send her rental income there. Said she's staying with her friend, Faith.'

Moppel shuffles the papers. Noisily. 'Gabby's arriving soon and she needs cash.'

'I thought her husband has this job with IBM...'

'He does. But they live in style, in a huge house in Vienna. Gabby's been spending on furniture, china. Bought a real pricey car. 4-litre Minerva saloon.'

'Minerva? I never heard of that.'

'They're made in Belgium. One of the classiest cars on the

continent.'

'Not like one of our good old tin Lizzies then?'

Moppel laughs. 'Not even close. Hers cost well over 1,000 bucks.'

Hudwalker whistles. An incongruity not even his wife has been able to stop. 'I'd like to help you out, Emil Junior. Believe me I would. But I just can't do it. Your father entrusted me to be your guardian till you were of age. I promised Dorinda I'd keep right on looking after her properties until she married or until she decided to take care of them herself. You understand, Junior. I have to stick with Dorinda unless she gives the word. And I don't think it's in her interests to sell right now.'

CHAPTER 7

Tulsa, June 1932

'It's been swell, Faith. I've loved staying with you.'

'You really think it's a good idea to have the baby in New York?' Faith Bowler towers over Doly. Concern crinkles her eyes, the desire to solace her small friend circles her arm around her shoulders, her lips into a kiss. 'Why not stay here with me? Tulsa's a great place. And I'll get a raise soon. I can take care of you both.'

Doly feels despair run through her like a piercing sword. 'A bastard brought up by two single women? An innocent exposed to society's wrath? Won't do, Faith. I have to give my child a better start than that.' She can't let Faith take over. Loving, yes. But also overbearing, and alarming at times.

'Like handing your own flesh and blood over to people you don't even know.' The tone which alerts Doly to Faith's dangerous mood. The glacial set of the eyes, the fury in the raised arm. She's eclectically temperamental, with hostile tendencies.

Doly is not about to tell Faith what she has in mind. She has money. She'll find a nice little place somewhere in New England, pretend she's a widow, bring the child up on her own.

'I've booked into a maternity unit. They'll see me through the birth and find an adoptive couple for my baby. All carefully vetted by the hospital.' She starts the ignition on her smart new Ford convertible. Bright, white, fast. Waves goodbye. 'I'll be in touch when it's all over,

Faith. Thanks again.'

New York City, June 1932

Doly's decided the best course will be to look after herself. She has to contact Hudwalker and take responsibility for her part of the estate. A tinge of regret that she's made over her third of the Villa Dohlen to her brother, even in such a good cause. But she still has her share in the twelve tenement houses and two public bath houses the three of them own together. The prestigious Castle Bath, out on Long Island, is particularly valuable. And brings in a substantial income.

Moppel answers his phone on the first ring. He's set his office up in Seaford, Long Island. Professes to be doing well. 'Well, I'll be doggone, Doly. Where've you sprung from?'

Sounds almost keen to hear from her. What's he want? Of course; make sure she reassigns the villa, now she's of age. 'I wrote you I was coming East.'

'Sure thing. So you're back in the land of the living now?'

Does he want to be permanently shot of her? 'If that's the way you like to put it. I thought we might meet up.'

'Why sure. Great idea.' He sounds genuinely delighted. 'All three of us, for a change. There's a surprise.'

'All three?' Doly feels her stomach lurch. Is he saying Gabby's in New York?

'Sure thing. You didn't know? Gabby's boat docks nine tomorrow morning. She asked me to pick her up.'

Doly draws in her breath. That could change everything.

'Problem is, I have a real full schedule. You free? Great if you could meet her for me. She's about due to give birth, so she'll be better off with you.'

Does he suspect she's pregnant too? How could he possibly know? 'What makes you think that?'

A jovial laugh. 'No need to sound shocked. Pretty much because you're female. What does a guy know about having a kid? She'll be much better off with you.'

Perhaps her guardian angel is back on duty. Gabby will be outraged at Doly's pregnancy but she'll come round and help. If only to avoid an open scandal. It could be useful to get Gabby's slant on things before letting Moppel know. Doly's pretty sure her brother would milk the situation, though she's not clear how or why. Gabby's astute. Not bad at business. She can steer her in the right direction.

CHAPTER 8

New York City, July 4th 1932

Gabby, standing at the *SS Berengaria's* rail as she draws into New York Harbour, scans the people gathered on the dockside to meet the new arrivals. Her eyes search for her brother, for the white hat he always wears in summer. Rolf wired Moppel, asked him to meet her and take her to the Buckingham Hotel. In mid-town Manhattan, surrounded by internationally famous art galleries, museums and concert halls. A place where she can await the birth of her son and enjoy the best New York has to offer.

No sign of Moppel. But—surely not?—that unmistakable head of hair, that all-too-familiar figure, waving both arms.

'Surprise, surprise.' she saw her mime far below her. A slip of a girl, her boyfriends always said. Dwarfed by the transatlantic liner, but—much bigger than the last time she saw her. Even from so high above. Round as a barrel. Like herself.

Doly instead of Moppel. A shock, a blow. Not a surprise. Nothing her sister does is ever a surprise.

Arms used as semaphores pretend delight. She waddles down the gangplank, checks the crowd again. Desperate to find her brother. He isn't there. Doly has come to meet her on her own. In a manner of speaking.

'My, my. I hardly recognised you, you're so big.'

On the offensive right away. Always that mocking tone.

510

'Aren't you even a teensy bit glad to see me?'

Gabby thinks back to last September, when she thought Doly dead. Wished she'd been kinder to her sister then. She puts on a forced smile.

'Doly, of course.' She pauses, works on the smile. No explanation, just that impish look. 'Did you marry someone out West?'

'Goose. Would I be here on my own?'

Good intentions flee as all the old resentments come flooding back. That wilful, simpering, grabbing little bitch has finally come to grief. Carrying God knows whose child. 'So who's is it?'

Small fangs glint white. Her sister pats the platform protruding her middle. 'Fancy, the both of us ready to drop our load at the same time.' Lips clench in a sideways smirk. 'And the same father.'

'*Same* father?' Gabby's voice squeezes sharp, cutting above the hubbub.

'Ralph.'

'Ralph?' A fleeting hope. Rolf's name was Rezsö when he lived in Hungary; he was never Ralph.

'I like to use the English version of his name. Rezsö Ferent. Your perfect husband.'

A jolt of possibilities. That time in Berlin, when he sank to his knees, swore there was nothing between him and her sister, he only kissed her cheek...

'Don't talk such rubbish.' How would the slut know who the father was? If she were telling the truth, and Doly is the most accomplished of liars, Rolf would only have been one among many. But he was on his Middle Eastern tour last autumn, while Doly spent a short time in South America, then settled in Oklahoma. Nowhere near Turkey, Iraq or Persia.

Doly's eyes slit in a smug smile. 'Suit yourself.'

Determined on Rolf's paternity. Fertile with it. Surely Tante Martha wrote she travelled on the same boat as Bandi last September, a trip to Curaçao? Doly is obviously near term, as she is. So the dates work out. Could it really have been Bandi?

She lets it go. For the time being. Nervous exhaustion has drained her, New York summer heat saps her energy. 'I have to find my luggage.'

511

Why the hell isn't Moppel here? Couldn't he have helped her out for once? Didn't he stay for months in the villa in Vienna, cosseted by Viktoria, fed by a devoted sister?

Her cases are waiting. She points them out to the porter, stands guard by the one she really cares about. The baby clothes. White and blue. Her son will start life with a silver dollar in his mouth. And be born in the Land of the Free. Rolf, proud in his fatherhood, promised the longed-for son by the gypsy, couldn't do enough to humour her. Booked her a First Class stateroom, filled it with roses. An insurance policy against the ominous clouds of political unrest darkening the minds of Germans. Pointing to future catastrophe, sooner or later.

'Why the hat boxes?' Doly's frown turns to a sneer. 'No one wears hats in New York.'

Maybe no one her sister knows. She has a duty to be well turned out when she calls on the Watsons. Company president Thomas J is now taking his International Business Machines to the very top. And Rolf with him.

'My new car's this way. I'll give you the ride of your life. Maybe we can even stay in the same hotel.'

What it means is that Doly wants her to help her cope with the Hudwalkers, Moppel... She has to try. She owes it to their mother's memory.

Gabby stares at the car. How very like her sister to drive a cabriolet. A small impudent two-seater in glaring white, top folded down. She can't stand convertibles for the same reasons she can't actually stand her sister, however hard she tries. Pretentious, unrestrained, frivolous. A damned menace to anyone who comes in contact with her.

'Where on earth are we going to put my luggage?' She's brought enough for a month's stay, together with the layette for the new American citizen she's carrying inside her.

Her sister lizards a pale, fissured tongue at her. 'You ever going to learn to travel light?'

Dismay turns to fury. Should she refuse to ride in that toy, find a cab? New York summer heat saps her energy. Crowds everywhere on Independence Day—there's a long line for the taxis. Swallowed air pinches, squeezing for space. An acquiescent shrug as she reluctantly agrees.

Tuning-fork laughter as her sister dumps her handbag, rubbish-crammed, behind the driver's seat. Full-moon eyes, still fringed with lashes, challenge the porter. 'You'll sort it out for us, won't you?'

He all but kneels at her feet. 'Sure thing, ma'am.'

'Great.' Doly opens the driver's door, eases herself behind the wheel, shoehorns her pregnant body in.

Sweat glistens the porter's face to polished ebony, dampens his vest. He hauls and nods, a workhorse servicing her beautiful sister.

He pushes the cart creaking with luggage to the back, twists a handle, pulls down the metal lid to form a platform. He heaps cabin trunk and cases on to it, lashes them into a pyramid with leather thongs.

'I guess that'll do it.' He pulls open the passenger door, helps Gabby into the seat. She's ballooning more than with her first baby. Boys carried high and forward. She's been told. She clings to the Prater gypsy's promise that she'd have a son. "Born in the pink," the woman had prophesied. As well as something else she'd confided to Rolf, and he had refused to tell her.

The porter's eyes follow Doly as he backs away. She flutters a wad of dollars at him. 'I knew you could do it.'

'That's way too much...'

'You deserve it.' Lady Bountiful tosses her hair, smiles radiantly. She twists the key in the ignition. Heat-expanded steel squeals the motor into life.

'Take it easy now,' the porter shouts above the squeal, 'or you'll lose your load.'

Her sister puts her foot down, hard. A rally skid out of the parking space. Still abundant auburn tresses in the wind. Stripes of red bunting on Independence Day.

Gabby billows a headscarf around her carefully set waves, ties it under her chin. To protect her hairdo. The very thought of it blown away by wind crowds out all other thoughts.

The car swerves, Gabby's insides try to catch up with her. She hears screeching, discordant, loud, punishing her eardrums. Inhuman shrieks of rubber melting on asphalt, brake pads burning on steel. Accelerated force has met fixed object; they've hit a hydrant.

She screams as her body is catapulted forward. Arms used as sandbags protect her head. She's bounced against the wooden dashboard, cushioned by scarf and hairpiece. Her body is jerked back against the car seat. Smell of singed rubber, shuddering, dust. Noises reverberate in her head, quiet, then sigh away. Uncanny silence.

Is she all right? She can move her head, her hands, her upper limbs, open her eyes. She's still in one piece, her torso held tight by a crumpled metal shell that was the car. And her legs? Pinned under an intruding front panel, holding her in a grip of iron.

What about her baby? Her hands are tingly, but they move. And explore her body. She feels her belly a tight drum, liquid seeping between her legs.

The child inside her shifts. Strong muscles contract, relentless forces she can't control. Full, scorching pains radiate out from her navel, spread down her thighs, catch at her knees wedged tight under the wooden console. She fights to open her door, to escape. The handle won't budge. Rigid metal is warped around her, she's caught like a sardine in a can.

Contractions grip her, ripple through. More pain, spurting swollen breasts into liquid, stabbing her eyes, dropping as tears.

Understanding leaps out of her addled brain. Birth pangs. Her son, the gypsy swore he was a boy, is about to be born. Too soon. 'Not yet.' Her voice a rattling window in a storm.

People are gathered round, staring at her. She gulps air to breathe, to demand action. Her throat muscles contract, produce a squeak no louder than the buzzing of a fly.

Insistent summer sun beats down, relentless, hot. Trickling her strength away.

Funnels of black swallow up consciousness.

'Help us.' Sound, movement by Gabby's side return awareness, slap her from passive into active. Doly is sitting in the driver's seat. Clearly alive.

'Are you OK? Can you move?'

Her sister's arms are gripping the steering wheel, her face masked by hair shocked into straggling locks. 'I think so. Yes.'

'The baby's started.'

'Damnblast. You're sure?'

'Of course I'm sure.'

'We'll get a doctor... '

'*You* get him.' Exploding outrage. 'My door's jammed. I can't even move my legs.'

Sun blazing right above their heads. High noon. Only a couple of hours since she disembarked. Recognised Doly standing on the quay.

What possessed her to follow Doly to this stupid little car? She knew even before she levered herself into the low-slung seat that the wayward fool would jerk in and out of gear, corner at speed. Why was she idiot enough to accept the ride? Couldn't she have waited for a cab?

That wasn't it. She went with Doly because she needed to know how her sister got into this mess, had to offer help. Acknowledging an illegitimate child would take all of Doly's bravado, all her defiance.

Lurching, ungainly with her lawful child, Gabby clutched the grab handle to keep her balance, to protect her baby. 'Don't drive so fast.'

'Always such a spoilsport. Relax. Let the wind blow the cobwebs away.'

That reckless, irresponsible tramp. She floored the gas pedal, lost control and hit the hydrant.

Utrinal muscles take over, overwhelm every nerve, every thought. The baby pushing to be born.

'I can get out.' Doly's shaking sibilants of guilt. 'I'll call an ambulance. They'll be here right away.'

She can get out; that mad impetuous bitch tearing along narrow downtown streets at over eighty is unharmed.

'Hold tight. You'll be OK.' The male voice of authority. A cop, knight in a squad car.

Her tongue is longing, parched. Water from the hydrant is spouting over the bonnet, out of reach. The putrid sweat of fear makes her gag, the blood vaulting through her veins returns thoughts of devastation to her brain.

Slow rhythmic pulsing as the baby inside her tries for independent life. The warped metal expands with her, burning against her hip, pinching bruised flesh.

The baby pushes, hard and insistent. Her skirt is wedged tight across her knees, the metal fiery.

Willing hands pull at the passenger door. It doesn't budge.

'Hold on there. Don't try to force her out. Wait for the medics.' She hears their voices re-echoing down a channel. Far away.

'Be here right soon.' Sir Galahad in NYPD blue armour trying for cheer.

A woman in the crowd offers her a glass of water. She swills it down, asks for more, splashes herself. Contractions bite into the furnace of the car. She can't stop them. She plunges in and out of consciousness, eventually brought to by the clamouring bells of an ambulance.

'The driver's sitting on the sidewalk.' Confident tones of a stranger's voice. 'Looks OK, but she's pregnant. Sure need to get her to the hospital real fast.'

Doly is pregnant—but not in labour.

The irony of it. The bastard is all right, while her child is stuck between her legs. Head crowning, delving between her thighs, unable to forge through. Held hostage by her feckless sister's showing off. To prove she can get anything she wants. Break the speed limit. Steal her sister's husband. Any man.

'Passenger looks in poor shape,' she hears another man say. 'The door won't budge. Gimme a hand to haul her free.'

They yank her out. Her voice, high and loud, crescendos with excruciating pain. The smell of blood, the lurch. Her skirt up to her waist, her legs spread wide, being split in two...

A moist rag over her face. The chloroform does its work, veiled void turns to vivid red, dark crimson, black.

A spiral of light whirls, tosses Gabby's thoughts like spangles, forces her back to consciousness

She's swaying on something hard. She opens her eyes, feels her belly. Flat. Her hands throb, she curls them up, spreads them out, feels for her child. Nothing. Her eyes squirt round. Where is her baby?

Clawing hands search for a solid hold, find a strap. She pulls herself up. 'Where's...'

'Easy, now. We're taking you to the hospital. Don't try to sit up.'

Doly's squeaking words behind her. 'I didn't mean to harm you, to hurt the baby...'

'Where is he?'

Strong hands push her down. 'Gee, lady. We couldn't save him.'

'Nooooaaa...' She knows wails of denial can't change what's
happened. But they go on.

Where have they put him? She pulls the cover over her face, feels
oozing wet, sees dim red light spreading around her, smothering her.
She aches for her son, joins her hands together, hugs empty arms to
her breast.

A sobbing disembodied voice behind her. 'It wasn't my fault. The
other car was coming at us in the middle of the road.'

Sympathetic male pats on Gabby's shoulder. 'You're young, you'll
have another...'

The pain disappears as blood drains from her head. She shivers, her
body stiffens to rigour.

Doly's raucous sobs behind her. 'I didn't mean...' Her sister's
babbling infiltrates the fruitless longing in her heart, her brain. Fury
floods thought back, lights up hate.

Gabby pushes off coarse sheets. Eyes wide, she twists round to look
at her sister. Can't do it. 'And you? Are you all right?' she asks. Clipped,
disjointed syllables.

The cover tucked back round her, a coat placed on top. 'Your sister's
fine, lady. Don't move.' A hand, not ungentle, urges her back. 'Lie
still.'

'I'll give you anything to make it up to you.' Doly's voice right by
her ear.

What does a murderess have to give? A sudden inspiration born of
grief, of loss, of desperation, surges through her mind. 'Anything? You
mean that?'

'Just say.'

Would she? Can she ask that of her? It would be a secret between
the two of them. Another family secret, but of a different kind. They
are well schooled in secrets.

The ether smell approaching. 'Don't try to talk...'

'I don't need that.' She flicks the hand away. Is this why the gypsy
refused to tell Rolf more, however much money he pressed into her
palm? Because she saw their baby dying—dead? Gabby reverts to the

517

North German dialect she and her sister spoke as children. 'Süster, ick wünsch mi nix as dütt. Geb mi dien Kind. Wen he mol sowied is—Sister, I want just one thing. Give me your child. When he's at the right stage.'

She pants to breathe. Shuttering lids shadow light. She sways with the ambulance, feels cocooned in the murmuring swish of tyres, claps her palms over her ears to blot out the memory of screaming rubber.

Doly's gasp, implosive breath, pierces through. 'Mien Kind? Keeneen soll mien Kind van me kregen—My child? No one's going to take my child from me.'

The thought that Doly would have a child she cannot possibly look after, while she... Gabby's hands clasp over her empty belly, fury guides her tongue. 'Rolf's, you said. So he'd be with his father.' Doly always lies rather than tells the truth. This time a wonderful, glorious lie. Not Rolf's. Gabby would stake her life on that.

'Still mine.' Defiant, shrill.

'I'll take him back with me. His father, no one, need ever know.' Her breathing steadies. 'You won't have to worry about not being married. You can start again, knowing your baby has a good home, devoted parents. Works out for both of us.'

'You think I can give away my child?' Doly's helpless little-girl voice.

She'll be doing her a favour, all of them a favour. Particularly the baby. 'You swore you'd give me anything.' She uses every atom of willpower to fight the limbo of emptiness. 'Is it a deal?'

No response, no words of any kind. Loud clanging bell to clear other traffic out of their way. Tolling her baby's death before life.

Cold rage brings strength. 'You didn't mean it then?'

'Mean what?' Doly's voice toneless, even.

There's only one chance. It will never come again. 'A barren pledge?' she whispers, delving the weak spot, taunting her sister's well-known pride. 'Going back on your word when it really counts?'

Fistfuls of silence punch the air.

'Right. Deal.' Her sister's voice cuts through the squeal of gripping brakes as the ambulance slows. 'We'll seal it in blood.' Doly lunges towards her, moist fingers slide along her cheek.

'You shouldn't move, honey.' The ambulance attendant leaning

518

towards her sister. Worried about her, already smitten. 'Not in your condition, not after that crash.'

'Change places. I want to sit by her.'

That demanding voice no man dares disobey.

Doly grabs her hand. Sticky, metallic wet on wet mingles between their palms. Thicker than water. 'A solemn promise.' Still using the language of their childhood. 'You have her. You have her when she's born.'

Gabby shudders as the gypsy's exact words come back to her. 'You are carrying a fine son. I see him born in the pink.'

THE INHERITANCE

A very rich landowner left two sons. His enormous wealth, consisting of houses, woods and pastures in a wide area, wasn't easy to split up.

'Let's not quarrel over our inheritance,' the younger brother said. 'Let's just draw lots and settle the whole thing.'

'Suits me,' the elder said. 'But bear in mind that one side of the land is much more valuable than the other.'

'I'll take my chance,' the younger brother said.

They drew lots. And luck was on the side of the elder son.

'Du hest beter käset as ik—you've chosen better than me,' the younger son declared. And ever since the elder son's inheritance was known as beter käset. Which sounds like Bederkesa. Which is the name by which the place is now known.

CHAPTER 9

'You two girls sure take some catching up with.' Moppel peers round the door and walks into the hospital room his two sisters are sharing. He sees Doly is holding a baby. 'Hey, kiddo.'

Doly's eyes are moist, her voice husky. 'Your new niece.' She wraps the baby's shawl closer around the child.

'Hold on, there. I can't hardly see her.' He pulls the shawl away and looks at the new-born. 'Looks just like you, Doly. Same shape face, violet eyes. Say, which one of you two had the baby, anyways?'

Moppel has finally turned up, though he's the last person either Gabby or Doly want to see. He's the one who could spot their secret, work it out. Gabby knows her brother likes to kid his sisters. Is it just that, or does he sense something? Damned close to the wind. She throws down the New York Times. 'Well, Moppel. Good of you to show your face at last.'

'Doggone it, Gabby, I'm here now. Right? So don't give me no hard time.'

'Trustworthy as usual.' Gabby, normally fond of her inept brother, can barely contain her anger. Couldn't he have put his own interests second, just for once?

'OK, Sis. So I didn't make it to the boat. Doly gave me a call and said she'd take care of meeting you. So what's the big deal?'

Nothing much. Gabby wouldn't have been involved in a car crash, her son would have been born alive. Detail, really. She feels like

521

screaming and knows she can't afford that luxury. She holds the paper up to cover her face, to suppress the threatening tears.

'Well, now I'm here, you might stop reading the news for a coupla minutes.'

Doly holds the baby out to her brother. 'Born only four hours ago, and beautiful already.' She kisses the top of the infant's head. 'Put her in the cot and cart it over to her mother, won't you?'

'Sure, sure.' Moppel stretches out both arms to take the bundle. He lays the baby down and wheels the cot to Gabby. A tooth-bared grin. 'Rolf's going to be real put out. I reckon.'

Gabby catches her breath. Does he know? How could he? Doly went into labour right after the crash. The hospital had no names to contact. 'What makes you think that?' She manages to control her voice, but two startled pairs of eyes stare at their brother.

'Say, you two girls lost all sense of humour? Guy was hoping for a son, right?'

Gabby avoids looking at Doly. Any more mistakes like that and he'll rumble them. This secret has to be between the two of them. 'I'm sure he'll be thrilled to have another daughter, Moppel. He adores Gemma.'

Moppel stares from one to the other. 'What is it with you two? Concussed, is that it?'

'That too. And Gabby's only recently given birth.'

Small eyes seesaw from sister to sister. Grow mean. 'You girls are way too pally to be for real.'

Gabby bends over the cot, kisses the baby's head to disguise a shudder. Moppel looks like a duffer, and he's lazy. But he's far from stupid.

Dollar signs in his eyes. 'I guess it's enough neither of you was hurt in that crash. Decided on sisterly love after a brush with death, that the way of it?' Assessing eyes turn on Doly. 'How come you're in bed? The doc told me you're fine. Scratch or two, is all.'

'I'm a bit shaken...'

The door opens, a nurse marches in. 'Congratulations, Dad. The baby's the spitting image of you. Except she's got hair.' She grins at Moppel conspiratorially as she winks at Doly. 'I thought you said your husband... '

An enormous thud as the huge vase of red roses on the bedside table between the beds crashes to the floor.

The door flies open and Walter Hudwalker rushes in. 'Is everyone OK? That sounded like a shot.'

'Father Hudwalker. How kind of you to visit.' Gabby forces a smile at the nurse. 'Sorry about that. I'm still a little groggy from the accident.' She sees the maternity nurse about to speak. 'I'm really thirsty. D'you think someone could bring us all a cup of coffee?'

'I'm not the maid, young lady.' The starched uniform crackles as the nurse stalks out.

Moppel perches on Doly's bed as Hudwalker sinks into the only chair. 'My goodness me. How in the world did that happen?' He stares at the mess of wet flowers and shattered glass.

'They'll send someone to clear up.' Gabby lifts the newborn out of the cot, holds her up for Hudwalker to see.

'The Lord be blessed for the precious gift of a sister for Gemma.' His smile is genuine. 'Mother Hudwalker's arthritis is playing her up. She'll be sorry to have missed such a glorious sight.'

'I'll bring the baby over to New Jersey before I sail back.'

'Very accommodating of you, Gabriele. Well now, what a strange coincidence.'

The sisters stare at Hudwalker.

He frowns back. 'I'm saying a pair of sisters three-and-a-half years apart, just like my own two girls. What are you going to name her? Or will you wait until you're back home?'

'Rolf leaves girls' names to me. Nina, maybe. Or Lisa. Those sound right in both English and German.'

'How about Rosa, Gabby? That works in both languages as well. Rosa for a beautiful rosebud. And to complement all the red roses your devoted husband sends.' Doly giggles. 'Anyone got a drink around here?'

Hudwalker looks stern. 'You're not in Germany now, Dorinda. Didn't have a drink in one of those Speakeasies, did you? Before giving your pregnant sister a ride?'

'No.' She reaches for her pack of Lucky Strikes, lights up.

'Not the best thing for the baby, Doly.' Gabby strokes the infant's full head of curls. Rolf will appreciate those, at any rate. Will he notice the baby's eyebrows, the tell-tale sign of the inheritance? 'Nina Dorinda maybe? That has a nice ring to it, don't you agree?'

'Named for her aunt?' Moppel peers from sister to sister. 'What a sweet thought. Sure good to see you girls getting along so well.'

Doly's eyes water. 'Sorry. Damn smoke's got in my eyes.' She stubs the cigarette out.

Moppel stands. 'I know this isn't the best time. But we don't often get together. Could I raise a little business before the coffee comes?'

'Business?' Gabby looks up from the doll-like child. Her hair, ample for the present, just like her biological mother's, has an auburn sheen. Darker than Doly's hair, more like Gabby's wig. A happy coincidence.

'You wanted to raise some cash, Gabby. The problem is the properties are owned jointly. Means none of us can sell unless the other two agree.' He blinks at Doly. She stares back. 'You and Rolf live in Vienna, Doly travels all over. Which tends to leave me in a bit of a hash.' He looks uncomfortably at Hudwalker. 'And Father Hudwalker here's in charge of Doly's investments. And doesn't like to act without her agreement.'

'I'm not sure this is a good time to sell.' Hudwalker hunkers down in his chair while Moppel leans back against the door.

'Why don't we settle which tenement buildings belong to whom right now?' Doly billows her bed coverings, exposing bare shoulders and arms. Hudwalker's eyes flutter. 'It gets so hot in New York.'

Hudwalker levers out of his chair, arranges the bedding more decorously around Doly. 'How d'you mean, Dorinda? How can you divide them without selling them all?'

'Cast lots. Put the names of the properties in a hat and draw them out, one by one. Then stick to our lucky dip.'

Gabby can hear the more-than-usual brittle note in her sister's voice, feels the constriction of guilt. Should she have asked for Doly's child? Is it a sin crying out to high heaven? Bad enough for her to go to hell?

Moppel is outraged. 'But some are much more valuable than others.'

'I'm willing to risk it. What about you, Gabby? Going to take the gamble?'

Gabby, light-headed with the mixture of grief and guilt, feels the weight of double parenthood. She's happy to let Doly have the best properties, if that's what the fates decree. 'Up to a point. I agree to drawing lots for the tenement houses. Everything except the East Side People's Bath and Castle Bath. Those are the really valuable ones.'

'Moppel?'

His bright red scowl flashes dollar signs. 'OK. Let's do it now.' He takes notepaper from his briefcase, writes down the addresses of the properties. 'I'll get some scissors from the nurses' station.'

'Maybe you'd better take control of your own real estate from here on in, Dorinda. I'm not as young as I used to be.' Hudwalker stands, picks up the flowers, walks over to the washbasin, puts in the plug and turns on the cold water. 'Now you're settled in the States, you'll be the best guardian of your own affairs.'

'Well, here we go.' Moppel is back in the room, takes off his hat and turns it upside down. He drops equal-looking pieces of paper into it, holds it out to Gabby.

'Eldest first.'

Four draws each. Gabby and Moppel examine their lucky dips, shrug. Doly has pulled the best ones. She doesn't even look at them. She takes one at random from her pile and hands it to Hudwalker.

The men gawk at Doly. Gabby, grieving at the death of her son, not thinking or caring about money, wonders whether the baby swap has unhinged her sister completely. Can she allow Doly to make this sacrifice? She is the elder, the one with the stable temperament. She gulps, splutters.

'You OK, Gabby?' Doly sounds calm, composed, then laughs. A long, shuddering laugh which ends with her lighting another cigarette. She blows a smoke ring. Ephemeral, large. 'This is to thank you for looking after us all these years, Father Hudwalker. For all the work you've done.' Doly's voice sounds lifeless, flat.

He stares at her, appalled. 'I can't accept this, Dorinda… '

'Then give it to the church. It's yours.'

'Dorinda, you're way too generous. You'll need this yourself.'

Doly's red cheeks burn brighter. 'I'll be fine, Father Hudwalker. After all, I've picked the jackpot.' She holds up a slip, widens a gargoyle mouth at Gabby.

525

Walter Hudwalker twiddles his hands. Listens as Gabby and Doly arrange for their brother to handle their American properties.

'Lucky the way Moppel is running a real estate business now,' Gabby burbles. 'Makes it that much easier for all of us.' Relieved to pass that burden on to her brother. She's already carrying more than she can easily cope with.

Hudwalker clears his throat, grunts. 'Moppel's still very young, Gabriele. Don't you think you should leave all your affairs with Rolf?'

Gabby considers Hudwalker to be even more pedestrian than her husband. 'He's looking after my shares, Father Hudwalker. Not doing too well there.'

Hudwalker opens his mouth. 'The markets...'

Moppel slits eyes at him.

He leaves the sentence dangling, takes a deep breath. 'The main thing is to take out plenty of insurance.' He sounds so out of breath that Moppel goes up to him and pats his back. Hudwalker waves him off. 'On all the properties, but especially the two public baths. They're used by crowds of people. Could go up like Christmas trees.' He blinks at Moppel. 'You will have them fully covered, won't you, Junior?'

The nurse comes back, a grim look on her face. 'Time for Mrs Ferent to get some sleep now, gentlemen.' She turns to Doly, removes the pillows behind her head. 'Lie right down flat.' She turns back to Gabby, holds out her arms for the baby. 'You too, Miss Dohlen.'

Hudwalker smiles. Muddling the two sisters happens all the time. He waves goodbye.

Moppel's unfocused eyes change to full alert. Pinpoint on Gabby, Doly, back again. 'What the hell is going on around here? I'll bet my bottom dollar you two been up to some game plan or other. No way you can fool me. I sure as hell am going to get to the bottom of it. Whatever the fuck it is.'

Gabby finds New York heat oppressive, her wig almost too hot to bear. Takes a deep breath, then picks up a handkerchief. She pulls at the hair above her forehead, raising the front of her heavy hairpiece imperceptibly, mops up the perspiration running down. Sees her brother and sister stare at her. Why should she care? It's time she came to terms with her inheritance, didn't worry who knows or sees the consequences. Now that she thinks about it she realises it's not for herself that she wears a wig, it's so others' feelings are spared. She makes herself look good for Rolf, for Mr Watson, even for Gemma—worries about everyone. Time to be more relaxed about it.

'You sure you're OK, Gabby? That car crash got to you?'

Maybe it has; maybe it's jolted her into reality. 'Just hot, Moppel. No big deal, is it?'

Small eyes squint shut. 'Sure thing. So long, you two.' He slams the door and is gone.

THE PHONEY MILL

A young miller needed to buy land to build his mill. He found a landowner only too happy to take his money. Because he's seen better days. But the man didn't want the clattering noise of a mill in full sail in his back garden disturbing his tranquillity.

The landowner thought he saw a way out of his dilemma. He offered the miller the land on one condition: the mill's sails were to turn in the 'wrong' direction. Anticlockwise instead of clockwise.

The young miller agreed. The landowner took the money, confident that the mill might be built, but it would never be a working mill. Mills, after all, always rotate in the right direction—clockwise. How could the young man ensure the sails would turn the wrong way round?

The miller began to build a fine mill. He started on the sails, carved them appropriately and hanged them to turn in an anticlockwise direction. And made it all work.

The landowner still has the noisy clappering of the sails in his back garden. And the people of the village talk of it as the 'phoney' mill.

CHAPTER 10

'You think he's figured it out?' Gabby puts her new daughter to her breast. The child suckles contentedly.

Doly lights up. 'How could he? Only Liesi and Faith even knew I was pregnant. Neither of them has much time for Moppel. He can speculate all he likes. Won't make one bit of difference.' She inhales deeply, turns away from her sister suckling her baby, explodes into coughs Gabby understands cover bitter tears.

'Rolf expects you to bring back your child, Gabby. He'll see Nina suckling at her mother's breast, look into those soulful Ferent eyes; he'll never doubt she's his and yours.'

Ferent eyes—Bandi's eyelids, Gabby recognises. Slow, tortoise eyelids. The irises are violet, like Doly's. Gabby strokes the locket dangling from her neck, her lips tremble. 'And the Dohlen inheritance puts a strange kind of seal on it.'

Doly laughs, a barking, hacking sound that covers emotions Gabby can identify with. Her sister is grieving, hurt. She's just lost a son but, unlike Doly who has to bear the loss of her child alone, Gabby has gained a daughter she can take back to a loyal, if boring, husband, a secure home. Conscience grabs her, squeezes tight.

'It's not too late to give her back to you, Doly. Come clean.'

'You'd do that?' Violet pierces forget-me-not blue.

'If that's what you want, she's yours.' Gabby is clear now. Her sister is suffering, unhinged by that. She must not take advantage of her, must give her the chance to keep her child.

Doly doesn't get up to take her daughter back. Instead she lights another cigarette. 'I guess I could leave the States. Take her on a round-the-world trip with me. India, China, the lot. Teach her to live in peace with all races, all religions. Turn any frog I meet into a prince—and marry him.'

'Is that really what you want to do?' A feeling as though she's stabbed herself in the back, a deep wound. Would Nina survive Doly's mothering?

'I said you could have her, damn you.' Doly flings the sheets off, walks over to her sister and her daughter, sinks down beside them on Gabby's bed. 'My keeping her would ruin both our lives. You have her, Gabby. I only ask one thing: love her with all you've got.'

Tears are streaming down Gabby's cheeks. 'I will, Doly. I will.'

'Let's never mention it again. Tell no one.'

'If you're absolutely sure...'

Doly stands, whirls round. 'You saying you don't want her because she's mine? You can't stomach that?'

'Wrong end of the stick, Doly. I can't explain it, but I really take to her.' Gabby removes her breast, flutters kisses on the baby's head, lifts her against her shoulder to burp her.

Doly watches her sister, nods. 'Right.' She blinks tears away. 'You won't believe me, but I think I understand exactly. Because of that I trust you.'

Gabby takes in the tragic face, sees realisation in the feverish violet. Has Doly unmasked her sister's secret passion for Bandi, as Gabby has worked out Nina's paternity? 'My solemn promise: I'll treat her as my own.' Great gusts of maternal feeling well through her. She's warming to this child, feels more strongly than she did when Gemma was born, knows she is the right mother for both girls. Because she will make sure they accept their inheritance—without rancour, free from shame and prepared to take on, and overcome, any challenges it might bring.

"Look after your brother and sister," their mother said, so many years ago. Gabby feels her mother's love envelop her, cherish her, savours the warm glow. She's genuinely trying to forgive her sister, and to help her. 'We have to be brave, Doly. Put all this behind us, never refer to it again. Not because of us: for Nina's sake.'

Doly blows another smoke ring: an enormous, perfect one enveloping the baby's head. 'I'll smoke to that.'

Gabby feels the locket heavy on her breast, feels it hard against Nina's head. She unclasps the necklace, puts the locket beside her on the bedside table, is surprised by its weight. She won't wear it now or in the future. She'll never allow it, or anything else, to chain her down again.

The hand life deals you is a given. What counts is how you play the game.
Emil Julius Dohlen